GAME OF REVENGE

BOOK ONE OF THE GAME SERIES

STÉPHANIE C.

Always remember, beauty can come from chaos, order can come from disorder. Go through the storm, it can only get better on the other side.

PLAYLIST

Scan Above or Click Here to listen on Spotify!

1. Demon time – Aaryan Shah

2. Debajo de La Mesa – Luis Miguel

3. Huele a Peligro – Myriam Hernández

4. Niña Amada Mía – Alejandro Fernandez

5. Think Twice – Celine Dion

6. Almohada – Pepe Aguilar

7. Lose Control – Teddy Swims

8. Dynasty – Miia

9. No Me Doy Por Vencido – Luis Fonsi

10. I have Nothing – Whitney Houston

PART 1

CHAPTER 1

THERE ARE A FEW moments in one's life where one decision could change the rest of their trajectory, change anything—from the people they meet, where they live, what they eat, what they learn, what job they do, to who they fall in love with. I wondered what my life would have been like had I stuck to my decision to escape from my stepfather's house when I was a teenager, instead of coming back after three days.

Would I have found happiness, peace in leaving this life behind, or just regret? Would I have gone to college or found another passion? Would I be married? Would I have found fulfillment? What if, that night, I stopped playing the game of the obedient daughter? What if I broke the rules of decorum and did what I truly wanted?

I was toying with the idea of causing mayhem that evening, ruining my birthday party, taking them all down with me in a spiral of pent-up anger and resentment. But when it came down to it, I always lost my resolve and managed to reason with myself, for better or worse, and I'd lock the rebel back in a box and focus on what was expected of me.

Instead of putting on my jeans and sneaking out of the house as my heart was begging me to do, I ordered myself to take a very deep breath. I walked toward the king-sized bed covered with a silky comforter and thousands of throw pillows. If anything, my bedroom always brought me peace.

Richard Anderson, my stepfather, had let me redecorate it to my heart's content years ago. I had chosen light-gray wood furniture with soft, gold-colored drapes and the most comfortable mattress money could buy. The room was elegant and airy, the light colors always calming and reassuring. It was my own little oasis in a house that had always felt too big, too empty for me.

For the evening, I opted for a long black dress. The color reflected my mood perfectly. As I approached the mirror, I noticed how the dress hugged my curvy features. It had a single sleeve on the right shoulder, tied up with a gold brooch. I picked up my makeup and started my routine, picking colors specifically to bring out my hazel eyes, straight nose, plump lips, and delicate oval face inherited from my mother. I undid my hair bun and let the dark-brown cascade of wavy hair fall down the middle of my back.

While I enjoyed parties and balls, this night was a bit different. Richard had organized the evening festivities in honor of my twenty-eighth summer. My stepfather had insisted that this year be a big celebration, but he really was just using my birthday as an excuse to invite the most affluent families in California. What he wanted was to show off his opulence. He wanted to use the opportunity to strengthen his professional relationships, show everyone how rich he was, and strut his beautiful daughter in front of eyes filled with desire, admiration, and jealousy.

When I finished my makeup, I tiptoed to the bed and slid my heels on, fastened my gold bracelet around my left wrist—one of the few items I had of my mother—and attached a pair of golden earrings to my ears, hanging with emeralds, matching the stone in my brooch. This was as good as it was going to get. I was grabbing my golden bag to put my cell phone in when I heard a knock on the door.

"Come in, it's open." Richard entered the room, a scowl on his forehead.

"Are you ready? You know I want us to go down the stairs together," he announced.

"I'm ready," I replied, pursing my lips.

Richard was a pale-skinned man in his sixties with intense blue eyes and wavy white hair. He was a bit short with a fairly full body. His eyes and smile charmed everyone who did not truly know him.

But I knew better.

I hated this man with every fiber of my being. I cursed the day my mother married him. I was only two years old then, and two years later, my mother died in a car accident and left me with this man for a father.

I had very few memories of my mother, but I remembered her perfume, her smile, and the sound of her voice. I remembered the feeling of being loved, of being comforted, of being fed. My mother was warmth and safety, all of which got ripped from me in an instant, leaving me in the hands of a stranger as a poor excuse for a father.

I didn't know anyone from my mother's family. From a young age, Richard had explained to me that my mother's parents had died, and he knew nothing about my father, who had abandoned my mother when he learned that she was pregnant with me. Richard never stopped reminding me that my mother was a starving artist who had left me with nothing and that, without him, I would be on the streets or in an orphanage.

The man was a bully and a nightmare who always treated me as a charity project instead of the daughter he claimed me to be. When I would disagree with him, he would threaten to kick me out "like the fucking orphan" that I was.

I had spent a good part of my childhood with Richard in Mexico, but after my eleventh birthday, he decided that we should relocate to LA, claiming it was where his business partners and dealings were. Richard always had a strong hatred for Mexico, but I never understood why. And even when he traveled back for business from time to time, he always refused to take me with him.

It always felt like, if he could, he would get rid of everything that connected him to his roots. He even took classes to remove his accent so people couldn't tell where he was from.

As I got older, he became more vicious in the mental games he played. He made it his mission to remind me that he had paid for the expensive bachelor's degrees in hotel management and English that I had obtained in New York and that I "wasn't worth shit" without him. It was his way of ensuring he would forever have his claws in me.

My attention was snapped back to reality as Richard grabbed my hand and brought me to the mirror.

"Well, very beautiful," he declared. "My guests will be delighted to see you! I think George will be happy as well," he said with a clever smile on his lips.

George and I had been dating since I returned to LA after my college graduation and had gotten engaged a few months ago. His ring was shining on my finger, the weight of it feeling uncomfortable. Richard had urged me to meet him, and eventually, I agreed. George was the son of one of the most powerful businessmen in LA, so for Richard, a relationship between the woman he introduced to the world as his daughter and George was a transaction he could not pass on.

While I had been reticent at first, eventually I agreed to date him. The truth was, I didn't really have high hopes when it came to men, but the long distance worked out. I went to Stanford for my graduate degree, and he gave me the distance I so craved in life.

Honestly, I considered George to be a decent man, but I hated the fact that he was Richard's protégé.

"Let's go," ordered Richard, slightly pushing me toward the door. "It's showtime."

I took a deep breath, plastered a dazzling smile on my face, and proceeded to walk out of the room and down the hallway as instructed. I would not have to endure this situation for much longer, I reminded myself.

When we got to the top of the stairs, Richard wrapped his arm around me. We trailed down the staircase together as the guests were cheering and shouting, "Happy birthday!" I forced myself to smile and accept the greetings, kisses, and hugs I received from all these strangers.

After all, in the eyes of California's elite class, I was the happiest young woman in the world. I had it all. According to them, I was beautiful, young, and wealthy, with a father who adored me and the perfect fiancé to top it all off. The world saw Richard as a very clever businessman and a good father to his only daughter—he played the part quite well.

"There you are, honey, more beautiful than ever," complimented George, kissing my hand. "Happy birthday again."

"Thank you." I smiled.

George was a tall, slim, but slightly muscular man with beautiful blue eyes that inspired peace. His light-blond hair was combed toward the right side of his face.

He grabbed two glasses of champagne from one of the waiters and handed me one.

"Thank you."

"Cheers, my dear," said George, toasting with his glass.

The evening was going as slowly as I had feared. I went from group to group with Richard and George by my side. I kept smiling and behaved as the pleasant, seductive, and attractive host Richard wanted me to be.

The celebration was taking place in one of the large halls of the house, which had been transformed into a dance floor surrounded by golden high-top tables for cocktail hour. The event planning crew had installed two bars at each end of the room. Near the entrance were musicians playing soft, instrumental music so the attendees could still hear each other talk.

There must have been at least a hundred people and more than a dozen waiters making sure there was no shortage of drinks and appetizers. I generally found this house, with its white walls and marble floors, to be quite stale. Even the paintings on the walls were devoid of color and life.

Richard had confused sophistication with boredom, as Iris loved to explain—a lesson I feared my stepfather would never learn. But this was no longer my home. Frankly, it never really was.

"Yesterday, Richard and I finally convinced Mr. Ramos to let us buy his property," boasted George.

"That's very good!" I replied, pretending to be interested in the conversation.

After a while, I got a little distracted. For the past thirty minutes, I had observed a broad-shouldered man with dark hair and tan skin staring at me as he made his way through the crowd. He was dressed in a tuxedo, like most men were this evening, but he had chosen a thin black tie instead of a bowtie. He kept a hand in his pocket as he mingled with guests, but he was clearly following my every move with his gaze.

I couldn't see his features very well, but I was sure I had never seen him before. I wouldn't have forgotten a man who looked like he fit—but also didn't. I turned to give him my back and wrapped my arm around George's, still feeling his gaze down my spine. George turned his head and kissed me on the forehead, likely feeling my discomfort.

"Are you okay?" he asked.

"Yes, just a little tired. You know I didn't want such a big birthday party. I would have preferred a dinner for two or to go to the movies."

"We must celebrate. Your father would have been very sad if you had not agreed to have this gala. Look around at everyone who came to see you! Only you could complain about a celebration like this."

"I don't really know these people, and frankly, their company doesn't do much for me."

As George was getting ready to retort, a group of guests joined us. As I smiled and accepted their compliments, Iris made her way to me.

Iris was tall and fit, a naturally elegant woman with warm, golden-blonde hair, defined cheekbones, and gorgeous blue eyes. Her stylish emerald dress, with a high cut on the front leg, brought out the shine in her eyes.

She had been my best friend since middle school, and one of the few people I truly trusted in this world.

"I came to save you! Olivier was taking all my time, but I'm here!" said Iris. She knew that, behind what I hoped was a sensational smile, I hid a lot. She saved me from the inquisitive crowd and took me by the hand to go to the bar.

"Tell Olivier that I was here first!" I joked.

Olivier and Iris had known each other for only a few months. I was very happy for her, but I couldn't help but think the relationship was going way too fast. Iris was a tender soul, and I didn't feel like Olivier appreciated that. He seemed to be in a rush to infiltrate himself into every aspect of her life, and I wasn't sure of his intentions.

I had shared my doubts with Iris, and since then, I felt that he was avoiding me. Iris promised that she hadn't said anything to Olivier, but his behavior seemed to indicate the contrary.

"You have to admit, this is a nice party," teased Iris as we managed to grab an empty table by the bar, a bit far from the rest of the crowd.

"I mean, I didn't expect anything less. He should have hired you, but no, he had to get the same designers his competition used. Instead, the man hired two party planners and made them compete against each other until the very last second."

"Wow, that's intense."

"It always is," I acquiesced.

"Well, I know you hate this, but all we can do is enjoy it," concluded Iris.

"Amen to that!" I declared as I gently tapped my glass to hers.

Iris and I had been best friends since the first week Richard and I had moved to L.A. I had been in school for about a week, a confused little girl who barely spoke any English. Other kids had made fun of me for that. All I wanted was to go back to the life I had been forced to leave behind—a whole different culture, different language, friends, and a home that still had memories of my mother.

But instead, I found myself in an unknown land where people looked at me with curiosity, and sometimes disdain, like they didn't know what I was or how to behave around me.

Then, one day, while I was sitting in the back of the school cafeteria alone, Iris came and offered me half of her sandwich. She had introduced me to other kids and made sure, perhaps without realizing, that I didn't continue to feel like an intruder in my new school. Richard had been thrilled because Iris's dad was a very successful fund manager—just the type of person he wanted desperately to be around.

Iris had been my confidant and gave me strength through her friendship. I missed our Sunday brunches and our escapades to the spa as retaliation against Richard or whatever was pissing us off. She was an excellent interior designer who was already making a name for herself in California. She had started a social media page before college, and was now booked months in advance. We dreamed of working together one day, with Iris deciding themes and decor for hotel chains I would be running.

"I wish Keisha and Chloe had made it," said Iris.

"Yeah, me too, but you know those lawyers and their crazy work schedules," I joked.

"I know." Iris and I met Chloe and Keisha at a college party, and the four of us had been inseparable ever since.

Keisha, Chloe, and Iris had been my everything at the time. It wasn't boys, but the promise of a career and the love I got from that group of wonderful women. We traveled together, protected each other, and took care of each other when one of us was sick. A real support system that made me feel like I finally belonged somewhere. Those girls had become like a family to me.

My mind wandered back to the man who had been making me feel uncomfortable all night. I looked for him around the room, but I could no longer find the man in black.

By the time the clock hit almost eleven in the evening, I was at my wits' end, tired of pretending I was having a good time, so I decided to announce that I needed some fresh air as an excuse to be alone. I quickly removed myself from the group that had interrupted my exile with Iris and claimed to be heading to the bathroom.

When I was finally out of sight, I walked down the hall to the enormous, two-island, all-white, marble-countertop kitchen. I moved through it, quickly exiting to the beautifully landscaped garden. It was an unusually chilly night in May, and the moon was full and beautiful, its light reflecting softly on the trees and their leaves.

I took a deep breath, feeling my shoulders relax instantly. I took off my shoes and walked over to a bench. I sat down on the stone and closed my eyes, letting my feet softly graze the wet grass, my mind drifting into thoughts of the new life I was about to start.

I found peace in thinking about my plans to get away from my stepfather forever. He wanted George and me to live with him after our wedding. I frankly didn't understand why he always wanted to keep control over my life, considering he despised me.

I had hoped that once I turned eighteen, he would make good on his constant threat of getting rid of me, but when I told him I wanted to go study in New York, he had been adamantly opposed. I knew that my reputation was my most precious asset in his eyes since, being his beloved stepdaughter, I was an extension of him. So, I started to party with folks he considered to be 'pretty questionable characters', and those wonderful times were documented all over social networks.

When he learned that I was dating "bums" as he called them, he let me go study in New York. I spent four wonderful years studying at NYU, and then I spent a year traveling Europe. When I returned to New York, after having job offers mysteriously rescinded, I agreed that I had to go back to California, temporarily. I eventually became suspicious that Richard had used his connections to close the doors for me in New York, but I had no proof.

Once I was back in L.A., feeling defeated, I eventually caved and worked at one of Richard's hotels. He eventually allowed me to work at his company, Hotel Estrellas, but with supervision and only when he was there.

Despite Richard treating me like a child, I loved it. I developed an interest in company management and had a desire to be at the round table of executives making decisions, but it seemed like Richard had different plans for me. He wanted to join his company with the McAllens's once I married George. He didn't want me working. He never saw women as equals. I knew that by how I witnessed his treatment of female employees. After that experience, I swore to myself that I would be independent and never need Richard in my life ever again.

That was when I decided to enroll at Stanford, and a month ago, I graduated with my MBA. As much as I wanted to be involved in Hotel Estrellas, I did not want to work for him. I had secretly secured a job in New York and planned on moving out of his house in a month.

A noise in the trees snapped me back to reality and I refocused on my surroundings. I stood up and peered the bushes, trying to find the source of the interruption. Suddenly, I felt a hand grab me by my waist and, before I could cry out, another hand placed a cloth soaked in strong liquid over my face. I tried to fight whoever was attacking me but to no avail.

When I realized I wasn't going to win, I felt fear invade my brain, and before I could try to strike my attacker one last time, everything turned dark.

CHAPTER 2

I HAD A THROBBING headache, but I was starting to regain a semblance of consciousness. I felt what I thought were car vibrations and heard the sound of an engine. There was a piece of cloth wrapped over my eyes and another over my mouth. My hands were bound in front of me with what felt like handcuffs, and my feet were bare. I was starting to come to, and fear washed over me once I realized what had happened. I had been kidnapped.

I hurriedly pushed the blindfold up on my forehead. I could tell that I was lying down in a very dark but spacious car trunk. I heard a man talk. It sounded like he was shouting from a phone. I tried to take a few breaths to slow down my heartbeat so I could focus on hearing.

"Si, la tenemos. We have his daughter," said the voice. The man he was talking to started screaming, but I couldn't make out what he was saying.

"Yes, but..."

The man on the other end of the phone call started to shout again.

"Si, la estamos llevando alla," answered the one in the car.

The conversation then ended.

"He is not happy?" asked another male voice.

"Que piensas, idiota!" shouted the other.

I did my best to keep calm. I, thankfully, remained fluent in Spanish after leaving Mexico and could understand the bilingual conversation perfectly. They were taking me somewhere, and someone was not happy with that, probably with the kidnapping logistics.

Perhaps something hadn't gone as planned. Since I was in the trunk of a car, with what appeared to be at least two men based on the tones of their voices, there was nothing I could do before the car stopped, other than count the seconds in order to avoid the panic attack that was threatening to consume me alive.

I desperately wanted to wake up, find out this was all a dream, that I was back in my room, but every time I reopened my eyes, I was faced with unforgiving darkness and the terrible smell of confined spaces.

The drive felt eternal to me. It seemed like we had been on the road for hours, and I was doing my best to try to keep track of how much time was passing by. Finally, the car came to a full stop, and as I heard doors open and close, I quickly pulled the blindfold back down over my eyes.

The trunk popped open and someone lifted me up, startling me, so as I was pulled out of the vehicle I punched the person with my tied hands, landing straight in their face. The self-defense lessons that Chloe had forced our group of friends to take, finally proved useful. The person let go of me, and I fell heavily to the ground. I quickly removed the blindfold and tried to stand, but the person I hit was faster. I fought as best I could, but the person held me back up as another much shorter and petite one appeared before me. It appeared to be a woman. She landed a punch to my face, stunning me.

I closed my eyes and screamed in pain, but the man took no pity on me and lifted me while holding my hands. I kept moving, terrified of what they would do to me, but another man intervened and lifted my feet. I understood that I had lost the battle. He pulled the blindfold back over my eyes violently as I heard a door open.

"You're going to pay for this!" screamed the woman in English, with a heavy accent. "I'm going to make sure your time here is hell, you spoiled bitch!"

At her words, a paralyzing fear rose inside of me—the realization that I could die.

"Put her in here," ordered the woman.

The men who carried me dropped me down on cold, wet ground. I winced as my side hit the floor, but I refrained from expressing my pain further. Someone came over and removed the blindfold from my eyes.

I had trouble seeing, adjusting to the light and space around me. At first, I couldn't make out my attackers' faces well because they were wearing masks, and we were in a room with barely any light. I could hear the sound of water dripping from the roof in a corner to my right.

I finally was able to see the figures of two large men, tall and muscular. The woman stood in the middle of the two, a bit shorter, with straight black hair cascading over her shoulders. All three of them were wearing masks and dark clothes. It was clear that she was the leader of the group. She looked at me with cold hatred, and a mocking smile danced on her lips. I wondered what I could have possibly done to this woman to justify how she was treating me.

"You're going to sleep here. I'm sure the accommodations will be to the taste of the *princesita*. Don't be afraid when rats and insects come to visit you," she warned, bursting out laughing.

She took a few steps in my direction and lifted my left hand. With her other hand, she smiled at me as she ripped the diamond ring from my finger. I wanted to strangle her, but really that ring didn't mean as much to me as it should. I didn't care if she had it. Thankfully, she didn't seem interested in my bracelet, the only jewelry I really cherished.

The woman walked out of the room, the two men following her. I was too scared to even say a word, my heart pounding in my chest, my legs shaking. I held back a cry of horror when they shut the door and I was left alone in the dark.

The only light source came from a window above a mattress on the left. As my eyes were adjusting to the dark, I saw some insects climbing on the wall to my right. Withholding a cry, I tried to get a little farther from it.

It was clear that I had been kidnapped, and the kidnappers intended to keep me there. I assumed they would want a ransom, probably from Richard.

He would pay for it—I hoped—not out of love but out of obligation. He couldn't stand being ridiculed. I had at least that for comfort. Richard wouldn't stand for being made a fool. In the meantime, I had to face the fact that I was so cold and tired, but I did not dare to sit down. How long would I have to stay wherever the hell I was before Richard helped me?

After two hours of standing, I reluctantly chose a place to sit—the only place in the room illuminated by the moonlight... the mattress. My tight dress wasn't the best of outfits for this situation. I was freezing and very uncomfortable.

The headache that had been creeping up on me was now pounding. I closed my eyes and forced myself to breathe deeply. No one would come to help me this evening, so all I could do was control my heart rate, try to stay calm, and save my energy for whatever was to come.

I woke up to the sound of voices and my head throbbing with intensity. For a few seconds, I forgot where I was. When I recognized the stinking mold and wet smell of the room, I stood up abruptly, my ribs hurting from being dropped to the floor earlier. The voices grew louder outside. It seemed like it was still dark. I had no sense of what time it was. Bile rose from my stomach, and I began to shout, "Get me out of here! Get me out of here! Help! Help!"

The door swung open abruptly, and someone stormed in with full force, pushing me violently to the ground.

"Karina! Stop!" ordered a man's voice.

Karina, who was about to hit me, froze. It was the same woman from earlier. I tried to quickly get up even though my left arm was hurting because I wanted to show these criminals that I was not afraid, even if I was terrified. The man who had given the order entered the room.

"Juan, take her to the other room, and untie her hands when you get there."

He just stood there, hands crossed behind his back. I was trying to see his face when I noticed he wasn't wearing a mask, but he had strategically placed himself in a dark corner, the shadows getting in the way. Perhaps it was for the best. If I learned anything from television, kidnappers didn't generally let their prisoners stay alive if they could help the police identify them.

"Yes, chief," replied the man they had just referred to as Juan.

Juan grabbed me by the arm to lead me toward the door. As I passed by the man who clearly gave the orders, considering how he had screamed at Karina and had decided my fate, I freed myself from Juan to charge toward him, but I was stopped in my tracks. As I pivoted to pull away again, I saw Karina rush toward me, raising her fist and landing a blow to my face, causing my ears to ring.

As I was recovering from the hit, Juan grabbed my arm and began dragging me away. Once out of the room, I let myself be guided. There was nothing I could do in this moment, and it wasn't worth getting hurt further for a futile attempt.

Juan pulled me through a very dark corridor. Finally, he opened a door, removed the handcuffs, pushed me into a room, and closed the door behind me. I stayed right behind it, desperately looking for a light switch to identify what new hell I was in.

I finally felt myself breathe when I flipped a light switch, and a very dim light came on. I was in a small room with a single window, much too small to escape from. There was a twin bed by the wall as well as a bedside table.

I was overcome with fatigue and fear, living the worst of nightmares, but at least there was a bed and no crawling insects—a slight upgrade from the first space. Tears filled my eyes and rolled down my cheeks as I sank on a corner of the bed. As much as I didn't want to admit it, I realized this unimaginable situation was becoming my horrifying reality.

I tried to stay calm, though. I couldn't let these assholes win.

About two days passed with me locked in the room. One of the men brought me food twice a day. I managed to sip a little bit of water, but I couldn't bring myself to eat.

If this was for money, I would hopefully be out of this place sooner rather than later. All I could do to keep my sanity was force myself to think of happy thoughts, to go back to memories that made me happy, and ignore the sense of doom that was threatening to engulf me.

To ground myself, I focused on memories of my wonderful college days, far from my stepfather. I focused on the wonderful trips I had taken with my friends, back when my life was filled with hope and excitement for what was to come.

Perhaps my mistake had been going back to California, back to my stepfather, who clearly was the reason I was taken in the first place. There was no other explanation. I couldn't fathom what he could have possibly done and what role I was to play in it.

It was, of course, always possible that my situation was just bad luck. People knew my family had money, and perhaps that was all it took for someone to decide they had the right to take my freedom, and my life, away from me.

CHAPTER 3

Four days. That was the amount of time that passed, and I was left alone in a dim room with a bathroom break only once a day, when one of the men came to get me to take me across the hall.

The first couple days, I screamed, cried, knocked on the door, but they didn't care. All I heard was laughter and mumbled conversations.

If I let fear consume me, I was done for. And I couldn't be. I had a life waiting for me out there, goals, ambitions, so much I wanted to accomplish. I had to believe it wouldn't end like this. It couldn't. I needed to escape. I needed to find a way.

I was losing track of time when one of my captors walked into the room. He was bringing me one of the plates of the day. He moved further into the room—as usual, avoiding any eye contact and always with a mask on—and he placed my plate on the floor, turning to quickly leave like he always did, as if being in the room with me for more than a few seconds would cost him something.

Before he was out the door, I gathered the strength to stand up and go to him, grabbing his hand in mine, hoping human contact would help me plead my case.

"Please help me. I can pay you double whatever it is they are giving you. You seem like a nice person. Please, I need your help," I tried.

He did not answer. He just stared at me with those bored, dark eyes.

For a moment, I thought he might actually help me. Instead, he removed his hands from mine, hastily moved to the door, and proceeded to close it behind him.

I held the doorknob but let the door close. I had been observing that door for days now, at times playing with the knob, toying with a backup plan, concocting ways to escape should I fail to appeal to his humanity, and I had. He would think that it was locked, but I knew better.

The door would not lock as he thought, because the doorknob did not close by itself as it normally would. I figured out that if I could hold the doorknob at the right time and with the right pressure, I could stop it from locking while someone who was not paying close attention would assume that it was. And this time, it worked.

I had learned to do this when I snuck out of Richard's house in my rebel days. You could hold a doorknob, close a door, and then slowly release it so that no one could hear it. I held my breath for a second to see if he would notice the different sound, but when nothing happened, I knew I was in the clear.

I was afraid to open the door, as I had no idea who was outside or what could be waiting for me. I stayed there, frozen with fear, for what felt like hours but in reality was probably only minutes, as I waited for the voices I could hear to dissipate.

I was conscious of my heartbeat pounding in my ears. Maybe I could try another time, now that I knew how to do it. I could always wait for another day to try to escape.

No, I would not let fear paralyze me. This could be my one and only chance to escape from this place, and not taking a chance at freedom could turn out to be a life-or-death decision. The man might pay closer attention next time. He might realize the door did not lock well. I might be too slow or too fast and lose my chance for real.

I didn't consider myself a very brave woman, but I also didn't usually let fear control my life.

I was choosing to fake the courage I didn't feel for a chance at getting my life back, for a chance at survival.

Taking a deep breath, I turned the doorknob to the right and slowly opened the door. Hesitantly, I peeked my head forward to see if there was anyone around. I saw a small, dimly lit corridor, but there was no one in sight.

I wasn't sure which way to go, but I noticed there was some natural light filtering through on my right. I closed the door without making a noise. Looking behind me almost every second, I started walking toward the light. The floor was cold under my bare feet, just like the room I was being held in. There was still no one in sight, and since the floor was made of cement, they couldn't really hear my footsteps.

I finally reached another door. It seemed to be my only way out, so I had to decide whether I was willing to take a chance on whatever was on the other side or go back to my prison.

I lingered there for a moment, listening attentively. I was met with bone chilling silence—not necessarily reassuring. I could, of course, go back to the corridor and head the opposite way, but I didn't have the strength to do so. I inhaled deeply. *Here we go. Life or death.* I assembled the little bit of strength I found deep in myself and proceeded.

Grabbing the doorknob, I twisted it slowly to the right. The door opened with a creak. I swiftly glanced behind me, worried that someone would've heard the noise. There was no one. I pushed the door a little wider and peeked through.

I found myself in a small, dark, and messy kitchen. There was some sort of a stove on my right, a fridge on my left, as well as a very beaten-up sink. There were several gallons of water on the floor and a skeletal kitchen island in the middle. That was where they must've been making my meals. That would explain the clatter I would hear from the room.

I proceeded to the back of the kitchen where I could see an open door. Considering the amount of light that was coming in, I hoped it led to the outside. After a few more steps, I thought I might actually have a shot at freedom.

I reached the open door and finally stepped outside. I found myself in a beat-up backyard where the grass and cement appeared to be competing for space. I noticed three black-and-silver motorcycles parked outside. There was still no one there, and I could actually see a road. If I could only run to it, I would be free. I would be able to stop a car and get some help.

I hesitated again for a second, worried about what they might do to me if they caught me. But now wasn't the time to be scared or change my mind. I told myself I had to keep going.

I scanned behind me one last time, then to my left and right, and started running low, trying to keep myself as close to the ground as possible, my dress making the task quite challenging. I stopped by the motorcycles, frantically looking for keys, but did not find any. Giving up on that idea, I continued running a little faster toward the open road.

Discovering a line of trees bordering the road, I decided it was my best chance for cover. I followed the road behind the trees for as long as I could. When I reached the end, all I could do was run or walk on the grass next to the road. There were no houses for miles, just empty land.

I had no idea where I was, and I hadn't seen one car pass by for the ten minutes I had been walking. The sun was out, bright and shining, beating on my bare back and shoulders. It looked like it would be hours before dark. My hope was to find either a ride or shelter by the time night came.

As if by magic, I saw a car speeding toward me—a pickup truck kicking up so much dust that I had to cover my eyes for a second and hold my breath.

The car sped past me, and I felt instant defeat. But as I was just about to continue my trek, I noticed the truck start to drift sideways as it came to a stop, blocking the street behind me completely.

Something didn't seem right, and I instantly questioned whether this person was a friend or enemy.

A man stormed out of the driver's seat, staring at me attentively for a few seconds. He then started slowly marched towards me, as if not to spook me. I didn't know if I should run away from him or stand my ground. It all depended on his intentions, and I had no control over that. As he got closer to me, I could finally see his face, although I couldn't make out his features very well.

An angry scowl creased his face. He was wearing a pair of dark-blue jeans, a white shirt, and a perfectly tailored gray suit jacket. He had a gun tucked into the right side of his jeans. He quickened his pace, his steps seemingly growing more urgent.

Panic invaded my senses, and I started running in the opposite direction with all my strength, my bare feet burning as they hit the hot concrete with force. I had to get away from this man as fast as I could. Perhaps another car would come by and help me.

Unfortunately, he was next to me in the blink of an eye. He grabbed me by the waist, spun me around, lifted me up, and before I knew it, he was carrying me on his shoulders. I was fighting him as best as I could, pulling on and scratching his jacket, kicking my feet—to no avail. He wasn't fazed, his toned body too built to feel any of it.

"Let me go!" I screamed. "Let me go! You can't do this! LET. ME. GO!"

He held me tight with his left arm behind my knees, seemingly unharmed by my attempted strikes. I could no longer kick him as his strong forearm held my thighs firmly against his chest.

"Stop it!" he ordered brusquely in perfect English. "There is no point in fighting. There's nowhere for you to go!"

"Ahhhh!" I continued to scream even louder.

My hands were tired from aimlessly smashing against his hard back, but I had to continue fighting. He definitely was not the savior I was expecting him to be.

We got to his pickup truck, and he opened the back door, shoving me in on my back. I looked up, horrified, as he was getting in, closing the door behind him.

What was he going to do with me?

I started kicking, trying to push him out and looking behind me to find a way to open the door at my back. He abruptly held my legs to stop the blows. With each of his hands holding my thighs apart at my knees, he pulled me violently toward him and positioned himself in between my legs and on top of me, his weight pinning me down. He was going to rape me—I was sure of it.

This couldn't be happening. My blood rose to my brain, but I couldn't move. I was now not only screaming but also crying from fear. The idea of a stranger penetrating me against my will made me want to die.

"Please stop!" I pleaded. "Please, I'm begging you!"

Now that I could not move my legs, he grabbed each of my wrists. I closed my eyes, waiting for impact. I was sure he was going to hit me. Instead, he just held my wrists together.

"Damn it, stop fighting me!" he said. "I don't want to hurt you."

I opened my eyes, confused at what he just said.

I was met with the glare of two dark eyes, filled with anger and exhaustion. Broad shoulders and thick, curly black hair framed a wide forehead, thick black brows, a straight nose, full sensual lips, a strong jaw, and a determined chin.

This man looked familiar. I had seen him before, but I didn't know where from. Why was he trying to take me?

While still pinning my wrists together, his hand pressing my bracelet into my skin, he used his left hand to pull a black tie out of his right jacket pocket.

When I realized what he was going to do, I started moving away, trying to get out from under him. But the weight of his body on top of mine kept me under his control no matter how hard I fought. He moved my arms down and tied my wrists together tightly behind my back with his tie, his chest hard and strong against mine. He then reached down under the right seat and pulled out a rope.

He momentarily lifted his body up so he could grab my legs and started tying them together too. I was still trying to free myself, aggressively moving to undo the knot he did with the tie, but he was too fast. He was already done with my legs and was grabbing my wrists again to make sure I had not done too much damage to his knot. He lifted me from the seat and put me on the ground of the car. Closing the door, he walked to the front of the car and sat in the driver's seat.

"Now, we can do this one of two ways," he said as he turned to capture my attention. "You can lie back down where I put you and make this easy for yourself, or you can continue what is obviously a pointless and stupid attempt to escape until I tire and hurt you. You choose."

"Fuck you!" I screamed at him.

He did not flinch and continued to stare at me, a paralyzing intensity darkening his eyes even further. My hands turned cold. I was afraid, and I knew he was completely serious, and more importantly, he was right. He had a gun and could shoot me if he decided it was not worth the struggle. There was nothing I could do in the middle of nowhere. I had to accept defeat, at least temporarily.

I turned my head to stop facing him directly and reluctantly lay back down on the ground on my back.

"Good, you are not as stupid as you seem," he mocked, with a satisfied smirk on his face.

I was fuming. I would make it my mission to remove that fucking smirk from his face.

It was clear he was associated with the kidnappers, but this was the first time I saw one of their faces fully. If I had to guess, this man was probably the person who showed up after I was taken to the house. It sounded like the same voice, with a very slight accent, and he had a similar physical build.

I closed my eyes and tried to calm down. It was important that I controlled my emotions and not show my fears to this stranger. While I didn't know what he was capable of, the strength and intensity emanating from him gave me goosebumps and made a pit drop in my stomach. He scared me more than I cared to admit. I felt like I had run away from hell, only to fall in the hands of the devil himself.

CHAPTER 4

WHERE WAS HE TAKING me? I wanted to ask him questions, but I did not think he would be in the mood to give me answers.

I turned my head slightly to the right to observe him. He was a tall, built man with golden skin, a bit darker than mine. I stared at his strong jaw for a minute, trying to decipher some emotion. I could tell he was furrowing his brows and was very focused on the mission at hand, getting to the next location as soon as possible.

I closed my eyes again. There was no point in torturing myself, trying to find answers to questions only he could answer but surely wouldn't. The sun was still coming in full force, warming my body. The warmth provided some solace, distracting me from what had the potential to be the end of my life as I knew it.

We were no longer on a straight path, I gathered, since the car slowed down, and I could now feel bumps and curves. As I painfully lifted my body to peek out the window, I noticed we were driving on a very narrow street bordered by very tall trees behind which the sun was starting to hide. It felt like we were going up a hill.

A few minutes later, the car came to a halt.

"Don't move," he ordered as he twisted in his seat to face me.

I did not answer and just stared at my kidnapper. He must have taken my silence as an agreement because he climbed out of the car. I could hear him chatting with another man.

"Llevatela al cuarto," I overheard him order.

They were about to lock me in some room again, and panic started coursing through my veins. Before I could do anything, someone opened the door behind me and shoved a bag over my head.

I started fighting my aggressor as he dragged me out of the car. But I had to catch myself as he pulled me to my feet.

"I wouldn't do that if I were you," threatened the voice of the man who drove us here.

I let out a whimper, unable to hide my fear any longer. I heard him sigh, he sounded a bit closer to me. I felt him untying the cord around my feet.

"Behave and nothing will happen to you," he explained in a deep but calmer voice.

He was right. I had lost the battle today, and I could only hope my failed escape didn't put me in a worse situation than I was in before. Someone grabbed my right arm.

"Ven," instructed the person.

This time, I followed without a fight. It wasn't worth it.

I could hear doors open and close. It felt like we had been veering through a maze of corridors for a few minutes before my tour guide and I came to a halt. He pushed me in a room and untied my hands. I heard him close the door behind me.

I cursed and angrily took the bag off my head.

I found myself in a small bedroom. It was simple, but at least it was clean. There was a small bed in the middle with two dark oak nightstands on either side. The mattress had no sheets or pillows. A full-length mirror was leaning on the wall across from the bed. There was a small chandelier in the middle of the ceiling, the only source of light since it was a windowless room, and there were no lamps.

The space did not really look like a bedroom that was in use. It would be hard not to get claustrophobic in this room. It was so far the smallest space my kidnappers had put me in, but at least it smelled good and there was light.

Someone knocked on the door.

"Yes?" I answered, confused.

I heard a key in the doorknob, and a short woman with long black hair braided all the way down her back entered, carrying a tray with food and water on it. She immediately closed the door behind her and stood in silence, staring at me.

She observed my dirty hair matted to my face, my dress ripped and covered in dirt, and my feet dark with dust and mud. I knew I looked a little rough, but I didn't realize how much until this moment. I likely didn't smell great either. The longer she stared at me in clear disgust, the more I realized how bad I must look.

"Ay dios, pero que te hicieron?" she inquired.

I didn't answer. They kidnapped me—that's what they did to me. The answer was obvious.

The woman put the tray down on the bed.

"You want to shower?" she asked in English, with a heavy accent. I could not utter a word. I just started crying.

"Ay, no llores. Come, come. Let me take you to the shower."

She grabbed my dirty hand and opened the door. She escorted me down a very short hallway and opened the only other door just a few steps away. She pushed me in very quickly.

"Be fast, and don't try anything, please. They are everywhere." She quickly shut the door.

"Thank you so much. What is your name?"

"De nada, señorita. I am Dolores. I will be waiting here for you. Please, rapido!" Dolores closed the door behind her.

I was touched by Dolores's kindness. This woman did not know me and yet seemed to have taken my well-being to heart. She also seemed scared, probably of the brute who drove me to the house and seemed to be ordering everyone around.

The bathroom was very simple. There was a small but well-lit white square sink with a nice size mirror above it. The shower was a walk-in. When I opened the sink cabinet, I found some toiletries. Who thought I would feel such happiness at finding some toothpaste and a toothbrush?

I also found a few towels as well as some body wash and shampoo. I started to brush my teeth with the same enthusiasm children show for chocolate.

I could see my pale, dirty, and bony reflection in the mirror, my face covered with dust with streaks of tears going through whatever was left of my foundation. The mascara from days ago emphasized the dark circles under my eyes. My dress was a lost cause.

I remembered that Dolores was waiting for me outside, very nervous. There was no time to waste. I undressed myself and got into the shower. The feeling of the clean, warm water penetrating my hair, running down my face and the rest of my sore body was invigorating. I could not get enough of the shampoo and the soap. I washed myself thoroughly, but I still felt the need to do it once more, as if that would erase this nightmare I was living. It still didn't feel like enough.

Once done, I proceeded to dry my hair and body with a towel. With my skin clean, I could see the bruises on my face, hips, arms, and wrists more clearly. I ignored them and wrapped myself in the soft towel. There was no way I was going to put back on that dirty, ripped dress.

I timidly opened the door. Dolores had a look of relief on her face. She saw that I was holding the towel around me and, thankfully, understood my predicament. She took me by the hand and quickly guided me back to the room.

"Stay here. I'll be right back," instructed Dolores.

I did as I was told, but of course, Dolores locked the door with a key behind her. I settled on the bed, feeling my body both numb and in pain at the same time, in dire need of rest, but my mind couldn't stop. My life was in danger, after all. I forced myself to lie down on the mattress, even if just to stare at the ceiling.

Ten minutes later, Dolores was back with a pile of clothes in her hands. She shut the door behind her and set the clothes down on the bed.

"Here you go: clothes, some underwear, a comb for your hair, lotion, deodorant, and also, sandals and bed sheets."

I could not believe my eyes. In tears, I got up and hugged her. Dolores hugged me back for a second and then took a step back. She gazed at me with what seemed like understanding and sadness.

"I have to go now," she said, and then she left, locking the door behind her again.

I started going through the pile of clothes. There was one yellow dress with thin straps that was simple and delicately embroidered along the bottom. There was also a set of gray female gym clothes.

I had no idea where Dolores could have found these gems, but I was very thankful for them. I used all the lotion my body craved and put on the gym clothes. They would be handier if I decided—or rather, was presented with the opportunity—to try to escape again. I combed through my wet and now very curly hair and braided it in place. *Much better*, I concluded as I stood in front of the mirror.

My small figure looked well protected in gym clothes. My face was still bony, but at least it was clean. I stored the rest of the things in the two nightstand drawers and proceeded to make the bed. There were now clean sheets sitting on the mattress. And they were soft, promising me at least some rest—something I hadn't had in too long.

Thank you, Dolores.

As soon as I was done making the bed, I turned to the plate of food Dolores had left me. It was an amazing quesadilla with a side of rice and beans. I almost swallowed the food whole. It was my first full meal in a week—or at least the first I accepted and devoured. I was enjoying the freshly squeezed orange juice and the very big, cold glass of water.

When I was done, I set the tray down on the floor by the door. Exhaustion was getting the best of me, and I let it. There was no point in thinking right now. I needed all the strength I could muster, to be ready for what was to come—whatever that would be. I got in the bed and fell asleep as soon as my head touched the pillow.

When I woke up the next morning, I felt very rested, but It took me a few minutes to remember the events of the day before. As I got off the bed, I noticed that the plate of food was gone. Someone must have come in to take it.

"Hello? Can someone hear me?" I inquired behind the door.

I heard a key turning in the doorknob, so I took a few steps back. Dolores entered with a smile on her face.

"Sleep well?"

"Yes, thank you so much for everything you brought me yesterday. I really needed a shower!"

"Si! And now you need bathroom again?"

"Yes, please. That would be great."

Dolores took my hand in hers, just as she did the day before, and guided me to the bathroom. I was thrilled to get to brush my teeth and shower again. I put the gym clothes back on afterward. As I was combing through my freshly washed curls, the bathroom door flue wide open.

A man who was wearing a mask dragged me out by my left arm. He pulled a bag over my head and forced me to walk.

"Pero porque tanta violencia!?" cried out Dolores, but he was not bothered and continued to walk fast even as I stumbled.

I tried to resist but to no avail. Finally, he opened a door and shoved me inside before closing it behind me.

I hurriedly took the bag off my head, finding myself standing in a big office with a thick, impressive oak table in the middle with oak cabinets filled with all sorts of books. The wood floor was half covered by a beige rug. The sun was shining through two very large bay windows across the room, and I could see an immense yard, bordered by trees peeking from behind the see-through white linen drapes. There was a table by the window, with a chess board and a record player.

A man was standing behind the desk closest to the window, staring outside.

He slowly turned around, and I couldn't help the gasp that escaped me. Facing me was the brute who so violently put me into his pickup truck and drove me to this unknown location. He continued to just stare at me, not saying a word, as I could feel the water from my wet hair roll down my neck and back.

I wanted to either scream at him or snap around and run away, but I restrained myself and held his gaze with a stoic face instead.

"I hope you find your new accommodations pleasing," he said with a faint smile on his face. I wondered if that was mockery or if he was just a psychopath. Authority seemed to emanate from his every pore.

"Well," I retorted with a hard swallow, "it was quite a low bar, considering I had rats as cellmates before."

"My apologies for that," he said with a slight bend of his head.

When our eyes met, I could have sworn I saw a flicker of amusement flash in his gaze, an eyebrow raised.

He didn't break eye contact as he made his way slowly to his desk. He stopped by the corner and leaned his back against it for support, his arms crossed, his gaze still fixated on me. His stance seemed like an intimidation technique.

And it was working.

He was wearing a pair of black jeans and a blue shirt with the first two buttons open. I noticed how tall he was again, his shirt tracing his muscles, letting everyone know he was a man to be feared. His tan skin indicated that he spent a lot of time outside in the sun. I got even more irritated as he just stood there, in all his glory, legs opened wide, looking like he owned the world.

I took a deep breath between clenched teeth.

"Who are you, and what do you want from me?" I asked calmly.

"My name is Alejandro," he said.

"I'd say nice to meet you, but I'd be lying."

"And I wouldn't believe you."

I rolled my eyes. "Since it seems like you can only answer one question at a time, let me ask you again, what do you want from me?"

Alejandro eased off the desk and started toward me, moving deliberately with his hands in his pockets. He came to a halt just a few inches from me. I swallowed hard, fear pouring through my veins, but I had to stand my ground. This asshole was not going to get the satisfaction of seeing me afraid.

"You privileged little brat," he grunted in a deeper voice that sent shivers down my spine. "Let me remind you that you are currently very far from home without anyone to protect you. Tread lightly. I don't accept insolence and have no tolerance for a spoiled, useless woman like you. I suggest you watch your tone when you speak to me."

My hands started to shake, but I quickly hid them in my pockets, doing my best to ignore the adrenaline coursing through me, telling me to run as fast as I could.

Instead, I held his gaze. It wasn't his words that scared me; it was the calm and yet threatening tone that made every hair on my body rise. It was the way he never broke eye contact from the minute he turned around when I walked in the room.

He observed my bruised face and wrists as his jaw clenched and lips got tighter. He looked disgusted by me.

"I need to know—"

"No, you don't," he said, cutting me off. "You don't need to know anything, and I don't owe you any explanation."

I let out an exasperated sigh.

"I have been held in captivity for over a week. I have bruises all over, and I am sore, and I am tired. I deserve to know what you want from me," I explained with a broken voice.

Alejandro backed up a few steps and headed toward his desk.

"You are your father's little pride and joy," he said with disgust. "Let's just hope he does what he has to do so you can get back to your little castle in no time."

There was no point in arguing with him. I knew I wouldn't get anything else out of him. And if he believed that my stepfather was going to do all it took to rescue me, it was my best card, even if I was starting to doubt it myself. If Alejandro or any other person involved believed that Richard wasn't going to help, my life would no longer be of any value to them.

"Are you... are you going to kill me?"

My question was met with silence and indifference.

I swallowed hard but pushed further. "What do you want from him? Money?"

"It's time for lunch," he said, ignoring my question.

He grabbed his phone and placed a call.

"Dolores, nos sirves la comida en mi despacho por favor? Gracias."

Everyone spoke Spanish in this house. I had no doubt now that I had somehow crossed the frontier to somewhere in Mexico.

Apparently, Alejandro intended to have Dolores bring lunch for the both of us in his office. Was he crazy? He kidnapped me, and now he wanted to, what, break bread with me? Who in their right mind would see this situation as normal?

"We will sit out here to eat our lunch," he announced as he opened one of the glass doors.

I reluctantly followed him out to a gray-stone patio with a nice off-white couch and a rectangular glass dining table with matching chairs. Two place settings were already set out on the table. Outside smelled of rain and freshly cut grass, but the sun was coming out, warming up the air and clearing up the skies.

The patio was big, but the bright-green yard was the size of a park, going all the way into what looked like the beginning of a forest. I could see part of the house as well. I was starting to realize that I was ironically being held captive in the most gorgeous Mexican hacienda I had ever seen.

I was enjoying the feeling of the sun caressing my skin after being away from it for a week. I wanted to scream that I refused to eat with him, but I was so excited to get to sit in the sun and breathe in some fresh air that I decided to swallow my pride and keep quiet. He pulled a chair out for me, and I reluctantly sat down. He took a seat next to me, at the head of the table.

"This is your house?"

"Yes." He raised a brow in my direction, looking annoyed.

"Do you usually use your house to hold people captive?"

He glanced at me. "No, not usually," he answered, leaning back in his chair and facing me.

He moved slowly, almost sensually, the way a panther moves right before it catches its prey. I was terrified, but part of me was fascinated. I considered if I should try to run again and take my chances with the animals in the forest instead.

Dolores came outside with a big tray. She had a younger woman with her to help set the food on the table. Dolores smiled at me, and I smiled back. Dolores and the other woman placed down various plates with chicken, beef, and pork, a good amount of corn and flour tortillas, and all the necessary condiments for fresh homemade tacos. They also set down a water pitcher and an orange juice pitcher.

"Muchas gracias, muchachas. Pueden retirarse."

The ladies immediately retreated with their empty trays.

"Ladies first," said Alejandro, turning to me.

The man spoke both perfect Spanish and perfect English, a slight accent present when he spoke English, but so far only when he was upset. I wanted to ask questions, but really, where he was from wasn't quite relevant to my current situation.

I wanted to pretend I wasn't interested in the food, but I was too hungry to be prideful. I started making myself various tacos and sat back down to devour them. Alejandro proceeded to do the same.

I forgot that I had company as I was enjoying what were, hands down, the best tacos I had ever had. As I was getting ready for my second serving, I noticed Alejandro glancing at me, seemingly amused.

"I bet they don't make tacos this good in your little castle."

"No. In my castle, as you call it," I retorted, "we don't eat Mexican food."

"Of course you don't. You and your family are the worst kinds of Mexican immigrants. You assimilate completely and lose all touch with your roots." He gave me a disgusted stare, his eyes dark with judgment.

I realized I might have offended him. He must have misunderstood what I was trying to say. If anything, I hated that Richard had banned what he called "dirty street food" in his house. But I did not owe this man any explanation.

"You don't know me," I said. "You know nothing about me, so stop pretending that you do to make yourself feel better about what you are doing to me—and god knows who else."

"I know you. I know your kind." His jaw clenched in warning, but I ignored it.

"My kind? What does that even mean? It's the stupidest—"

"Enough!" he cut me off, his lips tight. "I don't have to explain myself to you."

As I was about to answer him, Dolores stepped in. "Everything okay?" she asked, clearly concerned by the screams she overheard when she entered the office.

"Call Juan to take her back to her room. She's done here," ordered Alejandro.

Dolores hesitated, disappointed to see that lunch had taken a turn, but she clearly knew better than to contradict Alejandro.

"And you call me a spoiled brat," I said, standing up, "but you are the one being a jackass the minute someone disagrees with you. You, sir, are a fucking asshole and a criminal!"

Alejandro violently shoved his chair back as he got up, grabbed me by my left arm, and pushed me inside his office.

"I've had enough of you and your attitude."

"Then let me go home!" I screamed.

Dolores had already returned with Juan. He was still wearing a mask. He came straight to me, put a bag over my head, grabbed my right arm, and proceeded to drag me with him.

I was tired of being the cooperative victim and decided to give him a taste of his own medicine. I stepped on his foot, and he let go of my arm, in pain. As I was lifting the bag past my forehead, Alejandro grabbed me by my upper thighs and lifted me. He plopped me on his right shoulder like I weighed nothing and proceeded to walk. The bag was no longer on my head, but I couldn't see anything since I was upside down. I kicked and screamed.

Alejandro finally swung the bedroom door open, marched in, closed the door behind us, and threw me on the bed.

I opened my eyes wide, my pupils dilated with fear, realizing the error of my ways, provoking a criminal like that. And now he was towering over me, mouth open, teeth showing, panting, fury coming out his pores, the room seemingly too small for his presence. I had provoked the beast, and I was at his mercy. If he decided to rape me or harm me in any other way, there wasn't a lot I would be able to do to protect myself. My body was shaking, and my eyes were round with fear.

"Insolent brat," he growled as he bolted out of the room.

I quickly got up in a futile attempt to try to leave behind him, but he was already out, locking the door.

I screamed in anger and started crying. I was livid. Who did this man think he was? He kidnapped me, insulted me, and somehow expected me to do, what, behave? This brute had no idea who I was, but if he wanted me to be a nice little wallflower that wouldn't talk to keep him happy, he had another thing coming.

CHAPTER 5

Dolores brought me both lunch and dinner for a couple days, but I couldn't eat. On the third day, when she came to escort me to the bathroom to have a shower, she insisted that I wear the dress instead of the gym clothes, but I refused. After I was taken back to my room, I spent the day in bed, half asleep.

The next day, after I barely touched my breakfast, Dolores told me that I was expected to go to lunch, but I not so respectfully declined. Fear was causing me to be depressed, my earlier resolve to escape looking quite dire. This house, from what I could tell during my short bathroom breaks, was much better guarded than the previous location.

With all the men that stood guard around the premises, it felt like I was in the middle of a wolf pack, with Alejandro at the head. They clearly had a rotation, my every move under the gaze of at least three men. As time went by, nothing changed, no mistake, no avenue for escape.

If it wasn't for Dolores telling me the day and time, I would have had no notion of it, and it was affecting me tremendously. I was surprised when she came in with a small digital clock in her hand. The small amount of freedom and control that came in that moment was priceless, providing comfort and a semblance of normalcy to this hell I was in.

It was about seven p.m. on a Thursday, well over two weeks since I had been home, when Alejandro came into my room without knocking. He was dressed in all black, his hair wet, and his curls pushed back. I was still lying in bed and pulled the sheets higher to my neck as he made his way to my side.

"We are going to have dinner together tonight," he announced.

"I don't want to."

"It wasn't a suggestion."

"I'm not hungry," I tried to explain, glaring at him.

"Yes, you are, and you look like death."

I turned my head to avoid his gaze.

"I expect to see you for dinner in ten minutes," he ordered before he walked out, leaving a trail of masculine fragrance notes behind him, teasing my nostrils and piquing my interest despite my best judgment.

There was no way I was going to join this man for dinner—or anything, for that matter. Dolores walked in behind him and sat on the corner of the bed.

"Por favor, señorita, go to dinner. You need to eat."

I didn't answer. While I saw concern in Dolores's dark eyes, I was here in this house against my will. I didn't have to dine with my captor on top of it.

"He's a good man, señorita. Just, eh... bad tempered right now."

"A good man?! Que secuestra?" How could she call a kidnapper a good man?

"Ay, no sabia que hablabas español!" she said with a smile, pleased that I answered her in her native tongue.

"Si, vivia en Mexico por un tiempo antes," I answered, explaining to Dolores that I had lived in Mexico.

My first language was one of the few things from my life in Mexico that Richard wasn't able to get rid of.

"Ay, que bueno." She paused, seemingly contemplating what to say next.

"Yo se que las cosas son raras," she proceeded to explain. "But it's... esta complicado todo."

Dolores stopped, seemingly toeing the line between making me feel more comfortable and telling me too much.

"What?" I pressed. "What is so complicated? He just wants money."

"No, señorita."

"What do you mean?"

Dolores sighed but got up, ignoring my questions. She pulled the yellow dress out of the nightstand. "Let's go, please. I will help you get ready."

I hesitated.

"It's for your own good. You can ask questions, señorita. Maybe el patron will... I don't know." She sighed. "He is a good man, señorita."

I felt bad for Dolores. She really looked very concerned and clearly did not want to cause me any harm. Plus, I was hungry. I gave in and followed Dolores to the bathroom, admitting to myself that if I had any chance of escaping, I needed to feed myself and be as friendly as I could manage.

Dolores wasn't left in the dark as to my situation, and she also clearly had some information about my captor that could be useful. More importantly, Dolores was heavily hinting at a complicated situation and perhaps interests that weren't just financial, urging me to find my eagerness to survive, take matters into my own hands, gather information, and hopefully use it to find my freedom. Dolores gave me the hope I had been missing the past few days.

I showered quickly and slid the dress on. It was a tad loose on me, but I loved the embroidery on the dress. The top part was very fitted, but the bottom part of the dress was a nice flowing skirt that moved in harmony with every step I took.

Dolores sat me down and combed my hair, shaking her head as she noticed the bruises on my shoulder. She pulled two hairpins covered with small pearls out of her pocket and used them to pull my hair back, letting the rest of my curls fall down to my shoulder blades.

"Those are beautiful," I said. "Thank you." Dolores smiled and pinched my cheeks.

"Adding color to your lovely face," explained Dolores. "You are now ready for dinner," she announced. "Let's go."

"No head bag tonight?" I asked when Dolores started taking me down the hallway.

"No," she answered with a smile. "Juan is not here today."

"Why does it matter if Juan is here or not?" Dolores ignored me and continued walking.

I was starting to realize how big the hacienda was, as I could finally walk around more than the hallway without my face being covered. The ceilings were high, and we passed multiple rooms that looked like they were taken straight from a magazine, but there was no time to stop and explore—we were on a mission.

Dolores finally stopped in front of two big wooden doors. She knocked to announce us and opened one of them. She told me to walk in and closed the door behind me.

The formal dining room was stunning. The walls were decorated with some artwork I recognized as amate bark paintings. There was a beautiful chandelier in the center of the high ceiling. In the middle of the room was an eight-person, walnut dining table with hand-carved legs and chairs. A big bouquet of creamy white Dahlia's was in the middle. There was a china cabinet on the left wall. The wall on the right had a long painting depicting three very colorful birds, seemingly flying around each other with grace and elegance.

Across the room, I could see a bay window and, next to it, a small bar. Alejandro was standing there, pouring himself a whiskey.

"Do you want a glass?" he offered.

"No, thank you."

"Please, take a seat."

I kindly declined. I wanted to move around, stretch my legs. I headed to the table to take a closer look at the flowers. I knew there were native of Mexico. I smiled as I caressed the petals. I was also fascinated by all the works of art in the room. I walked to one of the paintings to admire it more closely. It was beautiful, inspiring both freedom and happiness.

"You like this painting?" he whispered right behind me. I felt his breath down my neck and shivered as I held back mine.

"Yes," I managed to answer. "Traditional papel amate paper. I love seeing how colors come alive on such a unique canvas."

"How do you know this?"

"I am not as uncultured as you seem to think I am," I said, turning around.

I hadn't realized how close he was standing. I was now facing him, looking into those deep-brown orbs. They almost seemed sad.

My breast lightly rubbed against his chest. We stood there for what seemed like an eternity. I was breathing in every inch of him, a bit startled by my treacherous body's reaction. His smell was so masculine, a mix of tobacco, a bit of bergamot, a trail of lavender, and a touch of sandalwood.

This man was a god walking amongst mortals, and as much as I wanted to be indifferent, I still found myself breathing rapidly.

But he was my keeper, his savage beauty only contributing to the sense of danger I felt every time I looked at him. I was keenly aware of my situation. I was in his hands, at his whim.

He made sure to remind me, with this invitation, pretending that I was a guest and not a prisoner. He was taunting me for some reason, standing way too close to me, but two could play that game. The reality was that it was in my best interest to be pleasant. My survival depended on it—however disgusting it might be.

He cleared his throat. "I, uh... I wanted to apologize for my behavior last time." He sighed.

I, on the other hand, remained frozen. I tried to speak, but my throat was dry. I couldn't think of what to say in this situation, with him being so frustratingly close. My captor had just apologized to me for being rude.

That wasn't what I expected. Brutes didn't apologize; they just took. Even Richard had never apologized to me, not when he had called my mother a slut, not when he told me it was a shame my skin wasn't as light as his, not when he reminded me that I was a poor excuse for a daughter.

I searched Alejandro's deep eyes, wondering what game he was playing. He seemed sincere, but then again, he was a criminal.

"Buenas noches."

Both Alejandro and I stepped back. We had been completely unaware that Dolores likely had been knocking. She entered the room, seemingly ignoring us, and proceeded to arrange the food on the table from the cart she had rolled into the dining room. She was serving pozole as the entree dish.

Alejandro and I silently sat down at the table. I was avoiding eye contact, while Alejandro was staring at me with inquisitive eyes. After setting down the pozole bowls in front of Alejandro and me, Dolores uncovered a plate full of chiles en nogada. I could not believe my eyes.

"I haven't had these chiles in so long," I exclaimed to Dolores, warmth filling my stomach. "Thank you!"

"My pleasure, señorita," said Dolores, proud of seeing her dishes bring a smile to my still very pale and bony face. Dolores rolled her cart out and closed the door.

I started savoring her pozole without waiting for Alejandro. He smiled and proceeded to eat as well. We both enjoyed the soup in silence. I was too ashamed of my slight attraction to this man earlier to say anything, and frankly, I was too hungry to care about anything other than my food.

If there was one thing that generally improved my mood, it was good Mexican food. When I was done with my soup, Alejandro stood up, moved the bowls away from us, and served the chiles en nogada. I was surprised but held back any snarky remarks. My kidnapper was literally serving me food.

"My mom painted that piece," he said in between bites, shifting his eyes to the artwork I had been observing earlier.

I was getting more confused by the second. This man, for some reason, wanted to share information about his life with me. What exactly was I supposed to do with that?

"It's beautiful," I admitted. "She must be very talented."

"She is. Her work is fairly famous around here."

He looked so proud, his eyes suddenly filled with love and tenderness. It seemed he was capable of some human emotion and had a good sense of family values. Although, it didn't stop him from destroying mine and who knew how many others.

This was the first time I had seen him smile, a real full and happy smile. It almost looked honest, making him look younger than he generally seemed. I couldn't help but notice his white, straight teeth and admire the look of sensuality he had with every movement he made. The way he moved his hand, the way he looked at me.

Why would a man like this, who seemed to have it all and could really have the love of anyone he wanted, remove someone from their home against their will for money?

"Does your mother live here?" I inquired. *Be polite,* I reminded myself. *Don't rush this. Get to know him. Take advantage.* The plan was to be civil, avoid provocation.

"At times. She is a citizen of the world, she says."

"Where is she now?" I pushed.

He stayed silent for a second but continued, "Hawaii." I didn't know if that was true or not.

We managed to keep a friendly and comfortable conversation for the next hour, as if we were just two old friends enjoying a nice meal. I felt my anxiety reduce a bit, and I went from pretending to care about what he had to say to actually wanting to hear more. I savored the sound of his voice, deep and strong.

I bit my lip every time I wanted to scream that he should let me go home, that this was the most confused I had ever been in my life. I had to make him think I was going to comply in order to gain some trust.

Dolores came back in to clear the table and served some wonderful tres leches cake.

I, surprisingly, did enjoy listening to Alejandro tell me about his childhood growing up in Mexico with barely anything but heart and passion for life.

He had managed to quiet my fears a little, but I was still alert, not losing sight of the plan to get to know my oppressor better, in the hope of being able to use any information in my favor. The more data I gathered, the better I could plan. And somehow, in some twisted way, talking to him casually like this felt very natural.

"When did you move to the States?" He cocked his head with a slight frown. "You barely have an accent," I explained. "I just assumed."

"Hm. An uncle was living in Texas. He got me a visa, and I moved there during high school. I knew it would be up to me to make my parents' sacrifices worth it, and there were a lot more opportunities there," he finished.

"And you clearly succeeded. This house is, in itself, a work of art, it seems. Do you live here full time now?"

"Not exactly."

I saw his jaw tense as he looked at a message on his phone. The door for questions was quickly closing—I could feel it.

"Why, then?" I dared to ask, unable to stay cordial any longer as I felt like I was running out of time. "Why kidnap me if you don't need the money?"

He glanced at me, his lips now forming a thin line. I almost regretted my question. It probably should have been an inner thought, but it was too late. Richard's biggest problem with me was always that I spoke my mind too much. Alejandro shook his head and closed his eyes.

He got up from his chair with such ferocity I feared he would hit me.

"I made it very clear this wasn't a topic I was willing to discuss."

I was fuming. The audacity of this man was not something I could handle. In what world did he live in?

"You expect me to join you for dinner, talk to you, and pretend that I am not here against my will, is that it?" I retorted, standing up to face him. "I don't know you, and abduction does not generally make a good first impression."

His lips tightened. My face twitched but I kept my head high.

"You could, alternatively," he stated coldly, "refrain from asking questions and instead enjoy the fact that I am making an effort to treat you as a guest in my house."

"A guest!" I laughed. "Really? Is this what you call hospitality in Mexico?"

"Watch your mouth," he warned, grabbing my arm.

"Or what? You will do what? Hit me? Call one of those criminals who took me and have them punch me some more?"

His eyes darkened to black burning fire, his nostrils flaring. He must have noticed the blood leaving my face, because he let go of my arms so brusquely I struggled to stay balanced.

"I don't hit women, but don't taunt me, Amelia, because I will throw you over my shoulder and lock you back in your room again," he warned under his breath.

"Great," I retorted. "I guess your preferred method of forcing submission is pretending to be a gentleman while you take their freedom away."

"You are an arrogant, stubborn brat!"

"And you are a fucking brute!" I screamed back.

Before he could say anything, I rushed out of the room with tears blinding me.

I had no idea where I was going, but I had to get away from this man. He had managed to make me feel safe this evening, but his behavior morphed into disdain at the drop of a hat, which angered and scared me even more.

It was very clear to me that he was the mastermind behind it all. Yes, he had a family, but so what? I was being forced to dine with a criminal, be cordial, and pretend we were two normal people getting to know each other under normal circumstances. No, staying there wasn't an option.

I flung the front door of the house wild open. I hurried out and started running down the stairs. Cold air hit me like a slap in the face as I was boiling, but I had to rush as I could hear footsteps getting dangerously close to me. As I finally made it to the bottom of the stairs, Alejandro violently grabbed my left arm and turned me toward him, staring at me angrily. I let out a frustrated groan. I was at my wits' end.

"Where do you think you're going?!"

"Away from you!" I screamed in tears. "Let me go! Please let me go home!"

"Don't you understand that you can't leave?! You can't leave! I cannot let you leave, but you are safe here. Calm down!" he ordered, shaking me.

I was still fighting him, trying to free my arms from his grasp. How on earth was I safe when I was at the mercy of a criminal pretending to be a gentleman?

He grabbed my other arm, pulled me closer to him, and held me firmly against his chest. Both my arms were on his hard chest as I was trying to pull out of his grasp. With his other hand, he pulled my face close to his, and he aggressively pressed his lips against mine.

I froze for a second, eyes wide open, keeping my teeth closed, trying to resist his ravaging lips from overtaking me. But the pain was too strong, and I eventually gave in.

His tongue penetrated my mouth deeply, demanding, ordering my submission. I fought him, but when I felt his arms go around my waist in a possessive embrace, I closed my eyes and kissed him back with the passion and desire he was demanding. I felt myself melt into his hands as he was molding me like clay.

I heard myself groan and opened my eyes.

What on earth was I doing? I pushed him away from me, almost falling as I took a step back, staring at him in shock. We were both gasping for air.

"Much better," he said, wiping his lips with the back of his hand. "obediente como deberías de ser," he declared with a smirk of satisfaction on his face and victory flickering in his eyes.

Ugh, of course.

I was furious at myself for letting him kiss and touch me like that. I was ashamed for giving in so easily, letting this man think he could control me by violently forcing me to kiss him and now calling me "obedient as I should be." I was at a loss for words.

I looked up and saw Dolores standing by the door, her hands on her lips. I scanned my surroundings, but it was too dark to see where the road led. We were clearly not off a public street. It wasn't going to be an easy escape in the middle of the night, even if I somehow managed to outrun Alejandro.

There was nowhere to go but where I ran from, in the house of this man who was looking at me like he had won something. I quickly ran past Alejandro and up the stairs. I was shaking, but I had to get away from him. Dolores took me by the arms gently when I reached the top of the stairs, guiding me to my room. I was in shock, and the walk was a blur, a wasted opportunity to continue to map the floor plan in my head.

When we got to the room, Dolores left me, with the door open, and returned with a glass of water that she set on one of the nightstands before leaving me alone. I quickly changed into the gym clothes that had been washed and neatly folded for me on the bed.

That kiss, and all the different currents it had sent through my weak and shameless body, was haunting me, and I felt guilty for it. Guilty that I took pleasure from my kidnapper. Guilty that I had a fiancé out there who was probably looking for me. *Oh gosh*, I hadn't considered how George was fairing with all of this. *Was he devastated? Was he trying to find me?*

There was no denying that Alejandro was attractive. There was no denying that he was trying to manipulate me into submission—through physical attraction apparently.

And with the way my body had melted against his, he probably believed he had succeeded.

He was going to fail—miserably. If anyone was going to do any manipulation, it was me, as I had everything to lose if I didn't play my cards right. He could physically harm me, force me—or worse, I could lose my life—and no kiss, however amazing and confusing it was, was going to change that.

CHAPTER 6

WHEN DOLORES ENTERED THE room, I was already awake. I had barely been able to sleep for most of the night, the searing kiss flashing in my head every time I closed my eyes.

After taking me to my daily shower, Dolores led me back to the room, where some new clothes were waiting for me on the bed.

"Espero que estén de tu tamaño," said Dolores with the brightest smile on her lips, proud of herself.

"Thank you, Dolores. I'm sure they will fit."

I couldn't help but get a little excited at the prospect of changing clothes more often. It made me feel like I was still a person. It made me feel like I still had some control over my life.

I started trying on the jeans and the shirts once Dolores left. Two pairs of jeans fit me perfectly. It was easier with the shirts. I settled for a yellow shirt with delicate hand-embroidered straps covering my shoulders. It had a tight fit around my breasts and was a little wider as it got closer to my hips.

This was perfect as it meant I did not need to wear a bra, which was a relief, considering I only had the ripped one I was abducted with. Dolores had brought me some sandals in my size as well. I was starting to be in a much better mood after putting the clothes on. I was starting to feel like a human again, and I wanted to hold onto that sensation as long as I could.

Dolores was trying to make me feel safe and cared for, I realized, but still, I was not any closer to understanding why I was in captivity, all the way in Mexico, with no return date in sight. It was also frustrating because, for however nice Dolores was, I couldn't get her to share any more information with me. Dolores clearly loved Alejandro very much, and for some reason, she wanted to convince me that Alejandro was a good man, despite appearances.

Dolores knocked and entered the room again an hour later.

"It's time for breakfast," she said. "Let's go."

"I am not eating with that man again."

Dolores pleaded, but I would not have it.

"Okay," accepted Dolores. "You eat in the kitchen, then?"

"With pleasure," I replied, relieved that I would still get to go out of the room even if I refused to eat with Alejandro.

Dolores escorted me to the kitchen. It was an enormous space, with dark-oak and glass-window cabinetry, complemented by an enormous kitchen island. On the right side, by the window, was a six-person, round table. I took a seat as instructed, but when Dolores proceeded to make chilaquiles, I got up to help her.

Dolores refused my assistance at first, but eventually accepted my help—just like Martha, my nana, had when I was fifteen.

She was the house manager, as I called her, responsible for a good part of my education and making sure the house ran without any issues. Together, Dolores and I set the table.

As I was getting ready to sit down, I noticed Alejandro leaning on the door frame, arms crossed, observing my every move. His dark-black hair was not combed as usual. Rather, it looked like he had let the wind play with it, or perhaps he had raked frustrated fingers through it. He was wearing a light pair of khaki pants and a black polo shirt. Dolores seemed as surprised as I was to see him.

"Hola, señor," greeted Dolores.

"Buenos días, Dolores. Me sirves el desayuno aquí, por favor," he said as he took a seat next to me.

Of course, he asked her to serve him breakfast in the kitchen.

Dolores hurried, setting some plates and cutlery in front of him. She quickly put the food and the drinks down. I was hoping she would stick around, as I did not want to be alone with Alejandro, but Dolores guiltily avoided all eye contact with me and left the room in a rush.

"I didn't know you cooked," remarked Alejandro.

"Every now and then."

Why would he know? We weren't friends. But perhaps he and his team of degenerates had been watching me for a while before taking me. That thought sent a shiver down my spine. I shook myself a little bit.

"It seemed like you knew what you were doing," he said with an air of surprise on his face.

What did he want?

"How long were you lurking in the background for?" I snapped.

"Long enough," he said with his usual mocking smile.

He was staring at me, his eyes tracing every curve of my body with a brief focus on my shoulder bruise. I shifted in my seat, aware of the slow heat rising through me, unnerved that, for some reason, his inappropriate gaze made me wonder what it would be like for him to touch me.

I couldn't divert my gaze for too long, not just because the man was built like some sort of Greek god, but it was more so the primal, angry look he had in his eyes as they ran over my body and my face that scared and captivated me. I felt naked in his presence, and while I wanted to look away, I was also fascinated. No one had ever focused on me like that before.

"I assumed you always had someone to assist with your every need," he mocked, interrupting my reverie.

I inhaled slowly, trying to find it in myself to be cordial. This man knew how to rile me up in just a few seconds. I bit my lower lip to resist the urge to retort. I could point out that, from what I could tell, he had resorted to crimes and who knew what else to amass his fortune, considering the size of the mansion he used for kidnapping purposes, but it wasn't worth it.

"I started learning when I was a teenager. I decided to take it more seriously when I was in college in New York," I admitted. "Richard was paying for part of my studies, and I didn't want to owe him any more than I already did."

"Why don't you call him Dad?"

"Because he is not my dad," I snapped back at him.

"I see," he said, deep frowns forming on his forehead, eyes glancing in my direction, a look of confusion in them.

I stopped paying attention to him and focused on my food, doing my best to ignore his persistent questioning gaze. Perhaps letting my disdain for my stepfather be known wasn't the right approach. Maybe I had made a tactical mistake.

"What did you study in college?" I was glad for the change in conversation.

"Hotel management and English at NYU. And I got my MBA a month ago from Stanford."

"Impressive, and here I thought you were just your father's little wallflower," he teased, leaning back into his chair to face me better.

"You know nothing about my life," I retorted curtly. "You shouldn't make assumptions about people you don't know—especially when it makes you, I don't know, a sexist for assuming that my goal in life is to stand around and look pretty."

He clenched his jaw and got up from his chair slowly. "Enough with the name calling Amelia," he warned.

"Enough with the stereotypes, then," I retorted, standing up, as he was getting too close.

I took a few steps back, trying to get as far away as I could but suppressed a gasp when I felt my back hit the cold wall.

He grunted, closed his eyes, and shook his head, both hands on his hips. He slowly looked at me, as if running out of patience, and took a step in my direction.

"Let's try this conversation again, shall we?"

What was perhaps meant to sound like a pleasant optional invitation to converse sounded more like a threat to me. He paused, as if waiting for me to consent, but he proceeded anyway as I remained silent.

"Why hospitality management?"

I was baffled. What was his game exactly? Was he trying to get to know me? Or was there some information about me or Richard that he was after? I couldn't read those dark eyes.

For some reason, he seemed to always be trying to befriend me, and none of this made any sense. But I couldn't think of anything related to my career that I should hide, so I decided to go with the truth.

"I enjoy customer service, and I enjoy managing a team to achieve excellence. I love the idea of participating in people's lives as they spend a few days or a week in a transient location, being able to contribute to a wonderful experience and a seamless process as they proceed with their lives."

"Do you want to work at a hotel or for a restaurant chain?"

"I think a hotel. It's the job I have lined up, anyway. I would love to manage a chain but would then want to proceed to management of the company, participate in the decision making of where to open hotels, what the brand is supposed to be about and all that."

I felt myself relaxing a bit. Talking about my dreams calmed me. It reminded me that my life was still a possibility as long as I was alive.

"It's such a great experience to get to observe people's behavior, try to grasp their wants, their needs, and package that for them in different locations around the world. Life is short, and I want to participate in making it pleasurable for people, but I also want to be one of the strategic minds behind the process."

"Where do you plan to work?"

"In New York."

"Interesting."

"Why?"

"I'd assume you would want to learn the ways from your family business in California."

"No, I don't want to work with him."

I stopped myself before saying too much. He didn't need to know that working for Richard was the worst thing that could happen to me, both personally and professionally.

He stared at me, as if expecting me to say more, but I kept my lips shut.

He spun around, went to the cupboard, and grabbed something I couldn't see. I held my breath, afraid that he was going to hurt me. But when he turned around, I saw a box that looked like a first aid kit in his hands. He placed it down on the table, opened it, grabbed some alcohol, some cotton, and a Band-Aid. He saturated the cotton ball with alcohol.

He then slowly drew closer to me, his gaze never leaving mine. Despite him looking like a predator getting closer and closer to his meal, I didn't feel fear, just a weird anticipation. I stood stiffly, my arms down by my sides, unable to make a move, anticipating his touch.

With a frown on his face, he dabbed the cotton ball between my neck and my shoulder.

"You are bleeding a bit," he explained.

I winced from the cold liquid sending a bit of pain coursing through me. I hadn't realized I was bleeding from the cut. It had been closing, so I had left it alone.

"I'm sorry about this. I never meant for any of this to happen." He seemed sincere, but I couldn't even think of a clever retort on how he was at fault in all of this.

We stood there in silence, my hands still locked by each side of my body, unable to move even an inch. He walked away, threw the cotton in the garbage can, then turned back to me with the bandage open. He placed it on my neck, his fingers lingering on my collarbone, lightly caressing my skin. I tensed a bit further, unable to look away from his eyes.

Barely breathing, I stood there, my lips shaking, anticipating his. My heart was beating faster and faster as his face came closer and closer to mine. With the tips of his fingers, he lifted my chin. I could feel his breath on my face, warming up my body and accelerating my heart rate.

He seemed undecided. As he got closer, I felt the edge of his lips starting to brush mine. I moaned slightly as he suddenly was pulling away from me.

He brusquely took a few steps back, his eyes wide. I still couldn't move, immobilized by the rush he had caused inside of me. I felt ashamed, angry at him for playing with me, leaving me wanting more, wanting what I shouldn't even be thinking about, what shouldn't be happening. He left the room in a hurry.

The way my body responded to him was overwhelming. I had never experienced such physical attraction and pain before just from the proximity of a man. A dangerous man, no less, who barely touched me and yet activated all my senses, making me pulse between my thighs.

"What happened?" asked Dolores as she returned. "He looked sick."

I didn't answer. I couldn't. I just stared at my feet, trying to hide my flushed cheeks from Dolores.

"Is it time to go back to my room already?" I asked, dreading being locked away again in that windowless bedroom, alone with my thoughts, but I still wanted to escape and be able to close my eyes and pretend I was safe.

"Yes, come." Dolores smiled.

I obediently followed but quickly realized that Dolores was heading in a different direction.

I gave her an inquisitive gaze, but she just kept smiling. Instead of heading to the back of the kitchen where my room was, she was taking me through the rest of the house. We got to the foyer where a big, thick, hand-carved mahogany table carried an amazing centerpiece with the most beautiful wildflowers I had ever seen, but there wasn't much time to observe as I followed Dolores up the wooden staircase. Where was she taking me?

We navigated through the warmly lit, light-taupe-colored halls until Dolores opened a wooden door and gently pushed me inside. I held in a gasp as I walked into a dream bedroom. It looked like it was taken straight from the 20th century and upgraded to meet the comfort of the current time.

The bedroom had a king-size bed on what looked like a cherry-wood bed frame, a gorgeous oatmeal-colored ottoman, a chaise by a gigantic glass door that was currently opened to a small balcony. There was an amazing glass chandelier providing a lot of the light in the space.

My gaze trailed on an exquisite reclaimed-wood vanity on the other side of the room as well as a full-size mirror. There was an open door leading to a bathroom, as well as a decently sized walk-in closet. I couldn't believe it.

"This is your bedroom now, miss," grinned Dolores, her eyes shining as she saw the excitement on my face. "El patron's orders. I already moved your clothes into the closet for you."

"Thank you, Dolores!" I said almost in tears.

I would now have my own bathroom and, more importantly, an amazing amount of natural light. Who knew that having sunshine and my own bathroom would cause me to be emotional? Sometimes it's the little things we take for granted that get to us when we no longer have them.

I walked to the gorgeous bouquet of pink and red Dahlia's on the nightstand.

"These are so beautiful!"

"From don Alejandro" she said, a small smile on her face. I didn't know what to think of this gesture.

Dolores stepped out of the room. I wiped the tears off my face. A window! I went straight to the small balcony where there was a table and two chairs on which I could sit. My view was of a beautiful yard. I could see a big pool and a gorgeous stone-paved patio. The sun was out, droplets of water from the rain the night before shining as the heat evaporated them. I could still smell the rain on the wet grass, the slight scent of eucalyptus creating a Zen atmosphere.

Perhaps some fresh air was all I needed to bring some sense of reality back into my head so I could stop the tingling sensation that coursed through my body every time I was in the same room as Alejandro.

I could make out the extent of the property, as the vast backyard was enveloped by towering, dense trees. I could glimpse the peaks of other mountains just beyond it. I closed my eyes, enjoying the sound of the birds and the heat bringing some calm back to me. I looked down, trying to gauge how far up I was. I wouldn't be able to climb down the balcony; it was a bit too high for that.

I despised Alejandro for keeping me captive and making me experience sensations I had never felt before, even with George. Still, I was very thankful for the new prison. I was a prisoner in the middle of paradise, trapped in a gilded cage.

CHAPTER 7

I HADN'T SEEN ALEJANDRO in three days. Dolores would set meals on the balcony for me and come for the trays later. I was dying to ask about Alejandro, but I was too prideful to do so. I had spent my days pacing, twisting my fingers, wondering how life was back in L.A.

How was everyone doing without me there? Was my stepfather worried? Was he looking for me? How was George? Iris, Chloe, Keisha, and Martha were the people I was the most worried about, the people I knew really did love me and would be worried sick about me.

I didn't know whether my abduction was a secret or a known fact at this point. I desperately wished I could hug them, let Martha braid my hair as she used to when I was little, and play in the doll house for hours with Iris.

I sat by the window, reminiscing about the life I should have been living. I would have been in New York by now, starting a new chapter, starting the career I had always wanted. Solitude had forced me to take a look in the mirror and re-evaluate the life I might lead if I ever got out of this house alive.

I also had a lot of time to reflect about my relationship with George. The arguments I had been trying to convince myself of—that marrying him was the best decision and the path of least resistance—were starting to waver. I was starting to realize how precious life truly was, and with that came doubts about spending any more of it with a man for whom I felt only a passive affection.

I wondered if Alejandro had asked Richard for ransom. I still couldn't comprehend what the motive was otherwise. Maybe Alejandro was going bankrupt? Maybe this wasn't even his property? Who knew.

I wondered if I would ever get to go home again. Sheer fear took over me at the idea of never being able to go back to my life, to the job I had worked so hard to get, to the future I couldn't wait to start, independent, away from my stepfather for good. When those thoughts crossed my mind, I finally reached my breaking point. The flood gates opened, and a scream rose up from within me that probably alerted everyone in the house. But no one seemed to care.

When I finally saw Dolores later that day, she never mentioned anything, just silently cleaned. But then again, for however sweet and warm Dolores was, for as much as she reminded me of Martha, she was still part of a team that obeyed Alejandro to the letter, including in the crime of taking my freedom away.

Eventually, on day four, as Dolores was bringing me afternoon tea, I tried to inquire further in a more diplomatic fashion.

"I can't thank you enough for taking such good care of me, Dolores."

"Es un placer, señorita."

"How long have you worked for Alejandro?"

"For at least eight years," she said, "but I have known him since he was a wild little boy, running around, playing futbol around our neighborhood. When he made himself, he took me and my family in, paid for my son's college degree. I insisted on staying here with him, working for him and his mother, in the only thing I love to do—cook."

"Do you also bring him tea every afternoon?"

"I do," she said, "but not lately. He travels to California a lot for his business. He hasn't been here for three days, if that is what you are asking," said Dolores with a smile. I smiled back.

Dolores seemed to be creating some sort of story in her mind about why I was asking. I, on the other hand, knew that my only interest was wanting to investigate what was next for me.

"He should be back this evening," said Dolores, patting my shoulder before she left me alone with my thoughts.

It was crucial that I make an effort to be nice to Alejandro going forward. I needed to earn his trust. It was the only way I would be able to perhaps make him tell me what this really was all about, as I still couldn't understand why he had abducted me in the first place, and that drove me mad. He seemed to have it all—some sort of business in California, and enough success to own a mansion.

Even if all of it was through illegal means, why continue? It couldn't just be about money. Also, I couldn't understand why Richard hadn't paid anything yet—at least as far as I knew. I assumed he would to avoid any gossip, but I didn't know what to believe any longer. Had I been in captivity too long? What was a "normal" time to wait before kidnappers started cutting limbs, raping, beating? No, no, I couldn't think of that. I couldn't let fear take possession of my sanity any further.

CHAPTER 8

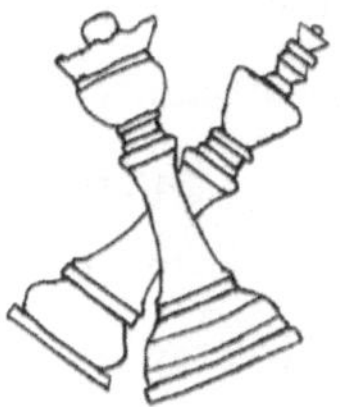

I WAS ALL READY for breakfast, waiting impatiently for Dolores to come get me to join Alejandro as she had told me she would. I had to hide my disappointment when she brought breakfast to my room instead. The same thing happened for lunch. I grew mad, mostly at myself for wanting to see him—for missing him? What was wrong with me?! I needed a hobby, something to do.

I could not continue spending my days waiting for some man's attention, even if that same man held my fate in his hands. Clearly, he wasn't really in a rush to get rid of me. And that was fine, as that would keep me alive, give me another chance. Until I saw him, though, I was stuck in limbo, unsuccessfully trying to get Dolores to talk, wavering between daydreaming about my life and being paralyzed with fear.

When it came time for dinner, Dolores came in and announced I was expected in the dining room. My body warred between excitement and anxiety at the thought of seeing Alejandro.

I picked an embroidered, flowing white dress for the evening that stopped at my knees. The cut in the back was fairly low and flattering. I let my hair fall completely down my back. I had straightened it and curled the ends with the blow dryer and straightening tools I had found in the bathroom, courtesy of Dolores. She had even provided me with some foundation, blush, and some mascara, which was all I needed to amplify my features.

It felt almost twisted to be putting on makeup to have dinner with the man who abducted me, changing my life forever—and probably for the worse. But going through the ritual of getting ready also gave me a feeling of normalcy in a way, a touch of my life back, memories of me and the girls eating popcorn in my college dorm, watching hundreds of makeup tutorials on YouTube to learn how to actually do our makeup and not look like clowns afterward.

Dolores finally returned, but instead of taking me to the dining room, she took me to the office patio.

There he was, standing outside, breathing in the fresh breeze the night provided, his presence somehow thickening the air around him. My heart skipped a beat when he turned around and looked at me. He was wearing a dark-gray suit and a white shirt with the first two buttons undone. He remained silent for a few seconds, his gaze seemingly taking in every inch of me.

"Do you want something to drink?" he offered.

"A glass of wine if possible."

Always such a gentleman, I thought. The kidnapper gentleman.

He poured some wine from a label-less bottle into two wine glasses and handed me one. *Was he trying to poison me? Where was the label on the bottle?* I made an effort to simmer down after he took a sip of the glass he had poured for himself.

"I see the food is already set on the table."

"I wanted us to have no interruptions tonight," he explained.

I focused on the wine in an attempt to hide my nervousness. I smiled when I noticed the beautiful bouquet of white and red Dahlia's on the table.

"This is delicious," I said as we sat down to eat. "I generally prefer a malbec, but this is perfect for tonight. It's a merlot, right?" I asked, savoring the feeling of the red wine teasing my taste buds.

"You know about wine?" He raised an intrigued brow.

"I wouldn't go that far, but I'm a great wine consumer," I teased, smiling.

"Are you now?" he asked in a low guttural tone, bending his head.

He looked at me with eagerness in his eyes. Just one look from those deep, dark eyes made me feel naked. I was trying my best to control my breathing. I had to keep my cool, and I had to remain charming.

"Are you a fan of California wines?"

"Not generally," I admitted. "I tend to prefer Argentinian wines, as well as some European ones generally, but there is a vineyard in California called Robledo Estates. They are not as big as the usual labels, but their wine is not cheap. I don't know how they managed to make European-style wines in California land, but it's perfection. They also don't add sulfites and the other usual offenders that other American vineyards tend to add, which is great."

Was I sharing too much? I wondered. I didn't need this man knowing more about me than he already did. But at the same time, sharing is how people bonded, and I needed him to think we were getting along. I had no choice there. And the truth was that I was enjoying it. Perhaps it was the lack of human interaction making me want to talk so much to my enemy.

I watched him bite his lip. Desire surged through me at the speed of light, taking me by surprise. He suddenly stood and heading to his office, pausing at a record player he had by the window and putting some music on. The melody filled the room and drifted outside to me. It was a sensual song by Luis Miguel, one of my favorite singers. Alejandro approached and asked for my hand. I hesitated.

This didn't seem like a good idea.

But at the same time, he was being cordial, and this was exactly what I needed him to be. When our fingers touched as I slowly slid my hands into his, I had to clench my teeth to remain in control of the swirl of emotions threatening to overtake me. Alejandro pulled me toward him in the most tender embrace, one hand resting gently on back while the other still held my right hand tightly. He slowly drew me closer to him.

I closed my eyes as every single one of my senses was on high alert, feeling every inch of his body against mine, breathing him in, getting high on the mix of his cologne and his intoxicating body scent, while fearing what I was getting myself into, or how my body felt. But seduction was all part of my plan, if it was needed, so I let go a bit.

"You play chess?" I asked, looking at the board game.

"I do." He answered in a low tone that made goose bumps travel down my arms.

"Do you know how to play?"

"No" I admitted. "I would like to though." Richard knew but had refused to teach me when I had asked.

"I could teach you" he offered; his gaze locked on mine.

I nodded, as we swayed in silence. How long did he plan to keep me captive for exactly, if he thought he would have time to teach me how to play? I closed my eyes for a few seconds, to block the fear that was threatening to rise inside of me.

"You like this song?" he whispered in my ear.

"'Debajo de la mesa,'" I said. "A classic and one of my favorites."

He leaned a little away from me to stare into my eyes. He was frowning and looked disconcerted.

"You are full of surprises, muñeca. Every time I think I am teaching you something, you show me that I am the one who has so much to learn about you."

The depth in his voice shook me to my core, shattering some of my restraints.

"How is it that your Spanish is so good?"

"I spent the first eleven years of my life here, in Mexico."

Something flashed behind his eyes. I had admitted to knowing where we were, but he didn't make any comment on it. I wondered if I should continue sharing more of my life with him. But the way he looked at me, almost like he was hanging on my every word, made me feel heard, so I continued.

"When we moved to California, I made sure to keep my mother tongue, to continue learning. It was all I had left of my life here, of my mother. I wasn't going to lose that because Richard decided to move to America."

"You didn't want to move?"

"Why would I? I was a kid. My mother was dead, but despite that, I loved my life here. Maybe he thought a new place would do me good. I don't know, but at first, I hated it. I didn't even speak a lick of English, and kids at that age weren't very nice. No patience, no tolerance, they made fun of my language, of my accent at the time, of my clothes. Things got better, though. I learned English easily, thankfully. I made friends, and I started loving life there. I started fitting in somewhat."

"I felt the same," he confessed. "I hated leaving my home behind."

"And now?"

"Now it's my home as well."

"Do you ever feel lost? Like you don't belong here or there? Sorry."

I glanced down at his shirt, his gaze making me feel like I was naked, like he was looking straight through me. Perhaps it was the wine, but those were words I had never uttered out loud—not even to my closest friends. I wasn't sure they would get it.

"I do. All the time."

I shifted my gaze to his. He did; I could tell he did. His intense eyes were searching mine, but I could no longer hold it in. He made me want to share that part of me with him, and it felt good.

"Really?"

"Yes. When I moved to Texas, at least I spoke a bit of English already. But it was hard. I felt like a traitor at times, leaving my family, my friends behind. I knew I was doing the right thing—for all of us, really—but I couldn't help feeling like a coward for leaving."

"You weren't a coward. You were pursuing certain opportunities. I am sure they get it. At least you came back, even if you don't spend all your life here."

"You don't come back?"

"No. Richard never wanted me to. And when I became older…I don't know, I just never did. I was afraid of what I would find here. I finally got to a place in my life where I felt like the US was home. I felt like I had finally started to integrate, to be at peace with the fact that I didn't really remember a lot of that life I had been forced to leave behind. I was afraid that coming here would, I don't know, cause an uproar in me, bring me back to those days when I felt empty, like I had left my soul behind."

I swallowed when I heard my voice quiver a bit. I stared into the depth of his eyes, afraid of what I would find. But there was no judgment there, just an understanding, a recognition.

"I get it. I was older when I left. But my mother still lived here. My uncle and I came back here every summer. I felt like I was happy in the US, but something was missing when I was there. But the same happens here, frankly. I find that different parts of me get something from each place."

"It's a citizen-of-the-world problem, I guess," I joked. "We don't belong fully anywhere, but we find pieces of us in different cultures—or you do, anyway."

"You shouldn't be afraid to visit," he encouraged. "Yes, you will likely feel something that might shake you to your core, but if you still have that ache in you, that bit of emptiness, it might be worth exploring. You are stronger than you give yourself credit for, Amelia."

I felt my eyes well up, and I batted my eyelids to stop the tears from falling. I knew he was right. I had always thought that deep inside me, but I just never found the courage to come back. I wondered how much I would remember and how much that would affect me.

I was afraid that I would feel my mother's absence a lot stronger if I went back to my roots. I was afraid that the peace, the happiness, and the sense of belonging I had worked so hard to get would crumble if the parts of me I had ignored found that thirst for home, for fitting. And this man, my kidnapper, was bringing it all out, on my skin, in the open.

I tucked my head into his neck, unable to resist the urge to feel his naked skin against mine. Yes, this was all part of the plan, but it didn't mean I couldn't enjoy the process just a bit, a safe amount, as long as I was in control. That conversation unleashed something inside of me, something I desperately needed to put back in the box where it belonged.

Alejandro gently grabbed my face with his hand, turning my head toward his. My parted lips were trembling in sweet anguish as I lifted my head further, those dark eyes showing me how futile my resolutions were. I closed my eyes when his lips touched mine.

It was a passionate yet gentle kiss. I heard him groan under his breath as my tongue slipped between his lips, hungry for him. I put my hands on his back, enjoying the thrill of feeling his muscles contract, and he drove me further into his embrace. He left my lips, and as I was about to beg for more, Alejandro kissed my jaw and made his way down my neck, kissing my collarbone. I moaned as I was clinging to him, looking for support, wanting him closer.

He pulled away from me so brusquely I had to hold the chair next to me for support. My legs were weak, so I quickly sat down.

"Who is it?" I heard him ask.

"Dolores, señor." I hadn't even heard the knock on the door.

He quickly ran frustrated fingers through his hair and fixed his shirt. I grabbed a glass of wine to drink it, trying to control my senses, and hide my heated cheeks.

"Perdon, señor," said Dolores when she entered. "Puedo hablar con usted un momentito?"

A look of concern crossed Alejandro's face as he went into the other room to talk to Dolores. I was doing my best to try to listen in, but they were both very careful. I could hear their voices, but I couldn't understand anything that was being said.

Alejandro walked back to my side, his hands in his pockets, his composure fully recovered, as if nothing had happened between us earlier. He looked angry, almost concerned.

"It's time for you to go back to your room," he announced, staring at me with distant, cold eyes.

"But—"

"This is not up for discussion," he interrupted before I could finish.

Anger gave me all the strength I was lacking as I stood to face him. He was gazing at me with cold eyes, his face devoid of the passion I had seen just a few minutes before.

"Who do you think you are?!" I yelled as I hit him on his chest with the sides of my fists. "How dare you treat me like this!"

He held both my wrists tight. "I don't have time for your tantrums, Amelia. I am now done with you, and you are dismissed. I won't ask you twice," he warned.

I felt tears of embarrassment rising to my eyes. I pulled myself away from him and went to find Dolores. We walked to my room in silence.

As soon as I heard the door lock behind me, I dropped myself on the bed and let out all my exasperation on my pillow. I had never felt such a strong hatred for someone before. My feelings were raw, as someone I shouldn't even be interacting with, someone I despised with all my being, had once again trampled my pride and my self-esteem.

I was sure of one thing: I had to regain control.

The night started with me wanting to get closer to him, being willing to seduce him if I had to, in a desperate attempt to stay alive, to find out why I had been abducted, to perhaps even negotiate my freedom or facilitate another potential escape. But it ended with my body trembling under his touch. When he kissed me, he made himself more of a threat than ever.

I somehow had allowed myself to think we had a connection, something so innate in common, that I felt like I was talking to someone who could fully understand me. His rejection also had a sting after I had opened up and shared so much with him. I was a proud woman, after all, but it shouldn't feel that way. My life was at stake. I had to stay strong.

CHAPTER 9

I WASN'T IN THE mood to see anyone when Dolores came to get me for breakfast, but I made an effort. I paired some of the new jeans with a simple, soft black t-shirt. Thankfully, Dolores had also added a few bras to my clothing.

I had assumed I would eat alone, but Dolores was taking me to the kitchen. As we walked in, we found Alejandro planted there with a woman passionately kissing him. Dolores cleared her throat to announce our presence—she was clearly not pleased with what she was seeing. Alejandro quickly pulled away from the woman and looked up.

I felt my stomach drop with a tightening in my chest. The woman spun slowly, staring at me with a curious smile. She was beautiful with thick black hair, small breasts, and wide hips. She was wearing very fit jeans and a red t-shirt that put her breast tastefully on display and looked great against her tan skin. She had five-inch, red stilettos on. She seemed familiar to me.

"Well, well, well," she said, "she looks a lot cleaner than the last time I saw her trembling on the floor."

"Karina," said Alejandro, a warning in his tone, "it's time for you to go."

It was the woman from the previous house—the one who had attacked me countless times.

"I know," she said, turning back to face him. "I don't want to be late. Thank you for an amazing welcome home last night," she said, leaning toward him to kiss him again. Alejandro let her do so and gently pulled away.

As Karina was leaving, she violently elbowed me in my left side. I pivoted, ready for battle, but Karina paid me no mind. Instead, she continued strolling to the door.

I felt like heat was emanating out of my body. I straightened my face, trying to look as emotionless as possible as I followed Dolores. Dolores made me sit down and declined the help I offered to make breakfast. I obeyed, as I felt capable of hitting Alejandro with a pan if I had it in my hands. I refused to look his way. Although, I could feel his gaze burning through me. He sat down next to me silently, leaning forward on the table in my direction.

"Good morning," he said.

"Good morning." I was too prideful to let him understand how much seeing him with another woman had frustrated me.

"How are you?"

"As good as I can be," I admitted. He didn't get upset at my comment. He just shook his head in understanding.

I now understood that my plan to seduce and outwit him may be harder than I originally thought.

When Dolores put my eggs in front of me, I focused all my energy into eating, even if I wasn't hungry. I had to find a way to remain calm and distract myself from the drowning heartache suffocating me.

Once Dolores was done serving the food, she quickly excited the kitchen. The tension in the room was palpable, like an invisible electric current coursing through the air.

Alejandro and I ate in silence. I knew he was observing at me, searching for my eyes, but I couldn't look at him. I just couldn't stand the sight of him. When I was done eating, I got up from my chair.

"Wait," said Alejandro, standing up. I stopped. "About last night…"

"I don't need to hear anything," I said. "I couldn't care less about anything that happened last night."

"You don't?" he probed, venturing closer to me.

"Why would I?" I aggressively bit back, taking a step further. "You are simply a criminal who not only kidnaps women but dares to touch them as you please."

"Amelia, we both know that's not true," His voice was low and deep as he reached out for me.

I backed up again. If I let him touch me, I didn't trust how I would react.

"Not true?" I scoffed, laughing mockingly. "Do you think I enjoy spending time with you—or really doing anything with you, for that matter? I don't have a choice!" I lied. "I am being held captive here by a criminal, against my will, remember?! My family and *fiancé* are probably out there, worried sick."

I made sure to emphasize the fiancé I wasn't sure he knew about. At that point, I was mustering up any anger that I could find. I was hurt because I was starting to trust Alejandro—against my better judgment—but he couldn't care less. I screamed, purposely pushing my nails into my palms to stop the burn behind my eyes from continuing any further. The last thing I needed right now were angry tears embarrassing me.

Alejandro pulled back from me, his lips tight, his eyes suddenly cold and empty. He put his hands in his pockets.

"You sure seemed to enjoy it," he pointed out coldly.

I rolled my eyes.

"I wouldn't be the first woman to fake doing so," I seethed between my teeth.

I saw his nostrils open wide and his jaw tighten as he raised his head, a look of pure anger in his eyes.

"Don't follow me," I warned as I started leaving the room. "I am going back to my lovely prison cell. Dolores can come lock me in as usual."

I rushed out, my hands slightly trembling, but I was proud of myself, even as his mocking laughter resonated behind me. I almost ran to the bedroom when I was no longer in his sight. I got to the room and started pacing angrily.

I closed my eyes, trying to erase the image of that woman kissing him, her toned body pressed against his. That woman, Karina, was the one who had treated me like trash when I got abducted. I recognized both her name and her voice. Of course, she was his girl. She was the reason why Dolores urgently interrupted us the night before. Alejandro must have left me to go to her, and as Karina had insinuated, they'd probably spent the night together.

The pain I was feeling was well deserved, because I must have been out of my darn mind and borderline delirious for thinking that a man like Alejandro would take me seriously, and I was borderline psychopathic for wanting him to.

Last night, I had, for a few seconds, allowed myself to get confused, to lose sight of my end goal, just for a little bit. I hated him with all my heart, for kidnapping me, for playing with me, for making me weak--even for just a moment.

But no more.

I would not allow myself to lust so much for such a despicable person. Because that's all this was—lust for a man who did not deserve anything from me. My games had somehow turned against me, but he wouldn't win. I would get a grip on the situation.

I needed something to keep myself occupied. Being left alone for so long with my imagination was torture and probably the reason why this man managed to have such an impact on me in the first place. I had made and remade the bed, cleaned my bathroom, washed and straightened my hair, and refolded my clothes. I was going mad.

In one of the vanity drawers, I found some office supplies, including a notepad and pens. I sat at the vanity and started to write, pouring all of my frustration, anger, and confusion through the ink. I always did that when I was overwhelmed about something. It was my own way to open up while sharing my troubles with the silent pages of what normally would be my diary. Putting ink on paper always soothed me, provided me with peace, clarity, and even closure. It was therapeutic for me. I wasn't the writer in my group of friends, but no skills were needed to write one's inner thoughts. I was so focused that I barely heard when Dolores entered the room, bringing me some food on a tray.

It was nine p.m. when I realized that I had been writing all day, only taking breaks to eat or use the bathroom. I needed some fresh air, so I decided to grab a glass of water and sit on the patio. The weather here in the month of July was still warm, and it had rained all day. I was enjoying the unusual cooler night, with the smell of wet soil still softly filling the air. I loved the little balcony, just sitting there, breathing it all in, and staring at a sky full of stars. It was beautiful and peaceful. One did not get clear skies like this in L.A., with the pollution in California.

Every night that I stepped on that balcony I was in awe. It felt wide, spacious, suburban, relaxing, even in my circumstance. I got distracted when I saw a couple guards doing their nightly walks. I had been quite annoyed the first time I had seen them just randomly appear and disappear, interrupting my view, reminding me that I wasn't on vacation. I would never be able to escape from this house—at least, it wouldn't be easy.

CHAPTER 10

I woke up feeling a little more at peace the next morning. Pouring my emotions on paper had seemed to be all the therapy I needed, or at least enough that I wouldn't lose it. I was pleased with myself, feeling like I had regained a bit of my sanity. Lying to Alejandro, telling him that our kisses meant nothing to me, had made me anxious, but now I knew I had done the right thing, and my pride was healing. My ridiculous confusion subsided, and my irrational attraction reduced.

When Dolores brought me lunch, she had a smile going from one ear to the other. She had brought a man with her, who was setting up a Bose stereo system on one of the nightstands. She dismissed him as soon as he was done, very excited to show me what looked like a new distraction.

"What's all this?"

"Gift from Don Alejandro!" she squealed.

I sighed. "I don't want anything from him."

"Please, it will do you well. You spend your days bored, and this will bring light to your days," she said. "Look, he even sent CDs with great music." Indeed, the man had put some CDs down next to the stereo before he left.

I considered insisting that Dolores take it back, but she was right. I loved to listen to music. I could spend hours in a day savoring melodies and daydreaming. It would help keep me sane. When Dolores left, satisfied that I had given in, I perused the pile of CDs.

There was a note on one of them that read, *Play track five.*

Fingers shaking, I removed the CD out of its case and put it in the player, skipping to track five. I recognized the song in the first second. It was the song, sung by Luis Miguel, to which he had taken me into his arms, moving me around so sweetly to the rhythm of the melody. I could feel my stomach warming up as I perched on the corner of the bed.

He wanted to remind me of that night—the night I would have given him anything, the night that had shaken me, and left me ashamed of desiring him. I got off the bed my anger flaring as I turned off the music. A slow smile tugged at my lips as a flicker of happiness crawl its way back into my heart.

But there was no point thinking about that night and fantasizing a different ending. The reality was that Alejandro was playing with me, enjoying torturing me, the way cats played with mice, the way I had intended to do with him. I was not going to give him that pleasure. I quickly changed the CD to a more palpable one, grabbed my notepad and proceeded to write, the pressure of my pen on the paper offering me some solace.

Waking up in this house had gotten easier, with last night being specifically therapeutic. The power of music had worked its magic. I had fallen asleep to the melodies cradling my thoughts and reducing my anxiety.

I still couldn't get over the 'gift' Alejandro sent over last night. Perhaps it was Dolores's idea, but considering the note telling me to play track five, I doubted it.

Under normal circumstances, the music player would have been a very sweet gesture. Perhaps, in this instance, it was his attempt to keep me distracted so that I was less of a thorn in his side.

Dolores had served me breakfast in my room again that day. She also replaced the flowers with a fresh bouquet of white Dahlia's. After I was done with my food, I took my glass of orange juice and headed to the balcony.

As I was opening the window, I heard a splash. Someone was using the pool. I peeked to see Alejandro gliding through the water from one end to the other, his wet muscles glistening under the sun, his movements strong but measured. He crossed the pool with such precision, such graceful force, my mouth opened ever so slightly. He was apparently a good swimmer—of course he was. I sighed. He rotated at a measure pace when he was done with his lap and glanced up in my direction. I quickly stepped back, but when I saw a devilish smile slowly appear on his face, I knew he had seen me. He continued to swim, and I couldn't help but lean forward a bit to shamelessly get a better view.

As I was starting to allow myself to enjoy all the small currents that were starting to trickle down my body, Karina came to the pool, wearing a very revealing green bikini. She took a perfect dive into the pool and swam toward Alejandro. She wrapped her arms around his neck and pulled him closer to her for a kiss. As her lips touched his, I felt my heart sink. But almost immediately, Alejandro reached out and untied her hands from his neck. He whispered something I was unable to catch, and swam away from Karina, exiting the pool.

I took a step back so he wouldn't see me when he started to dry himself, but he looked up in my direction one more time before he walked away. I went to sit on the bed. That was a weird interaction, to say the least. Why would he push her away like that if Karina was his girlfriend? A little bit of hope and happiness took flame inside of me. It didn't make much sense, and I was dying to know what exactly was going on between those two.

It doesn't matter, I reminded myself. At best, it just meant that Alejandro was the kind of man who treated women as nothing and only used them for sex. I shouldn't see his rejection or mistreatment of another woman as a victory for me. Rather, it was probably an indication of Alejandro being one more jackass in the world. Karina wasn't a great person either, so my sympathies were limited, and I couldn't help somehow feeling vindicated as I remembered how hard Karina had hit me.

In the evening, Dolores came to tell me that I was expected for dinner. I did my best to suppress the unsettling rush of happiness I felt. It was not the time to act like a giddy teenager. I had not forgotten about my mission: find out why I had been kidnapped and was still in captivity. See if I could touch the heart of my captor, and perhaps he would let me go.

I opted for a red crinkled dress with an elasticized waist, an off-the-shoulder neckline, and short sleeves. The dress hung closely to my curves and stopped a few inches past my knees. I did my makeup and styled my full-bodied curls with the pearl hairpins Dolores had gifted me. As I was finalizing my lipstick, a knock echoed on the door. I turned around, and there he was, standing in my bedroom, looking at me with those dark eyes that made my blood coursing through my veins a little faster. He was dressed in a black pair of jeans and a light-gray shirt, his curly hair was left wild and free. He slowly walked toward me. I could only stand there frozen, barely breathing, and unable to look away.

"You look beautiful," he said.

"Thank you." I could feel my cheeks warm up as I bit my lower lip, looking up at him from under my lashes. "Dolores has great taste."

"She does."

We lingered there, gazing at each other. I tried to remind myself to be strong, but I was satisfied as the dress had the impact intended.

"You sent me flowers again" I stated, swallowing hard.

"I did. You like them?"

"Yes, thank you. They are gorgeous" I admitted with a small smile. His lips slightly parted.

"I assume you came to get me for dinner?"

"Uh, yes. Yes, I did." He took a few steps backward. "Shall we?"

I brushed past him, and we headed to the patio outside of his office. Dolores had already put the food on the table. On the menu was some green ceviche with homemade tortilla chips for an appetizer as well as some beef empanadas. For the main meal, Dolores had prepared some braised spare ribs with squash and corn.

With such an exquisite menu, I was in heaven. Every bite was a food orgasm, and I could not get enough. It took me ten minutes to realize that Alejandro was slowly eating his food, seemingly distracted by my very strong appetite, smiling at every bite I took. Had I been moaning? I looked up with guilty eyes, and we both started laughing.

"It's just so good," I explained between laughs.

"Dolores is a food genius."

"I told you we don't eat Mexican food in my house. It's not because I don't want to. My stepfather just hates Mexican food and never allowed us to have a Mexican dish in the house, so whenever I get to eat authentic, delicious Mexican food, I just swallow it whole."

"Why?" inquired Alejandro, frowning.

"I'm not really sure, to be honest. Like I told you before, we left Mexico when I was young, and he's never wanted to take me back since—or let me go, for that matter. He refused to let me speak Spanish in the house, even though it's my first language, and any mention of Mexico was strictly forbidden. I had to learn English very fast to not anger him. My nanny was the one who helped me continue to practice my Spanish, thankfully, and since Richard was rarely home, she made me the most wonderful meals."

"I'm sorry about your mother—and your stepfather." He looked very pensive and a bit confused.

"What?"

"It doesn't sound like you like your stepfather very much."

I had made the mistake of hinting at that before, and here I was again, sharing more than I thought wise. I had been afraid to voice that out loud since I was still not sure why I had been abducted. Admitting that Richard and I had a bad relationship might put my life in danger even further.

"It's complicated," I said, straightening myself up. "As it is with most father-daughter relationships." I returned to my food, hoping that Alejandro couldn't tell that I was lying to him.

"I see." He paused. "Must have been hard growing up without your mother."

"It was."

"How young were you when she died?"

I swallowed. "I was four."

Talking about my mother used to be my favorite thing pastime when I was younger, almost like I was afraid I would forget her if I stopped. But eventually, it just hurt too much. The ache from the absence of the woman who had given me life got deeper and deeper, to the point that I had found myself crying every day.

So, I forced myself to stop thinking about her, stopped bringing her back with my memories for a while, as much as I could. That had brought me some peace over the years, to get to a point that I did allow myself the memories every now and then.

Since my kidnapping, though, thoughts of my mother kept creeping in, making me wonder how different my life would have been if she had stayed alive. How different things would have been to have had the love of the woman who gave me life.

"I remember some things—a smell, a laugh, a song she used to sing me to sleep. She used to call me her little Mariposa," I said, my tone softening, my eyes distant, my mind taking me back to playing in a garden with my mom. I swallowed the tears.

"Sometimes I try really, really hard to see her face in my head, but it's a bit... blurry. I don't have even one picture. Richard never let me keep one. But when I think of her, when I remember some of the time I had with her, I can feel how much she loved me."

I straightened myself, swallowing the lump that was forming in my throat and the feeling of emptiness I sometimes nursed at the injustice of life taking my mother away from me all too soon. I quickly wiped away a tear that escaped.

"But Martha was like a mother to me. And when Martha was too busy, I spent my time reading. I really miss it."

"What's your favorite book?" he asked, leaning in toward me, wiping another tear from my face.

His tenderness warmed my heart, and I was thankful that he let me change the topic.

"Hmm, if I am forced to pick one, it would be *The Count of Monte Cristo*."

"Really?" He paused, seemingly pensive. "Interesting choice, but then again, I'm not very surprised."

"And why is that?"

He looked at me, head bent—as a slow, sensual, devilish smile drew on his lips.

"Come," he said as he got up, offering me his hand.

I hesitated, but I couldn't resist the urge to touch him again. Alejandro led me in his office and we headed to the room in the back. I was in awe. The room was a small, cozy library. There must have been thousands of books in there. There was a small window and a nook there with a bar cart.

"You are not the only one who enjoys a good book," he explained. "How else is one supposed to dream, learn, or grow if one is not curious about the world, about the nature of human beings?"

"Agreed." I smiled. "This room is... perfect."

"Well, as long as I am home, Dolores can bring you here whenever you want, and you can borrow whichever books you want to read."

"Thank you!" I said, turning around and hugging him. I immediately realized what I had done, but before I could get away, his arms were around my waist. He was staring at me, holding me close, breathing me in.

I was getting lost in his gaze, inebriated by his smell. But I was still hurt by everything that had transpired between us over the last couple of days. I lowered my gaze and pushed him back a bit. He looked hesitant. To my surprise, he let me go and went to the bar cart, serving himself a drink.

I turned and started reviewing the books to distract myself. I stacked three of them to carry to my room later. Holding them in my hands created an excitement within me. The smell of a book to a reader was equivalent to the greatest high.

There was nothing better than disconnecting from reality and losing oneself in a good story for hours on end. It was Chloe's and my favorite hobby. We sat together countless times, reading or discussing novels in our book club.

Alejandro clearly believed the same. He was walking me through his collection, telling me about the ones he had read. I was fascinated. I didn't picture him to be a reader.

We shared our favorite stories until we overheard some noise in the office. Dolores had entered and was cleaning up. I got a bit startled, realizing that we had been lost in book talk for hours. The last thing I needed was yet something else to bond over with my kidnapper.

"I think I should go," I announced. "But thank you for the books," I added before I went to join Dolores, avoiding the urge to glance over my shoulder.

When I got to my room, I changed, got comfortable in my bed, and grabbed a book. I needed to disconnect and think about something else and travel away through fiction.

I spent most of the day on my balcony, reading. I had picked a fantasy story that was doing a great job distracting me from my thoughts. But in between chapters, the unanswered questions peered back in through the corners of the book to overwhelm me. I couldn't believe that my stepfather would leave me in the hands of strangers for so long.

And George...was he devastated? I felt a pinch of guilt every time I remembered George. I didn't think of him that much. What did it mean? For him? For us?

The fact that I lusted after the man who kidnapped me must mean something. Was I technically cheating on George?

I had good times with George, but nothing compared to the rush I felt when Alejandro was around me. I must just be confused, I told myself. George was a nice man and treated me well. What else could a girl want? Love? Love wasn't really a thing, as far as I was concerned; my stepfather had taught me that. Marriage was still desirable, but for comfort, convenience, and company. I had never felt any special attachment to any man, including George.

But with Alejandro, I was losing my usual rational and controlled approach to relationships. Of course, I couldn't trust myself right now. I was locked in a beautiful bedroom for days, held captive by the only man I had interacted with in weeks, away from Martha, away from my friends, my favorite coffee spot, my gym, and what was a promising career.

I shut my eyes to try to stop the rush of desire coursing through me as my lips remembered the taste of his. I decided it was time to do some exercise.

It had been too long. And then I'd take a shower with the coldest water my body could withstand.

CHAPTER 11

After an early breakfast, I was eager to peruse Alejandro's collection. I still had two books in my room to finish, but I couldn't help myself. Thankfully, he was home, so Dolores was able to take me to him around ten. He lifted his head as I walked in.

"Am I bothering you?"

"No. Already in need of more books?" He gave me a devastating smile, softening his features in a way that made my heart skip a beat.

"In need? No, but I want to explore—if that's okay."

"Of course."

I proceeded to go through his shelves, picking books and placing them back, a small pile accumulating in hook of my arms. After an hour, I plopped down on the chair in the corner and began to read. I managed to focus, even if I was aware that he was observing me. Once I got into the story, though, it got a little easier ignoring his presence just a few inches away from me.

We spent the day like this, talking every now and then, taking a break for a quick bite around lunch time. He even started teaching me how to play chess.

I really wanted to ask questions, but I figured I had time, and I didn't want to be sent back to my quarters too fast. I was enjoying a semblance of normal as we talked—as if I wasn't a prisoner, as if I was in his home by choice.

By the time dinner rolled in, Alejandro had removed himself for what he described as a work meeting, so I was obligated to go back to my room, a little disappointed to not be sharing a meal with him.

We had gotten into a nice routine since that day, with Alejandro working on his computer, stepping away every now and then to take calls, and me reading in the corner in his office.

Alejandro's office was now adorned with various shades of Dahlia's. I enjoyed them, but it was impossible to keep ignoring the uniqueness of the situation, with my life on hold while I built a rapport with the person who had taken it all away from me.

We were on the fourth day of this arrangement, my patience was growing short, so I dared to use our lunch break for a more serious conversation than what were our favorite cities in Europe.

"So, um, about our... situation. Well... really my situation. I know you don't want to give me any details, but you understand that I have questions."

"I don't know why you keep trying," he said, seeming more tired than angry.

Maybe I was wearing him down, on could only hope. I decided to tread lightly, praying that with all the time we had spent together, he would see me as a person who deserved to be treated as such.

"Because I have a whole life out there, out of this house. And while I don't understand and consider myself lucky that... nothing too bad has happened to me here... this is not normal."

He rose from his chair, shifting to face the window, gazing into the night.

"No. No, it's not," he admitted.

I took a deep breath and continued.

"So? You won't even tell me what you and your people want from me or my family. Why am I here? Why are we eating together every day in a place where I am a prisoner?"

He pivoted and took a few deliberate steps toward the desk, leaning against it.

"I am doing all I can to make you feel at home, Amelia, to make you feel safe and comfortable."

"I know. It's weird, but I see that. But this is not my home. This is YOUR home, and I barely know you. You want me to feel safe in a place guarded by I don't know how many armed men lurking around, who will probably shoot me if I step out of my allowed perimeter or something?" I paused, hoping for some answer, but he just stared at me, anger starting to twist his handsome features.

"You barely know me? Really?"

"I can't keep doing this." I sighed.

I pushed myself up and started pacing, agitation taking over. He was right. I didn't barely know him. I felt like I had known him all my life. And that was terrifying.

"It's been over a month since I've seen my family, my friends, my fiancé, people who care about me. What am I doing here, Alejandro? What kind of sick, twisted game is this?"

He clenched his teeth as I glared at him with my hands moving in all directions, my desperation for understanding taking over.

"So, you miss your fiancé now. Is that it?" His nostrils flared, but he stayed in place, his voice low and controlled yet making me shiver.

"I shouldn't be spending all this time with you here, Alejandro. Not when I am in a serious relationship with someone else." My guilt was taking over.

"This..." I said as I pointed around me and between us, "this is not my life."

"It's the best I can do right now. I can't give you back your freedom. Not yet."

"Why? What is it that you want? What are we waiting for?"

Alejandro shook his head and squeezed the bridge of his nose. He looked exhausted.

"I think this evening has ended," he concluded as he went back behind his desk.

He grabbed the phone and called the kitchen for Dolores. I could feel the burning sensation in my eyes as I blinked a few times to hold back my tears. There was nothing left to be said.

I had been around this man long enough to recognize the stance—the cold, controlled, almost icy version of him that emerged when he was done entertaining a conversation—in stark contrast to the man he showed when he kissed me or when he let his guard slip down just a bit. I had lost him for the rest of the night.

CHAPTER 12

I SPENT MOST OF the day after alone with my thoughts, aching for my life back, for answers, for the end of this limbo state I was in. I was pleasantly surprised when Dolores stopped by in the evening and told me to get ready for dinner.

I was still surprised when Alejandro was there to get me again. He was wearing a dark pair of jeans and a shark-skin-blue button-down shirt. His thick black curls were slicked back. I did not like seeing him in my space, filling my bedroom with his presence and his intoxicating scent. How was I to stop thinking of him when I saw him in my room, so close to my bed, looking all male and primal?

He stayed by the doorframe this time, thankfully, waiting for me to walk to him. I was wearing my favorite dress—a tasteful, see-through, white lace mesh dress with a corset-like top, thin sleeves, and a flowy skirt. It made me feel like a princess. I left my hair curly and adorned it with the pearl pins. My cheeks were flushed from all the sun I had been soaking in during the day on the balcony.

"Already done with yet another book?" asked Alejandro when he saw me holding one as I got to the door.

"Yes, I wanted to return it," I explained, glancing up at him. We were both at the door.

I made an effort to break from his gaze and proceed forward. We headed to his office.

"Are you okay with just some appetizers tonight?" he inquired. "I know you ate lunch very late."

"I am not very hungry, to be honest."

"How about I show you around the house a bit, then?" he offered.

I hesitated, but if this was another peace offering, I wanted to take it.

"I would love that."

I followed Alejandro out of the office. We headed to the living room. I had passed by there a few times without having an opportunity to stop.

The room was impressive. It was the perfect combination of modern and classic with thick, dark-mahogany wood and French-style doors. The furniture was exquisite, some of the wood in the chairs clearly hand-carved with extreme care.

"I have one more room to show you," he said as we headed to the main hall. Alejandro led me down a set of stairs that I had never noticed before. I thought we were going to a basement, but the stairs went a bit lower than that.

We arrived in a humid, dimly lit cave. I barely held in a gasp. It was one of the most beautiful wine cellars I had ever seen. The cave had very small, separate rooms holding different kinds of wine. The smell of dirt, mold, and wood providing the perfect condition for wine storing.

"I am a collector," he joked with a smile.

He seemed in his element, proud and protective of his cave and the jewels it contained. The workmanship was exquisite. The cellar was made of cedar-wood and bricks, with slight curves into the ceiling. The wood wine racks were floor to ceiling, blending seamlessly into the cave.

Alejandro proceeded to explain the importance of storing wine at a certain temperature and in a specific type of environment to allow it to continue to age gracefully once bottled. This was Alejandro's favorite place in the house and a big selling point when he bought it, he explained.

We stopped in the tasting room, adorned with a gorgeous wood counter-top containing drawers directly built into the back wall, as well as a table with a few chairs. There were about a dozen French and American oak barrels, laying on their sides in two rows, on top of each other.

"And I thought I was obsessed with wine," I joked as I glided to the countertop to admire the bottles on display.

"Well, I enjoy traveling quite a lot, and I love getting to learn about new places through their wine. You'd be surprised how much you can learn of people's cultures, their temperament and personalities through the cultivation of alcohol. It also helps to be in the industry," explained Alejandro as he came to a halt next to me.

"In the industry? Are you a wine maker?"

"Something like that," he teased as he grabbed a decanter he had already filled.

"So that's your job? Winemaker?"

"Not quite." He smiled. "I manage an investment fund. I started by buying tequila plantations here and exporting the products. It evolved into a passion for alcohol making and distribution, so I focus on the business side of things now."

He poured the red shiny liquid into two glasses and brought me one.

I swirled the wine a bit in the glass to get the notes flowing. I took my time appreciating the oaky smell of the wine, my taste buds enjoying the hint of sweetness. I lifted my eyes from the glass to find Alejandro too close for comfort. He was doing the same, savoring the wine, without ever moving his intense gaze away from mine.

"Hmmm, this is amazing!" I exclaimed.

"I'm glad you like it," he said, a sensual smile drawing on his lips, testing my sanity.

We sampled multiple wines, Alejandro explaining what was unique about each glass he poured. It wasn't hard to do, as he had multiple Coravins, allowing him to pour small glasses of wine without opening his precious bottles.

I was in heaven.

The alcohol coursing through my veins was a pleasant feeling. But the real source of intoxication was him. Always him. His dark presence, his passion for the wine, the way he slowly drank from his glass, lingering on all the notes of the wine with his eyes slowly undressing me.

I could feel my body responding to his toxic presence, his jaw so straight I wanted to draw it with the tip of my finger. Alejandro discarded our empty glasses, setting them on the table behind him. I already knew what he was doing—or at least I hoped. Alejandro walked back to me, his eyes burning through my soul, only stopping once his legs brushed against mine. He slowly and tenderly moved some of my curls away from my face. A burning sensation swept through me as the tips of his fingers brushed my cheek. He looked even taller in the shadows of the cave, the low light adding to his enigma and mystery. He ran his hand down my left arm, leaving goosebumps in its path. He caressed my wrist, running his fingers over my gold bracelet.

"This is an interesting piece."

"What?" I asked, too distracted by the sensations coursing through me.

"Your bracelet."

"Oh."

I looked down at the antique piece of jewelry I always wore. It was a simple gold band with Aztec designs. Richard had kept a few pieces of jewelry from my mother. This one was my favorite, and I wore it every single day as a way to feel closer to her.

"It was my mom's."

"I gathered as much. I like it."

"Thank you."

"I also love your hair like this," he whispered.

"Thank you." I was sounding like a broken record, my lips unable to make any sound more than basic words.

"You say you don't know me, but I know you" he added, his voice a bit hollow, his expression devastatingly ravenous.

My lips parted, inviting him, daring him. This wasn't part of the plan, but my thirst for him was intense, the wine dulling my inhibitions and blurring my sense of reason.

Alejandro suddenly put his right arm around my waist and took my lips with his, stealing the air from my lungs.

I urged my body to keep cool, but my hands had a mind of their own and craved feeling his muscles contract under them as he intensified his kiss, hot and wet. My fingers got lost in his hair, drawing him closer to me. Alejandro groaned and lifted me on top of the table, positioning himself in between my thighs. I felt heat rise between my legs, my labia pounding. Alejandro abandoned my lips to bury his face in my neck, kissing, sucking, driving me mad with painful but sweet desire.

"I know you're trying to fight it, but you want me as much as I want you."

I let out a shaky breath. I grabbed his back and pulled him closer to me, his words unleashing something in me. Alejandro was traveling lower down my neck, getting dangerously close to my inviting cleavage.

I so wanted to feel him there.

His hands lifted my legs and pulled me closer. I could feel his length growing against me, already hard and promising so much, accelerating my pulse, making me desperate to have him inside of me.

His hands hungrily traveled from my ankles to my knees, then to my thighs. I could feel my nipples hardening under the soft fabric. I was out of breath, so high on desire that I felt like I could explode. His hand made its way to my panties, his fingers sliding under them to touch my wet folds. I put a hand behind me for balance.

"Oh god," I whispered, feeling myself about to fall over the edge.

I desired nothing more. Nothing else mattered other than the sensations coursing through me in that moment.

Alejandro groaned with pleasure when he felt how much I wanted him. I moaned, my body trembling in anticipation, feeling the tips of his fingers, eagerly waiting to feel them warm and hungry inside of me.

"Can he get you wet like this?" he whispered in my ear.

I suddenly opened my eyes, confused, processing the wake-up call. He was referring to George. I was just a competitive game to him. He was using my attraction to him to satisfy his pride. I pushed him away violently.

"How dare you?!" I shouted as I shot up, trying to compose myself.

He was breathing very heavily, but he had this perverse look of anger and satisfaction on his face. That smirk, making me understand that he had done all of this to prove a point, to prove how much control he had over me.

Disgusted with myself, blinded by shame, I approached him and slapped him with all my strength. He grabbed my other hand and pulled me close to him, gripping my wrists and strongly holding them behind my back.

"UGH! Let me go!" I shrieked, hating my weakness.

"Stop moving!" he ordered, but of course I wouldn't. Having him so close and being so angry drove me mad, and I needed to get away, but he refused to let me go.

"Calm down!"

"Let me go! Let me go home! I can't take this anymore!" I yelled as the tears I was holding in rolled hot down my face.

Alejandro's smile disappeared to make space for tight lips and sudden concern in his eyes. He let go of his hold, and I shoved him away with all my strength.

"I hate you!" I screamed at him.

I was in so much pain I felt like I could faint. I ran away from him, going up the stairs as fast as my trembling body would allow.

"Amelia, wait!"

There was no waiting. I was choking. I finally reached the stairs and was about to run up to my room when I almost slammed into Karina. She looked at my swollen, red face with a satisfied smile. She was wearing a very revealing negligée, clearly ready for a night of passion with Alejandro.

I knew he had quickly caught up to me, but I couldn't look back. It would kill me. I continued running until I made it to the bedroom. As I broke down on the bed, I felt like life had just left my body.

CHAPTER 13

My body felt numb the next day, but I consumed some of the food Dolores brought me.

I didn't miss how concerned Dolores looked when she noticed I was barely eating. I was also less talkative and not as inquisitive as usual. Generally, Dolores and I would chat for bit. I would ask her questions about her life or about Alejandro's childhood. This time, she commented on how I hadn't moved from one side of the bed. She was right, as the only time I got up was to use the bathroom.

Nighttime rolled in fast, I didn't want to stay alone with my thoughts, but Dolores had already taken my barely eaten dinner away. I decided to sit down and write. I was disgusted and could not process what was happening to me.

If Alejandro had decided to take me right there, on top of the table, surrounded by wine bottles of all ages, I would have let it happen. Worse yet, I had longed for it to happen, while his girlfriend was apparently upstairs waiting for him. I had opened my thighs to him, hungrily. I had trembled in anticipation of his touch and felt the tremors of what it would have been like to have him inside of me, pushing and pulling until we reached satisfaction.

What I imagined was blind desire for me had just been a traitorous ruse on his end to satisfy his male ego. He wanted me to know that all it took was one touch from him to get me to do what he wanted, even as his prisoner. For some reason, that mattered to him. That was why he had brought up George.

I couldn't believe I had slapped him. I had never hit someone before, and I regretted it. All I wanted now was to leave, go back home, and forget I ever met him. I mourned the days I thought that passive happiness with George would be enough, that passive desire for sexual satisfaction was just how it was.

I wanted to un-taste his dark, hypnotic self and un-smell his intoxicating scent.

I wanted my ignorance back, my unawareness of how my body could come alive with just one look, just one touch, tortured by anticipation.

I had a career waiting for me that I hadn't gotten to start. I didn't know how long I could continue to take this sweet and torturous confinement with this man. While I had intended to be the one to seduce, I feared I was the one falling for my own trick.

After a shower, I was back to bed without the will to do anything else. Alejandro had not requested my company, which was for the best, despite the infuriating sadness I felt at not having seen him in two days. All I could think of were ways to escape or to find out why I was here in the first place.

Dolores forced me to eat half of a sandwich during lunch, but I didn't touch my dinner. When she returned to take my tray, I asked her to please take me to the library so I could return swap books.

My best guess was that Alejandro wasn't home, and I was hoping for some alone time in his office. I wanted to searched the place, see if I could uncover anything that could shed some light on my situation. Since Alejandro wasn't home, as had then confirmed Dolores, I saw an opportunity and seized it. Dolores didn't seem concerned about letting me explore in Alejandro's absence.

I took my time browsing the books. I would pull one, start reading it, and conveniently change my mind to try another one. Poor Dolores was being patient, but it was obvious that she was eager to go take care of her business. I ignored the sense of guilt I was feeling. I was, of course, abusing Dolores's kindness, but there was no alternative. I was desperate for answers.

Desperate measures were required.

Eventually, Dolores told me to stay there and not to go anywhere else. She had just received a message about a delivery she had been waiting for all day and she had to go pick up. Feeling like the worst person in the world, I gave her my most innocent smile and pretended to be absorbed in my new read.

As soon as I heard the office door close behind her, I tiptoed to Alejandro's desk. My hands were starting to shake, my heart threatening to jump out of my chest. I wanted to run as much as I wanted to search through everything. But I knew I couldn't cower. I needed answers. I had to be my own savior.

I pulled on some drawers, only to find them locked. Of course. There was a cell phone on the desk, but it required a code. Although, I could see that there were some unread text message notifications. Knowing I wouldn't be able to get any information from it, I set the phone back down.

I continued opening anything that was on the desk. I paused when I caught sight of something shiny hidden by the computer screen. My heart skipped a beat. It was my engagement ring. What the hell? Why would Karina give it to him?

I held it in my hand but started perusing the documents on the desk. Nothing jumped out at me. I was about to retreat and give up when I noticed a piece of paper peeking out from under the keyboard. There were two pictures.

The first one was a picture of what looked like over twenty decent-sized diamonds coming out of a bag with the letters MFG. The bag looked familiar, but I couldn't tell why. I muffled a scream when I saw the second picture—a dead man on a wooden floor with blood pouring out of his head from what looked like a bullet wound. I suddenly felt nauseated and terrified.

As I was about to continue my search, I heard someone at the door. Panic filled my lungs but I managed to quickly slide the documents back under the keyboard.

I stepped back and knocked down a decorative box from the desk as well as the phone. The ring slipped from my grip.

Before I could cover my tracks, Alejandro entered the room, glaring at me with rising anger. In the blank of an eye, he was next to me, grabbing me violently by the arm. My eyes were wide open with terror, and I couldn't see straight. I felt both cold and weak.

"What are you doing?!" he shouted.

"Nothing!" My stomach churned when I stared into his eyes. He looked enraged.

Alejandro scanned the room, his eyes landing on the mess I had made. Spotting his phone on the floor, he reached for it without loosening his grip on me.

"Did you use my phone? Did you?!" he barked, shaking me even more.

"Stop it! Stop!"

"How dare you look through my things?! Do you realize how dangerous this could be?"

"Todo bien?" asked Juan as he entered the room—with no mask.

Alejandro, lips curled back in fury and jaw clenched, shoved me toward the floor violently with panic laced in his gaze. I landed on my side on the hardwood.

"Todo bien," he answered, turning toward Juan. "Get out of here," he brusquely ordered. "We will talk tomorrow."

It seemed like Juan hesitated. I couldn't see him, but one look at Alejandro's face and I knew Juan would know better than to argue. I heard the door close as Juan left.

"Mocosa mimada," accused Alejandro, lifting me by the arm. "Don't ever, ever dare come close to my desk ever again!"

I wanted to cry—or better yet, disappear. Alejandro was livid. His face looked distorted with anger and panic. I was scared. Would he finally hurt me?

Alejandro shook me again. "Tell me! What did you see?! Don't make me ask you twice!" I needed to process my thoughts, but he wasn't letting me, so I let anger invade my being instead—the only weapon I had.

"Let me go, Alejandro! How dare you treat me like this! I am not your child, nor am I your property!"

Shock darkened his features. He apparently expected compliance, and I was not giving in.

"You are mine! You are under my roof, and you will do as I tell you!"

"No! No! Let me go! You are no one to tell me what to do! Let me go back to my room!"

"No, no." He shook his head in frustration. "Your insubordination has consequences, and I will teach you to listen, for your own good!"

He pulled me by the arm. I tried to fight him, but he was too strong. He dragged me to the foyer, and I started to head toward the stairs, but he redirected me by pulling me farther to the back. We were headed in the direction of the kitchen.

"This is what I get for treating you as a guest in my home, but no more!"

"Let me go!" I cried, desperate, but there was nothing I could do to set myself free of his grip.

When we got down the path to the old bedroom, I understood that he was taking me to my old cage. I screamed louder with boiling tears rolling down my face. Alejandro ignored my pleas and took no pity on me.

He pushed the room's door open, and shoved me in. I tripped and fell on the floor. Alejandro walked in, looking as if he was coming to help me stand, but he stopped mid-step, hesitated, and stormed out.

By the time I attempted to open the door, it was already locked. I screamed and hit it with every ounce of anger I could muster up.

I let myself fall to the floor, feeling completely beaten and defeated. After crying myself to resignation for an hour, I went to bed. At least there was now a lamp in the room. My arm was bruised from the fall, and I could still feel Alejandro's burning fingers imprinted my now angry skin.

I had never seen Alejandro so enraged. He looked possessed and was either overtaken by blind anger or some sort of terror. He perhaps was terrified that I would find out something of importance.

I thought back to the picture of the dead man. Maybe that was what he was so angry about. Maybe he was a vile murderer, and he had killed this poor man in the picture, surrounded by his own blood. I felt like throwing up. I forced myself to close my eyes, unclasp my fingers, and lie on my back, focusing on my breathing.

I could feel panic rising through me like poison, and I needed to take back control and not throw up.

I forced myself to take deep breaths and to think of when my nanny used to take me to the ocean when I was upset, the sound of the waves usually calming me down, the vast ocean reminding me of how small my problems were in the grand scheme of things. After ten minutes of breathing exercises, I was able to calm down. My body felt heavy, and I had no strength left to move. Eventually, I fell asleep.

CHAPTER 14

THE NEXT MORNING, DOLORES woke me up, a look of concern in her eyes. It took me a minute to remember the night before. As memories flooded my brain, so did anxiety and terror. I might have been sleeping under the roof of a murderer. I thought Dolores would be upset with me, but instead, she just looked worried. When I apologized, she told me not to and hugged. She did her best to get me to eat something.

At first, I refused but eventually I took a few bites to put Dolores at ease. I knew that I still would likely have to use Dolores's affection toward me in my favor. I needed all my strength if I was going to try to escape this hell I was in. I did not want to end up like the dead man in the picture.

I concocted a plan in my head all day. I had an imperfect visual map of the house and made an educated guess as to how I could try to escape. When Dolores escorted me to the bathroom that night, before bedtime, I knew it was my time to try. Dolores would hate me after what I was going to do, but I had no choice.

My plan was to grab the keys from Dolores, shove her in the room, lock her in there, and run. The only problem with the plan was that if Dolores screamed and was heard, someone could realize that something was wrong, and I needed enough time to escape.

I would have to knock her out. I knew there were a few guards around, but I didn't know how many. I was going to try to escape through the trees by the pool. It was the closest possible exit that I had been able to observe from the other bedroom.

But when the time came to assault Dolores, I didn't have it in me. Dolores had just given me a goodnight hug, and I could not bring myself to harm that woman—even to save my life. I was frustrated at myself, at my weakness, but I just could not push Dolores, let alone hit her. I had to find another way.

A few hours later, I heard someone at the door and quickly looked up. The door slowly opened, and I saw a man enter. This time, he didn't speak, but I had seen just enough of him earlier to know that it was Juan. He silently closed the door behind him. He was a lean but fit man with very square and harsh facial features and a deep scar on the left side of his face. All I could see were his eyes, filled with malice. Had Alejandro sent him to finally get the job done? Bile rose to my throat.

I quickly got up from the bed, but he got to me pretty fast and grabbed my arm. I pushed him away, but I was struggling to find my balance. He came at me again and grabbed me by the neck, pressing against it to choke me.

Terrified, I realized that if Juan had his way, I would die that night, so I kicked him in his knee. He took a step back as he lost his balance. I knew this could be my only chance to escape. But as I moved toward the door, he grabbed my ankle, bringing me down to the mattress.

I managed to grab the heavy lamp on the nightstand, and as I turned around, I hit him on his head with all my strength. He let go of me as he fell on the mattress, in pain, unable to grab me again. I hurried off the bed, opened the door, and ran outside as fast as I could—barefoot.

This was not how I had planned to escape. Instead of utilizing the plan I had been thinking about all day, I was panicked, and my arm and neck were on fire. I was wearing the yellow dress, so thankfully, I was comfortable enough to run. I carefully crossed the kitchen and headed toward the pool. So far, no one had seen me. I finally got to the patio by the pool, under my previous balcony.

As I was about to stop and refocus on my next steps, I heard some noise in the house, as if someone was heading in my direction. I panicked and started running at full speed past the pool, hoping to get to the other side and then through the trees—anywhere but here, or they would kill me. My run came to a brusque halt when I saw Alejandro right there, staring at me, sprinting and dangerously closing the distance between us.

"Amelia, STOP!" he shouted.

My heart skipped a beat as I looked into his panicked gaze. The sweat going down my spine turned cold.

I pivoted to run back in the opposite direction, to get away from him and run toward the house—unable to process and with no time to do so. I felt myself trip on something, and I violently fell on the ground, I felt my bracelet break, and pain immediately seared through my head where I hit it on the cement before falling on my back into the pool.

"AMELIA!" Alejandro roared.

He had probably come to finish what Juan had started, and I possibly had stupidly accomplished the task for him.

I heard Alejandro bellow at the top of his lungs. I was trying to swim back up for air, but no matter how hard I tried, I couldn't reach the surface. All I could see was my own blood. I was panicking, my limbs growing weak very fast.

I could hear muffled noises and felt waves as someone jumped in the pool. My eyes were closing, my body unable to keep me above water. I felt arms go around my waist and pull me up. I was gasping for air, and when I saw Alejandro holding me, I started to panic again. Was he there to drown me? I tried to get away, but he was not loosening his grip.

"Por favor, mi niña, I'm not going to hurt you," he pleaded.

I stopped fighting when I heard his shaken voice. He grabbed my face to stabilize me so I could breathe better. I started becoming more aware of a painful, cold sensation on the right side of my head. I winced and brought my hand to it.

"Don't move. Please don't move," begged Alejandro, his voice holding a slight tremor.

I searched his eyes, and I only saw fear and concern. I could no longer focus. My body felt weak and numb, and my eyes were closing.

"Amelia, stay with me! Stay with me! Call Doctor Rodriguez! NOW!"

Those were the last words I gathered before I got lost in a haze. I could somewhat hear voices but couldn't focus on them or open my eyes. I heard a lot of commotion, felt myself being carried out of the water and moved to a drier, warmer place. When I tried to open my eyes, I saw glimpses of Alejandro's distorted face pinned on me and calling my name with desperation in his tone. I saw a man I didn't know lean over me. I saw Dolores.

Finally, complete peace came as I lost consciousness.

CHAPTER 15

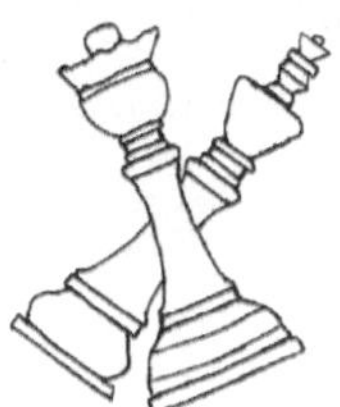

I WAS STARTING TO wake up from what felt like the worst hangover I had ever had. I did not recognize where I was and thus was very confused. I felt exhausted, but I did not know why. What day was it? Where was I? I tried to lift myself up but barely managed to raise my head. It seemed like it was daytime, from the amount of sun pouring in the room. Alejandro jump up in the distance and settled next to me.

"Don't, don't try to get up" he said gently, "you are still very weak."

My head started to pound lightly. I wasn't remembering much, but I remembered fighting off Juan, and I remembered running away from Alejandro and falling. I remembered hospital lights and a lot of noise. I remembered that I wasn't home. I remembered I had been kidnapped.

"No, no," I said between breaths. I was trying to push him away but was barely managing to touch him.

"Shh, please, calm down," he begged in a low voice. "You are okay. You are safe, and I won't let anything happen to you. I won't leave your side. I promise."

Hearing his words, seeing his distorted expression and his dark stormy eyes, somehow calmed me down a bit, and I let him lay my head back down on the pillow. Alejandro sat down by my side, concerned eyes looking at me, searching my face. I was starting to fall asleep again, but his presence was reassuring. I reached for his hand, and he grabbed mine and kissed it tenderly. My body was starting to relax and find peace again. I closed my eyes and fell asleep, feeling safe and protected.

"Dolores, she's waking up," I heard from a faint voice in the background.

I opened my eyes as wide as I could this time. Dolores was next to me, on my right, looking at me through relieved eyes. I saw Alejandro a little farther back.

"No te apures," said Dolores gently. "Here, let me help."

Dolores helped me lift my back a bit and squeezed a big pillow behind me for support. Alejandro was keeping his distance while looking at me with a concerned look on his face.

"What happened?" I asked.

"You fell," explained Alejandro, slowly moving to the end of the bed. "You fell, and you hurt your head," he continued, jaw clenching. He turned his head away, avoiding my gaze.

I remembered what happened. It hadn't been that simple.

"Where am I?"

I wasn't in my bedroom. The room we were in was massive, with a king-size bed and dark-oak furniture. It had a small couch by the bay window as well as an L-shaped table and a chair. There was a coat rack in the corner. The room was simple yet classic and felt strong, masculine. The walls were light gray, making the space feel peaceful and reassuring. The sun was shinning through, but it was more the warm, orange color of the beginning of sunset.

"In my room," answered Alejandro, suddenly searching for my eyes.

More questions stormed my thoughts, but Dolores was gently asking Alejandro to leave the room so I could get a little more comfortable and eat something. Alejandro reluctantly obeyed.

Dolores sat down with a preoccupied look on her face until I was done with the soup she had made me. While I did not have an appetite, the smell of the food revived my senses and made me feel stronger.

When Dolores left, I got lost in thoughts. I now remembered the events of the night before very well. I had attempted to escape and had once again failed. This time, I had managed to hurt myself. I was still confused, as Juan had attacked me, and I had no idea why.

I didn't know if it was of his own volition or if Alejandro had ordered him to do so. Alejandro might have gotten tired of having me around and decided to get rid of me when he realized that I might have seen something compromising in his office.

Nevertheless, Alejandro jumping fully clothed into the pool to save me would be inconsistent with him ordering Juan to get rid of me. So would him worryingly hovering over me.

There was a knock at the door. Alejandro entered, accompanied by another man. the stranger looked to be around his sixties, tan, tall and skinny, with very nicely combed gray hair. He was carrying a medical case with him.

"Amelia, this is Doctor Rodriguez," introduced Alejandro. "He has been taking care of you since the accident."

"Nice to finally meet you," said the doctor in a slight Spanish accent, shaking my hand.

Calling it just an accident was pretty audacious, I thought, but one look from Alejandro's face told me perhaps this wasn't a good time to discuss specifics.

The doctor examined me, listened to my heart rate, measured my temperature, and my blood pressure, and then asked me a few questions about my memory.

"It would seem you are okay," he said. "You suffered a mild concussion, so if you feel unwell, please let me know. It will be normal for you to feel tired, so please try to not become stressed, and do not engage in any aggressive exercise. You will have to take this medication for pain and inflammation for the next week or so, and I want to see you again in a week. If anything changes, please call me."

"Thank you, Doctor."

When he was done, Doctor Rodriguez left the room, and Alejandro left with him. Did the doctor know that I was kidnapped? I wondered what Alejandro must have told him and the hospital, as he didn't seem very concerned about my safety. Who could blame him? To an outsider, I likely seemed very well taken care of.

A few minutes later, Alejandro returned. He walked all the way to my side, his hands in his pockets, while he scanned my face with that preoccupied look in his eyes again.

"How are you feeling?"

"I'm okay."

I crooked my head to peek outside through the bay windows. If I got lost in his eyes for too long, I would forget about my doubt, my worries.

"Good."

Alejandro seemed out of words. He was standing there, wearing a pair of jeans and a blue polo shirt. He looked like he hadn't slept in days. His face was unshaven, and his hair was curlier than usual.

As I started to lift myself, Alejandro quickly closed the distance between us and grabbed my hands.

"Careful," he said.

"I know." I found so much comfort in his touch that I didn't want to let go.

I managed to stand up with his help. I felt a little dizzy so I held onto him for a little while. Alejandro seemed concerned about me and my safety. It didn't seem possible that he would have sent Juan to harm me.

"Why are you being so thoughtful?" I didn't mean to ask the question so brusquely.

"I'm not a beast, you know."

He sounded hurt. I lifted my head to look at him. Alejandro had a slight shadow on his face. I resisted the urge to touch his cheek and made an effort to stand by myself as I gently pushed his hands away. Alejandro accepted but remained close.

"Did you send Juan to hurt me?"

"What? Hurt you? What are you talking about?"

I searched his eyes, confused. Was he telling the truth? Did he really not know? He seemed honestly concerned, but I didn't know if I could trust him.

"He came into my room."

"I sent him to bring you to me. I did not send him to hurt you."

"He tried to kill me or...something else," I insisted.

Alejandro shook his head, frowning. "Amelia, you must be confused."

"I think I can tell the difference between someone who is trying to take me somewhere and someone who is trying to kill me, don't you think?!" I shouted.

"Juan works here. I can't imagine him trying to harm you. He has no reason to."

"And I have no reason to lie about this."

"You do," he corrected. "After all, you were trying to escape last night."

I felt anger rush through my veins.

"AFTER he attacked me!" I cried.

My breathing started to accelerate, and I felt the earth move under me. Alejandro caught me in his arm before I collapsed on the floor. I leaned on his shoulder and closed my eyes to try to make the spinning stop. Alejandro put his arms around me, holding me closely to his chest. I gestured toward the bed, and he slowly guided me there, then covered me with the sheets.

"You can't be your usual hotheaded self right now," he teased softly. I shot him a death stare. "Doctor's orders," he said, lifting his hands in the air.

I lay there, puzzled. I felt overwhelmed by his attitude. He was tugging at my anger. I couldn't fathom that he would have been the one to try to hurt me, but then again, he was holding me hostage. And say he had sent Juan to kill me, why would he then rescue me and take care of me instead of finishing the job? Why was he acting so nice all of a sudden?

Normally, this would be the moment he either stormed out or I did. Was he really that worried about me? But why wouldn't he believe me? I had so many unanswered questions, but I felt exhausted. I turned my head toward him, still sitting next to me, observing me, paying attention to my every breath, every wince. Looking in his eyes calmed me, reassured me, and caressed me, until I fell asleep.

CHAPTER 16

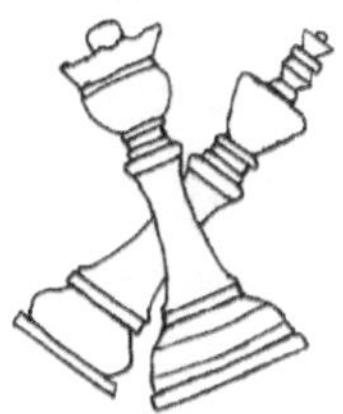

THE SMELL OF FRESHLY brewed coffee teased my nostrils as I woke up. Dolores was there, setting a tray with coffee on the office table.

"Good morning, señorita!"

"Good morning, Dolores."

She had added three vases with a variety of Dahlia's around the room. Dolores grabbed my hand and walked me to the table, refusing to let me do it alone.

"Dolores, do you know where my clothes are? This is not really my room—I mean, the room I was sleeping in before," I asked hesitantly.

"I put them in here, miss. Don Alejandro has lots of space."

"Thank you."

When Dolores left, I headed to the closet. I found myself in a large walk-in closet with oak cabinets and a good amount of light.

Alejandro had a taste for the fancy. I passed by all his suits, his jeans, his shirts, and got to the back wall, where some watches, belts, and perfume were neatly arranged. I wanted to smell them but got startled when Dolores returned. Instead, I wandered over to where my stuff was located. I went with a light, simple white dress with short sleeves, the skirt hitting just below my knees.

After selecting my outfit for the day, I walked into the bathroom. I was in need of a good and wonderfully long shower.

Alejandro's bathroom had a big walk-in shower that looked like it also could be used as a steam room. There was also a tub with jets. The vanity had two free-standing sinks and a very large mirror. This bathroom was the definition of convenience and luxury. I was discovering quite an elegant side of Alejandro that I really enjoyed. He called me spoiled, I thought with a smile, but then again, he clearly was quite particular and enjoyed his own taste of luxury.

I took a long, hot shower, feeling life slowly get back into me. I enjoyed putting some lotion on my body, appeasing my thirsty skin. I was starting to feel like myself again, despite the elevated bruise on my forehead.

When I stepped out of the bathroom, Dolores was setting food for me on a table on the balcony, and I went to join her. I wasn't hungry but was pleased with the idea of sitting outside. I noticed that Dolores put down two table settings.

As I was about to inquire, I heard the bedroom door open. I glanced over my shoulder to see Alejandro walking toward me, a grave look on his face. Dolores, after she finished setting out the most perfect breakfast, gave us some privacy.

"You shouldn't be standing for too long," he said, pulling out one of the chairs for me.

I sat down and let out a sigh. Alejandro put some eggs and bacon with some avocado on my plate and went to sit in the empty chair.

"Thank you."

"Did you sleep well?"

"I did. I feel much better. I just have a bit of a headache."

"Good. Did you take the pain meds?"

"I don't really think I need them. It will go away on its own," I said guiltily.

The truth was that I had completely forgotten. Alejandro shook his head and stood. A second later, he was back with the pills, and I didn't have the patience to argue with him.

"I could get used to this," I teased.

He gave me an unexpected smile and took a bite of his food. That twitch of his lips sent butterflies coursing through me.

"Thank you for the flowers." I added. "But, I'm curious, why Dahlia's?" He gave me one of those penetrating gazes that made the earth move around me.

"They remind me of you. Beautiful, elegant, bursting of life. And I noticed how much you like them."

A small smile on my lips, I looked away, feeling my cheeks flush and my pulse quicken.

"Where are you sleeping?" I asked shyly, still avoiding eye contact.

"In the connected bedroom next to this one."

I almost choked on my juice. I had noticed a door near the bed, but I assumed it was storage. He had a connection to my room, and the door did not have a lock from what I recalled.

"Is that why you so graciously gave me your bedroom? So you could spy on me?"

"Well," he said, sitting straight, his jaw tightening, "you did try to escape again, which of course was very stupid and put your life in danger."

Anger was flashing in his eyes. The audacity of this man knew no limits.

"Because Juan attacked me!" I yelled as I got up from my seat. "How do you think I got out of a locked room?!"

"Stop lying!" he shouted. He rose up from his chair so fast it hit the balcony railing.

I took a step back, my eyes wide with fear. My hands started shaking. I rushed in the room, livid, Alejandro on my heels. He caught my left arm and pivoted me toward him.

"You decided to run away when he came to get you, remember?"

"After he tried to choke me!"

"Why would—" Alejandro stopped talking. He frowned, shock and anger distorting his face.

"Let me go," I demanded, shaking myself to get out of his grip.

"Stop it" he grunted, shaking me. "Let me see," he ordered, a visible swallow going down his throat.

He pulled me close to him. I stopped moving, shocked by the electricity I felt rise all the way through my nipples as they brushed his chest. Alejandro grazed his fingers delicately over both sides of my neck, his gaze burning through me. I let out a slight breath, already aroused by the touch of his fingers.

Alejandro suddenly released his hold of me and rushed out of the room like the devil was behind him. *What is his problem?* I wondered. I went to the bathroom to take a closer look at my neck. I gasped when I saw the bruises surrounding my collarbone where Juan had choked me. My neck was tender to the touch, but I hadn't noticed the bruises this morning after my shower.

I got startled when I heard what sounded like furniture breaking, accompanied by someone shouting. It was Alejandro. My heart skipped a beat. He had ran out looking like he was about to go kill someone. Juan!

I sprinted as fast as I could out of the room, heading in the direction of the noise. When I reached the stairs, I saw Alejandro push Juan to the floor, punching him with so much force it looked like his head was going to penetrate the tiles. Juan was fighting back, but Alejandro, blinded with anger, was not letting him go.

"Stop!" I screamed. "You're going to kill him!!"

As Alejandro turned swiftly, I started going down the stairs.

"Stay where you are!" he roared.

Juan took the opportunity of Alejandro's divided attention to punch him in his stomach, and he fell on his side. Juan attempted to hit him again, but Alejandro was faster and hit him back. A few men, with Dolores right behind them, finally separated the two men.

"Take him out!" ordered Alejandro, shouting at the top of his lungs, "or I am going to break every fucking bone in his body!"

Two men were carrying Juan outside. "Te vas a arrepentir, imbecil! Te juro que me las vas a pagar!" Juan yelled. "Y tu tambien," he swore, looking straight at me.

Alejandro pulled Juan up by his collar while two of the men were doing their best to hold him back but failing miserably.

"Si te atreves a estar aunque sea a diez metros de ella, te juro que te mato."

Sheer terror crossed Juan's face. Alejandro had promised to kill him if he ever got remotely close to me again. When Juan was out of sight, Alejandro turned to me. I was latching the rail for support, my knuckles pale, feeling like I was about to collapse. Alejandro climbed up the stairs two at a time and caught me.

"You're okay. Come here."

He gently lifted me in his arms. I rested my face on his chest and closed my eyes, trying to stop the spinning. Alejandro set me down in his bed with some pillows behind my back so I could stay in a sitting position. He went to get a glass of water and brought it to me.

"Drink it slowly."

I took a few sips and gave him the glass back.

Alejandro sat next to me on the bed. He tenderly caressed my face. I closed my eyes, enjoying the heat emanating from his touch.

"Better?"

"Yes, better."

"I am so sorry."

"Sorry for what?"

"For not believing you." He paused. "If Juan had hurt you, I don't... I don't know what I would do."

I searched his eyes for humor or sarcasm, but none of that was there.

Alejandro moved closer, cradled my face with his other hand, and bent my head toward his. He leaned down and opened my lips with his. I felt his need as his tongue took and sucked, wanting to possess me. My body came alive. I pulled him closer to me, burying my hand in his hair. He groaned and intensified his kiss.

"Hmm, mi niña, you can't," he grunted. "You can't exert yourself too much," he muttered against my lips.

But lips still parted, I was struggling to calm down and lower my heart rate. He was right. I was enjoying the rush, but my head was still spinning.

"But I so want to," I whispered.

Alejandro groaned and grabbed my lips again passionately, aggressively, melting every inch of my body into his.

"Fuck," he cursed, pulling away, jaw tight, trying to exercise control, both of us panting.

I wanted to pull him to me again, but he was right. I had to close my eyes not to faint. Alejandro kissed my forehead.

"I do feel a little lightheaded," I admitted.

I snuggled my head into the crook of his neck to try to calm down and get back to a steady breathing rhythm. Alejandro ran his hand up and down my back in tender strokes. I was enjoying the warmth from his touch, the strength of his arms, focusing on that feeling of comfort. Eventually, I started to fall asleep. Alejandro slowly fixed the pillows and laid me down. Eyes half open, I held his hand and faintly smiled at him. How was I ever to fall asleep again without the feeling of him by my side?

CHAPTER 17

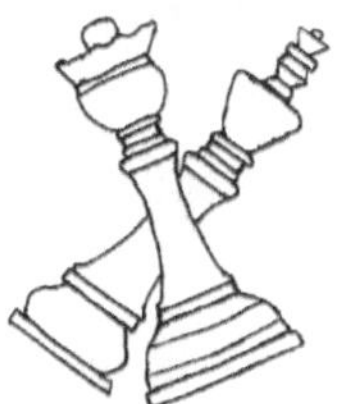

T HE NAP HAD SERVED its purpose. When Dolores woke me up, I felt better than I had in days. She brought me a light sandwich and a side of fruit. Alejandro was no longer in the room. I felt at peace, replaying that kiss in my head over and over again. Alejandro had made me feel wanted and cared for.

I was trying to focus on that, but I couldn't stop the picture of the dead man from invading my memory every now and then. I didn't think Alejandro had killed him, but I had no way of really knowing.

Perhaps if I knew the identity of that man, I could try to find out how he died. Why would Alejandro keep a picture of someone that he killed? Also, whose diamonds were those? I had forgotten about the picture of the diamonds! I was sure I had seen that bag before. But where would I have seen something like that?

"Richard!" I gasped. Richard had had that bag on his table in his office one time. I felt my heart drop to my stomach at the realization. Richard had that bag!

I had asked him about it, and he had told me that it was a watch! It was the same pouch with the letters MFG sowed on it. It couldn't be a coincidence. I had watched Richard store it in the safe he hid behind his movable bookshelf. That wasn't the only safe he had in his office, and certainly not the most hidden but it was where he kept his jewelry, so I didn't think anything of it. I hadn't even asked to see the watch, having no interest in Richard's affairs. I had just assumed it was from his collection and gave it no thought at the time.

A few days later, as I was perusing the library, unbeknownst to him, I saw him move a few items from the safe behind the bookshelf to the one hidden low in the wall, behind a big faux plant. I didn't think much of that either—Richard was always suspicious of the help, after all. Assuming I was right, Alejandro must have found out about those diamonds and kidnapped me for Richard to give them to him.

Where would Richard have gotten that many diamonds in the first place? They must be worth an enormous fortune, as both men seemed to be doing fine financially, and yet my freedom had been taken from me, likely in exchange for them. How would Alejandro have known about them anyway? Did they know each other? I wasn't sure what to do with this information. I wasn't sure if I wanted to confront him about it.

How greedy could a person be to kidnap another human being for some diamonds—however much they might be worth? Alejandro did not care about my life or what he was destroying by taking my freedom away for money.

I was starting to ground myself in logic and rationality. I couldn't allow myself to feel anything for someone like this. He acted like a gentleman, yes, but he had also kidnapped me. How could I reconcile the criminal and the gentleman? I needed to do something, distract myself. I opened every single drawer in the room to see if I could find anything useful to my situation, but there was nothing.

Of course, Alejandro wasn't stupid, and he wasn't going to leave anything compromising in this room, especially after he caught me going through his things in his office. I sneaked into his closet to explore. Alejandro had exquisite taste. I found a couple tuxedos—of course he had some. I loved a man in a suit. George wore them often, but they seemed to never quite fit him. I lightly caressed the satin lapel on one of the tuxedos, running my hand down to explore the feel of it.

I felt something in the left jacket pocket. I glanced behind me to make sure I was alone and pulled the piece of paper out. It was the invitation to my birthday party. Slight panic started to rise in my stomach. He was there, at my party, the day I got abducted! I searched my memory for guests. How would he have even received an invitation in the first place?

I remembered... I remembered the mysterious man that was staring at me from afar, sending a goosebump sensation down my back even when I couldn't see him.

It must have been him, planning and organizing what would turn out to be one of the worst evenings of my life! I was enraged. Of course, it wasn't news that he had kidnapped me, but getting acquainted with the reason and the details of the execution made his crime all too real, too raw again. I shoved the card back where I found it and stomped back to the room, pacing incessantly. I was starting to feel weak again, but I didn't care. I could not stay still.

When Alejandro knocked and opened our common bedroom door, I flew at him, pushing him.

"You were there, weren't you?"

"What?" he said, catching my hands to get me to stop hitting him.

"My birthday party. You were there!"

"Ah," he let me go. "Yes," he admitted, walking to the window.

"Criminal!" I shouted. "How could you so coldly calculate how to ruin someone's life—on their birthday, mind you. What kind of a man goes to a party, enjoys it, and engages in pleasantries while his people take someone's freedom away?!"

"Amelia..."

"No, there is nothing you can say. You are a sadist!"

"Enough!" he shouted, shifting to face me. His hardened face softened when he realized I was sobbing.

"Amelia, please..."

"Don't come near me!" I cried. "You disgust me!"

Alejandro looked like someone had punched him in the chest.

"How did you get in, in the first place? How were you invited?"

"Amelia, there is a lot you don't understand."

"Well, explain it to me! Tell me! I am not a child. I deserve to know, to understand! I can't keep doing this!"

I could feel my throat closing.

This wasn't just about the kidnapping. It was about the shame and confusion swirling through me because of how one touch of his could transport me to another world. It was about the struggle to reconcile what I felt and what I should feel, to find an explanation, a glimmer of hope, but realizing how absurd and illogical my behavior had been.

"I can't!" he barked. "Don't you understand?!" he pleaded, closing the distance between us. "I am trying to protect you! The less you know, the better!"

"Bullshit!"

"Do you think I enjoy this?" His lips hardened, and his nostrils flared as he grabbed my arm to make me look at him. "Can't you see what I am going through?" he whispered, searching my eyes for answers. "I have to protect you—now more than ever. I can't... I can't let them get to you, mi niña" he added in a deeper voice. "I can't tell you what I know, it will put your life in danger even further. Do you get that? Can you not trust me?"

Searching his intense brown eyes, I tried to understand what he was so afraid to voice. He looked conflicted, a tortured expression shadowing his gaze. He was pulling me again, destabilizing my resolve and the strength I thought reason could feed me. Panicked, I pulled my arms away with all my strength, going as far from him as I could.

"I can't trust you if you can't tell me. I can't trust you if you don't trust me, Alejandro."

His frown deepened, but I could not let what might just be me projecting what I wanted to see make me lose control of my emotions any more than I already had.

"Fuck!"

I shrieked at his growl, taking a couple more steps back. Before I could say anything, he was in front of me. I was breathing heavily, not sure if I was more afraid of him hitting me or kissing me, but Alejandro changed gears, left the room, and closed the door violently behind him.

I hurried to the bed, feeling myself about to collapse. My chest was tight, overwhelmed with all the emotions that were currently coursing through me. This conversation had accomplished the complete opposite of clarity. Alejandro seemed torn, and whatever he was hiding was eating at him.

There was no part of me that perceived him as dangerous or evil, and yet I couldn't bring myself to trust him, to let go. Letting go and trusting others wasn't something I was fond of, and how could I even be considering it in my situation?

Ever since I could remember, I was alone, with no family. It was always just me and Richard—the only man in my life with any impact, a man I despised. Martha had done her best to fill some of the void for me, and I loved her like a mother. But otherwise, I had to learn to survive on my own, and I had become quite protective of my space. Any other person was an intruder.

That was why my love life was the way it was. George didn't expect any-thing from me. He was nice and respectful, and he gave me all the space I wanted. Some women would mind, but I wasn't one of them. In any event, I always assumed that his interest in me was due to Richard, and I didn't care. The fact that he kept some distance was the perfect situation.

Alejandro, on the other hand, I had a deep need for, and that frightened me to my core. I felt his absence as much as I felt his proximity. I craved him, desired him more than I had ever desired any other being. I wanted to be with him. I wanted to listen to him talk, see him smile, and I had an inexplicable urge to make him happy.

But how did I explain this to a rational person? I was sure my friends would think I was crazy for lusting after my kidnapper. I could hear Chloe telling me to be strong, to not have 'dick blindness.' I laughed, the imaginary conversation with my friends providing some much-needed comfort. It must just be sex, I decided. It must be that. His masculinity was intoxicating.

Alejandro looked like the kind of man a mother would warn her daughter about. He looked dangerous and seductive, like trouble often was. I sighed. I was calming down. Since all this was just lust, I could fight it. I was a strong woman after all, one who had always been able to take charge and keep unwanted distractions at bay. I ran my fingers through my hair, feeling in control again.

I spent the rest of the evening content with myself. I couldn't resist going to Alejandro's closet a few more times, though. I had found his cologne, Mont Blanc Legend, and had opened it to take a whiff. It smelled just like him, the most perfectly masculine blend of bergamot, and sandalwood, inciting class and mystery.

I hadn't discovered any other useful documents or clues. When Dolores brought me some dinner, I was a little disappointed that Alejandro wasn't there. I knew I had pushed him away and potentially hurt him, but I was in the right. It really was for the best.

CHAPTER 18

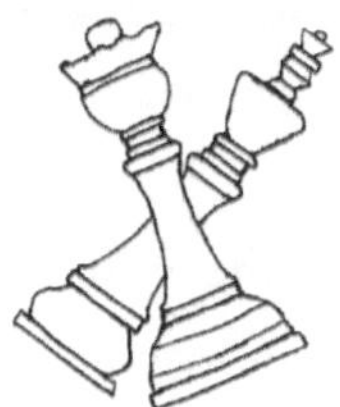

I WOKE UP STARTLED and a bit disoriented the next morning. I heard some noise, and it seemed like it was coming from the bathroom. I quickly got up without thinking, grabbed the lamp closest to me, and slowly tiptoed the bathroom to see what was happening. There he was, standing half naked, in all his glory, combing through his wet hair. My mouth turned dry as I admired the perfectly taut muscles on his stomach, tracing all the way down to…I swallowed hard, feeling like I got caught when my eyes met his burning gaze in the mirror.

"Why are you here?" I inquired, putting the lamp down on the table next to me.

"It's my bathroom," he answered simply.

"You don't have one in the other room?" I quipped, irritated.

"Yes," he mocked, "but all my things, including my clothes, are here, aren't they?"

I rolled my eyes. A slow smile grazed his lips as he gaze intensified.

"Well, that was your choice, wasn't it?" I continued, ignoring the heat I felt coursing up my body.

"I am happy to go back to the other room."

"So you can try to escape?"

"No, but—"

"You're not going back there."

"Fine," I snapped, exasperation taking over. "I can take the room you currently sleep in if that means you won't be barging in whenever you want to shower."

"I'll have Dolores transfer you there," he said as he past me, pausing in the doorframe. I tense, the smell of his soap invigorating me. "Now if you don't mind…" he added as he started unwrapping the towel around his waist, a mocking smile on his face.

Annoyed, I quickly stumbled out, closing the door behind me with my eyes tightly shut. I heard him laugh, mocking me. I decided to ignore him and go make the bed, giving myself something to distract me from the need I felt to run my fingers on his chiseled chest. Dolores walked in with a coffee tray.

"Buenos días, señorita!" she said as she set it down on the table.

"Buenos días, Dolores," I answered with a smile.

"Everything okay?"

"Yes, yes, I was only talking to Alejandro half naked!"

Dolores gave me a perplexed look.

"He just showered, and he is now getting dressed in his closet," I explained, trying to sound casual and not as flustered as I was.

Dolores gave me an awkward look. When I understood what Dolores thought, I quickly corrected her.

"No, no, he didn't sleep here, Dolores. Just seems to think he has to shower here."

"A, ya veo." She gave me a complicit smile.

"Would you mind please moving my things into the bedroom where he is currently sleeping? He agreed, and I don't want him barging in here half naked every morning."

"I understand."

I avoided her inquisitive stare as I went to sip my coffee on the balcony. I was basking in the feeling the sun on my skin; there was barely a breeze. I still had a view of the pool, shining in various shades of blue under the still burning sun of July.

A few minutes later, Alejandro came out of the bathroom and joined me. He was wearing a pair of jeans and a burgundy polo shirt. I couldn't help but admire his toned arms in the polo. He rarely wore polos, and I was enjoying seeing a more relaxed version of him. He stood next to me, staring at me.

"Such a nice day."

"And very hot," I complained.

"Yeah. If you promise to behave and not stupidly try to escape again," he said, shifting slowly toward me, "you could use the pool."

"So generous," I mocked. "Friendly reminder that I only tried to escape because I was attacked." He stayed silent.

I was too excited about being able to swim a few laps on such a hot day, and frankly, I was tired of fighting with him. Dolores had already provided me with a few gorgeous bathing suits that I was eager to use. I needed the distraction.

I moved to the bedroom where Alejandro was sleeping. It was slightly smaller, but I liked it better. It was a bit more feminine, with a light-oak king bed and matching nightstands. The closet was also a walk-in; Dolores had already placed my clothes as well as my notebook, but what got me excited was the record player.

I pursed my lips and put on the Luis Miguel vinyl and managed to put the needle on track number five. I then sat down at my new desk, happy to have found my notebook again.

I wrote until I looked up and saw it was dark outside. I found writing my fears and confusion therapeutic still.

I hadn't seen Alejandro all day, and when I asked Dolores for him around dinner, she told me he wasn't home. I decided to go swim a bit and take a dip in the Jacuzzi with Alejandro absent. It was the perfect timing. It would be easier at nighttime without Alejandro there. It would help release the tension in my body. If I was forced to stay here, I might as well enjoy the amenities.

I opted for a black bathing suit, very simple on the front, cupping my breasts on the sides, with strings going from my shoulders to my lower back. I grabbed a towel and made a pit stop by Dolores's bedroom to tell her.

I didn't want Dolores going to my room and getting concerned. Alejandro had told her that I could go to the pool, and she no longer locked my bedroom door. *Don't get too comfortable,* I reminded myself. *All this freedom is illusory if you can't leave the house.* But for a night, I would enjoy a nice bottle of wine that I selected from the wine cellar while soothing my nerves with the hot water caressing my skin and thawing my tense muscles.

The temperature in the pool was just right. It was no surprise as it had been sunny for days now. The skies were dark blue with the most beautiful stars shining from every corner. I could not get enough.

I swam a couple of laps then stopped to admire the quarter moon. It felt like a wonderful utopia. The property was surrounded by trees, and everything was so quiet. I could hear the faint sound of the music I left playing in my room since the windows were open. I could almost forget that I was a hostage tonight. I felt transported to another planet, swimming under the stars.

When my muscles turned limp, I decided to take it slow and go enjoy the wine in the jacuzzi. I had picked a lovely malbec, the right temperature for this heat if one didn't want to drink white wine. I closed my pupils, letting the water detangle every tired muscle in my body. I could feel the constant pain of anxiety that I had in my neck slowly fade away.

"I am glad to see that you chose to enjoy the place."

I jumped and squealed at the sound of Alejandro's voice. He was standing next to the Jacuzzi, wearing a black bathing suit. I was just staring at him, entranced by the moonlight highlighting every single muscle on his firm body. My mouth was agape, no sound coming out of it.

What could I possibly do when a body like his was just there, within reach?

I watched as he slowly slipped into the hot tub sighing at the feeling of the hot water on his skin. He walked next to me, never taking his eyes off me, and poured himself some wine into the glass he brought with him. Of course he came prepared.

He moved back to the other end of the jacuzzi and sat facing me. He savored a sip of the malbec, savoring the oaky taste. I swallowed and tried to slow my breathing.

I wondered what the wine would taste like from his lips.

Alejandro was still staring at me, where the water glistened off the tops of my breasts, his darkening eyes continuing to peruse my every curve, appreciating the sudden lack of coverage. His eyes looked like they were burning as he started to breathe heavier. Desperate to regain control, I distracted myself by pouring some more wine in my glass.

"I see you are loving the records," he commented.

"I am. Music is the most beautiful form of art humans could have ever created."

"I can't disagree with that."

"Spanish is such a beautiful language. Those songs just get under my skin and feed my soul."

He smiled. "You never cease to surprise me, and I agree."

My heart skipped a beat. I was starting to indulge in the lightness that a few glasses of wine were creating in my brain. I lifted my head to look at the stars for a few seconds.

"I love how magnificent the skies are here. I too often forget to look up, but here, the view... it's just magical."

"It is," said Alejandro, still scrutinizing my every move, my every breath.

I was enjoying the sensation of having my mind slightly turned off and my bodyweight carried by hot water. My senses were relaxed and yet entranced with just the mere proximity of this man. I was staring at him more, biting my lips ever so slightly, but I did not care. I didn't care if he saw the fire in my eyes, or if he noticed my accelerated breath. I wanted his hands all over me, between my legs, between my now wet folds.

"I think you are out of wine," I said softly, lips parted.

Alejandro's eyes flared. He slowly closed the distance between us, his eyes locked on mine, the tension in the air palpable. God, I would have given everything for him to kiss me. He was now standing right in front of me, his face bent toward mine.

He grabbed my glass and set both down behind me. He moved closer to me, putting each of his arms on my sides. We were both breathing heavily, my lips parted, waiting, inviting, hoping for his. Alejandro's hand began perusing my body under the water, starting from my thighs, coming up my hips, then my waist. I was unable to move. My hot skin felt every touch as an explosion of sensations. I moaned and let my head fall back, unable to pretend that I didn't want him to take me right here. Alejandro groaned.

"God, you are so fucking beautiful," he whispered.

He continued grazing his fingers up and down my neck, slowly going down my cleavage. I felt my nipples harden in anticipation. We both slowly moved our heads toward each other, hesitating in pain, not being able to resist being so close. When Alejandro's lips finally touched mine, I felt hunger, bold and raw, rise through me. I wrapped my arms around his neck, burying my fingers in his hair. Alejandro's growl vibrated through me.

His hand curved around my waist, pulling me closer, his other hand possessively grabbing my head. I moved my hand down Alejandro's back, feeling his muscles tense under every stroke.

"You have a girlfriend, Alejandro. We need to stop."

"I don't, muñeca. It's been a while since anything happened with Karina. I promise."

My blood rushed, the words being just what I wanted to hear, even if I wasn't sure I believed them fully.

"Still, we shouldn't be doing this," I said in a small voice.

"I know," he grunted. "But you, mi niña... you are driving me fucking crazy. I can't stop wanting you."

I moaned as he took my mouth back in his, feeling myself get wet for him.

"I can't stop thinking about you" he added in a raspy voice, as his hands grazed my breast, sending shock waves between my thighs.

I brusquely pulled away when I heard a crackling noise. We both scanned our right, but no one was there. I blushed with shame and desire, and the moment was over. I was so sexually frustrated I was sure I would combust into flames if someone lit a match around me. I felt like I was going to explode. But that would have been a huge mistake. I wasn't sure he was a single man, and I certainly wasn't. He and his girlfriend had kidnapped me, for crying out loud.

"I better go back up," I said, avoiding his eyes and quickly passing next to him to get out of the water.

I grabbed my towel, wrapped it around me, and sprinted to the house. I felt like if I did not get in my room in a few seconds, I would just collapse. When I got there, I let myself sit on the floor to regain my breath. I knew one thing: if I stayed in this house any longer, he would have me, body and soul, and I wouldn't be able to fight him.

When I was calmer, I took a cold shower and dried my hair. It was a habit taught to me by Martha. She always said I would get sick if I slept with my hair wet. Once done, I took refuge between my sheets. Thankfully, Dolores always left a glass of water on my bedside table. As the doctor had told me, exercise could make me a little dizzy, and well, the rise in physical sensation Alejandro stirred in me had the potential to be fatal. I chugged it as if I was dehydrated.

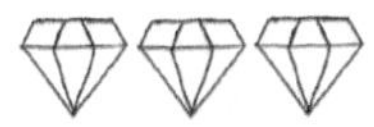

If I would feel all this guilt after the act, was it even worth it? I could never really allow myself to fully enjoy all the new feelings Alejandro was making me discover if, in the back of my head, I thought he was a criminal. I slid on the ivory silk gown I had with the matching robe. I didn't know if it was still the wine, but I was feeling brave and needed answers. I was itching for something—company, a fight, anything that got us in the same room as each other.

My earlier reasoning was obliterated by the still present tension in my body, begging for release. I had heard Alejandro's door a few minutes after I got into my room, so I knew he was in there. So much for the Jacuzzi relaxing my body, I was more worked up than before I went in.

I swallowed, and before I could backtrack, I knocked on his door, instantly regretting it. Alejandro came to open the door wearing what looked like boxers and a heavy robe. He also had just showered.

"Can I come in?" I asked.

He moved out of the way, shutting the door behind me.

"What's wrong?" he questioned with a frown.

"I need to know why I am here," I said calmly, turning to face him.

"Why all this questioning again?" he asked frustratedly, walking away from me, shaking his head.

"Can you really blame me for wanting to understand?" I pleaded.

He took a couple of seconds.

"No," he admitted, turning back to me. "No, I can't. But I can't tell you anything. Isn't it enough that I don't treat you badly?" he asked, his voice getting deeper. "Can't it be enough that you are safe under my protection?"

"No, Alejandro. No, it can't, and you know that. My real life is not here; it's in California. My friends and my fiancé are all probably worried sick. My life is on hold right now because I am here, in some sort of limbo, with no idea of why or how to get out of it. You must put yourself in my position."

He shook his head, his eyes closed for a bit. He marched to his dresser, picked up something and walked back to me.

"Here you go."

He handed me my engagement ring. I gazed up his face and was met with coldness.

"Take it," he said between clenched teeth.

He opened my fist and put it in my palm. I closed my hand and gave it no mind, my attention only focused on him.

"Why did you have it?"

"Karina had no right stealing it from you. I know you found it in my office," he explained.

I had forgotten about the ring, too troubled by the pictures at the time to care.

"But why are you giving it back to me?"

"You miss him, right?" he asked with a tight jaw and pursed lips. "You miss that guy?" Closing the small space that was between us, his gaze burned through me, stripping me to my core.

"No, not this again." I sighed. "I just... I just can't allow myself to... to feel... if I don't know," I admitted with tears burning my eyes, my throat tight.

Alejandro cupped my face in his hands, our foreheads touching, his breathing getting heavier, a grave expression on his face, his eyes half closed.

"Tell me, mi niña. Tell me how you feel," he whispered against my lips. "Tell me what you need."

My throat was closing, tears rolling down my face. When he talked to me like this, all I wanted was to lose myself in his embrace, pretend this was just a nightmare, everything but him and me in this moment.

"Don't cry," he whispered, kissing my tears away.

He grabbed my lips with the most tender kiss we had ever exchanged, causing more tears to come out. I rested my hands on his sides, gently pushing him.

"I saw pictures in your office," I finally confessed.

Alejandro took a step back and turned, shaking his head.

"Fuck," he muttered, bending his head in frustration. "What did you see?"

I could feel his anger, so palpable, as I stared at his tense, broad shoulders, and I wondered if I had made a mistake. Was this the part where he would choke me the way Juan had wanted? I swallowed a few times. It was too late to backtrack.

"Tell me!" he shouted in a deep voice, abruptly pivoting and grabbing me by the arm.

"Stop it!" I screamed. "Let me go!"

I backed up, hitting the bed with my legs.

He stood there, as menacing as when we had first met. He wasn't going to let me go without an answer.

"I saw the picture of a dead man," I finally admitted.

We both stood in silence for a minute, unspoken words in our gaze.

"Did you kill him?"

His frown deepened, his jaw tighter, his nostrils flaring.

"Would you believe me if I said no?"

"I don't know," I admitted. "Did you?"

"No. No, I did not kill that man."

I searched his eyes, but all I saw was anger and pain. I believed him. He looked tortured.

"Did you know him?"

Alejandro made his way to the bed and sat down at the end a few feet from me, his head buried in his hands. My chest was squeezing. I was worried. This man, so strong and impenetrable, now seemed beaten and defeated. I walked closer to him. Alejandro lifted his head to meet my gaze.

"That man was my brother, and he was murdered," he said with a broken voice.

My eyes opened wide in shock and shame. I was making him relive what was clearly a painful memory for him.

"I'm so sorry," I said, laying my hand on his shoulder. "What happened?"

Alejandro got up and treaded to the window.

"We won't be talking about that," he declared in a definitive tone. "What else did you see?" he asked, turning his gaze back to me.

I swallowed hard to try to get rid of the lump forming in my throat, but I still kept going.

"I saw diamonds," I admitted. "Is that why you kidnapped me? You want those diamonds?"

Alejandro rotated back and advanced toward me. "Yes."

I took a step back, feeling like he had punched me.

"So you think Richard will give you those diamonds for me?"

"Eventually. You are his daughter, after all," he reminded me in a cold and calculated voice.

"Why? Why would you do this when you have all of this?!" I asked, gesturing around the room.

"Those diamonds are worth over three hundred million dollars," he dryly explained.

I let myself fall on the bed, tears blinding me. Hearing the truth from him stated so carelessly was making this horrific situation all too real. I got up and started laughing uncontrollably, my voice laced with pain and disappointment. What did I expect? Why else would someone kidnap a person?

"If you think my life is worth more than three hundred million dollars to that shit of a man, you might as well kill me now."

Alejandro frowned and grabbed me by the arm.

"No, you don't understand," he said as he got interrupted by the sound of his phone ringing in his pocket. He let go of me and answered.

"What?" he shouted. "When? I'll be right there," he said as he hung up.

He walked to me and caressed my face. I pulled away. I could not stand him right now.

"We will talk more about this when I come back. I promise," he said before he darted out of the room.

I ran back to my room, dropped the ring on my nightstand, and got in bed immediately. I had to sleep. I had to sleep to stop feeling the indescribable pain that was threatening to tear me apart.

CHAPTER 19

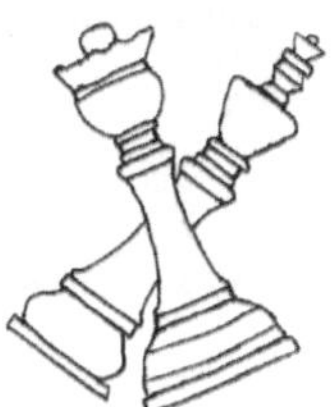

I HAD BARELY SHUT my eyes all night. I couldn't stop thinking about Alejandro.

I wasn't completely sure that trusting the words of a kidnapper about not being a murderer was the right approach. But at the same time, I couldn't fathom that this man would have it in him to take someone's life. At least not without reason.

There was a certain permanence to an act like that, both in terms of the life taken and the life of the killer going forward. What I saw was a man in pain, mourning the loss of someone dear to him, not an assassin. If the life of others didn't mean anything to him, I was not so sure I would still be alive. He also didn't have a good reason to lie to me. I was at his mercy, after all.

But he still was the man who'd had a group of people drug me and take me from my home. How could I want a man like this?

But reason didn't sway my emotions. I couldn't help wanting him with every single fiber of my being. Alejandro had taken possession of my body, and I was realizing that the man was dangerously close to taking possession of my heart. This frightened me to my core. I couldn't have that. I just couldn't. To allow oneself to feel this invincible, infinite pull to another was the beginning of death in my head. That was when one stopped being self-sufficient. This dependence on another being's life, mood, and affection was my worst nightmare, and wouldn't end well. It couldn't.

I told myself to be practical. How would a relationship with someone like that even work? What would he want from me? Some wife who would just have to deal with his lifestyle?

I reminded myself not to confuse a few passionate moments for a lifetime commitment. That was not what I wanted—ever. And why would someone like Alejandro ever want such a thing? He was the untamed, tall, dark, and handsome criminal who could have any woman his heart desired.

I was his captive. We had nothing in common other than the fact that certain circumstances had forced us under one roof for an indeterminate amount of time. Deep down, I didn't really beleive that, but I needed to.

Dolores finally got me out of my misery with a very strong cup of coffee and some fruits for me to nibble on. I chose to sit in the sun, trying to strengthen my resolutions and feel less miserable. As I looked toward the hot tub, all the memories I was trying to ignore flooded me with burning desire and need. I could feel his hands, caressing and possessing my body, melting me into submission.

No. I wasn't going down this route again. It was time for a good, cold shower.

Afterwards, I opted for a comfortable pair of light-blue jeans with a simple white shirt. I decided to wear a pair of beige, lace-free, Ultra-Flex Skechers that Dolores had added to my ever-growing collection.

I had a lot to think about. I had been playing with the engagement ring for a while. Many women would have felt so happy to have a man like George, to have a ring like the one I was holding around their finger. But that ring didn't quite fit me. Not anymore, I concluded while putting it on my finger. It never really quite fit me, if I was being honest. But I forced myself to keep it on, a symbol of that life I should have been looking forward to going back to.

In the afternoon, I asked Dolores if it was okay for me to go stroll by the pool, and she said yes. I felt a lot stronger, and the doctor was very happy to see how I was doing when he visited earlier in the morning.

Before I embarked on my walk, I decided to eat my lunch out on the balcony. As I opened the door, I could hear voices coming from the pool area. I peeked a bit to see what was going on and saw a woman talking to a man.

Her back was turned to me, but her frame looked like Karina. The man seemed annoyed and was pacing. Finally, he stopped in front of Karina and kissed her on the lips. Karina did not reject him. Instead, she wrapped her arms around his neck. *Who was this man?* He was tall and very built. He was definitely wearing some sort of police uniform.

Paying closer attention, I saw a nameplate I couldn't read, a badge, a radio, and a gun at his waist. This man was a cop—perhaps an undercover cop but definitely a law enforcement agent. Karina looked behind them, making sure they were alone, and grabbed the officer's arm as they scurried away. I made sure I was out of sight, and when they left, I went to sit down at the desk.

What the hell had I just seen? Was the cop looking for me, trying to rescue me? Why was he talking to Karina?

Clearly, he was something to her by the way they kissed. I doubted he was here to help me. If only Alejandro would trust me with more information, I would perhaps have a better idea of how to interpret what I had just seen. I wasn't sure if I should even tell him. I didn't know what he would do to Karina if he found out. Why would Karina try to help me in the first place? To get rid of me, perhaps?

So many questions with no good answer. When Dolores came to take me for a walk, I told her that I was under the weather and changed my mind.

"Do you want me to call the doctor?"

"No, no. I'm just still a little tired, but nothing to worry about," I reassured her.

I waited a few seconds before continuing.

"Dolores, what do you know about Karina?"

"Karina?" said Dolores with slight disgust. "She works for Don Alejandro."

"You don't seem to like her," I pushed.

"No. She doesn't know her place," Dolores said with contempt.

"Is she his girlfriend?"

"Ha ha, en sus suenos," laughed Dolores.

I also chuckled. I didn't know Dolores could be mean, but of course she was protecting the man she saw as a son. I had no complaints.

"Well," I pushed further, "I saw them kissing..."

Dolores sighed and sat down on my side for a minute.

"Bueno, they, uh, do... como se dice... things," she said with clear frustration.

"Don Alejandro is a man, and Karina knows how to use that. But Don Alejandro doesn't love her," she said, putting her hand on mine.

Dolores gave me a faint smile. I knew what she had in mind. She thought I was jealous, and she was trying to reassure me. I couldn't hide my smile or the little bud of hope flourishing inside of me, however silly. I tried to look away to hide my feelings.

"I don't care, really," I clarified.

"Señorita, mire, I know that things are...difficult...but Don Alejandro is a good man. He is a great man. He would never hurt anyone who didn't deserve it. He cares a lot about you."

I searched Dolores's eyes for mockery or lies, but all I saw was a woman, who could do nothing else but love, tell me what she really thought. I leaned in to hug her. I needed to feel the love and warmth of a person I could fully trust.

"Can you please tell him I need to talk to him?" I asked Dolores.

"He is not home, but I can tell him."

"Tell him it's very important," I insisted. "The sooner he can come home, the better."

"I will, señorita," she promised. "I am going to visit family today and tomorrow, but when I come back, I will make you a delicious caldo with dinner to give you strength," she said, looking at me tenderly.

"Thank you, Dolores. I don't think I would have survived so long here without you."

Dolores gave me another hug and got up to leave.

When Dolores left, I lay down on the bed, thinking. My instincts told me to tell Alejandro what I had seen as soon as possible. I wasn't sure if I was making a mistake, because if this cop was here to save me, I could ruin everything.

But the way both he and Karina scanned their surroundings to make sure no one else saw them gave me a bad feeling. Karina could not be trusted. It was anything but reassuring to see her talk to a cop.

I considered what would be the best course of action all evening, stress toying with my insides, but I always got to the same conclusion: I had to tell him. Dolores had told me that Alejandro was busy in meetings but would be back home as soon as possible. I would tell him everything when he came back.

CHAPTER 20

THE SOUND OF A door closing brusquely brought me back from my slumber. I had fallen asleep, waiting for Alejandro. Darkness filled the room. I turned on my lamp, but it didn't work. *That was weird.* I got up, guided by the moonlight, to flip the bedroom light switch on, but still nothing. I knocked and opened the door to Alejandro's room. He wasn't there, and his lights were not working either.

Great, a power outage, I guessed, and Dolores was not home. Wariness seized my chest. I didn't know who else was in the house, and I was hesitant to peek outside. The hairs on my arms were up—something was off.

But I figured if Alejandro was home, he could be in his office. I searched the space for matches in the dresser. Thankfully, I found some and lit the candle on top of the dresser to carry with me. I slowly and silently walked down the stairs. It seemed like there was no one in the house.

As I started trailing toward the hallway where Alejandro's office was, I was met with two very loud bangs.

Startled, I lowered myself to the ground. They sounded like gunshots, and the noise came from very close to me! Needles of panic invaded me. I didn't know where to go. *Where was Alejandro? Was he okay?* I heard more gunshots, a lot of movement and the sound of things breaking. It seemed like the noise was coming from the kitchen.

Shit!

I quickly swirled around, trying to find cover, my eyes getting more familiar with the darkness. I had no idea where to go, so I quietly started heading away from the kitchen, leaving the lit candle on the floor. As I was getting closer to the front door, a man entered, obstructing the exit. It looked like he was armed. I couldn't see him well but was hoping that it was Alejandro. The closer I got to him, I noticed that he was wearing a cop uniform. I took a couple more steps. There was someone here to help keep me safe. As I walked toward him, he started to look more familiar.

I recognized him as the cop who had been talking to Karina. I tried to hide by the stairs, but he had seen me already. I was frozen, just watching him close the distance between us at full speed.

"La tengo," he said with a frightening smile on his face. He lifted his gun and pointed it at me.

As I was trying to cover my head in a futile effort to avoid what seemed inevitable, I heard two gunshots, and I screamed as I felt some blood splatter over me. I looked up only to see the cop lying on the floor. Someone had shot at him from the other end of the stairs.

"Amelia!"

I knew who had just called my name, and I proceeded to run in his direction with the little bit of courage I had left.

Alejandro was standing there, gun in hand, covering for me so I could get to him. I heard a noise behind me, and I pivoted and saw more shadows holding guns coming through the front door. I finally got to Alejandro, instinctively covering him with my body to protect him, but he wrapped me between his arms instead.

Alejandro scanned behind him. He fired a few shots but quickly realized we were surrounded.

He violently turned around, never letting go of his grip on me, hiding me and firmly holding me behind him. I immediately heard the shot and felt him shake as it hit him. I screamed as we were both falling to the ground. Suddenly, I heard more men rush into the room. Thankfully, they came from our side of the fight. Running past us, they opened fire on the assailants, allowing us a path to get to safety.

We had to get out of the way. I put his arm on my shoulder as I looked for cover, my heart pounding. He got shot. Alejandro was hurt and bleeding. What the hell was going on?

"Kitchen," he said, eyes closing, jaw tight, grunting from the pain.

I grabbed the other gun he was carrying at his hip with a shaking hand, and we went toward the hallway to the kitchen. I had never shot a gun, but it might become necessary.

One of the men Alejandro's guards had shot was lying on the ground. One more second and he would have shot at us, and who knew what would have happened. Adrenaline was rushing through my veins, but I couldn't let panic invade me. One of Alejandro's men joined us and helped me carry him.

"Get us to my car," ordered Alejandro. "We need to leave."

We escaped through the kitchen and rounded the house until we got to the garage. We met up with another one of Alejandro's men.

"Let me drive," I said. "You're hurt."

Alejandro refused.

"Trust me," I begged.

Reluctantly, he gave me the keys.

The men helped him climb into the back of a white Range Rover. Alejandro removed his shirt and tied it around the part of his stomach that got hit with the bullet. He was losing a lot of blood, but there was no time to panic. I had to get him somewhere safe and seek help. Our survival depended on it.

"Julian, call Marcos," he ordered. "I will be in touch."

"But, sir, you are bleeding," pointed out the man.

"I have to get her out of here."

Alejandro did not wait and closed the door.

"Drive," he ordered. "I will tell you where to go."

I obeyed, and when the garage door opened, I slammed my foot on the gas pedal, the engine roaring to life as the car shot forward. A man was running toward us at an alarming speed, but the Range Rover was faster. He stopped in his tracks and shot at the car. I screamed but hit the gas even harder.

"It's bulletproof," reassured Alejandro. "Just drive, and don't stop!"

I followed the pathway, noticing a pickup truck following us. It was Julian, Alejandro's employee. He passed in front of us, heading toward the house gate where some of the intruders were keeping guard. They tried to stop him, but he hit the front gate without stopping, opening it for us to go through.

I drove for a few more minutes before reaching the property line. This land was much bigger than I had imagined. We finally made it to the street, where Alejandro told me to turn left. When it seemed like we were at a safe distance, I stopped and parked the car on the side of the road.

Alejandro's gaze was furious. "What do you think you're doing?"

I got out of the car, opened the back door to the left, and got in next to him. Alejandro looked really bad, pale, and was clearly in pain. He was holding the left side of his stomach. There was blood everywhere.

"We have to get you to the hospital."

"No," he said between heavy breaths. "It's not safe."

"You can't—"

"I said no! They will find us. They are here to hurt you, Amelia. I can't take that risk."

"I don't care. You're bleeding."

Alejandro bent himself in my direction and put his right hand on my face.

"I can't let anything happen to you." One look in his eyes, and I knew I wouldn't be able to convince him otherwise.

"Ok, then," I said, resigned. "Where are we going?"

"My other home. No one knows about it. We should be safe there."

"How long of a drive?"

"A little over an hour."

"You won't make it that long!" I sobbed, feeling pressure starting to build behind my eyes.

"I will. Please, drive." Alejandro winced in pain.

"No, you are not dying for me. I won't allow it!" I screamed, unable to stop the tears coming down my face. I looked away from his questioning gaze.

Think, think. What could I do?

"Where is Doctor Rodriguez?" I asked. "I can drive you to him."

"I don't think that's a good idea. It's possible they would find us there."

"If you want me to drive, that is where we are going," I declared in a finite tone. "Don't argue with me," I warned. "It will be of no use. Where is your phone? Call him."

Alejandro looked like he was going to object, but something in the way I glared at him must have made him back up.

"My right pocket."

I grabbed the phone from his pocket.

"Code?" I asked.

"3547. Look for Rodriguez," he added.

I found the number and dialed.

"Hi, Doctor, this is Amelia, calling you from Alejandro's phone. He has been shot, and we need to find you," I explained, trying to skip the pleasantries.

"His home," I said to Alejandro, "do you know how to get there?"

"Yes," he answered, closing his eyes a little.

"Doctor, we are driving to you now."

I hung up the phone, gave it back to Alejandro, and hurried back to the driver's seat.

"Let me know when I should turn," I ordered, looking at Alejandro in the rearview mirror.

"You can go straight for now," he said, a faint smile on his face.

"What?"

"It's very hot seeing you in charge," he teased.

I rolled my eyes but felt my heart grow a little. He must be fine if that was what he was thinking about. I followed his instructions and tried to keep him awake with incessant chatter. I talked about everything from my favorite ice cream flavor to my dislike of violent sports.

Finally, we got to a nice, gated house. Doctor Rodriguez was waiting for us at the entrance, and I stopped the car as close to the door as I could. Doctor Rodriguez helped me get Alejandro inside. He took us to the living room closest to the door.

"I don't have much time, Rodriguez. We have to leave," he explained as the doctor laid him on his back.

"What happened?" asked Doctor Rodriguez as he grabbed his tools.

"Got shot," said Alejandro, lifting his hands from his stomach.

I took a few steps back to give the doctor space to do his work. He had everything ready on the table.

"You are going to need this," he said, giving Alejandro a bottle of scotch.

Alejandro did not wait to be told twice. He grabbed the bottle and took a couple of gigantic gulps, wincing.

I was so scared I felt cold seep though my bones. I could not stand seeing blood. I could barely stand the smell, but I had to be brave for Alejandro. I brought a chair next to him and sat there. The doctor was at work, probing and cleaning. Alejandro seemed to be in terrible pain. He was wincing, growling, his eyes closed shut, his hands in fists. I would have given anything to take his pain away.

Doctor Rodriguez let me help with disinfecting the wound.

"I need you to go to the other room," Alejandro said to me.

"I'm not going anywhere."

How did he think I could just leave him there? I could barely move, terrified that something would happen to him, that he wouldn't make it. I erased that thought immediately, my heart falling to my stomach just at the possibility of losing him. I didn't think I could handle it. That realization was overwhelming—ridiculous, but very eye opening.

"I need you to go," he insisted, his jaw tense, his pain intensifying as the doctor proceeded to remove the bullet.

Doctor Rodriguez eventually convinced me to go into the other room, per Alejandro's request. I went out and pushed the door behind me, keeping it slightly open so I could still see.

I couldn't move. He was suffering, grunting, knuckles white from the lack of blood. I stood there in tears, hearing him scream, unable to make his pain go away, feeling completely useless. Eventually, the bullet was out. I still stood there, watching over him from a distance, for as long as I could stand.

The doctor was still in there with him. It had been over an hour, and the anguish was killing me. I was realizing that if Alejandro died, a part of me would too. I needed him to survive as much as I needed air to breathe. He needed to be okay.

After an eternity, the doctor finally came to get me and take me back to the room. I rushed to Alejandro's side, scanning him and desperately wanting to make sure he was okay. I tried my best to hide it, but I couldn't, my emotions raw on the surface.

"I gave him some mild sedatives. He wouldn't let me give him anything stronger, but he needs to rest," explained Doctor Rodriguez.

I nestled beside to Alejandro, holding his hand in mine, unable to keep my eyes off him.

A few hours later, Alejandro finally opened his eyes. Seeing those dark orbs immediately released some stress off my shoulders. The confusion on his face didn't last long as he fought me to sit up.

"You are lucky," stated Doctor Rodriguez, rushing to his side. "No organs were touched. I disinfected and sewed your wound, but you will need a lot of care and rest. Normally, you would have to be in a hospital, but I understand that is not possible under the...circumstances."

"Thank you, Rodriguez," said Alejandro, trying to get up. I jumped to his side to hold his arm.

"You really should stay here, Alejandro," insisted doctor Rodriguez. "You are in no state to be on the road. You lost a lot of blood—"

Doctor Rodriguez stopped talking when Alejandro lifted his hand, clearly indicating that it wasn't an option.

"Thank you, Rodriguez, but I'd be putting your life in danger as well. I already stayed here for way too long."

I begged him to let us stay longer, but my plea was in vain. "Doctor, what can I do? How can I help him in the coming days?"

Alejandro couldn't stop looking at me, as if he was seeing me for the first time.

"Let me write you some instructions," he said. "You will have to change his bandages a few times a day and watch his temperature. I have some painkillers I am going to give you and some bandage material. I don't have a lot on hand, but it should be enough for the first couple of days or so. You will need to go to a pharmacy to get antibiotics."

"Thank you."

Doctor Rodriguez gave me a bag with all the medicine and equipment he could, as well as some water for the road. He also wrote me a list of recommended foods I was going to have to find to help with the loss of blood.

He helped Alejandro back in the car, in the front seat this time. I climbed in the driver's seat, thanked the doctor profusely, and started driving under Alejandro's instructions.

Alejandro pulled out his phone and plugged it in the car charger. He made countless calls, trying to figure out who had attacked us and how his men were doing.

From what I could hear of the exchanges, it sounded like Alejandro's men had regained control of the house, some intruders had escaped, and others were dead. There were no fatal casualties on Alejandro's end, thankfully, but a few of his men did get shot, and some of them were in the hospital. Alejandro mostly talked to a man named Marcus, who was going to help him investigate who had attacked and why they had clearly tried to shoot me.

I had a million questions, but I had to bite my lip—for now. All that really mattered in this moment was getting Alejandro somewhere where he could rest, where we would be safe.

CHAPTER 21

ALEJANDRO FINALLY INSTRUCTED ME to swerve into what looked more like an actual neighborhood. We had been driving for an hour or so, and I was glad when he said we were getting closer.

I drove up a narrow, barely lit road. Thankfully, the skies were clear, the moonlight lighting the path for us. I could smell the ocean as we had rolled the windows down. I finally stopped in front of a brown gate with a security checkpoint. Alejandro told me the code to enter. The gate, he explained, would open and close by itself.

I took us down a fairly short road and parked the car as close to the entrance of the house as I could. The house looked quaint, two floors, very spacious with a white exterior and light-green shutters and doors. It was the perfect beach house—at least based on what I could decipher in the dark.

Alejandro grabbed some keys from the glove compartment and accepted my arm as he got out of the car. I opened the double doors to a gorgeous foyer with a small table and a gorgeous blue orchid plant. Alejandro pointed me to the staircase. We went up the stairs very slowly, so as to not strain him, and I stared at his face to watch for any sign of discomfort. I opened the first room as indicated.

I guided Alejandro to the bed and slowly set him down. I quickly but tenderly removed his shoes and what remained of his shirt. Doctor Rodriguez had run the bandage all around his waist, but it looked like he was still bleeding through. I went to turn on the light.

Before me was a gorgeous bedroom, all white, with a simple, gray wood king-size bed and a gorgeous window I imagined opened to a view of the water. The room was a coastal decor dream. The moon was high and full as it shed some light inside the room, and I could hear the sounds of the waves hitting the beach with all their strength.

"I am going to go find the kitchen," I told Alejandro. "You need some water to take your medicine."

"Come here," he said, lifting his arm toward me. I went to him and grabbed his hand.

"How are you feeling?" he inquired, searching my face for an answer.

"I just want you to be okay," I admitted, avoiding his gaze, my voice cracking.

"I am going to be just fine," he said sweetly, "all thanks to you." He paused. "Thank you."

I cleared my throat in an attempt to push down the rush of emotions that were going through me. I needed to be strong in the moment and think later. I quickly got up, wiping my eyes as I turned away from him.

"I will be back as soon as I can," I announced before I left the room.

I rapidly went down the stairs. The house was very spacious, clearly built to maximize the view of the ocean from every room, even though I couldn't quite see it in the dark. I passed what looked like a very relaxing living room and dining room then finally got to a gorgeous kitchen with white counter-tops and gray cabinets.

I proceeded to the big, stainless steel fridge in the kitchen. It was empty, but I found a box of frozen chicken wings and frozen fries in the freezer. The expiration dates had thankfully not yet passed, so I put both in the oven.

I plopped down on one of the chairs by the kitchen island. My brain was still trying to process the day. Everything had changed in just a few minutes. I could still hear all those gunshots. It had felt like I was in a war zone, and I really thought I was going to die. But at the last minute, Alejandro saved me.

I had instinctively wanted to protect him, but he chose to put his life at risk for mine instead, literally shielding my body with his and taking a bullet in my stead.

That memory made my blood rush, my body overtaken by a chaotic combination of fear and hope. He turned around and took a bullet that was, for some reason, meant for me. I was torn between the overwhelming joy I felt at knowing that he would sacrifice himself for me and the simmering dread I felt at the idea that he wouldn't make it. The sharp pain and panic I felt at the idea that I might not see him again overpowered my being, fear shaking me to my core.

I had to tell him eventually—about the cop and Karina. The sooner, the better. Because Karina probably knew of this house and seemed to be part of a plot against him or me, so he should know as soon as possible.

When the food was ready, I put it all on a plate, got some water and a bottle of Italian wine I had found in a cabinet and took it with me to his room. Alejandro was dozing off when I went in, but the smell of the food woke him up. I helped him sit up a bit and put some pillows behind him for support. I brought him the food and gave him the painkillers.

"Ah, you found something," he said.

"Yes, the only food there is in the whole house."

"I don't come here often," he explained.

"Where are we?"

"This is my childhood house—or I should say, neighborhood. When I went to college, developers, in conjunction with the government, forced people to sell their land at ridiculously low prices to build vacation homes. They kept some walls but destroyed everything. I bought it all back, and some of the other houses, and gave them back to some of the people who used to live here." Of course he did.

"That was very nice of you."

"It was the right thing to do," he corrected.

I had to encourage him to eat a little more. He was trying to put on a good face, but I could see him wince or his lips tighten with every movement. The painkillers were probably wearing off. His color was coming back, at least.

"I have to go to a pharmacy tomorrow and a grocery store."

"No, I don't want you leaving the house."

"I have to. We have nothing to eat, and the doctor gave you some medication that you need for inflammation and infections."

"Amelia…"

"Please, Alejandro, I have to, and in your state, we both know you can't stop me." He shot me a death stare, but I was right.

"I wouldn't be so sure about that."

I rolled my eyes, sighing frustratedly at him.

"They could find you."

"Who else knows about this place?" I asked.

"Only my mother and Dolores," he admitted.

"Dolores is out of town, and I heard you call her and tell her not to go back to the house. So that leaves your mother, who I assume has no idea what is going on since she is currently in Hawai, as you had told me."

Alejandro shook his head, out of a retort. He sighed.

"There is a store named Casa del Carmen. They sell everything, and there is also a pharmacy inside. I will go with you when they open."

I remained silent but took his plate away from him and refilled his water cup. He would eventually fall asleep, I thought.

"Do you know who attacked us?" I asked.

"Not very sure," he said.

"I have something to tell you," I confessed hesitantly. "This morning, I saw a man in a cop uniform at the house. He was with Karina, by the pool. They looked suspicious. It seemed important to them that they were alone. I think... I think it was that same cop who... tried to kill me."

Twisting my ring nervously, I sat by him on the bed, studying his reaction. His jaw was stiff, his nostrils flaring, his eyes suddenly filled with anger, as a shadow crossed his face. I hated the idea that he might be jealous, but it had to be done.

"Are you sure?"

"Yes. I know she is your girlfriend, but I saw them from my window. I couldn't hear what they were talking about, but I certainly saw them. They also... kissed," I said in a lower voice, my head bent.

"Bring me my phone." I got up and took the phone from the table where I had set it to charge. "Look at me."

I raised my chin, hoping he couldn't see the thunder pounding inside of me.

"For the record, she is not my anything. I've told you. I don't have one of those—yet."

I didn't say anything but was quite aware that he was studying me for a few seconds longer, then he turned his gaze from me to the phone in his hand, a frown on his face.

Alejandro called Marcos and shared the information, asking Marcos to call him back as soon as possible.

"You look awful," I told him once he hung up. "You need to sleep."

"You certainly know how to charm a man."

"I am not trying to charm you, Alejandro."

"That's too bad."

I sighed but relaxed when I saw his mocking smile, reassuring me.

Alejandro protested, but the state of his body and the narcotic medication were winning this battle. I removed the pillows and arranged them to make him comfortable. Alejandro was fast asleep within five minutes.

I got up to take a good look at him. I was admiring his long eyelashes, his straight nose, his sensual lips, that jaw that flared with frustration at me so many times, those crazy wavy strands he didn't bother to tame anymore, that strong neck, and those shoulders I enjoyed the strength of. I tenderly slid my fingers through his hair and gently kissed his forehead.

Catching myself in the act, I decided to bring the dirty plates to the kitchen and quickly wash them. I made sure all the exit doors on the first floor were locked. I got myself some more water and went back to Alejandro. I didn't want to sleep. I needed to check his temperature every hour. I felt like if I closed my eyes, something bad would happen to him. I wouldn't be able to live with myself if he died.

This stranger had somehow filled a hole in me, a hole I thought had disappeared some time ago. The idea that he would cease to be alive wasn't something I could even contemplate. And that was a new reality I wasn't equipped to deal with.

I grabbed a blanket from the closet. The temperatures were a bit cooler here by the beach. The sound of the waves was calming me down, and since it was late in the night, I knew the sun would rise in only a few hours. I wrapped myself in one of the covers and sat on a chair next to him, the rise and fall of his chest settling me.

I spent the rest of the night falling asleep for a few minutes, waking up confused, my back and neck hurting, with a slight headache. I checked on Alejandro, made sure his bandage looked good and that he didn't look uncomfortable. I would wipe his forehead when it seemed a bit wet.

I realized that I was covered in blood, so I jetted to the bathroom and washed my white shirt the best I could. Now it just looked like it had gotten discolored in the washer. I spot-cleaned my jeans to try to get rid of more blood stains. I almost cried when I found a toothbrush and a hairbrush in Alejandro's bathroom.

Reality started sinking in when I caught a glimpse of my face in the mirror, dirty with blood and dried tear drops creating lines on my cheeks. I found some soap and quickly washed myself, trying to take away the memory of the warm blood of that man all over me. I washed my hands, cleaned under my nails, and scrubbed my arms the best I could.

I was in dire need of a shower, but I didn't have the time or the energy for that. I had never in my life gotten ready so fast. The doctor had told me to watch for fever because it could indicate infection, and that would complicate things. All I wanted to do was keep taking his temperature and never leave his side.

Alejandro woke up in pain, so I gave him more medicine. He had asked me to sleep by his side, so I got onto the bed next to him and kept my hand in his until he fell asleep again. I intended to lie there for only five minutes, but I ended up falling asleep as well.

CHAPTER 22

I CURSED MYSELF FOR falling asleep in his bed. I must have been out for forty minutes. I got up, admiring the sun shining through the window. I was about to go to it to let some fresh air in when I noticed Alejandro moving a lot. I rushed to his side in a second. He looked troubled.

My breathing quickly accelerated, but I wasn't going to let my emotions get in the way. I snatched a small towel, dampened it with the coldest water, and wiped Alejandro's head. He was mumbling something. I got closer.

"Amelia... mi niña... don't leave... please."

God, he was calling my name, my heart sinked. I grabbed the phone and called Doctor Rodriguez.

"Doctor, he's burning up, I gave him the medicine, but he's still hot! I am applying cold compresses, but it's not helping."

"You have to go get him the medicine I prescribed, Amelia. He probably has an infection. We have to get the fever under control."

"I am going to the pharmacy at Casa del Carmen, it's the closest one, from what Alejandro told me. Can you make sure I can get the prescription for him there?"

"Yes, and if you need me when you get there, llamame."

I changed his bandage, disinfected the wound as indicated by Doctor Rodriguez, and put on a new bandage. I forced him to swallow some water, but he was still delirious. I could no longer understand what he was saying. There was no time to waste.

I grabbed one of his jackets, money from his wallet, the car keys, and the phone. I scribbled a note in case he woke up looking for me. I ran to the car and started driving. Thankfully, the phone GPS was working, so I managed to find directions to Casa del Carmen. I sprinted into the store with the prescription information. I had to compose myself. The last thing I needed was to seem panicked or scared and have someone call the cops.

The supermarket was gigantic, but after asking a few people, I finally got to the pharmacy window. The pharmacist ended up being a little suspicious based on the medication I was buying, so I called Doctor Rodriguez, who then dialed the pharmacy directly. The man—short with a thick figure—seemed distrustful of strangers. He was staring at me with a frown on his face. I tried to give him my best smile, but he was not biting.

"Ahora regreso," he said after he hung up.

He went to the back for an eternity. I was relieved when I saw him return with the medication.

I grabbed additional alcohol, hydrogen peroxide, gauze, and everything I needed to heal the wound. Thankfully, it all totaled an amount that Alejandro had in cash, as I was afraid to use the credit cards.

Once done, I ran back to the car and drove as quickly and safely as I could—although my shaking hands made it quite difficult—and got back to the house in record time. I parked the car and climbed up the stairs two by two. When I opened Alejandro's bedroom door, I saw a woman standing next to him, kissing him. She got startled when I entered the room, eyes shooting fire.

"Quien eres tu? Que le paso?" screamed the stranger, clearly concerned.

"Who are you?" I answered while I dropped the bags down on the floor.

There was no time for a conversation. I proceeded to open the medication and went to Alejandro, almost pushing the woman out of the way.

"Quien eres?" screamed the woman, violently grabbing my arm.

"Fuck off!" I shouted, pushing her away. "He is burning up. I have to give him his medication!"

I poured a glass of water. I lifted Alejandro's head off the pillow and forced him to swallow the pills.

His eyes were slightly open, and he was trying to say something, but he did not have the energy to do so.

"Don't talk. It's okay. I'm here. It's going to be okay," I whispered as I gently laid his head back down on his pillow.

I grabbed the towel, ran to the bathroom to refresh the water, and came back in to dab it on his forehead, trying to bring the temperature down. Doctor Rodriguez had also prescribed a shot. That was probably why the guy was refusing to give me the prescription at first.

With slightly trembling hands, I filled the syringe with the liquid and stabbed it in Alejandro's arm, as the doctor had explained.

Luckily, I had attended a first-aid training course in high school and learned the basics of administering a shot from Martha. She had a severe nut allergy, and I had wanted to be prepared should she ever need my help. Once again, I was so thankful for Martha and all she contributed to my life.

Alejandro was very slowly calming down. I was still wiping his face, caressing his hair, his hand, trying to reassure him with my voice. I had completely forgotten about the stranger in the room until I heard her clear her throat in frustration.

I got up to face her.

"Okay, I came here with Alejandro last night, you are the one I found here trespassing as I went to get him some medication, so I am the one asking questions here. Who are you?"

"I am Elena," she responded with an attitude and an accent. "Soy su mujer! Asi que quien eres tu?"

The woman took a few purposeful steps in my direction, her gaze inspecting me from my feet to my head. She claimed to be Alejandro's woman and wanted to know who I was. Elena was a bit taller than me; she was petite with curves in the right places. Her pitch-black hair went down the length of her back, and her brown eyes were shooting sparks at me. Jealousy poured through me like tar.

Then what was Karina? It wasn't my place to correct her. Nor was it my place to feel the green poison of jealousy coursing through me as she stared.

"I don't owe you an explanation," was all I had the strength to say.

"Amelia, Amelia."

Alejandro was calling for me again. I swirled around and went to him. I took his hand, refreshed his compress, and caressed his face. I almost bent to kiss him when I remembered Elena was still there, looking like she would jump at me at any moment if I kept touching Alejandro.

"My name is Amelia," I responded, shifting my attention toward Elena. "Alejandro and I got into a situation, and he got hurt. He saw a doctor last night, and I am trying to bring his fever down."

I didn't like her, but I reluctantly put myself in her position. I understood that she was worried.

"How did you get in here?"

"I live next door, in the house Alejandro bought for me," she quipped, every word emphasized by her beautiful, thick accent. "And I have a key. I check up on this house for him when he is not here."

She was more proficient in English than I thought at first. I was not going to speak Spanish with her. No reason to make her life easier.

"I see."

There wasn't much I could say when Elena jiggled her key set in my face to emphasize her point. She walked by me and went to Alejandro. She started caressing his head, and tears came out of her eyes.

I had to clench my hands into fists, burying my nails in my palm, to resist the urge to grab this intruder by the hair and push her out of the house. She seemed honestly concerned about Alejandro, and I could sympathize with that, but she was touching what was mine. I shook my head, trying to get rid of that idea, but I couldn't shake it. I knew he wasn't mine, but my heart had a mind of its own.

"You have to let him rest," I finally interrupted, lips tight, trying to end the torture I was feeling at seeing another woman close to him.

Elena got up reluctantly and walked to the window.

"He will be okay, right?" she asked, tears falling down her cheeks.

"I will do everything I can," I admitted. "And I welcome your help," I conceded in an effort to make peace—whatever it took for Alejandro to get better. "But no one, and I mean no one, can know we are here. His life is in danger."

Elena looked at me with scared and questioning eyes. I thought it was best to tell her this. I wasn't sure I could trust her, but her sorrow and concern for Alejandro seemed candid, and I didn't want the other people in the neighborhood to know we were there.

"Está bien," accepted Elena.

I was torn. I didn't want to owe her anything, but we needed groceries. I wanted to have some food for Alejandro to eat. I could ask her to stay with him, but the idea of leaving her alone with him made the hair on the back of my neck rise.

"Would you be able to go to the mercado? He has to eat," I explained, hoping she would be willing to run the errand.

"You go. I will stay here with my boyfriend," she said, her hands on her hips. "I don't know how to drive," she added with a satisfied smirk on her face.

I wanted to scratch that stupid smile off her lips. But I didn't think I had a choice. I had to accept Elena's idea. That would allow me to call the doctor. I gave Alejandro more water and took his temperature again. It seemed to be going down, and he was sweating a little less. I caressed his face. "I will be right back," I whispered before I headed back out to Casa del Carmen.

The grocery store was very nice and had everything. I bought some meat, fish, taco shells, bread, fruits, leafy greens, spinach, coffee, and everything needed to make some soup and solid meals for the week. I still had a good amount of money left from his wallet.

One of the employees was nice enough to help me store all the provisions in the car. I drove back like the devil was behind me. My hands were sweating, my heart racing as I imagined Elena touching him or kissing him. Alejandro was an asshole, like all other men, with countless girls adoring him, none of them enough to satisfy him. And he apparently expected me to be one more in his little harem.

I realized that this was probably the first time in my life that I felt real, raw, almost blinding jealousy. None of the men I had dated previously had ever elicited such a visceral reaction from me, likely because I was never really emotionally involved. Most of those men had been handpicked by Richard himself, which was likely a big part of the problem in the first place. In my anger, I almost forgot to call the doctor. He was pleased with the small progress and made himself available if I needed anything else.

When I returned to the house, I called out Elena's name so she could come help me, but she refused to join me. It had only taken about an hour, but I was concerned that Alejandro would wake up and decide to go look for me, so I moved as fast as I could, filling the kitchen with the provisions. I had bought a good amount of already cooked food, anticipating not having time to prepare anything from scratch for a day or two. I quickly heated up some fresh caldo de pollo and added some fresh spinach and cooked beans. I grabbed one of the Gatorades and the vitamins I had bought and hurried upstairs.

Elena was there, of course, settled next to Alejandro, caressing his face, holding his hand. As I got closer, I noticed that his eyes were slightly open. He looked at me and smiled. I ignored Elena and went straight to him. Elena reluctantly got up.

I placed a big pillow behind his back. He was still dozing off, but I brought the bowl with me and sat next to him, urging him to drink some of the soup. He didn't want to eat, but he didn't have the strength to fight me, so he let me feed him. My heart melted with relief when I saw his usual mocking smile slowly draw on his face. He was staring at me now, clearly enjoying being taken care of.

I almost jumped when I heard Elena scoff, having wishfully forgotten that she was still in the room. She suddenly walked to Alejandro, standing between me and him.

"Mi amor, que te paso?" she asked, almost crying, grabbing his face between her hands.

"I'm okay, Elena," answered Alejandro awkwardly. "I will call you, I promise, pero ya dejame descansar."

Elena lingered a little bit more but got the message that he wanted her to go and let him rest.

"I think you should leave your keys here," I said before I could stop myself. "It is safer that way—for her and for us," I doubled down, looking back at Alejandro, trying to hide my real motive.

The last thing I wanted was for her to just appear out of nowhere. Alejandro raised his eyebrows and looked like he was hiding a smirk. I was divided between pettiness and embarrassment for my behavior.

"Tiene razon," he agreed, never losing sight of me. Elena wasn't budging.

"It's safer for you, Elena. I have people trying to harm me, as you can see," he added, looking at her for a few seconds before turning his gaze back toward me.

Elena's eyes grew wide. She threw her keys at the bed and finally left, slamming the door behind her without a word.

I continued to feed Alejandro silently, avoiding his mocking gaze the best I could. I felt flustered and could feel my cheeks burning with satisfaction and shame at the same time. When I could no longer take it, I rose up.

"I think you can feed yourself the rest of the soup."

"I much prefer when you feed it to me," he teased with his usual smooth, deep voice.

The smirk was fully drawn on his face now. He was surely feeling better already. I ignored him, looking out the window. I hadn't realized how close the house was to the ocean. I could see the waves gleaming under the sun.

"You like the view?"

"It's perfect," I whispered almost to myself. "I find the ocean mesmerizing. A fascinating and terrifying reminder of how lucky we are to live but how insignificant we are in the world."

"Yes, this house is very different from the house I grew up in, but the view, the smell... it's all those little things that take me back," he said. We remained peacefully in silence, not wanting to ruin the moment.

When Alejandro finished the soup, I moved the tray to the table. "I have to change your bandage again. We need to avoid another infection."

Alejandro acquiesced and let me unwrap him and start disinfecting the wound before wrapping it back up with new bandages. He was scrutinizing my every move. I was trying to not get distracted by his inviting golden-tan chest or those arms that made me feel so protected when they held me close. His eyes caught mine when I looked up.

"What?" I asked, feeling a bit defensive.

"I love watching how you take care of me," he admitted.

His honesty tore me apart. He wasn't mocking me this time; he was letting me in.

Against my better judgment, I leaned toward him and kissed him. I felt his breathing immediately accelerate as he held my face to pull me closer to him. Heat climbed up my body, trying to consume me, as I enjoyed the warm taste of his tongue in my mouth. My hands went up to his face, wanting to hold him there forever, but I gently leaned backward. I didn't want to make him tired. I got up from the bed, clearing my throat, avoiding eye contact.

"You should rest," I said. "We don't want your fever to rise again."

I brought him the last pill that he needed to take on a full stomach, as well as the multi-vitamins. I moved the pillows and helped him lean back.

I could tell Alejandro was fighting it, but the last medication was supposed to help him relax and rest. After a few minutes, Alejandro was snoring. Satisfied with myself, I checked the time. It was nearly noon, too early to sleep even if I was exhausted, so I decided to take a better look around.

I ventured into his closet to get him a change of clothes and glared at some of the women's clothing I found there as well. I needed a change of clothes too, but I had too much pride to try those on. By the size, they would probably not fit me. They probably belonged to Elena, I thought as the vise of envy coursed through my veins.

I gave myself a house tour to appease my thoughts. There were three good-sized bedrooms and three comfortable bathrooms on the second floor as well as a laundry room. There was a smaller bedroom and bathroom by the kitchen on the first floor with a separate living room, as well as a half bathroom in the shared area. There was a three-hundred-sixty-degree balcony going around the second floor and gorgeous patios outside of every room on the first floor.

The side of the house that faced the ocean had many glass sliding doors, giving one the illusion that they were right there on the beach. There were two gorgeous living rooms, a reading room, a dining room, and an exercise room.

The house was simple yet gorgeous, and had a peaceful atmosphere throughout. All the light-blue, light-green, and white colors were carefully selected to create a vacation ambiance with some paintings bringing a rush of peaceful colors in certain rooms. This house was a beach lover's dream come true.

I spent some time in the kitchen, cooking chicken soup. I would eventually make him some hearty meals, but for now, he needed to regain his strength and stay hydrated.

I headed back upstairs and picked the room closest to his as mine. It was time to shower, so after taking his temperature again, I borrowed a pair of boxers from his closet, as well as the smallest short-sleeve white shirt I could find. I threw my jeans in the washer and placed my underwear and white shirt in the bathroom sink with some water, soap, and Clorox to soak for a bit.

As my clothes were getting cleaned, I took the time for a proper shower. The bathroom was, of course, equipped like a hotel, fully ready for unexpected guests. I put my jeans back on when they were ready and dry. I managed as best as I could with Alejandro's shirt, tying the bottom in a knot right above my hips in the back. The shirt kept falling over one of my elbows, but it would have to do for now. My shirt was clean but was still stained with blood, and it would take a bit more time to fix that. I found a bottle of hair mousse to help control my unruly curls. I observed my figure in the mirror.

I could see the dark circles under my eyes, and my smile lines showed. My face reflected the whirlwind of a mess my life had been since my dreaded birthday party, which seemed so silly now. So much had changed in the past few months of captivity, and I didn't really recognize myself. I remembered my life before, but it felt like I was watching a movie of myself, unable to distinguish reality from fiction.

After I composed myself, my feet took me back to Alejandro's room to check on him. His temperature was completely back to normal, and relief that the worst seemed to be behind him washed over me. There was no blood on the bandages for once.

I lay down on the bed next to him. I loved seeing him at peace like this, no frowning, just pure invigorating sleep. Every single feature on this man was perfect, created by the devil himself to drive my senses wild. I lay there, enjoying his masculinity without scrutiny or interruptions.

CHAPTER 23

WHEN I OPENED MY eyes later in the evening, I panicked as Alejandro was no longer next to me. I didn't know how long I had slept for, but I could see the sun setting, it's gorgeous orange light covering all the furniture with a soft glow.

As I got up, Alejandro was coming out of the bathroom. He had clearly showered and found a way to put a pair of beige linen pants and a white linen shirt on himself. I rushed to him as he was wincing with every step he took.

"What did you do?!" I squealed, wrapping his arm around my neck to provide him support.

"I can't just lie there like this."

"Showers can wait!" I retorted. "No strained efforts, remember? Are you bleeding?"

"No, don't worry about me," he said.

When he sat down on the bed, I lifted his shirt a bit. Yes, of course, he was bleeding a little, and he had gotten the bandage wet. I closed my eyes for a minute, trying to control the urge to slap him back to a fever. I quickly took the bandage off, medicated the wound, and put a fresh, dry bandage on, ignoring his grunts and the wonderful fresh soap scent on his skin. I checked the time on the phone. It was almost seven p.m. Ignoring Alejandro's slightly frustrated gaze, I grabbed some of his pills and gave him a few to swallow.

"Don't move," I ordered before I exited the room.

I heated up the soup, toasted some bread with butter, and brought it to him.

"Why didn't you wake me up?" I asked, watching him eat with a satisfying appetite.

"You need to sleep, Amelia. You were clearly exhausted."

"You should have woken me up so I could have taken you to the bathroom."

"No, I'm fine. I can handle it."

He was back, I accepted, rolling my eyes, but his pride was getting in the way of his recuperation. But he no longer had a fever, and he had a decent appetite, so I couldn't bring myself to scold him for long, even if he deserved it. He smelled great, and it was nice to see him look more normal.

"Did you make this?" He looked impressed.

"I did. My nana taught me how to make it. When she realized I was ordering food all the time in New York, she basically flew there for a month to give me lessons. She knew I didn't enjoy cooking, but she claimed every human needed to have that basic skill. There was no way to argue with that logic."

Alejandro smiled. He didn't give me one of his "you're a spoiled brat" responses this time.

"It's delicious," he complimented.

"Thanks."

"I haven't seen you eat," he pointed out with a frown.

"I have," I lied, "in the kitchen."

The truth was that I had completely forgotten to eat. I had a knot in my stomach that didn't seem like it wanted to go away, and it killed my appetite. The idea of swallowing anything right now made me want to throw up.

"I'd rather we eat together next time," he insisted, looking at me with suspicious eyes.

I ignored him and brought the dishes back to the kitchen when he was done. I filled two big glasses with water, putting one in my room and bringing him the other.

"You look tired, Amelia. You need to sleep. I am fine, and I can take care of myself."

I was hurt to have my assistance be so aggressively rejected.

"Fine. I can see that you feel much better," I said.

"Yes, you saved my life. And I won't let you put your health in danger for mine any further," he insisted.

I looked away flushed, trying to hide from his gaze.

"Okay, I will go to bed in the bedroom next door to you. Please, if you need anything, wake me up."

"You can sleep here," he offered.

"I think it's best if I sleep there," I countered, not wanting to be tempted. "Goodnight."

"Goodnight," he replied.

I exited his room as fast as I could, trying the simmer down the overwhelming need to feel his warmth over my skin. I desperately wanted to lock my door, but I had to leave it unlocked in case he needed me.

Something told me that I should run away as far and as fast as possible before it was too late, before he stole my heart.

I got into bed, but I couldn't sleep. I was worried about him and had millions of questions making their way back to my now less-exhausted self. Why would a cop try to kill me? Why was Alejandro literally protecting me with his life? Where was my stepfather in all this? This new place might be my opportunity to escape I realized. But nothing mattered, not even my freedom, until he was fully recovered.

After tossing and turning in bed for hours, I decided to go check on him. I swayed the door agape very quietly, padded silently to his side, and gently touched his forehead. He was okay. There was no way I was going to sleep if I didn't have my eyes on him at all times, I admitted to myself. So I put my pride aside, went to his closet, and looked for the most pajama-like clothing that I could find, which amounted to gym shorts. I changed and, ignoring my pounding heart, got in bed with the devil.

The sunlight was coming through the curtains, gently warming up the room that morning. Alejandro was peacefully sleeping next to me, still with no fever. I knew he was a bit sedated, because one of the medications the doctor prescribed was meant to calm him down and get him to sleep, and it was doing him a lot of good. I spent the day making sure he ate, downed his medication, and stayed hydrated, taking his temperature every two hours.

I dared to walk outside of the house when he was asleep, my bare feet enjoying the feeling of the warm, soft sand for an hour, relishing the saltwater breeze caressing my skin.

The ocean was quite tempting, but I didn't have the appropriate attire to take a dip. I roamed the house a little more when I got back inside, happy to have found a TV in the living room. So, for the first time in weeks, I managed to curl up on a couch with chips to watch a telenovela as Alejandro slept away in peace.

I had too much time to think, but the TV helped keep my thoughts occupied. The last thing I wanted to do was face my feelings or what was to come.

I realized that there was a phone upstairs—a phone I had used before and could use again—and yet there I was, ignoring a golden opportunity, enjoying the amenities of my captor's beach house while tending to his wounds—wounds he had gotten while using his body as a literal shield to protect me.

There was so much to process there that I didn't know where to start. Why wasn't I calling anyone for help? I could call Iris, give her the address. Alejandro was hurt, and there were no guards with him. But I wasn't going to do anything. I knew that. At least not until I was sure Alejandro was going to be okay. Only then could I make an attempt to go back to my life—whatever specks remained.

The idea did not fill me with as much drive or excitement as it should have. If I didn't do something while I had a chance, though, I might be stuck in Mexico forever, living a life that wasn't mine.

For some reason, even after the horrible attack just a few days ago, that possibility was no longer as scary as it should have been. I missed my life, my friends, Martha, and maybe even George, but in the land of my childhood, I was unexpectedly finding something I didn't know I needed, something I didn't think existed, and I didn't know what to do with that realization.

Around ten p.m., I went back up to check on Alejandro as I had done all day. He wasn't sleeping anymore as he had for most of the day; he was trying to get up. I ran to him, attempting to push him back on the bed.

"I do need to use the bathroom once in a while, you know," he protested angrily.

"That doesn't mean I can't help."

I helped him rise and accompanied him to the bathroom door. I could tell that his strength was coming back. He moved faster and stood taller, but he needed at least a few more days, according to the doctor, to let his body heal.

Alejandro gave me a death stare when I tried to follow him to the bathroom, and he closed the door in my face.

I found him so frustrating, but I understood. I patiently waited for him, but he didn't let me walk him back to the bed.

I helped him change his bandages, take his pain medication, and finally lie in bed. As I was about to let him sleep, Alejandro grabbed my hand in his and forced me to sit down by his side on the bed.

"Why are you taking such good care of me?"

As I looked into those already sleepy eyes, my stomach tensed. I was tempted to say out loud what I hadn't even admitted to myself yet, but I couldn't bring myself to.

"It would be quite boring around here without you."

Alejandro laughed, that guttural honest laugh that always made me feel so whole, his gaze creating a blanket of warmth all around me.

"That's all?" he insisted, searching my eyes. I didn't understand what for.

"Uh... yes," I answered, looking away, unable to handle the intensity of what I felt. "Well, I am going to go get some sleep," I announced as I started to get up.

"No," he murmured, refusing to release my hand. "Please, stay with me," he whispered, his tone low and pleading.

My heart swelled, threatening to swallow me whole. I couldn't let his words get to me; I just couldn't.

I tried to leave again, but he wasn't loosening his grip, his thumb rubbing my wrist. I could see that he was going to fall asleep any minute, the drugs already taking effect. So, I decided to stay for a bit, enjoying the feeling of my hand in his, waiting for him to drift away for a few hours.

It was six a.m. when I opened my eyes and realized I had slept in his bed—again. He, thankfully, seemed unaware. I snuck back into my room to shower, change, and continue sleeping since I was too exhausted to do anything else.

The day started with the sound of the waves calling to me and the sun warming my arm. I lazily opened my eyes. The last few nights had been a bit better, with me relaxing a bit at seeing Alejandro making progress, his wound healing, and thus being able to fall asleep for close to full nights in my room.

This morning, though, I found myself lying in Alejandro's arms, perfectly nestled, my head resting on his chest, his hand possessively secured around my waist, holding me close. A moan escaped my lips, as I decided to embrace the perfect comfort I felt, until I realized that he was awake, holding his phone with his left hand. I jerked back, lifting onto my arm. Alejandro smiled the most sensually teasing morning smile I had ever seen on him.

"Everything okay?" he asked, his eyebrows raised.

My cheeks flushed lightly. I turned away and quickly rolled out off the bed. Without a word, I escaped back to my room. I could smell him on me, my senses prickling, my body getting aroused. How did I end up in his arms? But I couldn't help smiling when I remembered the feeling of his warm skin against mine.

I showered but had to wear one of the shirts I had stolen from him again with my now worn jeans. When I was done, I went to see him. He was sitting in front of the desk in his room with a notepad, talking on the phone. I almost screamed at him because he wasn't in bed, but I knew it would be futile. I got closer and stared at him until he lifted his head up.

"Te llamo luego," he said before hanging up the phone.

He looked refreshed. He had clearly showered and changed his clothes, going for a pair of white pants and a light-blue shirt with rolled up sleeves. He still looked rugged with his beard unshaven, giving him a bit of a wild-man look that made my stomach tense and my hair raise.

Every inch of his body looked like fulfilling sex to me, my mind drifting to the forbidden. I shook my head to stop myself from continuing down that path.

"Let me see," I said, lifting the right side of his shirt. His bandage looked new.

"You changed it?"

"Yes, and before you ask, I took the medication this morning, except for the one that makes me sleep."

Feeling guilty, I rolled my eyes. Alejandro stood brusquely and grabbed my face in his hands. Before I could object, he kissed me sweetly but possessively. His kiss was slow and strong, surprising me with the intensity and overwhelming emotions it was raising in me.

"Thank you for saving my life," he said.

"You saved mine," I whispered, eyes slightly closed, breathing him in.

"I would never forgive myself if something happened to you." His guttural tone made me tremble.

I kissed him back, wrapping my arms around his neck. I pressed myself against him, enjoying the feeling of melting in his embrace. He deepened the kiss—his tongue, hot and wet, getting more and more demanding.

I could feel his erection, long and strong against me.

And, god, I wanted it.

I wanted to stroke it, lick it. I wanted him to slide inside of me so badly I felt desperate for it.

I heard Alejandro slightly wince, and I leaned back a bit.

"Sorry."

"Don't be,' he muttered, pulling me back to him, possessively grabbing my lips again, parting them with his impatient tongue. Alejandro's cell phone rang.

"Damn it," he grunted against my lips. I was grateful for the interruption to compose myself, even with all the pent-up frustration. If he kept going, I wouldn't have been able to stop him. A girl could only take so much, though. Alejandro answered the phone, and it sounded like it was Marcos giving him an update. I took advantage of this distraction to leave him alone.

CHAPTER 24

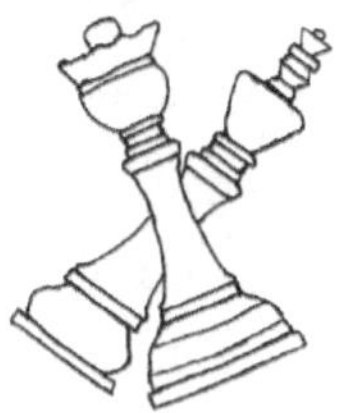

WE HAD BEEN IN the beach house for well over ten days now. The doctor had stopped insisting that he take the sleeping pills a couple of days ago, in part because he had thrown the rest of them at the wall, threatening to leave and go "*wherever the hell he wanted*" if he had to stay in "*this fucking room*" any longer.

Alejandro had, for the most part, stayed in bed, and I acknowledged that he seemed almost fully recovered. The wound was healing well and quickly, and there had been no further bleeding or fever.

For most of the week, Alejandro had tried to have serious conversations with me. He wanted to discuss what had happened in his hacienda. I had been avoiding them like the plague. All I wanted was for him to heal and get better. I didn't care about anything else—not Karina, not Elena, not my kidnapping. I feared that if we talked, everything would change.

Eventually, we got into a comfortable routine—when Alejandro wasn't drugged out—where we would talk about our passions. He even continued teaching me how to play chess. We were stuck in an amazing lull where nothing else mattered.

It didn't matter that he had kidnapped me; it didn't matter that a cop had tried to kill me; and it didn't matter that, sooner rather than later, this very unusual situation would have to come to an end one way or another. I was enjoying letting myself take care of him and getting to know him.

I realized that the more time we spent with each other, the more confused I was, but for now, all those emotions were shoved to the bottom of my heart, and I was, for once in my life, taking life day by day.

Against all my resolve, when I heard his voice calling for me, I ran to his bedroom. He was standing in front of his desk, so I went to his side.

"We need to talk," said Alejandro with a serious frown, a shadow over his face. "But coffee first."

"I will go make it," I said, rushing past him as he tried to leave the room.

"Amelia…"

"No, the doctor said you have to rest. You shouldn't even be up on your feet this much."

"I feel fine. I am perfectly capable of going to my own kitchen" he retorted, frustrated.

I felt a sudden rush of fear run all the way up my body.

"No! You have no idea how bad you were just a few days ago. You were sweating, trembling…you were dying! And if something happens to you, I don't…I don't know what…"

"Shh, shh," said Alejandro, a questioning look on his face, alarm in his eyes. I was crying, unable to stop the tears and the sobbing. I let Alejandro wrap me in his arms, caress my hair, and stroke my back.

"Mi niña, te ruego, no llores. The doctor said I am fine, I am feeling a lot better. I can't stand to see you cry."

I couldn't stop the tears.

"I'm sorry. I'm so sorry," he whispered in a clouded voice.

We stood there for a few minutes as I enjoyed the comfort I did not realize I needed. The past days had been a roller coaster of emotions, seeing a man I cared for almost die to save me, and now that I was able to slow down, it was all hitting me in shock waves.

After a few minutes, my breathing got under control; all that was left was the embarrassment from breaking down like that in front of him. I slowly pushed Alejandro back and avoided eye contact at all costs. "I'll go make coffee," I declared, rushing out of the room.

Once I got in the kitchen, I ground some beans and set the coffeemaker. The smell was bringing some life into me as I prepared an omelet with chorizo, spinach, and onion, with a side of toast and a bowl of fruit. The meal preparation calmed my turbulent heart.

I carefully carried a very heavy tray up the stairs to Alejandro's room. I set it down on the table on the balcony outside, thinking some sun and a breath of fresh air would help. Alejandro joined me. He leaned back in his chair, pensive.

"The irony of all this... you taking care of me."

"What do you mean?"

Alejandro shook his head, seemingly unable to find his words. He took a sip of coffee. Confused, I sat across from him, grabbing my cup of coffee. Was I finally getting to him?

"You are not eating?"

"Just coffee for now," I said.

Alejandro's eyes flashed with frustration. He glanced at me, took one of the small plates, and put some of his eggs on it. "Stop being stubborn," he said irritably. "Eat."

I knew he was right. I hadn't had a real meal since we left the hacienda. I had grabbed bites when I prepared his meals but hadn't been able to consume any more. This time, I forced myself to eat, and halfway through, I could tell my appetite was slowly starting to come back.

"So, I'm going to get straight to the point," started Alejandro, looking serious when we were done eating.

He hesitated, clearly conflicted about what to say and how to say it. I held my breath. From his expression, I knew it wasn't going to be good. "Everything seems to indicate that the men who entered my house were sent for you, to harm you."

"Why?" I asked, shocked and incredulous. "Why me? Why would someone try to kill me at a kidnapper's house?"

I realized how it sounded, but it was too late. Alejandro clenched his teeth, shook his head, and got up, frustrated. He started pacing.

He stopped behind the chair he had been sitting on, his fists squeezing around the top, jaw tight.

"I was really hoping to keep you sheltered from all of this," he started to explain.

"No," I protested, standing up, angry and shaking. "Not anymore. Too much has happened for you to continue to keep me in the dark."

I needed the truth, desperately, whatever it may be. I needed him to rip off the Band-Aid I didn't have the courage to remove. Let me see the truth, for however horrible. Maybe then I could reason with myself, stop these feelings that threatened to consume me on a daily basis.

Alejandro sighed, looking away.

"I know," he confessed, "but the more you know, the harder it is for me to protect you."

"It would seem like that strategy backfired," I retorted.

Alejandro looked like I had just shot him, but he shook his head, admitting there was no other option. He inhaled deeply and exhaled.

"I think... I think it was Richard."

The information hit me like a rock. I felt my knees weaken, and I leaned onto the chair for support. Alejandro took a step in my direction, but I lifted my hand, telling him to keep his distance.

"I'm fine." I swallowed hard. "Why would Richard try to hurt me?" My voice was slightly shaking.

"I am not sure," he admitted, "but in the past few weeks, he has not really acted as you'd expect a father would when it comes to you."

"He is not my father," I hastily corrected.

"Yes, and I get that now. We've tried to negotiate your ransom... but he hasn't budged..."

"Because he is not my father!" I screamed.

My stomach felt like it was twisting into knots. The truth was that I was hurt. Richard wasn't my father, but he was the closest to one I had ever had. The fact that he didn't care that I had been held captive for so long wasn't necessarily surprising, but it was still hurtful. To go from that to thinking he would actively participate in harming me was too much, even for him.

"I know, Amelia, but you can't expect that I would have known..."

"What? Known that he doesn't care about me, that he never did? That he treats me like his charity case, refuses to let me learn anything about my mother or her country? That he is a fucking asshole who used me to look good to his social network?"

"Amelia..." he reached out to me.

"Don't touch me!" I screamed, stepping backward.

My breathing was heavy, and I got dizzy, but I didn't care. I was livid, mad at Richard for rejecting me as a daughter, mad at Alejandro for wanting to use me against him so stupidly, making my palpable loneliness, my lack of a family undeniable, opening wounds I had repressed a long time ago. Mad at myself for allowing those men to hurt me.

"Richard CANNOT stand me. He NEVER loved me, NEVER wanted me. He kept me around out of pity... or obligation. He was never there for me, and you... you think he will part with something he considers valuable, for me?!"

I broke into a resentful laugh. Alejandro looked angry and concerned with no idea how to calm me down.

"You are JUST like him! All of you! You selfish bastards! I am sick and tired of being used, of feeling worthless because of you!"

He closed the distance between us in a second to grab me before I fell. I was blinded by pain, snapping because all the emotions I had kept bottled up for years were coming out in strong, destructive currents. I was fighting him, punching him, pushing him away from me.

"Amelia, calm down!" he ordered, shaking me. "Please! I don't like seeing you like this. Let me explain!"

"There is nothing you can say!" I yelled in tears. "Nothing!"

"I did not use you! This was never meant to happen!"

I couldn't see straight anymore. My knees were weak. I lost all my strength, shaking, feeling like my blood was leaving my body.

"You need to lie down," warned Alejandro, grabbing my waist, forcing me to lean on his chest as he took me to the bed.

I wanted to protest, but there was no energy left in me. I was drained. Alejandro laid me on the bed. He got up and brought me a shot of tequila.

"No," I complained, shoving his hand away.

"You are drinking it," he ordered, bringing the glass to my lips.

The smell teased my nostrils. I didn't want it, but he forced me to drink it anyway. My face cringed as the strong liquid went down my throat, immediately waking my body up. Alejandro poured me a second one.

"Again."

I chugged it, my eyes shooting sparks at him.

I agreed to lie down, closing my eyes. Shame took over a bit. My outburst wasn't a proud moment, but I was rightfully troubled. How could Richard try to have me killed? Why would he do such a thing?

"I'm so sorry," he whispered, his voice thick with emotion.

His words shook the gaping hole in my chest and caused tears to continue rolling down my face. I turned away from him to avoid his gaze. Alejandro got up and went to sit down on the patio to give me some space. I took a third and then a fourth gulp of that tequila, straight from the bottle Alejandro had left on the bedside table next to me, desperate to numb the pain and to stop feeling. Before long, my eyes were closing, my brain needing to shut down to process everything.

PART 2

CHAPTER 25

Alejandro

THERE ARE A FEW moments in one's life, where one decision could change the rest of their trajectory. Mine changed the day my brother died. One could argue that it got altered when I decided to help some low-life criminals get their property back. But I disagree.

The moment Richard Anderson put a bullet through my thirty-year-old brother's skull, he unleashed a chain of events that inevitably led me here, led me to her.

She was doing her best to sleep, but I could see her tossing and turning from the window. My fingers itched. I wanted to be next to her, to soothe her pain, make her feel safe, but I knew I was the last person she wanted to be with right now—after Richard, or so I hoped.

My life had crumbled in front of me less than a year ago. One phone call, telling me that David had been found dead—wrong place, wrong time—was all the police could give me. David was only four years younger than me.

My little brother was a good person, a good brother, a good son. We had spent some of our life apart when I had moved to the States, but our relationship never wavered. I was the big brother, supposed to protect him, but I had been unable to stop this fucking son of a bitch from killing him for some diamonds that weren't his in the first place.

Growing up, I was always keenly aware of the crimes that happened in Mexico, of the gang activity, my father having been a prominent member of Los Zetas. My mother sheltered us as much as she could—until it was my turn to be recruited. That was when she sent me to Texas.

By the time David grew up, they had moved, and life had changed enough that it was okay for him to stay in Mexico. David, I knew, was my mother's favorite, her little boy—the softer soul of the two of us, as she called him. To have to watch her go through the pain of losing him, after losing my father to the gangs, was heart wrenching.

My mother had instilled in David and me a respect for right and wrong, a respect for life, that was shaken to its core when David was killed. One of the few things my father had taught me was how to hold a gun and shoot to kill. I had witnessed my fair share of crimes in my life, so I was more than ready to pull that trigger, to kill Richard.

But I couldn't do that to my mother. I couldn't risk going to prison after she begged me not to, begged me to not risk my life. I was all she had left. She didn't want me to soil my hands. I would have no problem taking Richard's miserable life. No hesitation. I didn't see him as anything but a dead man, but I resisted the urge for my mother. Instead of killing him, I tried to use legal means, but to no avail.

And so started this torture, a partnership with a criminal, a process of infiltration into Richard's friend base, all to get close to him and get the diamonds. Instead, what I got was Amelia. And now I was in my beach house, wounded, protecting the stepdaughter of my brother's murderer—from him, apparently.

And nothing was going to stand in the way of her safety, not even my thirst for revenge. And I wouldn't change that for the world.

CHAPTER 26

Amelia

My nap did not last long, as my sleep was restless, my brain working overtime to process what my life had become. When I dared come back to reality, Alejandro was standing outside, with the window closed, pacing while on the phone. I resisted the urge to go get him and force him to sit down. This man was stubborn and refused to act like someone who had gotten shot. I sighed as I was aware of my own recklessness. I did have a concussion a few weeks ago and clearly still needed to take it slow.

It was past lunchtime, and I was dying of thirst. I got off the bed and took the stairs to the kitchen, where I drank all the water my body craved for and swallowed some Advil to calm the throbbing in my head. I hoped Alejandro was wrong. I even hoped he was lying, but something deep in my soul told me he wasn't.

I suspected something was off, considering how long I had been held in captivity. And every now and then, a voice seethed deep inside wondered if Richard was happy I was missing, If this was going to be his way to play the victim card further, having lost his only daughter. But still, to hear that he might not only be happy I got taken, but be involved in it? That he might have tried to get me killed? What was I supposed to do with that?

I knew Alejandro and I had more to talk about, but I was scared to hear more, to make it more real. I was filled with pain and resentment, and Alejandro wasn't immune.

After all, he also used me as a tool to get something from Richard, the same way Richard had used me my whole life to play the martyr husband who sacrificed everything for a child who wasn't his.

There was no reason he couldn't benefit from the situation while being a real father to me. But he chose differently for us. And now, for some reason or another, he considered me useless to him, so he had sent cops to kill me—the same way Alejandro would pack me up and send me back to Richard in a second if he gave him the diamonds.

I took a deep breath as anger started to course through me again. I wiped away a few tears. Even if Alejandro had hurt me, I did not want him to die. But anger I could deal with. In anger, I found strength. I found walls to use as protection.

I prepared a few quesadillas and brought them to his room with some water. He was still outside. I couldn't handle seeing him right now, but he had to eat. I still needed to make sure he was okay. I wanted to go call him, but that would be too much. He would eventually walk back in and find his food, so I took my tray, grabbed the bottle of tequila, and went to my room, locking the door behind me.

Away from anyone's eyes, I could allow myself a moment of weakness, a moment to cry and feel all the pain I had been hiding. I sat on the floor by the balcony, with alcohol as my best friend, enabling me to get lost in the ocean view, enjoying the sound of the waves.

I hated Richard, but that man was also the only father—or semblance of one—that I'd ever had. And now he wanted to kill me, for some reason that I would, of course, have to know about. I felt more alone in the world than ever.

The feeling wasn't new. If it hadn't been for my nana, I didn't know how my life would have turned out. Nana had filled the void left by my mother.

Martha had taught me how to cook, how to dress, how to care for my curls. She had sung to me when I was sad, bathed me, healed my bruises.

I still wished my mother was alive. I still wished I could remember what she looked like more, and I desperately wanted to hear her voice at times, but Nana had certainly done the best she could for me, filling in the role with grace, patience, and unconditional love. But Richard was never there.

I had to fend for myself, go to school, rely on my friends' parents for help with my homework and always either came back to an empty house or to a man who screamed at me when I tried to hug him.

I was always conflicted between my resentment toward him and the love that I did feel for him as the only parent in my life, for better or worse. But there was no room for love anymore—not for someone who would rather have me dead than have to part ways with money, or diamonds, or whatever it was Alejandro was after.

I got startled when I heard a few knocks. Alejandro was the last person I wanted to see. I closed my eyes and decided to stay silent, hoping that he would give up and go away.

"Amelia? Open the door!"

I sighed. Of course, there was no scenario in which he would just retreat and let me be.

"I want to be alone!"

Alejandro knocked again. "I said open the door!"

He knocked again, violently, when I refused to listen.

"Godamnit, Amelia, if you don't open this door, I will break it!"

He sounded so angry I thought twice about whether I wanted to open the door. When he pounded on it again, I could have sworn the room shook. Worried that he might hurt himself and start bleeding again, I wiped my eyes and opened the door.

"What?" I snapped.

Alejandro just stood there, breathing heavily, his eyes wide with anger and his jaw clenched. He almost looked like he was going to kill me, so I took two steps back.

"Are you okay?" It wasn't the reprimand I was expecting, his eyes searching mine anxiously.

"I'm fine," I lied, walking away. I feared that if I let him get any closer, I would start crying again.

"We have to talk," he said, closing the door behind him.

"No, we don't." I walked back to where I was sitting, grabbing the bottle of tequila.

Alejandro slowly sat on the bed.

"I'm sorry," he started. "I can't imagine how it feels to find out that your stepfather is not who you thought."

"That's the thing," I said dryly, "I should have known."

"What do you mean?"

"I should have known the minute I got kidnapped that I'd be doomed. I should have known he wouldn't bother."

"I see now that your kidnapping was a pointless move. Clearly Richard doesn't give a fuck about anyone but himself."

"Sorry to disappoint," I said sourly, facing him, my cold brown eyes cautiously scrutinizing him. "What's your plan now that you know I am completely useless to you? Kill me? Get rid of me? Sell me to the highest bidder?" I asked, hands in fists, a dry mocking tone showing resentment, a sour smile on my lips.

"Amelia," he said, getting up. "If you would let me explain—"

"Explain what?" I cut him off. "You are all the same, and I somehow always end up a tool in your little fucking games!"

"I am not the one who took you!" he yelled, grabbing my arm to force me to face him.

"You really expect me to believe you?" I laughed.

Alejandro let go of me so suddenly I struggled to remain standing. He put some distance between us, hands on his hips, as he started pacing.

CHAPTER 27

Alejandro

THIS WAS IT. I needed to tell her everything. I had tried my best to shelter her from the truth this whole time. I held out as long as I could, but with every passing second, I could feel her slipping through my fingers, and that wasn't an option. It was obvious she had been drinking. I couldn't blame her after the news I had dropped on her earlier, so I ignored the signs and continued to explain.

"Richard, your stepfather... he killed my brother."

"What?"

Her beautiful face was contorted and pale, the new information sobering her up.

I took a deep breath. She walked to me, looking at me like she was seeing me for the first time. I wasn't sure what she would see. But I needed to tell her everything.

"About a year ago, your stepfather got involved with some men of questionable character here in Mexico. They did a few shady business transactions together, to say the least. Richard decided to double-cross them and attacked one of their stores with some men. He wanted to steal a bag of diamonds from their safe, and he succeeded.

"My brother… he was an architect, and those people had reached out to him just a few days before Richard decided to break into the store, to hire him for some projects. David knew who they were. After all, our father used to be involved in some of those gang activities before he got killed, but he agreed anyway. He wanted their business, figured he could get paid well and use the money for good. He went to the meeting as scheduled. That evening was the time Richard chose to strike."

I stopped talking for a minute, tightening my jaw to control the pain those memories brought.

"Why? Why did he kill him?" She looked horrified, her eyes wide, her mouth open. My heart sank, knowing I couldn't spare her the pain she was feeling.

"It wasn't personal. He was… in the way. Collateral damage."

"So, you took me as revenge?"

"Not exactly." I paused. "I tried everything I could to find out who had killed my brother. When I found out it was this man, who lived in California and was rich, with no reason to steal, let alone take anyone's life for money, I wanted to kill him even more, watch the blood slowly drain out of his miserable body. I was going to do that, Amelia. I'm not going to lie. I fantasized about the day I'd get to put a bullet in his head, take away his pitiful life the way he had taken so many, the way he took David's."

I started to pace again.

"Are you going to kill him?" I paused, the thought still so tempting.

"No, that would be too good of a punishment for him. My mother suffered a lot with my father's involvement in those illicit activities. It took everything for her to keep David's and my hands clean, including sending me to the US. I wanted to kill him.

"Fuck, after what he did to you, I want to still. But she made me swear I wouldn't become a criminal like my father, even if it was the least that bastard deserved. But when he killed my brother, I went to the police, opened an investigation, and hired a private detective. Nothing came out of it. The police claimed they had done their best and said that there was nothing tying him to the robbery. He even had an alibi: dinner with you, apparently.

"But since the store owner is the leader of one of the most dangerous and sophisticated gangs in Mexico, I thought that perhaps this was more than a simple murder. Turned out I was right. They had a video of everything that happened. The store cameras, that the police claimed were not working at the time of the crime, had caught everything. They showed me the tape. I saw Richard, killing my brother in cold blood, like he was a fucking dog. He didn't even bother covering his face. He wanted them to know it was him."

My voice slightly shook as I spoke, and my jaw clenched. I felt anger boiling my blood, my muscles tense. My throat was dry, Amelia's expression making me feel like I was watching a car crash that I couldn't stop. The last thing I wanted was to relive those events, see my pain reflected in her gaze, but she deserved to know.

"Why didn't you bring the video to the cops?"

"The gang refused to give me the footage," I explained, "unless I helped them get their diamonds back. I agreed because the cops are all corrupt. They know they can't go against this man."

"And that's why you took me?"

We got interrupted when we heard a knock at the door.

"Are you expecting anyone?" she asked, a suspicious look on her face.

I rushed out of the room to go to mine, with Amelia right behind me. I grabbed my iPad from the desk.

"There are cameras everywhere," I explained. I opened the iPad to look at the live footage. "It's Elena."

"At the gate?"

"No, the door, there is no separation between her property next door and mine from the beach," I clarified.

She rolled her eyes, like she always did when she was frustrated. I wanted to explain. God, I had so much to explain to her, but I was out of time. I pressed a few buttons on the iPad to open the house door and let Elena in.

"We can finish this conversation later."

"Can't she wait?" she asked, doing her best to hide her annoyance with me.

"I asked her to come here," I clarified.

I could hear Elena coming up the stairs. She knocked and opened the door without waiting, walking to me directly.

"Alejandro, mi amor!" she squealed, grabbing my face and touching her lips to mine.

I gently pushed her away, annoyed that she kept doing this even after I told her last week that there could be nothing between us—and many times before that. We had known each other since we were kids. And while we dated a while back, since then, we had our fun, always with very clear terms—or so I thought.

"You're still here," she said, turning to Amelia, visibly displeased.

Amelia shot both of us a death stare and stormed out of the room before I could stop her. I knew things didn't look very good for me. But Elena had been helping me since I had put the plan together to befriend Richard, and there was much left to do now that I knew Amelia was in more danger than I thought.

CHAPTER 28

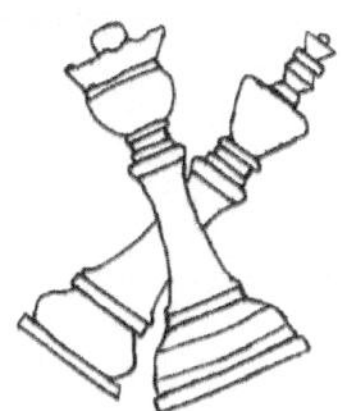

Amelia

My heart was pounding, divided between the horror of finding out that my stepfather was a murderer and the need to erase the pain and suffering from Alejandro's life. My heart broke when he told me what happened, when I saw his face contracted, his eyes wet, fighting his sorrow the best he could. He was still mourning what was a sudden and shocking loss.

But then Elena strolled in, and again, we couldn't finish our conversation. I did not have the stomach to see them together, and I had a lot to process. I needed some fresh air. I needed to put as much distance between me and them as possible.

I ran out of the house, heading to the beach. The sun was setting, the air warm and a bit dry, but there was a nice breeze bringing the smell of saltwater to my nostrils. I walked all the way to the waves and pulled my jeans up as much as I could as I dropped down in the sand. I needed to feel the water, hear the sand moving with the waves, distract my senses before my emotions got the best of me. Alejandro had dropped so much on me in all of ten minutes.

Richard was a murderer, and Alejandro wanted revenge.

How could he? I thought I knew Richard. I knew he was a despicable human, but to go from that to shooting people in a store to steal some diamonds, however much they might be worth? He was rich. Why would he go through all that trouble?

Richard was always greedy, desperate to belong to la crème de la crème of California. California-rich was another kind of rich that one mostly had to be born into. Richard always had a chip on his shoulder because he felt like he never had enough money to belong. But was that all it took to get him to think that he had the right to take lives?

The question now though was whether I could trust Alejandro with the location of the diamonds. I was starting to see him in a different light. It wasn't less confusing, but assuming everything he said was true, he had suffered a great loss because of Richard—a loss he had the right to seek revenge for. He had lost a bother to Richard's greed.

I was sadly collateral damage in all of this—me for the diamonds, my freedom for justice for his brother. Now I was stuck with him and his girlfriend in his beach house.

I winced when I remembered Karina. And then there was Elena. The animosity I felt towards her was the only emotion that felt normal, that I could cope with. Was the beach house where he went when he disappeared before, to be with her? Instead of this pinch of jealousy I was trying to stop from growing, I should have felt sympathy for Elena. Alejandro did, in fact, cheat on her with Karina, who might or might not be my stepfather's aid.

He had put his life in danger for mine, a fact I kept conveniently ignoring even though it was always in the back of my mind, pushing me toward a conclusion that I desperately needed to believe but one I wanted to avoid at any cost.

I made an effort to shut down my brain. The sound of the ocean was very calming, the smell of salty sand providing me some comfort. From where I was standing, I could see what I assumed was Elena's house on my right. It was smaller, but it looked very chic. On my left, it seemed like there was a separation between the properties. I leaned my head on my knees pulled up in front of me, distractedly running my fingers through the warm, grainy sand.

Listening to the rhythmic movement of the water always had a calming, centering effect on me, but it was no match for the ache I felt every time I thought of Alejandro. My desire for him hadn't gone away; it had evolved, with Alejandro intertwined with every corner of my soul. And to me, that was the most terrifying peril.

I could not let myself have any sort of need or dependence for someone who would probably get rid of me as soon as he got what he wanted from Richard, or rather, would give up and send me on my way. I was ashamed to admit this to myself, but the idea of escaping my captor and regaining my freedom had been put in the back of my mind the past couple weeks, as an eventuality, as opposed to something I was actively seeking.

But I could not allow Alejandro, or anyone else, to have such paralyzing control over me. That had always been a core principle for me. I had to find my footing, keep my walls up, for as much as they threatened to crumble under his gaze. After an hour, feeling resolved, I stomped back to the house. Elena could keep him. After all, I had George, the perfect candidate for someone who did not want to fall in love.

I perused the kitchen for a quick meal, warmed up some soup, grabbed a glass of water, and went to the small office I had seen. Thankfully, there were some books there. I grabbed a couple, as well as a notebook and a few pens, then made my way back to my bedroom, keeping the door unlocked this time.

Alejandro did not bother me all evening. I was trying to focus on the thriller I was reading, but all I could think about was him, in the room just next door, probably making love to that woman. I couldn't hear a breath, but I could imagine. I paced, exercised, showered, did all I could to distract myself and refrain from knocking on his door.

After all, I had the perfect excuse—we had a lot left to discuss. But my pride was stronger, and I eventually fell asleep, dreaming that I was in his arms instead.

CHAPTER 29

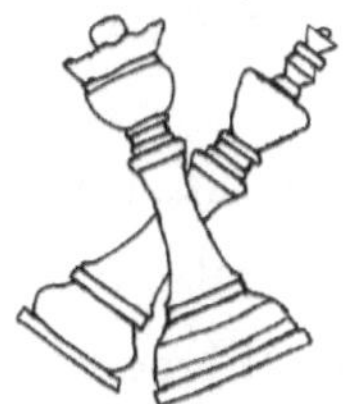

Amelia

THE NOW VERY FAMILIAR susurration of the waves softly crashing on the sand and the strong sunrise lighting up the whole bedroom brought me back to reality. I reluctantly got up to brush my teeth and wash my face, but I quickly returned to bed for a moment, enjoying the reflection of the light on the curtains, the peaceful sound of the sea, the room coming alive with a rainbow of colors.

I heard a knock on the door and got a bit frazzled as I was only wearing my underwear and Alejandro's shirt. I was ecstatic when I saw Dolores walk in. I got up and ran to her, giving her a hug. Dolores hugged me back, tears in her eyes.

"I am so happy you are okay!" she sobbed.

"Stop it. You are going to make me cry," I said, tears obstructing my view. "How did you get here?"

"Don Alejandro told me what happened. He didn't want me to go back to the house even if security tripled! So I came here to keep you company," she said, smiling sweetly.

"I'm so glad!" I hugged her again.

"I brought you some clothing," said Dolores as she put a pile on the bed. I giggled like a teenager as I grabbed a light-pink, flowy cotton skirt and quickly slipped it on in the bathroom. I kept on Alejandro's shirt for now.

"Thank you, Dolores. I've missed you so much!" I took her in my arms again. When I lifted my head, I saw Alejandro standing in the doorway, smiling at us.

"She refused to stay at her home like I asked her to," he explained.

Alejandro looked great, more relaxed, as he was quickly regaining his strength from the bullet wound. If I didn't know any better, I would think nothing ever happened to him. He was wearing a pair of light jeans with a white short-sleeve shirt, his eyes teasing my senses, my body vibrating under his gaze. Why was it that every time he was in the room with me, it felt like we were the only people there?

"It is safe," added Dolores in an attempt to appease me.

"Yes. No one knows she comes here—or that we are here, for that matter."

"And I will be coming every day," she announced, turning to Alejandro. "Tienes que descansar. You have to stay in bed as much as possible," she ordered.

I was glad to see that someone else would take charge of forcing this man to recognize that he got shot.

"The doctor also said I need to move around," he tried to protest.

"I will make sure you rest," she countered, dismissing his statement. "I am going to go make breakfast. Amelia, I will bring you more clothes, okay?"

"Thank you!"

Dolores left and shut the door behind her. Alejandro walked to the door and locked it. I took a deep breath.

"I see you are enjoying my shirt," he teased as he slowly walked toward the bed.

"I didn't exactly have anything else to wear," I retorted, not in the mood to play games.

"Fair. I should have thought of that."

"Do you need anything?"

"We do have a conversation pending," he answered.

"We do." I sighed.

"Sit with me." He eased onto the edge of the bed, facing the window. I followed.

"I am sorry that you got caught in the middle of all of this."

"Me too."

I understood deep down that he might have felt like committing a crime was the only way to have a shot at avenging his brother. I didn't have any siblings, but my friends were like sisters to me, and if someone ever tried to hurt any of them, I knew there wasn't much I wouldn't do to protect them. So, in that sense, I understood. That didn't mean I wasn't still bothered by what he had done to me. It didn't mean I wasn't still hurt.

"That night," he continued, "I was a guest at your party, but I wasn't there to take you. As far as Richard knows, I am a prospective investor in his company, so he invited me to your birthday party."

"He doesn't know you kidnapped me?"

"No"—he paused—"because I didn't. He thinks you are with Mathias and his people—the man he robbed. He has no idea about my brother or that I have anything to do with this."

My eyes squinted, confused.

"I told you; I did not take you. You weren't part of the plan. I was at your party to find the diamonds. Mathias had some of his men and mine break into your house, taking advantage of the distraction created by the celebration. My job was to be a guest and keep my eyes open in case Richard or you decided to go to his office."

I swallowed hard, trying to get rid of the lump that was threatening to choke me.

"I see. And I take it they didn't find the diamonds?"

"No, they broke open two safes in Richard's office, but no diamonds were found. Mathias got desperate and ordered his men to take you, to use you for ransom in exchange for the diamonds. I tried to stop them. Putting lives in danger wasn't what we had agreed on, nor was taking anyone hostage, but it was just me and two of my men against ten of his.

"They grabbed you and hid you in that house. I rushed there to get you away from them, but I had to play it safe. I could not seem too eager to help you, or they wouldn't trust me. These men are dangerous, Amelia, and I just could not leave you with them. But at that point, I also couldn't simply bring you back to your house. It was too late. They had already contacted Richard; the news was out in California."

Alejandro stood up and started pacing slowly, hands in his pockets.

"They could have raped you. Their idea of using you was to cut off a finger and send it to Richard. I couldn't let that happen. I had to let you suffer at their hands for a bit so that Mathias would think that, even if I took you with me, I would be willing to hurt you if it came to that. He needed to trust I wouldn't mess anything up for him. He eventually accepted that you be under my watch.

"That day you tried to escape from where they had you, I convinced him that I'd be able to keep you from escaping and I'd use you when needed to get the diamonds. Your attempted escape helped me convince him I would do a better job watching you than his people. But he still insisted on sending Juan and Karina to check on you, to make sure I was still holding you captive. I couldn't give you special treatment in front of them."

I could not peel my eyes off him, feeling like if I did, I would realize that this was just a dream. He was frowning, frustration seeping out of his every pore This would explain some of Dolores's anxiety and comments when Juan was around the house.

"If it looked like I was treating you like a guest, or really anything more than a means to an end, Mathias could insist that he take you back in his custody. And I would kill him and every single one of his men before I would let that happen. There was no fucking way I would let anyone of them put single finger on you, fuck the consequences. But I had to gain his trust, so I had to pretend I would be willing to torture you if need be."

I felt my throat close up a bit, tears threatening to roll down my face. He had gone to great lengths to protect me.

"Since you were taken, Mathias has been negotiating your ransom with Richard. It took us a bit to realize that he was stalling us. He cried on live television for you, Amelia, but eventually, he told us to go fuck ourselves. Right after that, we got attacked in my house."

"How did they know where we were if they don't know you are involved in this?"

"Our best guess is that Juan or Karina told the cop. That cop you saw... he worked on the robbery investigation. It's now clear that he really works for Richard, and that's why we couldn't put a case against him for murder. Juan or Karina must have told him where you were. That might also explain why Juan attacked you before. Richard doesn't know my real name, so he might just think I am one of Mathias's men or that the hacienda is his property."

Alejandro put his hand on my shoulder.

"We think Richard sent the cop to kill you with the intent to frame Mathias for your murder. He'd pass this off as a failed rescue by Mexican law enforcement and would, of course, keep the diamonds."

I closed my eyes, trying to process it all.

"He's always liked to play the role of the amazing father who does what it takes for his poor, unfortunate stepdaughter," I said as I got off the bed. "He has to show the world that he tried to rescue me. But if I die, he gets to be the mourning father that everyone in California feels bad for and admires for doing his best to save me. And he gets to keep the diamonds. At this point, I serve him more dead than alive."

"Something like that."

My heart was broken as I felt my stepfather's treason in my core. I found a certain twisted comfort in getting confirmation that Richard had never felt an ounce of affection for me.

I let myself fall back on the bed and dropped my face in my hands to try to hide the tears. Alejandro sat next to me and wrapped his arms around me. I pushed him away, but he did not move. Instead, he pulled me closer. As my head laid on his chest, I let the tears flow down.

"I can't imagine what it must have been like for you, growing up alone, with this poor excuse of a man, pretending. I'm sorry no parent was there to protect you, love you, care for you," he spoke in my ear, his voice deep.

I felt his every word, forcing me to look inward and taking comfort in his presence, his strength, his arms around me.

"I'm sorry about your brother."

"I know."

I got up and walked toward the window, wiping my tears, deciding that I would not shed one more for Richard.

"So, what now?" I asked, searching his eyes for answers.

"I don't know. It's pretty clear now to Mathias that using you is not the path to get those diamonds. And if Richard doesn't have them in his home, there is no way for us to get them. Mathias is a dangerous but loyal man, and he knows about what happened in my house. He is looking for Juan and Karina, who might have some information about the diamonds, but that's not very likely. The cop died, and the rest of the men either escaped or are dead as well. We have to come up with a plan."

Alejandro stayed silent for a few minutes, giving me some time to process. I was still confused, in shock and overwhelmed, but a soft fire was now growing inside of me. I was free of the guilt of having feelings for someone I thought was a criminal. Alejandro, just like me, was a victim of the circumstances. Another victim of my stepfather.

"But now," he started, slowly rising to his feet, "now you know the truth" he added, advancing towards me. "You know that I never meant for you to be involved in this. I had to play the game, but only to keep you safe."

"Yes," I acknowledged, staring out the window.

I felt relieved; I couldn't deny it. Relieved that Alejandro was a good man, caught in an impossible situation.

If what he said was true, he hadn't kidnapped me, and had saved my life at least twice. I wanted to hug him, kiss him, thank him, tell him I would rather die than let something happen to him, but I stopped myself. I didn't want his pity, and I didn't want to allow myself to feel all the emotions he raised in me.

There was something else.

I knew where those diamonds were.

If I was right, that bag I had seen was the same one Alejandro was looking for. I knew the code to the safe that they clearly did not know about, and I had seen Richard put the diamonds in. The best part was that Richard had no idea that I memorized the code, let alone that I saw him move the bag to that safe. He didn't even know I was aware of that one, as he had only opened the other two in front of me knowingly, but only sharing the code for one.

I had to decide if I wanted to trust Alejandro with that information, and I had to do it fast. I wanted to help him, take the pain away, make Richard pay for what he had done, and allow Alejandro to move on, but that required me trusting him fully and putting my last card on the table.

"Do you think Richard will continue to try to kill me?"

"For as long as we try to use you for ransom, I think he might try. Amelia, look at me," he said, turning my chin so I could face him. "I swear on my life, I won't let anyone harm you. I am going to get you out of this."

I knew in my heart, despite all my doubts, that he was telling the truth. He had saved my life before. For some reason, it was important to him that I be safe.

CHAPTER 30

Alejandro

SHE WAS SIZING ME up. Always. For the past few weeks, I had seen her walls come down just a bit and then go back up even higher than they were before. But even her frowning eyebrows couldn't hide her beauty. *This isn't the time*, I reminded myself, telling my dick to calm itself down.

She had finally learned the truth. I told her why she was here, what had happened. I felt the pit in my stomach lessen now that I could finally be honest with her. I could only hope she understood why I couldn't tell her before, that I never meant for her to be caught in the middle of this fucking nightmare—even before I met her. I lost myself in her gaze, those wide brown eyes sucking me in every time she looked at me. I wanted her to believe me. I wouldn't let Richard or Mathias hurt her—ever.

My hand was still holding her face in my direction. I caressed her chin with my thumb, unable to resist. She made one of those barely perceptible little moans that made my dick twitch once more. I needed to control myself. This was the time to reassure her, gain the trust I've been wanting for the past few months, make her feel safe with me.

"I want to find the diamonds. If I do, all of this ends. Richard has tripled the security at his house, so no one can enter. We've tried. My only option is to continue to play the interested investor, see if I can earn his trust," I explained.

"You won't," she said. "Richard trusts no one, except maybe George."

"Ah, your fiancé," I said dryly, my eyes darting toward that stupid fucking ring she had been wearing.

I should have never returned it to her. I didn't plan to. But a masochist-like need to see her reaction to it had led to me giving it back to her. I wanted to read her, see if she really did miss the fucker. I couldn't help it.

Every time his name left her beautiful, sensual lips, I wanted to grab his fucking head and run it through the wall. I wanted to rip that ring off her finger and make him swallow it. They had looked so perfect together at her party, all proper, a matching set of class and elegance. I didn't know her then, but I was still impacted by her beauty, her grace. There was a fire in her gaze, a fire I had no doubt George didn't know what to do with. A fire I wanted—no, needed—to possess.

"Yes. He sees him as the son he never had," she explained coldly.

"Is that why you were dating him? To please Richard?"

I tensed. Not my favorite topic, but I needed to know where her heart laid as much as I needed to breathe.

"I AM dating him because he is the right man for me," she said defensively, lips hard and eyes slanted as she looked at me with irritation.

Her words were torture, causing jealousy to burn me alive.

"You are sure of that?" I asked, getting closer to her again.

Amelia let out a shaky breath, while trying to keep her face emotionless, but I knew the truth. I had touched her before, and she had let me. Not because of fear, but because her breath accelerated every time I got closer to her.

I enjoyed seeing how nervous I made her, how irritated she got when she caught herself moaning for me with her lips parted.

"Yes." *Lies.*

"Hm, I beg to differ."

I gazed into her honey-brown eyes, her determination fighting her hunger for me. She stepped backward until she felt the cold window glass on her back, her hands behind her. She let out a little scream. I smirked and advanced towards her. I stopped right in front of her, my chest lightly brushing against her braless round breasts. She stood there stiffly, her arms now straight by each side of her body, refusing to give in, fighting every reaction.

But her chest was moving up and down at a fast pace. Her lips were slightly parted, her eyes searching mine.

I was boiling. I wanted to take her right there, satisfy this desire that had been consuming me since I brought her to my house—fuck, since I saw her at the party. But I knew I needed to take it slow. I had to, or I risked losing her, and that just wasn't an option for me.

I lifted my hand and removed her hair from her face. Amelia was doing her best to keep her eyes open and not succumb to temptation.

"Does he make you tremble in anticipation like I do?" I asked in a guttural tone, my lips now less than an inch from hers. She let out a sigh.

My breathing was accelerating as her smell invaded my every thought, my dick threatening to push out of my pants if it got any harder. "Does he kiss you like I kiss you?"

"Please stop," she whispered. "You can't do this."

"Do what? Touch you like this?" I asked, my fingers going up her left thigh and under her skirt. "Grab you like this?" She moaned as she closed her eyes.

I continued as my hands wrapped around her hips, drawing her closer to my dick so she could feel me, hard and hot against her, so she could see what she was doing to me. I needed to feel her. I needed her to be mine, every inch of her body, every inch of her soul... mine.

She gasped, and I lost it. My mouth grabbed hers, possessing her, drawing her to me, taking and demanding that she give me all of her. Amelia moaned, her hands gripping me for support. I put the full weight of my body onto her, pre-cum wetting my boxers.

I wanted her, hard and raw, right now. I needed to be inside of her, to take away all the hunger and sexual frustration that had been torturing me since I laid eyes on her. Screw the consequences. But I refused to do it with that bastard's ring on her finger.

"Remove it," I ordered, my voice raspy.

"What?" she asked with half open eyes, confused.

"That ring. Remove it from your finger, or I will do it for you." I gritted out.

She hesitated.

I held my breath, tension constricting every one of my muscles, while I wondered if she would do it. I needed her to show me she wanted me enough to forget about her fiancé, to put him aside, just so I could touch her.

She sighed, but she raised her trembling hand and removed it from her ring finger, her lips parted, her gaze fixated on my mouth. Hope spread through me like wildfire, as I lowered my head to hers again, taking her lips with mine. I heard the metal hit the floor with a satisfying clunk.

I proceeded to unbutton my shirt that she wore, revealing two inviting perky breasts, round and slightly swollen, yearning for my touch. I abandoned her lips, slowly going down her neck to grab one of her nipples between my lips.

Amelia let out a gasp, grabbing my head to keep me close. Her nipple fit perfectly into my mouth, her breasts large enough to almost fill my hand. I sucked and dragged my tongue, drawing circles around her nipple.

I was famished.

She called to god, and I swear I was just seconds away from exploding in my pants.

Fuck me.

I drove my right hand under her skirt and into her wet panties, parting her legs.

She was so fucking wet, all for me.

Looking lost under her long lashes, her cheeks flushed. I slid the tip of my index finger along her most sensitive part, making her moan even louder and hold onto me for dear life. She was wet, burning, and oh-so ready for me. I was hungry, kissing and sucking her breasts, her neck, her lips, devouring every inch of her skin with my mouth as I slowly rubbed her. She tasted so damn good, my restraint was falling at a fast pace.

Amelia was no longer holding back, her hips moving back and forth against my hand, begging for mercy, her moaning rising higher and higher with each stroke of my fingers. I had never seen anything more fucking sexy than Amelia chasing her satisfaction on my hand, not caring that my eyes were burning a hole through her.

"You are mine," I muttered in a deeply breathy tone as I continued to rub her in circles.

She needed to know who she belonged to.

Her movements quickened against my hand as I rubbed her faster.

"And you are going to come for me now, mi niña, aren't you?"

She grabbed my head to hold me close and let the explosion of her orgasm invade every inch of her as she screamed in pleasure and shook under my hand, every part of her body tensing and then relaxing. Amelia, breathing fast, eyes half closed, seemed to lose control of her legs. I held her close so she didn't fall to the ground.

She snuggled her head in my neck, looking for support. I caressed her back and kissed her head to make the feeling last longer as she was slowly coming back down from ecstasy. I lifted her head, kissing her sweetly, bringing her back to me. We were both trying to catch our breath.

My dick was hard as a fucking rock, but it was going to be for another day. I got more than I could have wished for. I got Amelia to come all over my fucking fingers, and that was all the victory I needed for today.

Our escapade got interrupted by a knock on the door. Amelia quickly straightened herself. She pushed me away, fearing that someone would see us, even if I did lock the door.

"What?" I brusquely asked of whoever had ruined the moment.

"Call from Mr. Fernandez," said Dolores. "He said it's important."

"I'll call him back," I replied, my eyes unwilling to leave hers.

Amelia seemed suddenly shy, her cheeks still flushed. She looked anywhere she could to avoid my gaze.

Concern coiled my stomach at the thought she might regret what happened between us.

"That's Mathias," I explained before she could get any ideas.

"You should go call him," she said, clearing her throat. "It might be important."

I cupped her head and lifted it to meet mine. "We need to talk about this when I come back."

Before she could object, I slowly kissed her until I felt her starting to melt against me again. I sighed, but this was important, so I stepped out and closed the door behind me.

CHAPTER 31

Amelia

As Alejandro left the room, I closed my eyes and put my face on the window, trying to feel something other than the lingering memory of his hands on my body.

Those three little words, "*You are mine,*" had been my undoing, shattering what was left of my reserves.

I unraveled, lost all control and self-respect, rubbing myself against his hand like I was possessed, chasing that high, no matter the cost. I was still enjoying all the sensations that had made my body shake and my knees weak, as Alejandro had just given me the most intense orgasm of my entire life, just with his fingers and his mouth.

I was lost.

So, so lost.

I had experienced nothing even close to this with any other men, including George, and Alejandro had only used his fingers on me. I couldn't even imagine what it would have been like if he had been inside of me.

I didn't want to shower just yet. I was still on a cloud, enjoying his smell on me, his own body's version of his Mont Blanc cologne, and the very vibrant memory of what he had awakened in me. The way he had touched me, my body releasing its frustration, fast and hard. I was also thinking about what it was we would have to discuss when he did come back.

Eventually, Dolores brought me some scrambled eggs and toast. Dolores also carried a piece of luggage filled with clothes with her.

"My daughter lives two houses down. She gave me some clothes for you. You are about her size. Don't worry, she doesn't know who you are," she explained.

She bent down to pick up the ring I had dropped on the floor when Alejandro ordered me to take it off. I felt guilty, but in the moment, there was no way I wasn't going to remove the one thing that stood between me and his hands on my body. Especially since part of me was suspicious that George was also involved in all of this. Dolores put it on the nightstand in silence.

"Did Alejandro give you back your house here too? I know you said his mother was your neighbor," I asked, dying for anything to take my mind off what happened by the window.

"Yes," she answered with a smile. "I love this land. When Alejandro gave my kids and me our house back, I couldn't believe it. My daughter lives there now with her husband, and soon, I will be an abuela."

The joy beaming out of Dolores's face was contagious. No wonder she wouldn't leave Alejandro's side.

She explained that she had been with her daughter since she left the hacienda and came here when Alejandro shared our location with her and finally allowed her to join us. Alejandro was refusing to let her stay in the house so she could spend more time with her pregnant daughter, but she insisted on coming over to cook and clean and make sure we had everything.

"Your soup is delicious," said Dolores as she sat next to me on the bed.

"Thank you! If you say so, I believe you." I smiled.

"How are you? Did Don Alejandro tell you?"

"Yes, yes, he did."

Without a word, Dolores gave me the hug I didn't know I needed. I held onto her for dear life, a few tears escaping from my eyes.

"I'm glad he told you. I'm glad you know now. I am sorry I couldn't tell you, y por lo que te hicieron. Tu eres inocente en todo esto."

"Thank you, Dolores."

I swallowed the tears that were threatening to continue to show my feelings to Dolores. Those words, for some reason, triggered me. I was starting to realize that I wanted more from Alejandro than someone who felt bad that I got caught between him and Richard.

He had awakened a need for much more, a need for feeling loved and wanted. What the hell was I supposed to do with that?

CHAPTER 32

Alejandro

THOSE LONG CALLS WITH Mathias always put me on edge. I spent most of the day dealing with him and his stupidity. I had bit off more than I could chew with this fucking mess, involving myself with the worst my country had to offer—highly sophisticated cartels that operated under the radar with such precision most people barely knew they existed.

When we partnered to get the diamonds and take Richard down, I was desperate and angry, filled with sorrow, mourning the loss of my only sibling. I had hired my own little army, though, to protect myself. I could not show any weakness as I entered this world. My mother had begged me to let it all go, but I still wanted Richard done for. I needed to destroy him, reveal to the world the kind of rat that he was.

But now I was paying the price of this alliance, and I would pay it ten times over to keep Amelia safe. I believed Mathias now when he said he didn't send his men to my house. If he had, I would have been forced to kill him, teach his team a lesson—that I was not to be messed with. Otherwise, Amelia would remain in danger even after all this was over. He was my first suspect. No one else knew where Amelia and I were. But it quickly became clear that Richard had infiltrated Mathias's team.

Who knew for how long, but Karina, among others, had been working with Richard. It also explained why Juan tried to kill her and disappeared right after. If he hadn't, I would have killed him myself. And if my men ever found him, they had orders to bring him to me alive, so I could finish the job. He had dared to hurt her, under my roof. I wanted to rip his head from his neck with my bare hands.

As for Karina, I had met her shortly after David's death. We had slept together a few times, but that woman was a viper. A violent, hateful creature who had been a traitor.

She showed up to my house, unannounced, multiple times during Amelia's stay. I couldn't push her away too much, I didn't want to raise any suspicions that my prisoner was getting to me. Karina could report anything amiss to Mathias. I had to be indifferent, and almost cruel to Amelia in the eyes of everyone. If I didn't, her life would be in more danger than it already was. That was why I let her kiss me in front of Amelia.

She and others had orchestrated a mission with Richard. Not a rescue mission I thought, tension building in my shoulders again as I sipped on my glass of scotch, but a murder mission. Richard wanted to kill his only daughter, the girl he had presented to the world as his most precious love. It was all a lie.

I got it now, Amelia's reaction every time I said his name.

To think that I called her a spoiled brat so many times when, in fact, she was just another tool to Richard, another means to an end, his only goal to be as rich as possible, no matter the cost.

When I remembered the state she was in when I had found her running barefoot on the street, fear eating her from the inside out, the shadows under her eyes, her bruised body... I wanted to destroy everything in my path, erase the pain all this had caused her. As luck would have it that day, she had given me the perfect argument to have her stay in my house instead of with Mathias's people.

But to keep her safe, I had to play the part of the villain. That day, when I found her going through my things in my office, I lost it. Mathias's men were with me, and I couldn't let them believe that Amelia had found anything she could use against Mathias once she was free. Otherwise, he would take his diamonds but still have her killed. I also had to make sure they didn't think she saw their faces.

I would never forget the terror in her eyes that night, when I put her back in that small room. I had hurt her, and that was something I had to make up for during the rest of our lives if she would let me.

The balance between protecting her and showing her no mercy in front of others was the hardest thing I ever had to do. The more I got to know her, the more she got under my skin.

My first mistake had been kissing her that night. I knew it was wrong, I knew it was stupid. But I couldn't stop it. I couldn't stop thinking about those lips. I had felt her breast rub against my chest when she admired my mother's artwork. I had seen those brown eyes dilate just a little, her plump lips parted. I knew she had felt it too. So, when she ran out of my house that night, angry, I took advantage.

I didn't want to want her, I thought she represented everything I despised, but still I gave in, and I kissed her.

When she let me taste her, I knew I was done for.

She had upended my life with each look, her rare smiles, her temper. She seduced me, and before I knew it, all I wanted was to be with her, glide my hand over her perfect curves, get to know her, and fuck her senseless, until all she knew was the feeling of my dick inside of her, until that fucking ring on her finger disintegrated into dust.

In her I found a kindred spirit, someone who could understand the deepest part of me, someone I wanted to share everything with. I wanted to own her, possess her, infiltrate myself in her every thought.

I wanted to possess her days; I wanted to haunt her nights.

I had managed to never fall for anyone my whole life. People who got married to someone for the rest of their days had always confused me. There was so much to try, to experience. So many women to fuck and lots of many places to see. I never wanted restraints, limitations, someone else whose need I had to consider.

Neither Karina nor Elena had tempted me. And yet here I was, drinking to calm an erection I had been fighting for months now, trying to control the urge to go back upstairs and make her mine, to finish what I had started. I wanted to hear her moan my name again; I wanted to feel her drip all over my fingers again. I had fallen hard for a woman I was holding hostage.

Just my fucking luck.

In just a few months, I had developed a core need for Amelia to be in my life, to experience living with her, to travel with her. I wanted—no, I needed to bury myself inside of her. I needed it like I needed air.

We were stuck in an impossible situation. She deserved better than me. She deserved better than this, but she would be mine, nonetheless.

But I had to fix things first. I needed to get Mathias off my back by finding those fucking diamonds. I needed Richard behind bars. Only then could life go back to some semblance of normalcy.

I could focus more on my job and on winning Amelia's heart, no matter the cost.

The first thing I had to do was set things straight with Elena, and there was no time like the present, I thought, as someone knocked on my door. Elena entered timidly. This wasn't going to be an easy conversation, but it needed to be done.

"Hola, amor," she cooed as she came to meet me by my desk. She set her arms around my neck.

I removed them gently, toying with the balance between being firm and hurting her.

"Hey. Let's go for a walk," I suggested.

The last thing I wanted was for Amelia to see her here. I didn't want anything to put the progress we had made in jeopardy—even though seeing Amelia go into jealous mode was sexy as hell.

Elena and I exited across the patio, slowly walking onto the beach. She was a gorgeous woman, young, with her whole life ahead of her. We had been best friends when we were much younger.

I always thought she and I would end up together, until I had to move to the US. We lost touch, and she started dating my brother. That was when I realized that Elena and I weren't in love and never had been. I didn't feel anything at all when I found out about their relationship.

Since his death, we had grown closer, understandably so. And yes, we both caved and fucked a few times. That was a big mistake. I had made as much clear to her. She had decided to help with infiltrating Richard's circle, and that had complicated things between us. After the way she reacted to Amelia's presence when we came here, I knew I needed to set things straight with her.

"So"—I cleared my throat—"the other day, when I came here—"

"I know," she interrupted before I could finish.

She looked at me with those black coffee eyes, her thick lashes hiding most of them. She was pouting as she slid her arm in mine.

"I'm sorry, Alejandro. I just panicked. You were hurt, and I... I lost it a bit. I just miss him so much. You've been my only company since... since what happened."

I felt my throat close. It was still hard for both of us. I knew the pain she was going through. She also lost someone—someone she was in love with. However, I still needed to set things straight.

"But I am not him, Elena. You can't just fill the void with me."

"Why not? We slept together already, and you enjoyed it."

Tears were rolling down her beautiful face. My heart sank, her sorrow reflecting mine. I couldn't morph into my brother for her, however much she needed it. While I had entertained the idea in the past, driven by pain, there was someone else, someone who made me feel alive.

"We are great friends, Elena. Let's not ruin it. Please. We fucked, yes, but it was a mistake, led by grief and nothing else."

She closed her eyes for a bit. "Fine," she sighed. After a long pause, she continued. "It's because of her, isn't it? You love her, don't you?"

There wasn't much left to say between us, so we continued walking in silence until we made it to her front door.

"We are still on for the trip?"

"Still on," I confirmed.

She gave me a hug, a parting one, hopefully a return to the friendship we should have never jeopardized for a few nights of comfort.

CHAPTER 33

Amelia

A LONG, WARM SHOWER was just what I needed to distract myself from my thoughts. I felt newly invigorated because Alejandro wasn't the ogre I had built him out to be in my head. I was feeling reborn, relieved, almost happy about my circumstances, which could have been so much worse it seemed.

As usual, Dolores did not disappoint. She had done much more than borrow some clothes from her daughter. She had asked her to properly shop for me, as evidenced by the fact that most of the clothes still had their tags on them. I arranged all the clothes in the closet, happy to see that Dolores's daughter had thought of all the details, from shoes to underwear, and had coordinated the outfits.

I chose to wear a beachy short blue dress with small white flowers. I liked how it perfectly grabbed my breasts. The bottom had fringes and stopped a few inches above my knees. I enjoyed the hair products and fluffed my curls. I lathered on some sunscreen and put on some of the new makeup.

No matter what I did, the memory of the morning was always there. I could not help grinning like a teenager when the feelings flooded my brain, but the enjoyment was always followed by a bit of guilt. I was starting to feel free to let what had been rising inside of me for a while now flourish, but what was the point?

While he never meant to harm me, there was still a purpose for him, a purpose I now knew I could help fulfill. While his words made my heart flutter, I was ashamed I let him touch me like that after what I knew and what I didn't know. The other issue was the decision I had to make: whether to tell him about the diamonds or not.

The afternoon was coming to an end, so I went looking for Alejandro. He was nowhere to be found. Dolores was already gone, but she had left the house spotless and the kitchen filled with food and small cakes.

the sun was setting, I ventured down to the water for fresh air. After just a few minutes on the patio, I heard some voices coming off the beach in my direction. As I got up to take a look, I spotted Alejandro and Elena, her arm wrapped around his, peacefully strolling by the beach, slowly heading to her house. I felt like someone had just punched me in my stomach. I quickly headed back to the house. The last thing I wanted was for them to see me see them together.

I ran inside and went directly to my bedroom, violently closing the door behind me. I started pacing with anger. *How could I have been so stupid*? Spending the day looking for him, dreaming of our next moment together, when I knew damn well that he had a girlfriend, a girl he had known since he was a child, even if he had denied it. Someone he had a lot more in common with than me—the woman he had called spoiled. How could I possibly compete with that?

I heard some voices coming from the living room. I was tempted to go there and just scream, but my pride was stronger. I piled up all the shirts I had borrowed from his closet to bring them to his room and drop them in his hamper. I no longer needed them, nor did I want them.

While I was about to leave his room, I heard footsteps outside his door. My heart skipped a beat as I expected to see Alejandro with Elena in his arms, but Alejandro walked in alone, looking even tanner, wearing a pair of cotton pants with a light-gray shirt. I was doing my best to keep my cool.

"How are you?" he asked.

"Good, where were you?"

I bit my lip, but jealousy was now driving the ship. I was blind with it and, frankly, was throwing caution and calm behavior to the wind.

Alejandro lifted his chin, looking at me through small eyes.

"I had a few things to take care of," he answered, hands in his pockets.

"You don't say," I said coldly. I could feel my face boiling.

"What's bothering you?" he asked as he got closer to me.

I took a deep breath, turning around in an attempt to avoid his gaze.

"I'm not bothered," I lied. "Just curious; you disappeared."

Alejandro gently grabbed me by the arm, slowly turning me to face him.

"What do you really want to ask me?"

He was scrutinizing me, following my eyes wherever I was trying to hide them.

"Okay." I sighed. I didn't have anything to lose as long as I could keep my cool.

"What exactly is your relationship with Elena?"

"She is a good friend," he explained. "We grew up together. She's always been there for me."

"Friends? Please. How stupid do you think I am? Friends don't act like that. She was kissing you when you were sick, that day I found her in your room. She kissed you again the other day."

"I see. And? Are you jealous?" he teased.

"Jealous?" My tone was higher than I intended.

I gave him my best fake laugh.

"Jealous of what? You and her?" I ripped my arm from his hold.

"Well, you are asking me for an explanation you think I owe you, aren't you?"

The audacity of this man, putting it on me to define what was going on between us. It enraged me.

"That doesn't make me jealous!" I shouted, my lips thin with frustration. "I have a right to know where you were."

"And what gives you that right, Amelia?" he pressed, his brows lifted, with that irritating smirk.

It was as if he thought he was asking me a question he knew the answer to.

"Forget it. I don't have time for this," I said, brushing past him to leave the room.

My feelings were getting the best of me, and it was time to do what I did best—flee. But Alejandro held me by my arm as I attempted to leave.

"She's not my girlfriend, Amelia." He smiled.

I rolled my eyes.

"Hmm, you have to stop doing that," he warned.

"What?"

"Rolling your eyes like that."

A trembling sigh left my throat. "Why?"

"It makes me want to punish you."

Jesus and all the saints. What the hell was he doing? Why did I feel like a current was forming in my stomach? I cleared my throat. No, I wasn't going to get distracted.

"Well, your *friend* certainly seems to think you are much more. She told me she was." He smirked, and I snapped. "What?!"

"I love seeing you like this."

I turned my head away, trying to hide the heat I felt rising to my face again. My pride told me to stop this, but my heart needed to know.

"Why does she act like you're hers, then?"

"Well," he said hesitantly, "we used to date when we were younger, but we broke up a long time ago. She then dated David until his death. She is a little protective of me, that's all."

I pulled against his firm grip, walking away from him, my arms crossed for self-support.

"She seems to be in need of a clarification from you," I pushed.

I knew what I saw. And he wasn't helping.

"I agree," he admitted. "If it will make you happy, I will clarify things with her. Frankly, I have before, and I did again today."

Alejandro started walking toward me again. I needed a distraction, or I would end up on that window again, the thought causing a painful wave of desire to invade me.

"What about Karina?"

"Ah, yes, well, Mathias and I have been planning what to do for a while, and in that process, she and I got... close... but it wasn't serious."

"You guys slept together."

"Yes," he answered with a low, patient voice.

I wanted to slap the calmness out of his face. Jealousy was blinding me, even if deep down I knew I had no right. We were having a staring contest, Alejandro waiting for me to react.

"When was the last time you slept with Elena?"

Alejandro lifted a brow, surprised by my boldness I assume, but I didn't care.

"You said I could ask, and I see no need to tiptoe around the topic."

"Very well. Elena and I slept together a few weeks ago, give or take," he admitted, jaw tightened, eyes darkening. I noticed his Adam's apple move down as he swallowed hard.

"That's what I thought," I said, trying to hide the pinch I felt in my heart. "It's no wonder she is confused. And she was dating your brother, for Christ's sake. Who does that?" He flinched. Jealousy was searing through my veins.

"It was a mistake on our part. We let grief get the best of us. But I was very clear, even afterward, even today. It was before you, Amelia."

I shook my head. "Goodnight, Alejandro."

I rushed out of the room and headed straight to the bathroom, where I could let out a scream of frustration. I decided to take a bath. I needed to control what clearly was a desire to destroy every other women Alejandro had ever touched.

I had hoped the episode earlier would have satisfied my itch, calmed down my desire for this man, but I feared I was more on edge now than I was before.

As the day started, my mind was made up. I needed to swim, try to exercise more, to calm my hot head... and my heart. After having a small fruit bowl for breakfast, I slipped on a pink bikini I had found in the luggage of clothes.

The bikini fit well, thankfully. It didn't cover as much as I would normally prefer, but it was the only one I had. I rubbed some oil in my hair, some sunscreen on my skin, and covered up with a long, white, cotton shirt. I put on a pair of beach sandals, and after I grabbed a towel, I headed outside.

The sun was warm but not too hot. The air was dry and just perfect for the first week of September. I enjoyed the feeling of the salty wind and a light amount of sand hitting my body.

I set my bag down on one of the long chairs located under the pergola, removed my cover up, and then walked as fast as I could to the shoreline. I cherished the feeling of the cool water on my skin, the sound of the waves, and the feeling of freedom and awe for the force of nature I always experienced when I floated in the ocean.

I swam to my heart's content, unable to hide the smile of satisfaction that drew on my face after each lap, enjoying how the water carried me around, making me feel weightless and worry free, as if the ocean had taken all my responsibilities, all my problems, and washed them away.

Nature had a way of forcing a person to live in the moment, and I needed that more than anything. The crash of the waves filled my brain every time I dived, making me focus on the task at hand instead of the turmoil inside of me. I loved swimming. I used to go to the ocean in California as much as possible, even when it was cold.

The very expensive swimming lessons Richard had forced me to take, because the daughter of some business contact was going, actually were a blessing for me, providing me with an outlet to exercise and relieve stress.

I swam until my arms and legs felt to heavy to keep me afloat, the numbness a welcome relief, anchoring me as exhaustion began to simmer my raging thoughts. Collapsing onto the sand, I scooped up a handful and rubbed it against my skin letting the gritty texture exfoliate the remnants of tension.

It was close to an hour when I gave up. I reluctantly headed back to the pergola. The sun was now hotter than before, so it was the perfect time to hide in the shade and take a nap.

To my surprise, there was Alejandro, standing by one of the poles, shirtless and in white-linen pants, scanning my body from head to toe, with no shame or discretion. I felt weak in my knees, recognizing my own raw desire in his eyes, but I had to walk to the pergola. It was too late to change course.

CHAPTER 34

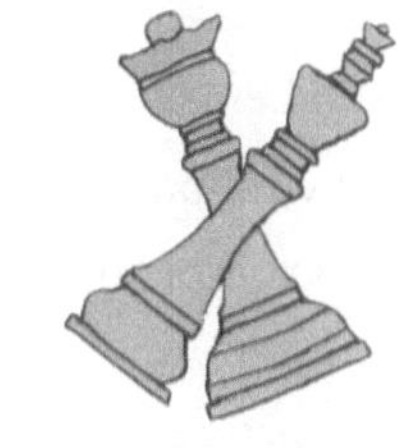

Alejandro

I HAD BEEN WATCHING her since she strolled out of the house, wrapped in a towel, headed to the beach. At first, I just wanted to make sure she was safe, but when that towel came off, I lost any sense of pride or decency. I couldn't take my eyes off her.

It was obvious that Amelia was an attractive woman, but my god. My dick thickened up immediately when I saw that pink bikini, her round breasts slightly overfilling the top, her defined stomach, and that ass. That plump, tight ass in a thong bottom, separating those defined butt cheeks I wanted to lick, bite, possess.

I didn't think Dolores realized what kind of bathing suit her daughter had snuck into that luggage she so proudly brought to Amelia when she showed up here. I would have to give Andrea a great Christmas gift for this favor.

Amelia was finally out of the water after swimming laps for an hour and doing some sort of exfoliation by rubbing sand over her skin. I knew she swam for fun. After all, I'd had to get files on everyone that was close to Richard, but this was my first time seeing her. She seemed in her element, even if I held my breath every time she went under the waves.

She was walking toward me now, her peaceful expression tensing as she noticed me standing under the pergola. I had no shame. My eyes roamed every inch of her body, the fire in my stomach intensifying with each sexy little step she took, her wet skin glistening under the sun, her breathing a bit accelerated. She fixed her bra a bit, to no avail.

"Good morning," I said, never taking my eyes off her and slowly, indecently making my way to her face.

"Good morning," she replied when she got to me, grabbing the neatly folded towel she had left here and wrapping it around herself.

Ignoring me, she sat on one of the long chairs, drying her long brown curls. I knew I should be more discreet, but I was staring at her, imagining how she would look with those now wavy curls wrapped around my wrist.

The things I wanted to do to her...

On the table between us was some champagne and orange juice in a pitcher that I had brought with me so it would be ready when she came out of the water. I walked to the drinks and poured a mimosa, handing it to her. She grabbed it but avoided any eye contact with me.

"Thanks," she muttered, her well-mannered behavior stronger than whatever hatred she felt for me.

"You're welcome."

I sat on the long chair across from her. I had a whole speech prepared, but I was rendered silent, so I focused on the now wrathful waves of the ocean instead, swarming just like the turmoil inside me, at being so close to her but yet feeling so far.

I took a big gulp of my drink to try to simmer down, but I couldn't help and look to my side to look at her.

She was enjoying the beach view, a pensive look on her face. The wind was blowing her wet, curly hair around. Her brown eyes slowly met mine, her stare now perusing my naked chest, all the way down to my raging boner. She bit her lip, her gaze going back to my chest and my arms. I had never been more thankful for staying fit. Her lips parted ever so slightly as her breath quickened.

I felt my pulse quicken when her eyes drew back to mine, burning raw desire emanating from her every pore. Every muscle of my body was tense, urging me to jump on her and make her mine. She held a gasp when she realized I was now looking at her, my eyes burning.

Amelia quickly rose to her feet. Before she could leave, I grabbed her arm, turning her to face me.

"Amelia, you have to know... Elena, she means nothing to me. She's just a good friend. I told you this already. We made a mistake, both overtaken by our sorrow, but that was it. We are just friends."

She shook her head, her beautiful lips thin.

"I don't know if I can believe you," she admitted.

"I know. I get it. Amelia, I didn't plan for this. I didn't know I was going to meet you—not like this. There are many things I regret doing, many things I wouldn't have done if I knew how my life was going to turn out—if I knew you."

She shook her head with force and backed away from me. I took a step toward her, but I stopped myself, turning my hands into fists instead. As much as I was hurting, I needed to give her space, to give her time, even if we were running out of it.

She turned around and walked fast toward the house.

I sat back down on the chair, running my fingers through my hair, holding my face in my hands with my eyes closed. How had things gotten so fucking complicated so fast?

To think that, at the beginning, when I came up with the plan to befriend Richard, my first thought was to seduce Amelia, the daughter I had heard so much about in my investigations. She was his pearl—or so I thought.

She was a young, beautiful, twenty-seven-year-old woman, and I was a thirty-four-year-old man who knew the effect I had on women. It wouldn't have been hard. But she was in a fairytale relationship with Richard's pet, George, and I understood from Richard that they were to wed. I figured that avenue was closed, as Richard wouldn't take kindly to me messing up his plans. She ended up in my home anyway, in my arms, ruining every plan I had laid out for myself, becoming my center, my core. And I didn't know how to get her to see me, to trust me. But I would try it all. Defeat was not an option.

CHAPTER 35

Amelia

I ONLY STOPPED WHEN I got to my room, a safe place. I was very conflicted. He seemed to care about what I thought, and that made me want to trust him, but I had learned not to trust or believe anything other people said without proof.

Men lied, after all.

I grew up with the worst of them all, so why would I ever put my heart in the position to be trampled on? Alejandro was danger. The way he looked at me was borderline criminal. The way my nipples tensed earlier, just from hims gaze, was unbearable.

I was never going to solve the emotional turmoil raging havoc within me. I knew that, so all I could do was resist falling for the devil as much as I could while we had to live together.

And yes, I was mad. I knew I shouldn't be, but I was. The fact that he had slept with Elena and Karina annoyed and worried me. I wasn't convinced that there was nothing between him and Elena. I shouldn't care; I knew that. Alejandro wasn't mine, and I had George—though I clearly had to break up with him now after the window episode. The worst was that all I felt about that future breakup was relief.

Why did he have to show up shirtless? I admired his presence and the aura of control that filled any space he was in. He was the kind of man who would never go unnoticed anywhere he stepped foot in. Then, for the second time, I got to drool over his muscles as they beautifully contracted under his bronze skin. His arms, looking so strong...I had felt myself get wet. He hadn't even touched me.

My hands had wanted to play with his hair. And that erection...it was unmistakable. Seeing his blatant desire for me was like a drug. But I wouldn't give in. I couldn't cave without losing control. And I feared that, once I did, there would be no turning back.

I spent a pretty uneventful rest of the day trying to decide whether I should tell Alejandro about the diamonds. That was trust—telling him something that might either keep me alive or put me in harm's way. But I knew where they were, and if I could use that information to help Alejandro, I knew I would.

That admission scared me to death because it meant that I cared for him, a lot more than I wanted to admit. He did save my life, after all. That was one of the key facts that made me feel like I could trust him with this, and part of why I wanted to help him.

Most of my day was spent listening to music, writing, and daydreaming, forcing myself to remember my life before all of this, before him. The job I had been looking forward to. My freedom from Richard. I didn't find the same enjoyment in those thoughts that I used to, but I still found comfort in them. I entertained myself until bedtime.

I chose to wear a white, slightly see-through, silk sleeping gown to go to bed. It was a cool night, and I loved feeling the air travel under my gown, caressing me, while I allowed myself to think about Alejandro's touch.

It wasn't really a choice at this point, more like an obsession, an escape, something both my body and soul craved to no end. I couldn't help but stand by the bay window, listening to the calming sound of the waves, admiring the black sky slightly lit by the moon and the stars.

I wanted to go to Alejandro's room so badly my body ached at just the idea of being near him. I wanted to feel him again, but my pride was stronger, as long as I kept my distance from him. I was afraid that once I got to feel him inside of me, there would be no going back to the guards and rails I was so fond of.

But when I heard a knock at the door, my treacherous body reacted. I turned my head back to the sea, but I each of his steps resonated, as his shadow he approached me.

He leaned on the other side of the bay window, also mesmerized by the night. I bended my head slightly, looking at him from the corner of my left eye. I couldn't stop myself, my eyes traveling along his lips, his jawline, his neck, hardened by the shadow of the moon. I wanted him desperately, my resolve slowly making way for anticipation.

When I glanced back up, he was staring at me with those sensual, dark, possessive eyes I could lose myself in. He was walking to me now, looking deep into my soul. He kissed me with his hungry lips, mine parting in complete surrender. I stood there stiffly, my arms locked, refusing to give in, even as my body was begging me to, my self-control holding onto a sliver of resistance. He moaned, but he lifted and shook his head, brushing past me.

"Good night," he said heavily.

Those words, the idea of him walking away, led to a panic, and before he could leave, I grabbed his hand with mine. I looked up, trying to tell him what I couldn't voice out loud. He groaned and grabbed my lips with so much ferocity I had to hold onto him not to fall, my heart beating faster and faster as he slid his arms around me, pulling me closer, my body yielding to his every touch, his every caress. Alejandro's hands roamed under my nightgown, leaving a trace of trembling anguish everywhere he touched.

He slowed himself down, his fingers caressing my face, gliding down to my neck, the side of my breast, my hip bones, relentlessly teasing me. I was letting go, grabbing his hair, feeling his strong shoulder, as I held him close.

He grunted as he lifted me off the floor and set me down on the bed. He stood over me, taking off his shirt. He lifted my gown above my head and took a minute to admire what he had revealed.

"You are so beautiful," he whispered.

I got a little shy, hiding my body a bit with my hands.

"No, mi niña, let me see you. All of you."

The desire in his eyes showed that he was dying to be with me as much as I wanted him. I felt reassured and removed my hands as he devoured every inch of my body with his gaze.

Breathless, I admired every single muscle contracting as he lowered himself on top of me.

"I'm sorry for the bruise you had here," he said as he slowly, sensually kissed my forehead. "And here," he added as he tenderly ran his lips over my jawline. "I'm sorry I let that happen to your neck," he added in a guttural tone as he sucked on my throbbing vein.

"No one else will ever hurt you again," he added as he teased the other side of my neck. "No one else will ever put even a finger on you," he swore as he kissed my jaw again.

He proceeded down to my ribs.

"I'm sorry," he chanted before every part of my body that he licked, sucked, kissed, every movement healing my heart, as tears filled my eyes. His words and his tenderness released a little bit of the pain I held inside at the physical impact this kidnapping experience had placed on me. Each of his kisses, each caress, repaired some of the harm.

He trailed his way along my neck, grazing my nipples in the process as his hands went up and down my thighs, lightly touching me in my most intimate parts. He was driving me crazy, giving very little, making me very desperate.

I pushed myself against his hands, but he was not budging, suddenly in complete control, kissing my belly, my hips, my inner thighs. My body was on fire, tight, shaking. I grabbed his head to pull him closer, but he refused. With a soft, guttural laugh, he grabbed both my wrists and held them tightly together above my head.

"Not just yet."

I let out a moan when he finally wrapped his lips around my nipple, slowly rolling around it with the tip of his tongue, sending a surge of current between my legs.

"Oh, yes" I whispered almost to myself.

I bent my head and screamed at the intensity, still in tears. I heard him groan in response as he grabbed my lips with his, his hand wiping a tear that had escaped.

"Please," I whispered against his lips, begging him to take me.

"Patience, mi niña," he moaned in my ear as he grunted.

Alejandro finally let my hands go, and he grabbed a condom from his pocket, took his pants off, and paused as he observed me, his dick so stiff it looked like it should hurt. He opened the foil and rolled the condom on his length.

Before I knew it, he slid inside of me with all his glory, a deep sigh leaving his throat.

I whimpered, in pain and pleasure, my body trembling as it adjusted to his generous girth. He started rhythmically thrusting in and out of me, deeply, eagerly, and strongly, sending fireworks through my blood.

His hands were grabbing me, pulling me closer, his mouth kissing me as I felt the fullness of him still thrusting inside of me, stretching me to let him in, deeper and deeper. It felt like he wanted to dive inside of me more than my body could allow.

It was so excruciatingly delicious I could barely handle it.

"You feel so good baby" he panted.

My nails dug into his backside; I was panting, feeling my body going wild, getting ready to explode. Nothing but what I currently felt mattered. Alejandro filled up every inch of my body and soul as I got overwhelmed by a completely agonizing and liberating explosion.

"Alejandro!"

"God, I love watching you come for me" he breathed.

Alejandro groaned, coming to a halt as he reached his release, pouring his climax inside of me. It was perfect agony.

Alejandro leaned down next to me, grabbing me into his arms, kissing my forehead. remained like that for a few minutes, Alejandro now tenderly kissing me and stroking me leisurely, extending my ecstatic numbness with every touch, as I started feeling heavier.

I hadn't meant to sleep with him, not when jealousy was still torturing me. Not when I didn't quite know what to make of us, what to make of what I felt, what was next for us. But I also wanted him too much to deny myself any longer. I could no longer fight my need for him. And right in that moment, I had no regrets. I was in heaven and couldn't help the smile that drew on my face as I fell asleep in the arms of my keeper, in the arms of the man who had changed my life forever.

CHAPTER 36

Alejandro

I HAD BEEN WATCHING her sleep like a creep for over ten minutes now. How could I not? My girl was lying so peacefully in my arms, that frown erased from her face. She was smiling in her sleep. Her cheeks slightly flushed when she opened her almond eyes and realized I was already awake, my head in my hand, leaning on the bed, looking at her.

"Good morning," I said as I caressed her face.

Amelia closed her eyes, seemingly savoring my touch. I never wanted this moment to end.

"Good morning," she answered, her voice sleepy.

That sound went straight to my dick. I'd spent the better half of the night inside of her, making up for lost time, making up for all the pain I had caused with every orgasm that shook her, but I needed more. I was very far from satiated.

I pulled her close to me, her small and firm body grazing mine, the warmth of her skin driving me wild.

"Again?" she asked with a small voice as my erection against her stomach made my intentions clear.

"Do you not want to?"

"Well, I didn't say that," she teased, her eyelids still a bit heavy with sleep.

I leaned to grab a condom in the nightstand. I rolled it along my already hard shaft. She wrapped her arms around my neck as my hands glided over her naked body, owning every curve of her. Hunger rose inside of me as I took her lips in mine and got on top of her.

I did not make her wait this time as I slid through her wet folds and filled her up until every inch of me was inside of her, making her moan with satisfaction.

Amelia was going to be the death of me, of that, I was sure. I never wanted to start another day if it wasn't like this, with my dick buried deep inside of her, while I gazed into her lustful eyes.

She started moving against me deeply, as if she was famished for me.

I fed on her need as adrenaline rushed through of me.

"Fuck, you take me so well baby" I let out as I intensified my movement, even as I feared I would hurt her, the way she grabbed my ass to bring me closer telling me she wanted more. And I gladly obliged with every thrust, going as deep as she wanted me, faster and harder.

Her cunt was so fucking tight, it squeezed my dick so well, I was losing myself in her. I was suffering; I was in fucking heaven. Her eyes glazed over, those little moans she let out destroying any restraint I had. We were both fully awake now.

"Oh, Alejandro," she moaned.

My name on her lips like this was my fucking kryptonite.

Something cracked inside of me with the terrifying realization that Amelia had me wrapped around her little finger.

And I wanted nothing more.

I grabbed her head and her hip to stabilize her as I wildly thrusted inside of her as if I wanted to escape from my own body all the way inside of hers. The headboard was loudly protesting, but I didn't give a fuck.

I was a man possessed by the woman who was under me, grabbing me like her life depended on it.

My thirst for her was insatiable as she moved against me, with me, in perfect rhythm, taking every inch of me as her fingers dug into my flesh further, until we lost ourselves in each other. I came, long and hard, my dick throbbing with intensity.

CHAPTER 37

Amelia

WHEN I WOKE UP again from my slumber, Alejandro was putting his pants on. He came to the bed when he realized I was awake, and I held him by his arm before he got up again.

"We need to talk," I said.

"What's wrong?" he asked, his eyebrows scrunched.

I sat myself straight on the bed, holding the sheets on top of me. Between the best orgasms of my entire existence, I had made a decision. Alejandro got closer, caressing my anxious face.

"Tell me," he insisted.

"I know where Richard has the diamonds, and I want to help you get them." I clenched my jaw.

He paused, searching my eyes for something I couldn't give him. I was telling the truth.

"We searched both of his safes."

"There is a third one."

Alejandro suddenly got up from the bed. He seemed furious, and I didn't understand why he was reacting so aggressively. He looked like he had gotten stabbed.

"That's not possible. We searched every inch of that office."

"It's very well hidden, but it's there. He thinks no one knows about it."

I wrapped the bedsheet around myself fully and got up after him.

"I don't want you involved in this," he said as he turned to face me.

"I don't understand…"

"Forget you said anything," he urged as he seized my arm to force me to look at him.

"Well, what do you want exactly? Richard is not going to hand you the diamonds, Alejandro, and I want to help you avenge your brother."

Alejandro looked confused for a bit, but then his features softened. He understood. He grabbed my head and kissed me.

"I'll find another way."

"What other way? You told me that it's impossible to break into his house now, and I am telling you I know where they are in his office, and I can get them for you." He shut his eyes for a second, as if in pain, trying to keep his composure.

"I said no. That fucking asshole clearly will stop at nothing to satisfy his greed, including killing YOU! I will NOT put you in danger like that!"

"But—"

"This is not up for discussion, Amelia," he declared coldly.

I was frustrated, but I didn't know what to say. I didn't think I would be able to convince him—not right now. He wanted to protect me, which made my heart swell, but he was being overly protective. There was no other alternative. This wasn't over.

Seemingly satisfied by my silence, Alejandro left me alone. Dolores must have been waiting for an appropriate moment, because as soon as he left, she knocked. I rushed to put my nightgown on before letting her in, but by the smile on Dolores's face and her slightly red cheeks, I knew she knew Alejandro had spent the night, and frankly, I was too happy to hide it.

I quickly showered, put on a nice white, long, airy dress, which accentuated my breasts, with an audaciously low back. I felt the right amount of naked. My body was already in dire need of Alejandro's touch again, and I wanted to feel attractive, to entice his desire for me and feel his need burn through me again and again and again. I resisted any attempt of my brain to try to reason with me, to urge caution. I didn't want to.

I spent my entire life being cautious, tiptoeing around what made others happy, including losing part of who I was. I wanted this for me, for once, even if it would eventually end. I detangled my bouncy curls and let them loose, enjoying the slight highlights the sun had added.

I went straight to his room, but he wasn't there, so I went downstairs. I found him on the phone, pacing and shouting in Spanish. When he saw me, he hung up. He clearly didn't want me to listen to his conversation.

"Everything okay?"

"Yes, yes, it was just Mathias."

"That didn't sound like a very friendly conversation," I noted.

"He's getting impatient. Our arrangement doesn't really serve him anymore at this point."

"So he won't give you the video?"

"We'll see," answered Alejandro coldly, clearly choosing unilaterally to end the conversation.

I rolled my eyes but resisted the urge to say anything.

"Anything from Richard's end of things?" I insisted.

"No. As of this morning, he passed on the negotiations to George," said Alejandro with a hard voice.

"George? Oh god, he must be so worried."

I realized I hadn't given much thought to how he must have been feeling this whole time.

"Do you care?" asked Alejandro, lips pursed.

"Well, he is not responsible for Richard's sins," I explained. "And he's always been good to me," I admitted.

"Good to you?" said Alejandro with a cold laugh. "That's hardly a reason to date someone. And you dated him for, what, about two years?"

What was his problem?

"I don't have to explain my choices to you," I answered, my voice slightly elevated.

"You're right. You don't," he said menacingly, getting closer to me, "but I am asking you anyway."

I swallowed hard, a bit scared by the fire I saw on his face.

"He is a good man, that's all. Richard thought he was a perfect match for me, and frankly, it didn't matter much. He was a nice man and respected my space. That was all I needed. What do you want to hear exactly? That I was in love? What for? Why would anyone ever give another person such control over their life, their emotions?"

I felt a pinch in my heart that I didn't quite understand.

"I see."

He didn't seem satisfied by my answer, his face more serious than before.

"Do you still want on marrying him?" Why did it sound like a threat?

I didn't know how to answer. That was always the idea. It made sense, but now clearly a lot had changed.

"It was part of the plan," I admitted. "George and I make sense." At least we used to. Before Alejandro. Before my suspicions that George might be complicit in my stepfather's illicit activities.

"I thought you were stronger than to play it safe, Amelia. I've seen you—the real you—and you don't strike me as the kind of woman who would be satisfied with a placid relationship, who would settle for a cookie cutter placid life."

"How dare you!"

I was getting more and more frustrated by his comments. What did he want from me exactly? Was there even a perfect answer to those questions? My options had been laid out for me, and I had accepted them out of convenience.

Then, Alejandro had thrown all my safeguards away and turned my life upside down in just a few months. I didn't know what I wanted.

I knew I needed him more than I had ever needed anything in my life. But all those questions, they were scaring me.

I found myself missing the comfort and predictability I had found in my relationship with George. Not this all-consuming need for someone that I didn't even know how long I really had them for. And now what? He wanted my doubts exposed, my sorrows palpable? Why?

"What do you think is better?" I shouted, trying to deny my pain. "Someone like you? Someone who sleeps around without caring about the feelings of others? Why would I ever put myself at the mercy of someone else like that?"

Alejandro gave me a death stare that almost sent me running, but I held his gaze. This wasn't the time to show weakness. I didn't mean what I said, but I didn't know how to take it back. So, I panicked and doubled down.

"Is that really what you think of me?" His eyes flashed with anger, as his jaw ticked.

"Isn't it the truth?"

"Amelia," he said, cornering me at his office door, "not every man is Richard. You don't have to settle for someone just because they feel like the safe choice, the easy choice."

Those words hit me hard. I felt like someone had punched me in the stomach. How could he, with just one sentence, threaten to shatter years of self-preservation? How could I have been so transparent? I quickly moved away from him, walking as fast as I could, but he was right there on my heels, grabbing me, turning me around, forcing me to face him.

"Why are you doing this to me?!" I cried, unable to stop the tears. "What do you want from me?"

"I am not saying I haven't slept around. But why wouldn't I, as long as I make things clear and am honest?"

He looked at me with eagerness in his eyes. "But with you... you..." He let out a frustrated sigh. "I want you, just you. I fucking need you more than I have ever needed anyone. Don't you get that?" he said, grabbing my face. I squeezed my eyes shut and shook my head.

"I want you to be mine, all mine, body and soul, and I want you to let me in."

My knees started to weaken, but I remained stiff as I considered him dangerously close to making me lose my sanity, but he had no pity.

He kissed me, prying my lips open, plunging his tongue into my mouth, demanding that I let him in. I was pushing my arms against his chest, but a rush of desire and helplessness had already invaded my body.

Alejandro held me so close, possessively, while he cupped my face to kiss me. I was out of breath, his hunger quickly becoming mine, until I forgot all the objections I had. His rhythm slowed as his tongue reminded me of what was to come.

He lifted me from the floor and wrapped my legs around him. He grabbed my lips again as he carried me up the stairs to his room. My alarmed brain was still trying to tell me to stop it, to let go of him and lock myself in my bedroom, where I would be safe. But time stood still, and all I was aware of was him and his fingers leaving trails of fire on my skin.

Alejandro put me down and locked the door behind us. I stood there, my parted lips shaking, anticipating, waiting to feel alive again. Alejandro came back to me, holding me in a trance.

His gaze never leaving mine, he grabbed a condom from his nightstand and slid it on. He cradled my face and kissed me slowly but passionately, torturing every inch of my body with his touch. He pushed me gently onto the bed as he proceeded to rip his clothes off. I lifted my hands over my head, inviting him to get me naked. I groaned as I felt his girth against me, hot and firm. Alejandro slowly slid himself inside of me, and I moaned as he grunted.

He was going deep inside of me, but with a slow torturous rhythm that made me want to beg for more. He was sliding in and out of me, and yet, I already craved more of this, more of him.

"You are all I want, mi niña. You. Only you."

I wanted to say it back, but I couldn't, no matter how much my heart bled at my silence. I couldn't. Still, his words sent a shiver spreading all over my body, and his deep thrusting into me intensified. He was going faster and faster, the pressure in my belly growing.

Finally, he sent me to oblivion faster than I could process what his words were awakening in my soul.

CHAPTER 38

Alejandro

Neither of us was sleeping. We were just trying to regulate our breathing, unwilling to let the other go. I wanted us to stay just as we were, but I was running out of time.

"I won't be here tonight," I said, kissing her forehead as I finally broke the silence.

"Where are you going?" she asked, concern darkening her features, a frown on her face, her eyes shooting small daggers through me.

"I have to go to California."

"What for?" she asked, lifting her body a bit to face me.

"I have a few business meetings that I can no longer delay." It was so much more than that, and it was clear she knew it.

"Are you going to see Richard?"

I moved to a seated position, feeling my jaw tighten as the weight of it all wore me down. She looked terrified, and I hated that it was because of me. But I had no choice, not if I wanted to keep her safe.

"Yes," I admitted. "I told you I had approached him for an investment opportunity, and he has been trying to meet with me for a while now. I can't just disappear."

"You don't have to go!"

"I do. I need to get close to him. It's my only shot at getting those diamonds."

"He is dangerous, Alejandro! He tried to kill me, and I am the closest thing he has to a daughter. What do you think he will do to you if he finds out who you are?"

Her almond eyes were fully round now, her cheeks slightly flushed.

"Are you worried about me?" I asked.

At least there might be a silver lining with this trip. I didn't want to worry her but knowing that she was scared for me gave me hope.

"Ugh!"

She tried to get off the bed, but I wouldn't let her. Before she could get away, my arm was around her waist, forcing her to come closer to me. I lifted her head so she could face me, as she was avoiding my gaze.

"I will be fine, I promise. There is no reason for him to be suspicious, and I will resist the urge to punch that asshole to death for what he tried to do to you."

"I just don't want anything to happen to you," she whispered.

I wanted to reassure her, but I couldn't. I was going to socialize with a criminal, after all, with the man who murdered my brother. I kissed her, but there wasn't much I could do that would put her at ease. And I had to go. I had to try to do something, see what Richard was thinking, figure out a way to get those diamonds before Mathias lost his shit and tried to use Amelia again to get to Richard. I got up, showered, and started packing my luggage. Amelia just stayed there, in my bed, my sheets wrapped around her, watching my every move.

"I have to go," I said as I bent to kiss her goodbye, "but I will be back in three days."

She wrapped her arms around my neck, bringing me into a kiss. I held onto her as long as I could.

"Please be careful. Please. Come back to me. Come back alive," she whispered.

I took her lips in mine one more time, her words strengthening my resolve even more. I needed to protect her, at all costs. I wanted revenge, but I wanted her more.

"I promise I will be. All I want, Amelia, is to get back to you, put this whole nightmare behind us, and focus on you and me."

She let out a sigh, her body slightly shaking in my arms. God, all I wanted was to stay here with her, keep her safe. But I couldn't do that without getting rid of both Richard and Mathias, and those diamonds were the key. I kissed one more time before I left the room.

CHAPTER 39

Amelia

THE IDEA THAT RICHARD could hurt him was unbearable, but until he had the diamonds, I feared Alejandro would get more and more desperate, and eventually, Richard would figure out that something was wrong.

Alejandro got ready at the speed of light. His every movement increased my anxiety until he left. Lost in thought, I took a quick shower and put my clothes back on. I then proceeded to the kitchen to look for Dolores, but instead, what I found was Elena by the entry door, luggage in hand. I did my best to keep a stoic expression and hold back the shock and anger coursing through me, even as I felt my stomach drop.

"You are still here I see," she said.

"What are you doing here?" I asked coldly, unwilling to waste my time on pleasantries.

"I am waiting for Alejandro. We are going to California," she answered with a smile that made me want to smack her out of existence. "From the look on your face, you didn't know we had plans," she added, enjoying her victory, knowingly stabbing my heart with every word.

"He seems to have forgotten about you," I said with a smile, in an attempt to save face. "He already left."

"What?" Elena, disconcerted, fumbled through her purse until she found her phone. She placed a call, impatiently waiting for an answer.

"Alejandro," she said, her perverse smile back. "Donde estas? No se suponía que íbamos a ir al aeropuerto juntos? Ya, ok, entiendo… es que no sabía que tenías que ir tan temprano. Ok, not a problem. I have the later flight, so I'll see you at the hotel tonight." she emphasized her last words as she looked at me to make sure I heard and understood. I did.

"Just a misunderstanding," she explained as she hung up. "My flight is later than I thought."

"Or he's trying to avoid you. He did tell me you guys used to date, you know. It seems like you need to learn how to move on."

Elena laughed, but I could tell I had hit a nerve.

"I don't know what he told you, but I have known Alejandro since we were children, and we were always in love. Sure, he experiments with girls like you every now and then, but he always comes back to me. I dated David, but I always wanted Alejandro. After all, I am the one by his side, and sooner or later, he will realize that he has to get rid of you. You are a liability for him and a temporary adventure," she said, lifting her chin.

I struggled to keep my cool, the seed of doubt growing inside of me.

"What do you mean?"

"Alejandro tells me everything, sweetie. I know who you are."

"I don't know what you are talking about," I lied, my voice slightly shaken.

"You are the daughter of the man who killed his brother. How do you think Alejandro would ever be able to do more than amuse himself with you? How could he ever love you when the man who raised you murdered his brother in cold blood? That is all he thinks about when he is with you. Hurting you hurts Richard."

I had to find every strength I had in me not to pass out. She knew everything. Alejandro had confided everything to Elena. I was at a loss for words. Elena's words had erupted a volcano inside of me. I kept a stoic face, but inside I was drowning, and Elena was holding my head under water, that nauseating smile on her face, basking in her victory. I could only hide so much.

"Well, I see you are well informed."

"Yes, I am. I was even at your party with him when you got taken."

I felt like I had been hit by a bulldozer.

"If it was up to me, I wouldn't be here," I said. "I'd be back in California, and since you know everything, you know I am only here because he wants me here."

I was grasping onto straws, trying to hide my distress. I felt betrayed. Alejandro had embarrassed me, humiliated me to the lowest level. I was just a toy to him, a girl he enjoyed for the moment. And he had humiliated me by letting someone like Elena, a woman he clearly was attached to and respected, know exactly what place I occupied in his life.

"He is using you to get revenge, idiota. Why else would he sleep with you? He would never love an American girl like you, not when he has me, a true native, who grew up with him, who understands him."

Elena's audacity and vulgarity irritated me to no end, but everything she said made sense. Otherwise, why would Alejandro have told her so much? I wanted to disappear, run anywhere, as far as I could. But Elena was staring at me, measuring my reaction, and for the sake of my pride, I had to play the game, even if I was dying inside.

"I am not going to fall for your tricks. I know what game you are trying to play, and trust me, I am too much woman for you to ever be able to make me feel anything but sympathy for you. Have a safe trip."

I walked away, doing my best to control my trembling hands and the tears that threatened to embarrass me further. I went to Alejandro's office, the closest room I could find. I needed to be alone. I wouldn't let Elena see me cry. But as I got to the office, I realized that Elena wasn't ready to leave. She headed to the living room, leaving her luggage by the door. Great, that bitch was going to stay here. I was desperately hoping to find Dolores, but it was clear that she wasn't in the house.

I locked the door behind me, letting myself fall on the floor, my heart broken, feeling defeated. How could I have ever thought that Alejandro wouldn't feel some contempt toward me? Would he ever be able to not see me as an extension of Richard, in some shape or form, after what I told him?

I knew he was attracted to me. Perhaps he even cared for me. But I was never supposed to be with him. I was an accident that he dealt with as best as he could. I didn't know what to make of his words. I felt foolish and stupid for even daring to consider that Alejandro and I could be more than an unfortunate situation.

Whatever it was that we had, I was not sure it could survive when we got back to our real lives. I didn't see how we could possibly overcome all that had happened and whatever was to come for us. I didn't see a path to happiness. I just couldn't really understand what he would gain from how he treated me and saving my life.

Maybe it was all a game to him. Maybe he didn't believe what I had told him about my relationship with Richard. Maybe he did sleep with me for revenge. I wanted to hate him. But I also couldn't let anything happen to him.

If only I could leave this place and never come back. Give him his life back, keep him safe. Get as far as I could before I lost whatever shred of strength was left in me. Before I gave him my heart.

Elena would be willing to help me if it meant I would be away from Alejandro. The only way Alejandro would let me go is if he didn't have a choice and if he thought I would be safe.

Regardless of whether he wanted me to be his, it was clear that he didn't want to be responsible for my death either.

I had revealed that I knew where the diamonds were, but that only protected me against Mathias. I needed something else, to force Richard's hand, to force him to "rescue" me.

If this situation was a normal kidnapping, in which the abductors were asking for a reasonable ransom and, more importantly, if that information were to go public, Richard would have no choice but to make sure I came back alive. It would ruin him if people knew he didn't do everything he could to save me.

I contemplated my plan for what felt like an eternity. I wasn't afraid, but the idea that I would stop seeing Alejandro hurt me to no end. I only found strength in knowing that I was going to do what was best for him, and if I didn't leave, I would end up falling in love with someone who would never be able to truly love me back.

Determined, I got up, wiped my tears, rinsed my face with cold water, and marched to the living room. Elena was sitting on a chair by an outlet, charging her phone.

"I have a proposition for you," I announced as I slowly walked to her and sat on the couch.

I felt calm and collected, with the type of coldness and detachment I had when I was focused on a task, any feeling or doubt put on pause for later.

"Why would I do anything for you?" asked Elena, straightening herself to face me.

"Because you want me out of your way, and because I have a life and a fiancé to go back to."

Elena seemed a bit skeptical, but I gave her a slow, determined smile that seemed to put her at ease as she lifted her brow.

"In case you need some convincing... I don't know if Alejandro told you, but I know where the diamonds are."

Elena shifted uncomfortably in her chair. She clearly was surprised by this piece of information. I found strength in Elena's shocked face. I would manage to get her to do exactly what I wanted.

"Even though he knows that, he insists on keeping me here with him, to protect me. My stepfather, after all, doesn't care about me, and if he finds out that I know where the diamonds are, he will have me killed without a doubt. As a matter of fact, he already tried for less than that. He tried because he didn't want to deal with the issue. That's how Alejandro got shot. He was protecting me."

I felt a bit of guilt, seeing her start to get angry, but Elena deserved it. Plus, if she did help me, she would get what she wanted—Alejandro all to herself.

"But I know Richard more than anyone else. If it were to get out to the press that I was still alive, and that my kidnappers are asking for something like a mere two million dollars for my ransom—a relatively trivial amount for someone like Richard—he would have no choice but to pay it to guarantee my safe return."

"Mathias wouldn't allow that."

"He would if we made a deal with him. I know where the diamonds are, but Richard doesn't know that, and I am the only person who can get close enough to Richard to get them for Mathias.

"If Mathias guarantees Alejandro's safety and gives him the proof he needs against Richard to avenge his brother, I will get him the diamonds. I hate Richard as much as the next person. And since Richard tried to kill me, I think Mathias will believe my genuine hatred for that man. More important-ly, they are all in a bind right now. They have no choice."

"Why would you want to help Alejandro?" asked Elena, standing up.

"I already told you. I miss my life. I miss my freedom. And I have a fiancé waiting for me. Alejandro won't let me leave. This is the only way to force his hand, get me back safe to my home, and get Alejandro the video."

Elena remained silent for a few minutes, deciding what to do with that information. But I knew that if she wanted Alejandro as much as she seemed to, she would do anything to get me out of that house.

"Está bien. Where do we start?"

I explained my plan. Elena took a picture of me against a wall, holding that day's newspaper. The idea was to send a copy of that picture with a letter asking for two million US dollars to Richard and leak it to the press in California. Richard would have no choice but to pay, and Alejandro would have no choice but to return me to him. Simultaneously, Elena would tell Mathias about the plan and present it as Alejandro's plan so that Alejandro would not be harmed as a traitor.

Elena had provided me with both her and Mathias's cell phone numbers in case I ever ended up needing them. I wanted to slap Elena, but I had to admire her strength and dedication. She was efficient and embraced the idea with no fear. I recognized a bit of myself in her. I was jealous of her.

Alejandro had reminded me so many times about how different I was and how he saw me as a spoiled brat, even if he tried to take it back later. But with Elena, he could have it all—someone who had grown up with him, embedded in the same culture he had assumed for a while that I had rejected. I couldn't bear the thought, but I knew Elena was the perfect woman for him. Not me.

When Elena finally left, I went to the ocean, where I could cry and pretend that I wasn't. My heart was destroyed. I felt like I couldn't breathe and that I was dying inside. The burning sun on my skin temporarily distracted me from the pain that was threatening to take my life.

CHAPTER 40

Alejandro

ELENA WRAPPED HER ARM around mine as I took a deep breath and stepped into the devil's den. We had gone straight from the LAX airport to Richard's office. As far as he was concerned, I had been in Europe for business and had been back in town for a week.

This wasn't our first meeting, of course. I had carefully crafted and executed a plan for the better part of a year and presented myself to Richard as a rich trust fund guy with more money than I knew what to do with. He only respected what he perceived as old money. Richard eventually bit and asked me to consider investing in a new resort he wanted to open in Miami. As far as he knew, I was very interested but still needed to be convinced.

I had even met with him while Amelia was in my care. He had played the card of the concerned father quite well, crocodile tears rolled down his face many times. He'd almost fooled me, telling me how the kidnappers were refusing any of his offers to pay for his daughter's ransom.

He didn't know he was talking to her keeper. He didn't know I was on the phone the multiple times Mathias tried to reason with him. I knew the truth, the darkness in his soul.

Today's meeting was for him to show us the latest plans the architects had put together, see if that would whet my appetite. He always seemed in a much more pleasant mood when Elena was with me, his ego flattered by the smile of a woman, so as per usual, she came with me to this farce of a meeting.

Elena was the irresistible Mexican beauty I had fallen in love with, as far as he was concerned. She made me more human, more trustworthy. That didn't seem to bother him, though, probably because she fit his expectations as my arm candy. Someone who was there just to decorate the room.

The Hotel Estrellas offices were impressive. Everything was neat and clean, but it was all glass and white marble, devoid of any semblance of life. Everyone was dressed in black, conservative suits, and no one smiled. For an entertainment conglomerate, one would have thought their offices would be more welcoming. But no, they all walked like they had a stick up their ass.

I clenched my teeth when we finally stopped at Richard's floor. It had gotten easier over time to resist the urge to put a bullet between his eyes and to give him fake smiles, and shake his hand instead.

But today, it was as if I was going to be face to face with my brother's killer for the first time. I was a nervous wreck, and I wanted to strangle him slowly until I saw life leave his eyes. He had not only taken my brother, but he had tried to harm Amelia, his own family. I had to keep my composure. I had to get this fucking asshole to trust me, and I had to find a way to get access to those fucking diamonds so that Amelia could be safe.

Elena lightly rubbed her hand on my forearm when the door to Richard's office opened to allow room for the bulky, blue-eyed man who had destroyed my life as I knew it. Who had broken my mother permanently, who had taken my brother away.

The fucking irony of it all was that he was still Amelia's father, and I wouldn't have met her if this criminal hadn't taken my brother's life away. That was fucked up in so many ways.

"There you are!" he cheered as he grabbed my hand with a strong shake.

"How are you, dear?" he asked as he kissed Elena on both cheeks.

He always stared at her a bit too long for my liking. While I didn't love her, it didn't mean that I wanted her to have to subject herself to this creep ogling her.

But she, as usual, accepted him with grace and gave him her best smile as we got seated at the four-person table Richard kept in his office. A tall, skinny man dressed in brown tweed and wearing big round glasses was already seated.

"Josh, this is Rick, the investor I was telling you about."

"Nice to meet you," answered Josh as he timidly shook my hand. Rick was the name I used a part of the identity I invented to get close to Richard.

"How was Europe?" asked Richard as we sat down while he poured me a glass of whiskey and Elena a glass of wine.

He never asked; he always assumed he just knew what we must drink. I wasn't sure if it was a power move in his head or part of his desperate need to fit into a society that would always see him as the wannabe white Mexican with a slight accent he tried so hard to hide.

"Great. A successful trip, I would say. The Bacards have agreed to open the hotel on Lake Como in two years."

"Congratulations!" he said as he put his hand on my shoulder.

I flinched. It took everything in me to not remove it and break his fingers.

"Thank you, Richard."

The words felt bitter on my tongue.

He knew what that meant. It meant I had an in with one of the most prestigious French families in the world. It meant that, with me, he could belong in the aristocracy. And even if I had learned through Amelia that this man hated his own country, his own people, he didn't know I was from there.

As far as he was concerned, I was of Spanish descent and had lived most of my life in America. Fucking idiot. I did know the Bacards—they were one of my biggest clients—but the rest was all lies. And he would never get to meet them.

"What about you, Elena? Did you enjoy Italy?"

"I loved it! All the shopping I did!"

"I'm sure. You women and your purses," he joked, shaking his head toward me like we shared a secret.

"So," I interrupted, eager to get the meeting done, knowing that, by the end of it, I would agree to open the hotel with him no matter the cost, as a step closer to gaining his trust. "Show me what we have here. It's time for another hotel, don't you think?"

Richard beamed as he instructed the architect to walk me through the mock-ups. I barely listened, my mind drifting back to Amelia, wondering if she was okay, if she was nervous, if she was thinking of me. She didn't understand, but I would do anything it took to keep her safe and to keep her with me, including getting in bed with the devil himself—with my brother's killer.

CHAPTER 41

Amelia

I SPENT THE REST of the day and most of the next in a haze. I cried, slept, and cried some more. When Dolores came in the evening, I had done my best to put on a good front. I didn't want Dolores alerting Alejandro about anything.

In the afternoon, Elena called the house phone. I had feared that call all day, but Elena reported that everything had gone according to plan; the newspapers and certain local news channels had picked up the story.

I didn't bother to pretend I was happy. After all, the farce was over, and I had gotten what I wanted. I hung up the phone and went back to my room. It was really happening. I would leave Alejandro, never to come back.

The idea of never being with him again filled me with panic. I regretted what I had done a few times, but Elena's words replayed in my head like a broken record. And I knew I had done the right thing, found a way to help him, to give him his life back. The only act that gave me a channel to express my frustration was writing in my makeshift journal.

The sun was setting when I got startled by the front door banging loudly against the door frame.

"Amelia! Amelia!"

My heart dropped to my feet when I heard Alejandro calling my name. He sounded furious and almost dangerous. I could also hear another voice, but Alejandro was shouting.

With trembling hands, I slowly opened my bedroom door and got a bit closer to the staircase to see what was going on. Alejandro was in the foyer, in a dark-gray suit, his face looking like he was about to murder someone. Elena was there, crying, begging him to calm down, but all he did was berate her.

"Por favor, mi amor. I did this for you!"

"You had no right! Get out! Get the fuck out of my house!"

"Lo hice por nosotros!"

"I don't know what you wanted to accomplish here, pero ya te lo dije un million de veces, no hay nada entre tu y yo!"

Alejandro grabbed her arm and took her to the door, pushing her outside. Elena did not dare to continue knocking after Alejandro kicked her out. When Alejandro got back to the foyer, he looked up toward me. I stared into pure madness. Alejandro looked like he was capable of the most heinous revenge in that moment.

I panicked and ran back to my room. Before I could close the door, he was there. I put all my weight on the door, but he pushed it open so violently I almost fell as I took some steps back. Alejandro slammed the door so loudly I thought I felt the ground shake.

He closed the distance between us in a second, his jaw tight, his eyes dark as night, his lips curled back in fury. He just stood there, looking down at me, breathing heavily, hurting me with just the darkness in his eyes. Alejandro grabbed the lamp that was behind me and threw it against the wall, the ceramic shattering everywhere. I let out a scream.

"Why, Amelia?! Why did you do this?!"

The words were missing. I had no idea what to say. I had a knot in my throat. Even if I wanted to, there was no way to say a word without struggling to breathe.

Alejandro frowned and took a step back.

"Do you despise me so much that you would put your life in danger like this just to get away from me?"

God, of course I didn't despise him. But what could I possibly say after what I had done?

"Answer me!" he shouted as he grabbed me by both arms. "Why would you do something so stupid?!" he insisted as he shook me.

"Stop! You're hurting me!" Alejandro immediately let me go.

There was nothing I could do to stop the tears from coming.

"I'm not letting you do this. I am NOT giving you to him!" He shouted through gritted teeth.

"You have to!" I pleaded, finding a bit of strength to put some sense into him. "There is no other way for you to get the diamonds! There is no other way for this to end well for all of us!"

"You're wrong!"

"You really think you can get so close to Richard that he would, what, just hand them to you? Come on! He won't hurt me, not after everyone knows that I am alive and that all he has to do is pay two million dollars. And Mathias won't hurt me, because I can get him the diamonds. Can't you see? It's the only way out of this fucking mess! You can finally get your revenge!"

"Fuck my revenge, Amelia! Fuck the diamonds! I don't care about any of it anymore. Can't you see that?"

His words shook me to my core, but there was no going back.

"This was always going to end poorly, Alejandro," I said as I wiped the tears off my face. "This is the safest way, and frankly, it's the only way. Both our lives are on pause, and they have been for months now."

"I see. So, all this is about George, is that it? You miss him so much that you'd risk your life like this?" he mocked coldly.

"It's about everything! Whatever this is! It was bound to end! I get to go back to my life, and you get to go back to yours—with Elena!"

"I don't know what she told you, but Elena has nothing to do with this!"

"How does she not? You told her everything!" I screamed, my trembling voice betraying me. "She knows about all of this, about why I'm here. She's been involved in this the whole time, with you!"

"I needed her help! I needed her help to trick Richard, to get him to believe in my intentions, that's all!"

"None of this matters!" I said, walking away from him. "You know I'm right. This is the only option, and it's not your decision anymore."

A lump was forming in my throat. I felt him walk to me, stopping right behind me.

I closed my eyes, anticipating his touch, desperately wanting him to grab me, to tell me everything was going to be okay, to make love to me and wipe my tears away. But he passed by me and left the room. I went straight to bed feeling numb and understanding for the first time in my life what it was like to lose the only man I had ever fallen in love with. I could no longer hide that fact.

CHAPTER 42

Amelia

ALL I WANTED TO do was sleep, even with the sun shining brightly through the window. Dolores kept trying to convince me to eat, but even that seemed like a chore. Once I felt up to showering, I went through the motions and then returned to my bed. Everything hurt a lot less when I was in the comfort of my safe space.

My mind kept going back to the fight with Alejandro. How I finally realized just how far I'd fallen for him. And just the thought that I would never see him again made it hard to breathe. Now that I knew what it felt like to have someone else's life matter more than my own, I knew I would never be able to be happy with George. And now, because of events I had initiated, I wouldn't be with Alejandro anymore either.

Dolores had told me that Alejandro wasn't home. He was probably trying to find a solution to what I had done, but even if part of me hoped that he did, my plan was bulletproof. Now that I couldn't deny that I was in love with him, there was nothing I wouldn't do to help him, even if it meant losing him.

It was late in the evening when Alejandro came back. I was sitting on my patio, trying to let the beautiful sunset distract me from my sorrows. I had decided to wear a very flattering but comfortable long, green dress with a very low back. Alejandro simply sat next to me, not saying a word, staring at the ocean.

He was avoiding my gaze, but I couldn't stop staring at him, admiring his gray suit and dark-blue shirt, paying attention to every detail of him, burning him in my memory.

We remained like that in silence as Dolores walked in. She could feel the tension in the air as she set various fish dishes, tapas-style, on the coffee table between us. I wasn't very hungry, but I ate anyway, just to have something to distract me from the nervous knot in my back. Alejandro had been tortuously silent, and it was getting to me.

"Where were you all day?" Not only had I broken the silence, but I couldn't even pretend not to care anymore, annoyed at myself.

"Trying to fix this mess," he answered coldly, slowly turning toward me. "But you won, Amelia. Tomorrow, I am taking you to Richard."

Alejandro got up, his back turned to me. I wanted to go to him, but my feet were glued to the ground.

"What do you mean?"

"Your plan worked. There is no convincing Mathias now. He wants you to go back home and get him the diamonds. So tomorrow evening, I will drive you to an abandoned factory by the border. Richard will meet us there."

"But is this safe? What if things turn out wrong?"

"They won't. I will have backup. I will make sure you are okay and that he doesn't try to hurt you again."

"Isn't tomorrow a little soon? I thought—"

"You thought what?" he asked brusquely, turning around to face me. "You got what you wanted, didn't you?"

Alejandro closed the distance between us, standing in front of me with his jaw clenched. I didn't know what to say. It was all becoming too real.

Yes, I had gotten what I wanted, but it was far off from what I needed. He shook his head and stared at the floor. I couldn't talk, my heart was bleeding, I wanted him to hold me, but I was stuck in place. He started heading towards the door but changed his mind and walked back to me.

"You didn't leave."

"What?"

He looked up at me, the intensity in his eyes threatening to consume me.

"When we came here. You didn't leave. You had my phone, you had my keys, hell, you even had cash. You could have left, but you didn't. You stayed with me. You took care of me, nursed me back to life. Why did you? Why didn't you leave me here?"

"I... I don't know."

My throat burned with the tears I was fighting too hard to keep from showing.

"You don't know?" he pushed, as he grabbed my arm. "You had your freedom at the tip of your fingers, Amelia. But you chose to stay. You chose us. You. Chose. Me."

"Alejandro, please, don't. It's too late."

I felt defeated. He was pushing me to look inwards, to admit something to him. To admit what shouldn't be. I couldn't bring myself to do it. It would ruin everything.

He brusquely let go my arm and took a step back, and shook his head to himself.

"Be ready by five p.m.," he said as he quickly left the room.

I sat down. I couldn't believe it all had happened so fast. I had hoped I would have had a few more days to savor every last minute with Alejandro before this had to end. I wiped the tears off my face.

I was conflicted.

Part of me regretted what I had done, and I felt guilty, like I had betrayed Alejandro. But I was doing this for him. He was caught in an impossible situation, a sort of limbo state, and I was caught in it with him. This had to end somehow so we could both move on with our lives. I also did it for my own good.

The longer I stayed with him, the more I would love him and not want to leave him. The harder my heart would break when we eventually went our separate ways. There was no point in delaying the inevitable.

I got up, knowing what I wanted to do, not caring about any consequences. We had one last night together after all. I was going to make the best of it.

I headed to Alejandro's room. I didn't knock. He was standing by his bed, wearing his dark-blue silk pajamas, shirt open. He was staring at me, confused and frowning. I walked straight to him, pressed my palms to each side of his face, and pulled him to me for a kiss.

Alejandro kissed me but removed my fingers from his face, holding me at a distance while he took a good look at me. My cheeks flushed, feeling the weight of what felt like rejection, but he was not letting me go, still holding my hands, an inquisitive look on his face.

"Tell me what you need," he asked between shallow breaths, showing me he needed me as much as I needed him.

So I bit my lip and took a risk.

"I want you to make love to me tonight."

Alejandro muttered something under his breath and pulled me back to him, kissing me, while his hands pulled my dress above my head, leading me to the bed.

I could not get enough of his lips, his hands roaming every inch of my body, my fingers exploring his hair and every muscle in his back. I had a dire need to at least show him how I felt. He removed my bra and grabbed my nipples between his lips, as my hand formed a fist around the sheets.

He licked and sucked my body all the way down to between my legs.

"Alejandro…"

"I need to taste you" he said as he removed my underwear.

I was trembling in anticipation. Alejandro parted my lips and dived right in. My body arched as he deliciously twirled my clit with his tongue. The sensation was so intense I tried to pull back, but his hands held my legs in place around his head.

"Oh god!" I screamed, panting, my fingers lost in his hair.

But Alejandro had no mercy and continued to run his tongue in circles. He groaned against my pussy, and I felt the vibrations inside of me.

Alejandro licked and sucked over and over again. I had never felt anything more delicious in my entire life.

He moved his hands to my breasts, rubbing my nipples between his fingers, multiplying the intensity of what I felt ten folds.

"Alejandro!" My toes curled and my legs shook as I writhed in delicious torture.

I didn't know what to do with myself, I felt so good, so unbelievably high. I had lost all notion of time and space.

I was oblivious to the world until a high pitch left my throat as every single nerve in my body vibrated, and I came for what felt like an eternity.

Alejandro continued to lick me lazily, driving me down back to earth. I slowly opened my eyes, as he got up.

"You're so beautiful when you come for me" he said as he took his pants off, his dark gaze drawing every inch of my body.

I still wanted more. I still needed him inside of me with urgency.

As he got back on the bed, I climbed on top of him.

"I want to feel you, I don't want anything between us" he stated, his voice hoarse.

I shook my head, I also wanted to feel him and only him, skin to skin.

Alejandro seemed surprised, but he groaned and grabbed my hips to move me against him. He slid inside of me as I let out a sigh.

"Fuck!" he growled under his breath as my movements accelerated.

He grazed my breast with his hand, bringing my nipple to his hungry mouth. I moaned a plea, pleasure coursing through me, a prickling sensation running down my body as he licked and sucked. He brought his thumb between us, rubbing my sore clit, as he moved to sucking on my other breast at the same rhythm he rubbed me.

"Oh, Alejandro!"

"I know, mi niña."

He grabbed my hips, pulling me closer, his other hand wrapping around my head, bringing my forehead to his, both of our mouths open, panting.

I reveled in seeing all his muscles contracted, his face contorted, the silence between us louder than words.

I didn't know how long I rode him like that in silence for. There was nothing else in the world that mattered other than the two of us in that moment.

I felt a current rise in me again, taking me closer to the edge.

I could tell he was as close as I was, his fingers digging further into my skin.

"I am not giving up on this, you hear me? I am not giving up on us. I am NOT losing you. I know you feel the same way."

His words shattered my heart into a million little pieces, tears escaping and rolling down my face as Alejandro kissed the trails away. My heart exploded, wanting to tell him those words. But as he started pushing me down on him more aggressively, penetrating me deeper, I rode him until he drove me to madness.

I woke up to Alejandro facing me on the bed and carefully removing my hair from my face. After the night we spent together and the stark contrast with what was to come, I wanted to tell him so many things, but nothing really felt right.

"I am going to have to leave today," Alejandro said. "And I will be back when it's time to go."

My throat started closing again as I restrained my tears.

"Are you sure it's safe for you?"

"Yes, I won't be alone. In any event, I want to be there. I don't trust Richard. I want you to be safe."

"What do we do after that?"

"Well, you will have my phone. You let me know when you have the diamonds, and we will meet for you to give them to me. Mathias insists on meeting with us as well."

"So... I will see you again?" I bit my lips, concerned edging around my heart.

"I am not letting you do this by yourself, Amelia. And as far as Richard is concerned, I am Rick Hernández, a man with a lot of money to invest, so he won't mind seeing me around as I feign interest in his company. He already invited me to a private event at your house soon."

"I can't believe he is organizing parties while I am technically kidnapped."

"Oh, he played his cards right. He said you wouldn't want him to act any differently and cancel, and he needed to continue living and be strong—for you, of course. Fucker."

I shook my head in disdain. I would feel no regret taking those diamonds away from Richard.

"Once you hand me the diamonds, all of this will end, and you can go back to living the life I took you away from," said Alejandro, jaw tightened, his voice deeper than usual. "If that's what you really want." His eyes darkened, searching mine.

"I didn't do this to get away from you," I explained in an impulse to let him know. "This is just the only way Mathias will give you the video you need against Richard. We both know our... situation could not continue as it was forever."

"You should have let me handle it. I could have found a different way."

"Like what?"

"I don't know," he said, frustrated as he got up. "But this arrangement puts you in danger, and I would have preferred to avoid that at all costs, even if that meant... It doesn't matter anymore."

I got off the bed and went to my room as Alejandro went to the bathroom. I desperately wanted him to finish his thought, as I could tell he had taken my decision quite personally. I wanted to explain, but that would mean admitting to him that I loved him, putting myself at risk of getting hurt. I didn't know if he was, or would ever be, ready for that.

CHAPTER 43

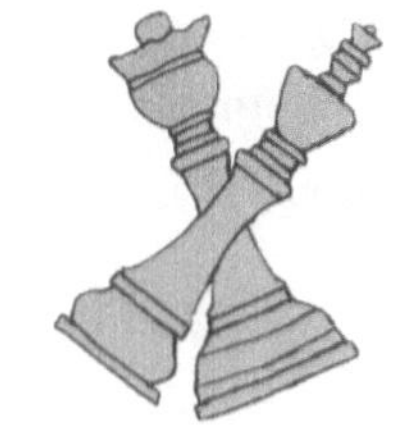

Alejandro

I DIDN'T WANT TO leave her. But I had just a few hours to finalize the plan. Yesterday, when Richard had agreed on where to meet him for the exchange, my guys and I, as well as Mathias and his team, had gone to scope out the grounds, see where we would come in from and decide where we would position shooters to make sure we were covered. We didn't trust Richard when he vowed for a peaceful exchange. That wasn't his style.

I met the men I had hired, and we spent hours planning in a hotel room. I then headed to Mathias's shop. It was an unassuming location, one story, a bit dingy, with jewelry cabinets and disinterested workers. The place had always been mostly empty every time I had gone.

Mathias was sitting behind his dark-oak desk, smoking what I imagined was his twentieth cigarette of the day. He wasn't a man that gave the impression of being a criminal. He dressed in business-casual clothing and had a warm smile.

Richard had a similar look to him. Many took him for a kind man, but I knew better. I knew the darkness that laid behind his eyes. I saw the deep lines across his forehead that so many took for worry lines. I saw the fire in his eyes when he wanted something.

Thankfully, Mathias and I had grown to find common ground in our mutual hatred for Richard. Mathias also realized that, although I wasn't part of his world, I had all the experience needed to manage it and all the funds required to exert power when needed. And he respected that.

"How did it go?"

"Good, all set on my end. The teams are coordinating to make sure we are covered on the grounds tomorrow."

"Great. Are you coming?"

"I am." Mathias sighed.

"You know, you don't have to. I can make sure the exchange is made with minimal casualties. I need her alive as well."

"No. I get that, but there is no way in hell I'm not going. She is staying by my side until the very last minute."

Mathias hesitated and shook his head.

"You don't think he will recognize you?"

"I don't intend to get close."

"Yes, but who knows what could happen?" He pushed.

"If I get exposed, I'll deal with it. But she's either going with me, or the deal is off."

"Alejandro, mira, I'm the one who calls the shots here."

"Not when it comes to Amelia's safety you don't. I thought I had made that clear." We stared at each other in silence for a while.

"Fine," said Mathias as he shook his head. He walked to the back of the room and poured us each a glass of scotch. We drank them in silence, preparing for what was to come.

Once we agreed on the final details, I drove back as fast as I could to the beach house, the sun already setting. We didn't have a lot of time.

I arranged for Amelia and Richard to be followed once she was with him. I also planned on giving her back the bracelet that broke when she fell in the pool. I'd had it fixed, but I also had someone add a tracker in it so I would know where she was at all times.

The thought that I had to hand her back to this fucking criminal, that I had to let her go with him, drove me fucking nuts. I hit the steering wheel with my fist as hard as I could to take the pain away.

"Fuck!" I howled, feeling impotent.

It had taken everything I had in me to stay calm when I saw the news on my phone while on the plane ride back to Mexico the other day. Amelia had somehow convinced Elena to help her let the world know she was still alive, forcing Richard's hand. It was a brilliant idea. But it broke me. I didn't know what to make of it.

Amelia had set it all up—that I knew. Elena was great, but this ten-step process had Amelia's name written all over it. Neither of them denied it either.

It wrecked me, thinking that, after all that we shared, it had been so easy for her to throw it all away.

Our time together hadn't been enough to make her walk away from her previous life—a life without me, without us.

I couldn't blame her. After all, she spent months thinking I was a criminal, while I had more time to see the real her, to fall for her. And now she was slipping through my fingers. I was grasping onto what I could, but I was failing.

What gave me a sliver of hope were those tears I couldn't handle. It was the fact that she didn't escape when she had the chance. It was the way she had looked at me. The way she asked me to make love to her last night. The way she rode me like she wanted to engrave every second of us in her brain.

I wasn't going to give up, not now that I knew what it was to live. Life without her would be a death sentence. I had no interest in that.

This mess had to end, she wasn't wrong in that. But that didn't mean there would be an end to us. This would be a new beginning—with Richard behind bars and Amelia free. I just had to make sure that when she got her life together, she still wanted me to be in it.

CHAPTER 44

Amelia

DOLORES AND I ANXIOUSLY waited for Alejandro to come back. I wore the most comfortable clothes I could find—a pair of light-blue jeans, comfortable lace-less sneakers, a white t-shirt, and a gray sweater. I washed and dried my hair without too much care and put no makeup on. I didn't want to raise suspicions by looking too put-together. I needed to play the victim part.

I hid the ring in my pocket. I stored the paper on which I had written Alejandro's, Mathias's, Elena's, and Dolores's phone numbers.

I reminisced on the last conversation between Alejandro and Elena that I overheard. I hadn't meant for Elena to pay for the consequences of my plan, but I couldn't help the hint of a smile drawing on the right side of my lips when I recalled Alejandro telling her they were not together, followed by a pinch of guilt, thinking of Elena's pain.

When Alejandro finally got back home, he didn't come in. He waited in the car for me to come out. It was all feeling like a dream—no, a nightmare—from which I desperately wanted to wake up.

I yearned for the time before I decided to be so clever and put an end to things. But there was no going back. Dolores walked me to the door slowly. She suggested I take some clothes with me, but of course, that wouldn't make a lot of sense. I was supposed to have been in that terrible room in the first house, being treated miserably this whole time. Generally, kidnapped people didn't get a whole closet of clothes given to them that they got to keep. I wanted to tell Dolores that it was okay, that she would give me the luggage she had prepared when we saw each other again, but I didn't think that would happen.

"Cuidate mucho," sobbed Dolores as she hugged me in front of the door. I did my best to not let tears roll out of my very wet eyes.

"Thank you for everything," I whispered before letting go. I silently got in the front seat. He looked concerned and very focused, and he avoided my gaze.

"We will meet with some of my men when we get closer to the meeting point. You will then have to get in the back with two of them next to you. We are going to an abandoned area with barely any structures left standing. Richard wanted to make sure there was nowhere to hide. He will ask to see you from a distance before he leaves the money. Then you will be allowed to walk to him as we take the bag."

"I assume he will bring some people with him as well?"

"Yes, the rule is that four people show up on each side, but I will have more of my men close if things take a turn."

We continued the rest of the drive in silence. I couldn't bear to see Alejandro's face so distorted with concern and anger, but every time I tried to talk, he gave me a cold answer, clearly not in the mood. If that was how he wanted to spend our last time together, then so be it, I thought, ignoring the hot pain I felt searing in my stomach.

After driving for an hour, Alejandro suddenly pulled the car to the right side of the street, his hands strongly wrapped around the steering wheel, his profile looking sexy and menacing at the same time. He pulled something from his pocket and handed it to me.

"Is that... is that my bracelet?"

"Yes, I had it fixed."

"Thank you."

I put it back around my wrist, hiding it under my sweater. My throat closed a little bit. That was very thoughtful of him.

Alejandro and I sat in silence for a few minutes. He shook his head, seemingly wanting to say something. Instead, he started the car back up and drove at the speed of light.

As Alejandro had explained, after a couple hours, we met with his team. I sat in the back, and two of his men sat on either side of me, with their masks on, and one more in the front seat. Finally, as we got closer to the exchange location, Alejandro stopped.

He looked at me through his rearview mirror. I felt like he was saying goodbye.

Without a word, he put his mask on as one of them put a bag over my head.

I let the tears that were haunting me roll down my face in the darkness.

After another thirty minutes, the car came to a stop. My heart started to beat faster as a hand landed on my arm, prompting me to get out of the car. Another person grabbed my other arm, and we started walking.

"Aqui la ve!" screamed the person to my right. "Ahora traiganos el dinero!"

I knew that Alejandro was the man on my left. I could smell him, feel his proximity to me. I desperately wanted to lean on him, tell him that I had changed my mind, beg him to end this and take me back to his home. We could just live there. I could change my name, get a job there, whatever it took so I could stay with him.

I was starting to reach for his hand when I felt the bag on my head suddenly being lifted off. It took me a few seconds to understand what was going on as my eyes were trying to adjust to the dark. I could see a couple black cars in front of me with four human shapes standing there, one holding a bag.

I thought I saw Richard, but it wasn't very easy to see facial features with barely any light in this dark location. I could see that we were in the middle of nowhere, with some remnants of what used to be a house on my left. I looked up to Alejandro. He was avoiding my gaze, staring at my stepfather instead, as one of his men was slowly walking to a pillar in between us to put the money down.

"Don't be afraid," whispered Alejandro as he turned to look at me.

I could only see his eyes—those eyes that I now would never wake up next to.

"I don't want to go," I whispered back.

Alejandro shook his head.

"I don't want you to, but it's too late. I can't risk your life by backtracking with his men here. I promise, I will see you again, even if it's the last thing I do." His words sent shivers down my spine.

The man on my right pulled me away, a gun pointed at my head, as Alejandro suddenly let go of his grasp on me. I continued to look back as I saw Alejandro also grab his gun and point it straight at my stepfather. I was forced to look forward so I didn't fall. The exchange was being made. The man stopped halfway as the money was put down.

"Walk to them very slowly," he ordered, "or I will shoot."

I felt like I was having an out-of-body experience. My emotions were on pause, far away, and I was just automatically going through the motions.

I made my way cautiously toward Richard and his men as the gun was still pointed at me, while another of Alejandro's or Mathias's men headed for the money.

After what felt like an eternal journey, I finally got to Richard, who was looking at me with tears in his eyes. He grabbed me as I turned around to confirm Alejandro was okay.

From what I could see, all three men were already standing by their car, with Alejandro still standing outside, looking my way, his gun still in his hand. Richard rushed me inside the back of the car and got in next to me as two of his men got in the front. Before I could digest what was going on, the car started speeding away.

I screamed as I heard three gunshots go off.

I jerked around to peer to through the back window, but it was hard to tell what had happened, who had shot. I could see the other men Richard had brought with him shooting at Alejandro's car. Someone on Alejandro's team was on the ground, clearly hurt, but the car was already too far for me to be able to tell if it was Alejandro.

Richard pulled me and forced me to sit low as I heard more shots.

I screamed again and started crying, praying for Alejandro to be alive and unharmed.

The drive home was silent. I feigned sleep the whole way. I did not have the strength to pretend to be happy to be reunited with Richard. He had hugged me and told me how relieved he was that I was safe and finally free. I had thanked him and returned his hug, but then I had claimed to be tired and avoided any other conversation.

I had no idea how long we had driven until we got across the border, then eventually through the main gate of Richard's house. We made it back to California at last.

"You are finally home," said Richard, grabbing my hand.

"I am so happy to be here," I mustered, forcing my most innocent smile. "Thank you, Richard. Thank you for rescuing me."

"Of course! I know we have not always been on the best of terms, but you are my daughter."

I resisted the urge to slap him. His hypocrisy was remarkable. The man deserved an Oscar. I smiled when I saw my nanny, in her maid uniform, run down the stairs to the car.

I hugged her with the little strength I felt, and we started crying.

"I am so happy to see you, my baby!" said Martha as she wiped the tears from my face.

"Me too, Nana. I missed you so much!"

Martha took me into her arms, completely ignoring Richard, and guided me to my bedroom as she ordered another one of the maids to bring food to the room. I was relieved to get away from Richard. I was overwhelmed with pain and resentment, and I could snap at him anytime and blow the plan.

All I could think about was whether Alejandro was okay, fear threatening to make me lose my mind and start screaming. But I couldn't crack—not yet. Both of our safety depended on how I handled the next couple days.

Martha was a tall, full woman with kind, golden-brown eyes and a deter-mined, sharp nose, who was always neat and clean and never worked without her light-blue maid uniform. She almost always wore her brown wavy hair in a bun—to keep her strands from slowing her down, as she had explained when I had inquired.

"Do you want to take a bath?" she asked as we sat on the corner of the bed.

"Yes," I said, anxious to avoid any sort of conversation about the abduc-tion.

It was always very hard for me to lie to Martha, but for her own sake, I had to try. Martha quickly got up to go run me a bath. I eventually followed her in and waited for her to leave before going back to the room and finding my cell phone. Martha had taken it out of the bag I left behind the night of the party and had kept it charged for me. I almost cried with happiness.

Hands shaking, I emptied my pockets. I put the ring on my dresser and opened the piece of paper with all the phone numbers that I had carefully folded and shoved in my jeans pocket. I called Alejandro. When I heard his voice, my knees got weak, and I had to sit back on the bed.

"Alejandro? Are you okay?"

"Amelia, I was worried sick. Are you okay?"

"Yes, I'm in the house, in my bedroom. You didn't get shot?"

"No, one of my men did, but he is okay. Richard didn't do anything to you?"

"No, I'm fine. I'm good. I just... I just wanted to make sure you were okay. I thought you got shot... I thought..."

"I'm okay, I promise." We stayed silent for a couple of seconds. "Listen," started Alejandro, "we need to talk." He paused. "When I saw you walk away from me, I..."

I was startled when I heard a knock on the door. George walked in before I could say anything.

"I'm so happy to see you," he said as he sprinted to me.

"George!" I said, more startled than happy. "I have to go," I whispered as I quickly hung up the phone.

George grabbed me and kissed me like never before. I should have felt joy, peace, but I felt nothing.

"I've missed you so much. I am so happy you are okay!"

"I am." Ashamed, I didn't know where to look.

"Did they do anything to you?"

"No, no, they didn't. I'm fine. I am, but I'd rather not talk about it."

"Of course. I understand."

I got saved from what promised to be an awkward conversation when Martha returned. She insisted that George let me rest. Martha never really cared for George. She always saw him as a reminder that Richard ruled over my existence. She said I was settling rather than living my life. And I always knew she was right. I was just more comfortable admitting it to myself now. I was eternally grateful. I wasn't ready to deal with George or the guilt I felt.

"Now you go take that bath I prepared for you. You can talk to George later," she ordered as she closed the door behind him.

I obeyed, and when Martha left, I started undressing myself. I welcomed the smell of Eucalyptus and mint that was filling up the air and the hot water that was slowly relaxing my muscles in the bath. I took a few slow and deep breaths, hoping that the relaxing smell would slow down my heartbeat. It felt weird to be back.

My mind was spinning, taking me back to just last night. To a time when I felt safe, felt cared for, felt whole. And how over the course of a few months, I came to find comfort in my new life. This place no longer felt like home to me.

I also thought about Alejandro. How much I missed him and wanted to be in his arms. And with those thoughts, George came to mind. What would I tell him? I had technically cheated on him, and I felt awful.

But I now knew, even if I couldn't be with the man I loved, I could not marry a man I didn't want to be with and fake a happy marriage for the rest of my life. It would be impossible now, after Alejandro had created a thirst for more in me, both physically and emotionally.

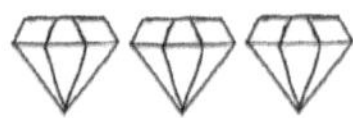

It was already very late in the night when I finally got to bed, imagining Alejandro holding me as I fell asleep.

CHAPTER 45

Amelia

Waking up in my bedroom after all the time I was away felt a bit surreal. I was confused for the first few minutes. As the memories started pouring back in, I felt a surge of anxiety rise through me. It was time to put my best acting skills in place. I was to reach out to Alejandro once I got the diamonds so we could meet and I could give them to him. The idea that I would get to see him again filled me with joy and excitement.

Alejandro and I had never really discussed what we were or what we would be—if anything—once he had the diamonds. I figured he would stay with Elena, get his revenge, and move on with his life, without me in the picture. But part of me hoped he would ask me to be with him. He'd alluded to that a couple of times, and he had saved my life, after all. Surely he cared for me. But did he? Or was that just guilt he felt that he had put an innocent life in danger in his quest for vengeance? Would he break my heart?

I impatiently looked for something to wear in my closet, still lost in my thoughts. Alejandro could never be mine. Our lives were on two different tracks. It just wouldn't work out.

But I also couldn't ignore the memories of the way he held me, the way he touched me, calling me "mi niña." In those moments, I could have sworn...

The idea of being with him scared me, though, with the way I felt for him. Having another person's will take over me and absorb me wasn't part of my plan. That was why I had dated George. He felt safe because he didn't cause a storm to rise up inside of me with just one look. The fact that I didn't love him meant he had no control over me. But I would give my life for Alejandro.

I put on a pair of dark-blue jeans and a simple pink t-shirt. I finally found the courage to go downstairs, joining Richard in the dining room for breakfast. I was hoping that he would be absent, but there he was, wearing jeans and a gray dress shirt, reading the newspaper while he enjoyed his coffee, not a frown of worry on his face.

"Hello," I said as I grabbed my usual chair to his right.

"Hi! You're awake! Did you sleep well?"

"I did, thanks."

"I'm glad. How do you feel? George said you seemed...distant yesterday."

I rolled my eyes. "I'm sorry. Did he expect smiles and giggles?"

"I guess that was a bit... insensitive. I'm sorry. I imagine it wasn't the most pleasant time for you for these past few months."

"No, it wasn't," I responded between my teeth, avoiding his gaze as much as I could. "Why did you take so long to come for me?" I asked, honestly hurt at his lack of concern for me.

"It wasn't like that," he explained. "These people, these criminals, they wanted everything. They made the negotiations for your safety hard, Amelia. You can ask George. We tried everything to get you here. You should be thankful that I risked my life and paid a large sum for your return."

I wanted to punch him, but instead, I focused on forcing myself to eat the lovely fruit bowl Martha had put there for me, even if the fruit tasted sour in my mouth.

"I know you tried your best."

I lied. I needed him to think I was as naive as before. It wouldn't be wise to let him know how livid and heartbroken I was. I needed his full trust, and I frankly wondered if he had doubts about how my abduction really was, considering I had spent a few months away. After all, I came home with no bruises, showered, and in clean clothes.

"They would have hurt me if it wasn't for you making sure that I was in one piece. I think they knew you would make them pay if they touched me or hurt me. Thank you, Richard. I won't forget what you did for me, that you gave your money away to save my life," I said, angry tears shining in my eyes.

"You are welcome, child," he said, grabbing my hand, a satisfied smile on his face.

I resisted the urge to pull my hand away. Instead, I gave him the most thankful and loving smile I could muster. I wanted to yell, "Murderer!" at him, but that wouldn't help.

"Hey, honey," a voice said from behind me.

When I turned around, George was there with Iris, Chloe, and Keisha. Tears ran down my face as I rushed into the arms of my friends. It felt so good to wrap my arms around them. I reluctantly left their embrace to hug George, who kissed me.

"I am so happy you are okay! I was worried sick. I can't believe those savages kept you for so long!" said Iris in her usual high-pitched voice, wiping tears of happiness off her face.

"I can't believe you were gone for so long," whispered Chloe, the strongest of us, unable to stop the tears from rolling down her face.

Keisha hugged me again in silence, her shoulders shaking. I wanted to grab them by the hands, go to my room, and tell them everything, but that might put their lives in danger, and that would force me to admit out loud that meeting Alejandro had changed everything for me.

"I will be working from my office," said Richard as he got up. "Oh, I almost forgot, Amelia, on Friday, I am hosting a small dinner here to celebrate your return."

"That's tomorrow!" I protested, horrified at his insensitivity.

"Yes, but I can't really cancel. I have a very important investor coming, so it's a two for one."

I wanted to scream, the lump in my throat threatening to choke me. Iris looked at Richard, her mouth open, Chloe muttered something under her breath, and Keisha shook her head, shocked by his indifference. George, on the other hand, was avoiding my gaze, refusing to be on my side—as usual.

"Don't you think it's way too early for that, Richard? I haven't even been home for a day!"

"I know, but I've had this one on the books for months, and this guy is hard to pin down. I know it's very soon, but the sooner you get back to your normal life, the better. It will do you good to socialize and see other people. And it will be a very small family affair, really," he explained as he walked out of the room under my angry stare and Chloe's slit eyes.

"What a fucking asshole," said Chloe once he was out of sight.

"Every time I try to see the good in the guy, he disappoints." Iris sighed.

"Some people are just fucking bad, Iris. I have been telling you this. That fucking guy wasn't trying to get her. We hired an investigator, you know," said Chloe, grabbing my hand. "But wherever those fuckers had you, it was impossible. Not a trace."

"And now this jackass wants to throw a party. That is so ridiculous," said Keisha, fuming.

"Well, in his defense, this is important for the development of the company—"

George stopped talking after I glared at him, flames in my eyes. But as I thought more on it, a dinner was just the right distraction I needed to sneak into Richard's office and steal the diamonds.

Iris, Chloe, Keisha, and George stayed with me for a couple hours. I had to feign interest in whatever story George was telling, but having my friends there made things a lot more bearable. Their presence also was delaying further what promised to be a very uncomfortable conversation between me and George.

It was three in the afternoon when my guests left and gave me some space. I needed to put some order in my life and distract myself from the fact that this highly coveted investor was probably Alejandro.

I turned on my laptop and started going through my emails. I only cared about reaching out to the hotel in New York. I was supposed to have started working with them weeks ago. They had heard about my kidnapping from what I could tell by the emails. I decided to dial Clyde, who was the person who had hired me. It was a very pleasant call and served as practice for what I would tell people when they asked how I was and about what I had been through.

Clyde told me to take as many weeks as I needed; the job was still mine if I still wanted it. He understood I needed time to deal with life, considering where I had been for the past few months. I was extremely relieved to hear that.

Now I at least had a plan for after I gave the diamonds to Alejandro. After all, the arrest of Richard so soon after my kidnapping promised to be a scandal, and I didn't want to deal with what would happen.

I would make sure to be out of town as soon as Alejandro had the diamonds. I would go hide some place where I could be at peace and could think, and when I was ready, I would move to New York and never look back.

I had called Alejandro a couple of times already. We needed to plan the next steps, and I needed to know if he was attending the event. The third time, around eight in the evening, someone finally picked up the phone.

"Bueno?" I paused for a second, hearing the voice of a woman. I knew it was Elena's.

"Can I speak to Alejandro?" I asked coldly.

"Amelia! Como estas?"

I could picture Elena's irritating smirk, even through the phone.

"Is Alejandro there?"

"He's showering. You want to leave him a message?"

"Just make sure he calls me back. It's important." I hung up before Elena could say anything else. Jealousy was almost as strong as love sometimes, and I had to close my eyes to refrain from throwing the phone at the window.

Why was she there? And why was she answering Alejandro's phone?

It was nine p.m. when Alejandro finally called me back.

"Hello."

"Amelia?"

"Yes."

"You called me? My phone signal has been bad all day. I tried to call you earlier."

"Yes," I answered coldly. "I wanted to confirm that you will be at the dinner tomorrow."

"Yes, I am the guest of honor from what I understand."

"Great, I will make sure to have the diamonds then, and I will give them to you at the party."

"Are you sure? There really is no need to rush. I don't want Richard to suspect you, Amelia. He won't hesitate one second to hurt you. If you tell me where they are, I can—"

"I'm sure," I interrupted.

We remained in silence for a few seconds, my heartbeat thumping in my ears.

"I fucking hate this. The idea that you are sleeping in this criminal's house is unbearable, Amelia. I need to see you."

"We will see each other soon." I swallowed, wondering how I would be able to control myself with him so close to me at the dinner.

"Amelia, about this dinner, you should know—"

"Don't worry about me, Alejandro," I interrupted. "The sooner I can give you those diamonds, the sooner we can both move on with our lives."

I hung up the phone and put it on silent, unable to control my shaking hands. I would not give him the pleasure of hearing my voice quiver. He called me back, but I rejected the call. I knew he wouldn't text me. We had agreed to not have anything in writing, just in case Richard got a hold of my phone.

I didn't want to let him know how much I was suffering, how much—against all my fears—I wanted him to be mine. Deep down, I knew if he said the words, I would follow him to the end of the world. But right now, he was with another woman, and it felt like an arrow was shot through my heart.

It was six in the morning when I opened my eyes. I could not, for the life of me, go back to sleep, so I decided to start packing my bags. I filled up two suitcases with clothes and hid them in my walk-in closet, making sure I locked it behind me.

I would have to tell Martha, but there was no need to leave evidence of my plans around. After the dinner, I would leave and go to a hotel. I, thankfully, had a good amount of savings. After all, Richard did provide for part of my monthly expenses, and since my return from Europe, I had made sure to be smart with my savings and investments. I could survive on my own for a few weeks before moving to New York for work.

I had spent the day tracking Richard as discreetly as I could, looking for a chance to get my hands on the diamonds. Unfortunately, Richard spent the whole day in his office, so I couldn't yet get to the diamonds. As was expected, the security had significantly increased in the house, and while they didn't really seem to pay much attention to me, their presence made me quite uneasy. He always used to work from home, at least part time, I reminded myself, so that wasn't abnormal. There was no need to panic. He would need to get ready for the party at some point, and I would go in then.

Martha came to my room around four in the afternoon. She had checked on me ten times already during the day and had forced me to eat two meals. Dolores and Martha would be great friends, I thought, smiling at the memories of Dolores bossing me around when it came to meals.

"I need to talk to you," I started, inviting Martha to sit on the bed next to where I was sitting.

"What's wrong? I can tell something is bothering you," said Martha as she sat.

"Remember that job I told you about in New York? Well, it's still available for me. So, I plan... I still plan on moving there."

Martha had a look of horror on her beautiful, long face. "But you just got back! From being kidnapped! You should stay here, let me take care of you, make sure you are okay!"

I gestured to Martha to lower her voice. "I am fine, Nana, I swear. And I won't leave immediately, but I won't stay here either. I am going to go to an Airbnb tonight after that stupid dinner."

"Why? It's not safe!"

"Trust me, it is. It's safer than here."

"I know you don't like Mr. Richard, but..."

I took Martha's hands in mine. "You know I hate him, Nana, and you know the only reason he keeps track of me is because he wants me to marry George—for his business."

"I know, but it's too soon for you to just... go!"

"Nana, it's happening. I just wanted you to know." I sighed. "And I will still see you, no matter what happens after today. Promise me you will always be there, Nana, no matter what. Know that I will always be there for you. And if, one day, you want to come to New York with me, you will be more than welcome. I know you said no last time—something about rude New Yorkers or whatever—but the offer still stands." I blinked back my tears, my throat burning.

"Oh sweetie" she said, water in her eyes.

"You have been the only person in my life that has been there for me since day one, unconditionally. I love you so much, and I am so thankful for everything you have done for me, all the sacrifices."

I stopped as tears rose to my eyes again, making my voice shake.

"You're making me cry!" she squealed in tears and hugging me tight. "Why are you saying all of this? It feels like you are saying goodbye to me, sweetie."

"I just want you to know how much you mean to me, that's all."

Martha looked at me with suspicious eyes. She knew I was not being completely truthful, but she also knew all she could do was wait. I wouldn't say anything else.

"What about George?"

"George? Well..." I said as I got up. "I will break up with him tonight, after the dinner."

Martha looked shocked, but she couldn't hide her relief. She never approved of George because she always knew my heart was not in it.

"What made you change your mind?"

"Well, let's say I... I now know I would be miserable, and it's also not fair to keep leading him on. He deserves to be happy, the same as I do."

I felt like I was under a microscope.

"I am going to start getting ready for that dinner," I announced as I cleared my throat, my cheeks slightly flushed, feeling foolish for being so transparent. Martha knew me too well.

"Okay, sweetie, okay. All I want is for you to be happy." Martha got up and gave me a big warm hug before she headed to the door.

When she left, I proceeded to get ready. Just the idea that I was going to see Alejandro in only a few hours filled me with warmth and desire. I couldn't help it. But it was followed by sadness and jealousy, knowing that it would be the last time. Even if it was for the best, it was tearing me apart.

One horrifying thought that I hadn't considered before made my bones chill. What if Richard had moved the diamonds somewhere else, somewhere safer? What then? What if I now could never get to them? Would Mathias give me more time? Would he trust that I wasn't suddenly lying or had a change of heart, that I didn't tell Richard everything instead? Alejandro wouldn't get his revenge, and who knew what Mathias would be capable of in that moment. I shuddered as I paced in my room.

There was no point in thinking about that. I would get there if that was the case and deal with it then.

I opted for an ivory, sleeveless jumper that curved around my breasts in a flattering way, with a low back. The legs were wide, making it look like a dress at times. I straightened my hair and curled the ends to add some volume and dimension. I took my time with my makeup, enjoying using my dear beauty products again.

I slid the ring on my finger. While I planned on giving it back to George at the end of the night, I didn't want any questions as to why I was not wearing it. I didn't even think they knew I was wearing it when I was taken.

When Martha came to tell me George had arrived, I finished packing and asked her to discreetly put my luggage in my car for me so no one would notice. I put on my gold Louboutins, grabbed my small Chanel purse, and headed to the foyer.

George was there, talking to Richard and what looked like two couples. Those were friends of Richard, two of whom also worked at the company. There was no sign of Alejandro. I went down the stairs and grabbed the hand George was offering.

"You look stunning," he said as he kissed me.

"Thank you," I said timidly as I slowly moved my head away.

"Welcome to my abode!" said Richard.

I turned around to see Alejandro standing in the entryway, looking my way, a frown on his face. Elena's arm was in his, and she was wearing a gorgeous long, blue dress, her usual perverse smile on her very red lips.

Alejandro was wearing a sharp, black Hugo Boss suit that fit him to perfection, his hair combed backward, his face freshly shaven. I was having a hard time swallowing as George grabbed my hand and headed toward the group.

This was going to be a long night.

CHAPTER 46

Alejandro

"Thank you for having us," I said, grabbing the hand Richard offered.

As I looked in Amelia's direction again, my eyes were drawn to the hand George was holding as they headed to us, that fucking ring back on her finger.

Seeing him hold her, as if he had any right, as if that woman wasn't mine, made my blood boil. But for her own safety, I had to be patient. I had to play the game, no matter how much it destroyed me.

"Nice to see you again," he said to me, shaking my hand and then Elena's.

"This is my fiancée, Amelia," George gestured to Amelia.

Little did he know just how well I knew her. Little did he know she removed that ring on her finger just a few days ago just so I could make her come.

"Amelia, this is Rick Hernández, and his fiancée, Elena," he said, continuing the introductions.

I shook George's hand and then Amelia's, rubbing my thumb on the soft skin of her wrist, keeping her hand in mine a little longer than would be appropriate. But I didn't care. She looked at me with wide eyes. I could tell her breathing was slightly accelerated as she fought to remove her hand from mine.

"As you can see, my very brave daughter is finally back home. I wanted to cancel our event today, but she insisted that we have it and take advantage to celebrate her return. She is eager to move on from the unfortunate incident and take her life back by the horns!"

I bit my tongue and tightened my jaw to suppress the urge to punch Richard's head until his skull cracked open.

"I can understand wanting to forget such unfortunate events," I said, holding her gaze. "It must have been a terrible experience."

She shifted her position and looked away from me, her eyes on Elena. I followed her gaze to Elena's ring finger. Yes, she was wearing an engagement ring. It was all part of this fucking farce I got myself into. I needed to explain it to her before it was too late.

In this moment, though, all I wanted to do was remove George's fucking paws from her, wrench that ring from her finger, and take her away from this house, where she would be safe. I just needed to convince her to leave with me. She wasn't going to spend one more night under Richard's roof.

We proceeded to the lounge area by the dining room. There awaited a table with some hors d'oeuvres and a sizable bar with a bartender. There were about twelve people in attendance, mostly couples. So much for a small family gathering.

George took her away to a small group of people while I got stuck with Richard a little bit longer. I wanted to peel Elena from me, but she was just doing what she was supposed to do—making us look like a couple in love.

I couldn't think. All I could focus on was Amelia. Her beautiful hair cascading down the back of her white jumper, accentuating every curve of her body.

George put his hand on her back. I tightened my grip around my glass and chugged it. I didn't know how much more of this I could take. Amelia finally walked away from George and headed to the bar. I excused myself immediately and quickly walked to catch up with her.

"Two shots of Ardbeg please," I heard her order.

The server gave her a quizzical look, but he obliged. She chugged both shots and asked for one more.

"I didn't take you for a scotch girl," I breathed behind her neck, standing so close that I could smell her perfume.

Fuck, I wanted to kiss her neck, mark my fucking territory. Instead, I slowly positioned myself next to her.

"Two champagnes, please." I turned toward her.

"I'm not."

"Good. Wine suits you better."

She took a slow, deep breath as she downed her third shot and winced.

"I don't have them yet if that's what you came to ask."

"I don't care about that, Amelia." I knew she was pissed at me, but it didn't mean her words didn't sting.

"Then why are you even here?" she asked aggressively.

"For you, to make sure you are safe."

A dark sound barely resembling laughter came out of her throat.

"I am, so if that's all you wanted, you can leave. I can bring them to you when I have them."

"That's not what I am here for. Why was George in your room today?"

"Alejandro... please... this is not the time."

I held her arm as she was about to leave me standing. She gasped and looked around to make sure no one was looking at us.

"If he keeps touching you, It's not going to go very well for him." She opened her eyes wide. She knew I meant every word.

"Let me go," she hissed between her teeth.

"We need to talk."

"Everything okay here?" asked George as he caught up to us.

"All fine," answered Amelia quickly as I reluctantly released my grip, focusing my attention on that poor excuse of a man.

George was frowning as he looked back and forth between us, a quizzical look on his face.

"What did I miss?" asked Elena as she walked to me, grabbing my hand with hers.

"We are just getting to know each other," I answered, my murderous gaze still focused on George.

"Yes," acquiesced Amelia, "but excuse me, everyone. I'll be right back."

She almost ran out of the room, George following behind her. I started tailing him, but Elena stopped me.

"You are going to blow our cover," she said between gritted teeth.

I took a deep breath and closed my eyes.

"What am I supposed to do here? She is in a house with a man who tried to kill her. And this other fucker can't stop touching what's mine."

"You will also put her in danger if you do that."

She gave me a frustrated look, the one she had when she was trying to tell me to stop being such a guy.

She was right, of course. Richard was glancing in our direction now. I needed to calm down, but it was easier said than done. I hadn't seen her for two days. She seemed okay, but I needed to make sure. And I needed George away from her.

I had left Mexico right when they did. Some of my men and I followed them into California until they got to this house. I was staying in an Airbnb close by with my team, armed and ready to extract her from this fucking house if it came to that.

I was also tracking her with the bracelet. I had already infiltrated the guards Richard had in his house with one of my own. So he was able to keep me abreast, let me know she was safe. But that wasn't sufficient. Once I got the diamonds, I wanted her out of this house. I would then do whatever it took to get her to trust me, to love me, to be with me. But all that had to wait. I had to find it in me to be patient.

CHAPTER 47

Amelia

I STOPPED TO BREATHE in the hall when I felt like I was finally alone. I closed my eyes, resisting the urge to cry. There was only one way out of this hell: getting Alejandro the damn diamonds so I could disappear forever. As I started heading toward Richard's office, George got in my way.

"Everything okay?" he asked, looking concerned and confused.

"Yes, but George, we need to talk." There was no time like the present.

"Okay, right now?"

"Yes, I don't want to wait."

He accompanied me to the library for a little bit of privacy. I was anxious. The last thing I wanted to do was hurt him, but it would be much worse if I disappeared on him without an explanation. We settled down on the couch, and I nervously ran my fingers up and down my arm.

"I've been doing a lot of thinking, especially when I was in... captivity. I had a lot of time alone to... ponder, figure out what I want to do with my life. I... I know we have been dating for a while now and—"

"What are you saying?" he pressured as I started to hesitate. I sighed. The faster I uttered the words, the better for all parties involved.

"I don't think we should be together anymore. This relationship is not working for me. It's... it's not what I want."

"I don't understand."

"I am so sorry."

"Amelia, you… you just got back from what I imagine was a very traumatic situation. I don't think you should be making any drastic decisions right now."

"Well, this experience gave me a chance to think about what I really want, and this relationship of convenience isn't it, George."

George leaped up, anxiously combing his fingers through his hair. He didn't seem sad. He seemed furious.

"You can't do this to me. Richard, he… he won't let you do this. I have plans! I… I… don't understand why you are doing this! We are perfect for each other!"

"But I don't love you."

"So what? Marriage is not always about love."

"What else would it be about, George? Business?"

He sat back down next to me and grabbed my hand. "You know that Richard and I have plans for our companies. I need to show my dad that I am serious, both professionally and personally, so this merger can happen, and I can finally get the role I deserve in his business. Do you understand that?"

I was now the one to violently spring up. I didn't want to be close to him. I had sometimes doubted that he loved me, but clearly, George was not any different than Richard, using me for selfish business purposes. I felt a surge of anger that quickly made space for relief and almost happiness.

There was nothing for me to feel guilty about. I wasn't breaking his heart. I was destroying his pride and his selfish agenda, and I could not care less about those two things. It was funny that one could feel like this about a relationship after two years of dating.

"You will have to find another wife for this, George. While I thought it was fine for me to marry you even if we didn't love each other, I at least thought we would make a good team, and we were a good fit because we let each other be. But now, I don't want to marry a younger version of my stepfather."

"I think you need to slow down and really think about what you are doing," he warned as he got up again.

He looked like he wanted to slap me. I took a step back, suddenly scared he would harm me.

"Richard won't let you act so stupidly. He will stop giving you money, kick you out of his house, do whatever it takes until you get back in line."

"Is that so?" I mocked, suddenly enjoying the exchange. This was the most honest conversation George and I probably ever had. He always had that condescending tone when I didn't agree with him.

"You doubt it? You know Richard stops at nothing for his business."

I bit my tongue. This was not the time to get angry. It was the time to be smart and enjoy my victory silently.

Richard's free days were quite limited, after all. And I had no intention of taking any money from him. I had a great job waiting for me in New York and what promised to be a great career ahead of me. I sighed, pretending to have suddenly realized what my rebellion could cost me.

"You wouldn't do that to me!"

"Yes, I would, and so would Richard." He paused and grabbed my hands.

"How about..." he said, feeling suddenly victorious, "we head back to the dinner and pretend this conversation never happened? It's normal for you to be a little frazzled right now, baby, but sleep on it. You will see how wrong you are. You're just confused."

I pretended to accept defeat and grabbed the hand he was offering me, a smirk on his face. I knew I had the last card to play, but I would let him think he won—for now.

We headed directly to the dining room, hand and hand, as we had noticed some of the guests proceeding in that direction. I took my usual seat to the right of Richard, with George next to me. Alejandro was seated across from me with Elena. Alejandro was not taking his eyes off me, but I chose to pretend he wasn't there and feign some interest in George's incessant business chatter with Richard.

George was quite annoying and frankly clingy. He wouldn't stop grabbing my hand, hugging me, touching my hair. If this was his attempt to convince me to stay with him after that "romantic" plea, he had another thing coming.

Alejandro loudly scratched his throat, his eyes fixed on me. I diplomatically moved a little further from George.

"So, Rick, when is the wedding?" asked Richard, clearly trying to get George to shut up and turning his focus on his guest of honor.

"Next August," answered Elena as she caressed Alejandro's arm.

He flinched slightly. I noticed it, now that I was all too familiar with his most faint facial expressions, but he confirmed what she had said with a smile. My imagination was misleading me. I shifted uncomfortably in my seat. I felt like I was going to pass out.

"Amelia and I are thinking about next year as well," said George, grabbing my hand. I could have stabbed him with the daggers shooting from my eyes.

"Are you now?" asked Alejandro, a brow raised, menace in his eyes, as he glared at George's hand on mine. I quickly removed my hand from the table.

"I am glad you guys are finally talking about a date!" said Richard. "I was starting to wonder. Congratulations to both couples! This is great!" he said as he raised his glass.

We all cheered, my cheeks feeling flushed with embarrassment, as Alejandro gave Richard a death stare. This was more than my heart could take. Alejandro seemed at the brink of blowing our cover, and I was seconds away from doing the same.

"I need to use the ladies' room," I told George and Richard with my best smile as I slowly got up and left the room.

It was now or never, I concluded.

I headed in the direction of the bathroom, and when I was sure no one had followed me, I changed course as soon as I was out of sight. I walked as fast as I could while looking like I was taking a casual stroll, avoiding windows as much as possible so none of his guards saw me. I couldn't afford to raise any suspicions.

My heart was beating so fast I could hear it. I kept glancing behind me to make sure no one had seen me.

I snuck into Richard's office, locking the door. My legs were shaking, but it had to be done. I checked to make sure Richard hadn't added any cameras. With the increase of security guards in the house, I had to be quick, and I couldn't make any noise.

I kept the light turned off, using my phone as a flashlight. I slowly moved the small plant in the corner next to the couch. It was quite a clever hiding place as the safe was actually behind the plant, with a door the exact same color as the wall. One would only know it was there if they had seen it opened in front of them. But kids saw everything.

I used to play hide-and-seek with Iris all the time, and the space under Richard's desk was one of my favorite hiding spots because Iris was always too scared of Richard to look for me there. While in my hideout, I had seen Richard store precious items in that safe multiple times. I had never bothered to snoop, but I had memorized the code for it as well. And now it was paying off.

With trembling hands, I punched the code in. The door did not budge. I almost panicked and ran out, but I had to try again. I inhaled deeply and slowly plugged in the numbers again, pausing after each one. I pulled the door again, and it opened. I should have felt relieved, but all it did was make me even more scared.

But there it was—the bag of diamonds that had changed my life forever.

It was very heavy. I quickly removed the diamonds from their current bag and dropped them in the replacement one I had brought with me, arranging them between Kleenex so they wouldn't make any clunking noise. I added some rocks I had taken from the beach years ago to the MFG bag and put it back in the safe where I had found it. It would either buy me time or piss off Richard if he went looking for it. A win-win.

I closed the safe and put everything back where it was. I now had to find the courage to leave the room. I slowly opened the door to make sure there was no one.

The coast was clear. I closed the door behind me, walking as nonchalantly as I could, trying to act normal even if fear was gnawing at my stomach. I decided to head to the smaller library. It was far enough from Richard's office. As I was about to open the door, I held in a scream when I realized someone was behind me. Thankfully, it was Alejandro. I entered, and he followed, locking the door behind us.

"Are you following me?" I whispered with frustration.

"I wanted to make sure you were okay."

"Well, as you can see, never been better," I answered sarcastically.

I was staring into stormy eyes, his face looking contorted.

"Are you really going to marry him?"

The question took me by surprise.

"Don't we have bigger things to worry about?" I snapped, defensive.

"Answer me," he demanded.

"I don't want to talk about it," I said, trying to pass by him to get out of the room. It suddenly felt like it was collapsing on us.

"Stop walking away from me," he grunted as he grabbed my arm to keep me there.

"Why do you care? Aren't YOU also getting married? I owe you no explanation about my relationship with George. None!"

"Amelia, that's what I've been trying to tell you," he said in a grave voice. "I'm not marrying Elena. It's all a lie."

"Really? Ugh, how can you say that? You gave her a ring! Doesn't that mean you changed your mind about being with her?"

"No, no, it doesn't. You know she was helping me with Richard, with the plan. You know that. When I met Richard months ago, she was with me, and we played the relationship game so I could seem less... suspicious. And yes, eventually I told him we were engaged. He helped me buy the ring. I needed him to feel like I trusted him. I needed him to feel like we were bonding. He was flattered enough to even offer to host an engagement party. This was all calculated, Amelia. We are not engaged." Alejandro looked disgusted by his words.

I removed my arm from his hand, my heart pounding, reason muddled by pain and jealousy.

"You got engaged. You have a past with her. I can't believe this means nothing."

"Might I remind you, Amelia, you are also wearing another man's ring around your finger right now? A man you also have a past with?" he pointed out as he grabbed my left arm, holding it to emphasize the ring under the light.

"Does that mean you love him? Hmm? Does that mean you already forgot about us, how I made you come, how you screamed my name?"

"Stop it," I pleaded as I felt my throat closing up.

"Tell me, muñeca," he continued, taking no pity on me, "because as far as I am concerned, no matter whose ring you are fucking wearing on your finger, you are mine," he growled as his nostrils flared, his jawline straight. "We are both faking it, but we both know how we feel about each other. Don't deny it."

My heart shattered into a million pieces. But I found the courage to use my free hand to grab the bag of diamonds from my purse and put it in his hand. He looked shocked, as if he didn't think I would have actually gone through with it. His jaw clenched, and he closed his eyes as he hid the pouch in his pocket.

"Don't do this. Please." His plea felt like an arrow though my chest.

"You have to go. You got what you wanted," I added with a broken voice. "Your nightmare is over."

I could not hold the tears in any longer. Alejandro pulled me toward him before I could escape. His arms wrapped around my waist as his mouth met mine, desperate, passionate, forcing my lips to part, demanding that I let him in. I fought the kiss the best I could, pushing and punching him, but he was not budging, getting dangerously close to breaking the few walls I had left to protect my heart.

I calmed down, caving into his desire, becoming clay in his hands. I kissed him back, burying my fingers in his hair, taking all he had to offer, our lips intertwined as if this was the last time. We both stopped to catch some air, our hearts pounding out of our chests.

My tears were taking over again as I pushed him away. He had the diamonds. It was over. I had to get away.

I left the room like the devil was behind me—and he was. I could hear him following me. The pursuit came to a halt when I almost ran into Martha, who was looking at the two of us with an extremely confused look on her face.

"What's wrong?" she asked, looking protectively at my distorted face.

"Nothing, Nana. I have to go. If they ask for me, say I left. Give this to George,' I said as I removed that stupid ring off my finger. "And don't let anyone follow me," I said as I continued my way out of sight.

I did not turn around to see what was going on. I headed to the patio, knowing it was the quickest way to the garage. I focused on slowing my pace down, not wanting to raise any suspicions from the guards, one of whom was staring at me with interest. I grabbed my cell phone and pretended to answer a call.

"Okay, now I can hear you better. I must have a poor signal inside of the house for some reason."

I pretended to walk like someone who was a little inebriated would and laughed to my heart's content, as if I was partaking in the funniest conversation of my life. The guard dismissed me as I continued my ruse until I got to my white Audi. Whatever happened to Richard, this car was under my name, and it would remain mine. I was still shaking, but I was feeding on the adrenaline rush as I turned the car on and drove away from my childhood house, I hoped for the last time.

On the way, I stopped at a grocery store and bought a lot of comfort food and wine. After I checked into the Airbnb apartment, I opened the wine and chugged straight from the bottle. My heart was aching, and I couldn't stop the tears, but the wine would eventually help me pass out. I already had a few missed calls from Alejandro, George, and Martha.

I simply turned the phone off as I waited for the alcohol to flow through my veins and take the pain away. Iris, Chloe, and Keisha were just a few minutes away if I needed them. I wasn't alone. Despite George and Richard, I did have people who cared for me, and that was priceless.

CHAPTER 48

Amelia

THE NEXT MORNING, WHEN I turned my phone back on, I had close to a hundred missed calls and a slew of messages. The first person I called back was Martha. In tears, she told me that Richard was furious that I just walked out of the dinner without so much as an apology, but the worst was that, early in the morning, the cops had shown up to the house with a warrant for Richard's arrest.

He was accused of murder, among other crimes. It was all over the news already.

I acted as shocked as I could. Part of my surprise was honest. I didn't imagine it would happen so fast. I couldn't help but feel a bit of sadness for Richard, even if I knew he deserved everything that was coming his way.

George had also called and texted to ask where I was and tell me about what had happened. Alejandro had texted me, asking that we meet, but as tempted as I was, there was no point in answering him. I did call my friends back. I did not want them to worry about me, but I felt like, now that Richard was behind bars, and Alejandro hopefully had made Mathias happy, maybe I could tell them what had really happened. But I wanted to wait until what surely was going to be turmoil settle down. I had to be sure this was over. We planned to meet for dinner later in the week. I reassured them that I was safe but explained that I just needed to be alone for a while.

The call I did not expect was the one from Steve Dressler, the chairman of Hotel Estrellas. According to his voicemail, he wanted to discuss a very serious matter in light of Richard's arrest.

When I called him back, I got his secretary, but when I said my name, it was clear that she was given orders to insist that I find time to see Steve with utmost urgency.

I couldn't think of what could possibly concern me, but I agreed to meet him for coffee the same day. I put on a pair of jeans with a white shirt and a gray blazer, trying for business casual. The rare times I had seen Steve, he was always in formal attire, and I felt like I had to dress a bit more formal so as to not look like a child next to him.

When I arrived at the coffee shop, Steve was already there, seated in a corner on the only two-person sofa by a decorative fireplace. I was concerned the place was too loud, but once I got to Steve, I realized he had picked a spot that was a bit sheltered from all the noise. He got up to shake my hand and offered me a seat.

Steve was a tall man of average build, who always wore tailored suits, and his blue suit that morning was no exception. He had a bit of a long but rectangular face, his all-white hair rightly shaped on his head, with thin lips and a straight nose, giving him a serious look.

"Thank you for meeting me on such short notice, Amelia, and I am really sorry for disturbing you like this. I know you went through a horrible situation, and you just got home. And now you have to deal with your stepfather's arrest. I am so sorry for everything you are going through."

"Thank you," I managed to say. Steve seemed very honest and candidly concerned about my well-being. "Richard's arrest was a shock, and I am not sure what happened," I lied.

"From the sound of it, he got involved in a pretty messy situation with some gang in Mexico, but there is a video of him taking part in a robbery and killing a man in cold blood. I just can't believe this is happening. You think you know someone—I'm sorry," he said, stopping himself. "I know he is family."

"Don't worry, Steve. Richard and I really did not have the best relationship."

"Really?" he asked, a bit surprised. "That wasn't my impression."

"Richard is a con artist, Steve, and he needed the world to see him as the hero who took care of poor me, so that's what he portrayed. And I played the game well."

Steve didn't just look confused; he looked concerned, his face turning white, his forehead getting a bit sweaty.

"Oh boy."

"What's wrong? Are you okay?"

"Uh, well... I don't really know how to say this. I came here because... well... since Richard is in prison, as you can understand, he can't remain our CEO, and he will lose his shares in the company."

"I get that. You have to protect the business, even if it's mostly his."

"His? Uh, this is starting to be concerning..."

Steve took a second to think before continuing. "Richard only owns fifteen percent of Hotel Estrellas, Amelia. There are moral clauses in the shareholder agreement, and in his employment agreement, and since you have both a right of first offer and a right of first refusal; we can't sell them to anyone unless you don't want them. But more importantly, his power of attorney should be revoked, and the management of your interest returned to you, unless you decide to appoint someone else."

"I don't understand. I... I have no interest in the company."

"You do, Amelia. Your mother left you her shares. Richard was, of course, appointed by the court as your representative, but when you turned eighteen, you gave him the power to manage your shares and represent your interest in the company, didn't you?"

"Is this meant to be a joke?" Nothing he said was making any sense.

"No," he hesitated, the truth only too obvious. "You didn't know, did you?"

"No. No, I didn't. I...I don't understand. Richard always told me that the company was his, that my mother was a lowlife artist with no family, that I was his burden for marrying a pregnant woman. What are you trying to tell me?"

"I think you will need a lawyer, Amelia...I think it's clear that, all these years, Richard has been taking advantage of you, enjoying your dividends based on your ownership in the company, pretending that you assigned him the right to represent you and manage your assets for you. He said that he had tried to get you involved, to have you take over your inheritance, but that you were never interested."

"How is this possible?! How could he have gotten away with this?! How did I not know?"

My voice and body were shaking. I was almost hoping the conversation was just a bad dream I needed to wake up from. Steve looked like he was hoping for the same thing.

"I'm really sorry about this... Richard had us all fooled. I am so sorry, but I am sure there is a way for you to make him pay. The shares remain yours. You own forty percent of the company, and if you want them, you have a right to Richard's shares. You are a rich woman, Amelia."

I couldn't process his words. My fight-or-flight mode was activated. I wanted to run. I wanted to break something.

"How did he manage to get away with this? There were no red flags on the company side? Didn't he have a document to sign? Why would I never take an interest? I have talked—not with you, necessarily—but I've shared my ambitions with some of the directors at cocktail hours and even during the short period when I worked at the company. How did this never come up?"

Steve looked distraught, clearly understanding what I was implying.

"I'm sorry, Amelia. We just... didn't know. It's not unheard of that a wife or child will have their husband or father just handle the business aspect of things. You've had a bank account set up for you like a trust since you were a kid. He has always been the one to manage it and represent you. The account is under your name. I assume now that he has been using it for his personal affairs. We had no reason to doubt him. He presented signed and notarized documents, and you seemed to have the perfect father-daughter relationship."

This had to be a fucking joke. I could not believe what I was hearing. My whole life felt like it was a lie. Everything Richard had told me about my mother was all fabricated by his greed. On the other hand, some things started to make more sense now.

"That's why he kept me," I said, almost to myself. "That's why he kept me after my mother's death. He wanted her money, and keeping custody of me was the only way for him to get it. That was the reason for all the fake hugs and all the bullshit about loving me like his own daughter. That's why he never really wanted me to go away, and that's why he wanted me to marry George... George must have known what was going on. Everything makes so much more sense now. I was so stupid! How did I not know this! I should have known, but deep down, I guess I had always hoped he did love me, in his own weird, twisted way."

"You couldn't have known, Amelia," Steve offered, patting my twisted hands. "He has clearly been covering his tracks since you were a toddler. He repeated the lies to you and everyone else since then, so you had no reason to doubt him, even when you turned eighteen. He probably made you sign documents, and you didn't even realize. Why would you? Once that was done, he took it over. Selling them without you knowing would have been harder, but as long as he had your power of attorney, he could reap the benefits. But I will help you, Amelia. I promise."

I was skeptical and very quickly learning from my mistakes. I needed a lawyer—a very good one.

"Thank you, Steve. I think we need to call for a special meeting. I need to have all the information, all the relevant documents."

"Yes, anything I can do, I will."

I left encounter distraught, fueled only by a desire to hit Richard with my fist until he took his last breath. I couldn't take it anymore. I called in reinforcements, and within thirty minutes, Chloe, Keisha, and Iris were at the apartment.

Chloe arrived first, Keisha and Iris showing up shortly after. Chloe gave me the longest hug before she turned to beast mode.

"I knew it. I knew it. You weren't just kidnapped randomly," she said as we all sat on the couch with mimosas at three p.m.

"What happened, Amelia?" asked Iris in her soft voice.

"We are here for you. You know that, right?" said Keisha as she grabbed my hand.

"I know. I can't believe you are all here. You all have been here for how long?"

"We flew in a few times," answered Chloe. "We didn't trust Richard was handling this. And he wasn't. We came back when we saw the news that you were alive and all they wanted was two fucking million. We made sure every newspaper in the fucking country picked up the news. If you didn't come back alive, Richard would be done for."

"He wouldn't give us any information. Nothing. George either. They told us the police didn't want anyone getting involved, that your life would be in danger if people interfered," added Iris.

"Iris called us. She knew something was off," said Keisha.

"Well, he never cried. Never. He was agitated, but that wasn't the reaction you'd expect for a daughter, or even a daughter-in-law," explained Iris.

"I don't know what to say," I said, fighting the tears.

Chloe and Keisha had jobs working in big law firms, things to do, yet all three of them were here and had tried to help me get back to my life. If only they knew. But I didn't know how to tell them. I didn't know how to say the words.

"You don't have to talk if you don't want to," said Iris. "But we are here. You know that, right?"

"And we will find those bastards who took you. I promise you they will pay. I don't know what they... what they did to you." Chloe took a break to swallow.

Seeing my strongest friend wobble was all I could take. I exploded, tears leaving my body as if I hadn't cried in years. My friends, my family, my sisters, they held me until I didn't have any emotions left in me, until I was too exhausted to feel anything. Only then could I tell them everything.

"I got taken because Richard stole diamonds from some cartel in Mexico. They wanted the diamonds back."

Iris put her hand over her mouth, holding in a gasp. Keisha's eyes grew wide, and Chloe shook her head.

"I don't know what dealings he had with them, how he knew to steal those diamonds in the first place. But that's what happened. They took me on my birthday when they couldn't find them in his safe. He wouldn't budge, though. They tried to negotiate with him, but he wouldn't give them the diamonds in exchange for me."

"Fucking bastard," said Keisha.

We all stayed silent for a bit. Iris held me in her arms while Keisha kept my hand in hers. Chloe kneeled in front of me, her hands on my knees. She was too perceptive to be satisfied.

"How do you know all this?"

I hesitated. Talking about Alejandro... that was the hard part of it all. Harder than the kidnapping. Harder than Richard's betrayal.

"I tried to escape a couple of times. The first time was just a few days in. Well, I did escape, but the person who I ran into on the street, he... he was semi-connected with the kidnappers. He took me, against my will, to his house and held me there. He didn't hurt me," I quickly added. It was important to me that they knew.

"He kept me there, but I was fed, clothed, staying in this gorgeous house with this... mysterious man who tried to make me comfortable but wouldn't tell me much of what was going on. Until he did. He explained who he was—his name is Alejandro—and why I was taken.

"His brother got killed when Richard attacked the shop to take the diamonds. He wanted revenge. The cartel told him they would give him the video of the crime, showing Richard clearly shooting people, including his brother, if he helped them find the diamonds. He lives here, too. So he got close to Richard to break into his house and look for the diamonds. When they didn't find them, the cartel decided to take me. He wasn't able to stop them."

"Bullshit," said Keisha. Iris shot her a stare. She sighed. "Sorry."

All I could do was smile. Any of my friends would stab Alejandro for me if they could.

"I believe him. I believe him because when Richard found out where I was, he sent people—not to rescue me, but to kill me so they wouldn't have something to hold against him anymore. Alejandro saved my life. He took a bullet for me, using his body as a shield."

Tears started pouring out of me again at the memory of the man I loved bleeding all over, almost dying in my arms.

Chloe eyes went wide.

"Oh my god," said Iris.

"That's some crazy shit," said Chloe.

"Yes, yes, it is," I said as I laughed and cried.

"Anyway, I plotted with Alejandro's girlfriend to get that picture of me in the news, asking for two million dollars, to force Richard's hand. Alejandro was furious."

"Did he hurt you?" asked Keisha as she swallowed.

"No," I answered, smiling against my better judgment. "He didn't want to risk my life for the diamonds."

Chloe searched my eyes, a small curve drawing on her lips. Keisha just looked startled, her gaze bouncing between the both of us.

"Okay. What is going on?" asked Iris.

"He seems awfully concerned about the safety of someone he kept captive, doesn't he?" asked Chloe.

I swallowed, hard. I needed to say it.

"I slept with him."

"What the fuck?" Iris blurted out.

Our heads quickly swiveled in her direction. Iris, my most prim and proper friend, the only trust-fund baby of the group—well, until now—didn't generally use curse words.

"What?" she asked, the picture of innocence.

We all exploded with laughter when she looked at us with a confused look on her face.

"'What the fuck' is exactly right," said Keisha in between bursts of laughter.

"Okay," Chloe said, trying to bring some order to our cackling. "Where is he now?" she asked, searching my eyes.

I stopped laughing. I couldn't use my words. I just started crying again as Chloe took me back into her arms.

We talked for another three hours. It felt good to tell others, to certify how fucked up my fate had been for the past few months. Too much had happened. So much had changed that my life no longer fit the old lifestyle I once had.

But I couldn't help the relief that came with telling my best friends the truth. That I had fallen for Alejandro. It felt crazy to admit that I wanted him above all else, even if I didn't think I could be with him after everything that had happened. I had never planned on giving my heart away. It was always a risk that I didn't want to take.

My mother had, and I paid the consequences of that, living in a house where I was rejected by the only parental figure I had. What was the point of love, of putting oneself at the mercy of another? None of it mattered now, though. He had his diamonds. He had his revenge. And I now apparently had a company to run.

I called Nicholas Constantinou as soon as the girls reluctantly left. Keisha thought he would be perfect to help with the legal battle I had coming. Chloe and Keisha did not practice in California, and this wasn't really an area of expertise for any of them. But it was perfect for Nicholas. He had called me shortly after I had returned home after the kidnapping, but I had not yet called him back.

Nico was my high school boyfriend. He had always been a good friend to me, making many men and women quite envious of me, considering that the man was your typical tall, dark, and handsome, eligible, rich bachelor. More importantly for me, he was a very successful trust and estates attorney with experience in shareholder disputes. He was out of town when I called, but we FaceTimed for over an hour.

Nicholas was livid. He never got along with Richard. Within twenty minutes of hanging up the phone with him, I had received five emails from Steve and other executives at the company, sending me and Nicholas all the documents we needed to review. I saw the power of attorney, my mother's will, and all the dividends that had been transferred to an account set up under my name over the past twenty years.

Within two hours, I was able to drive to Citibank, with Nicholas on the phone, to solve what had clearly been fraudulent transfers from that account to Richard's accounts over the years. He was quite clever and never emptied the account completely. All future automatic transfers were canceled, and I was now finding out that I had over eight million dollars to my name. Nicholas had also pulled my tax records. I was ashamed to admit that I had never bothered with them.

Richard had an attorney that took care of both our taxes, so I usually sent him my W-2 and 1099s, and he took care of it. I never really made a lot of money, so it wasn't a problem. I didn't expect any tax returns either because of all the money I got from Richard—or at least what I thought was his. Richard had managed to pay taxes on the dividends on my behalf—I'm sure because an issue with the IRS would have indeed caused his farce to crumble very quickly from what Nico explained.

The only thing that was keeping me from running away right now was Nicholas's calming voice telling me that everything was going to be okay, reminding me that this was a best-case scenario, really. Now, money I didn't know I had was mine.

CHAPTER 49

Amelia

HIS MESSAGES KEPT COMING. And as much as it made my heart bleed, I continued to ignore them. I had been staying at the Airbnb for three days already. Iris and Chloe had visited every single day to keep me company. Keisha had gone back for a court date. Chloe, as a transactional lawyer, could really work from anywhere. Iris was her own boss, so she also had some flexibility. I welcomed all the love they brought to me.

Martha had also stopped by, cleaned, even though I protested, and made sure I had healthy food to eat. Nicholas had filed a complaint against Richard for everything he had taken from me. I also found out that half of the house was mine and that I would probably be able to get the other half as retribution for what Richard had stolen from me. I now had control of forty percent of his company—my company. Always mine, I reminded myself.

Richard was in prison, facing the trial of his life. George was under investigation, as well as the tax attorney, the notary, and frankly, the whole board and officer slate of Hotel Estrellas. I should have felt happy, but I was scared and anxious to be dealing with all these chaos alone. I wanted to run to New York, but everything had changed.

I now owned a company I had always wanted to be a part of—even more so now that I knew my mother had left her shares for me. It was the opportunity of a lifetime. A position I thought I would have had in ten to fifteen years was now falling in my lap. Nicholas had explained there was no doubt Richard's fifteen percent would also become mine.

All the courses I had taken at Stanford were flowing through my brain, and before I knew it, I was writing business plans and growth strategies for the company. I knew what had to be done. I declined my job in New York. Thankfully, they were very understanding of my situation.

I needed to also adjust my perspective, I realized. Considering how dire things had been, this was a good thing.

But when I slowed down, when I was left alone with my thoughts, he always found a way back in, my mind traveling back to Alejandro. How right it felt when he held me in Richard's office. How safe I felt. I wanted to feel him again. I yearned for the times he kissed every inch of my body. I longed for the time we danced together. I kept going back to the fact that he saved my life. To the fact that he seemed legitimately hurt when I walked away from him. To the fact that he still called and texted, every single day, to ask how I was doing, to ask if we could talk. To tell me he wasn't giving up on us. I read his messages countless times, and I desperately wanted to answer. To tell him that I wanted him. That I felt his absence in my bones.

But then I remembered Elena. I remembered how he pointed out that I didn't fit in his world, and anger and jealousy added themselves to the mix. Then came pure fear, my trust issues, my terror of loving and not being loved back.

CHAPTER 50

Alejandro

RICHARD WAS FINALLY IN prison. The man who had murdered my brother was going to rot in a cell for the rest of his life, assuming Mathias or I didn't decide to dispose of him there. I had a promise to keep to my mother. But the fact that Richard had tried to murder Amelia changed everything. If it wasn't for the fact that I didn't know how she would react if she ever found out that I murdered him, I would already have given the order. But something told me that Mathias would finish the job regardless.

My mother was happy. As happy as a parent who lost a child could be. I should have been celebrating, but my mind was elsewhere.

Everytime it grew quiet around me, the storm inside me resumed.

She wasn't with me, but she was everywhere.

I knew where she was at all times. And yet I couldn't go near her. She had made that clear. I was to give her space if I had any chance of making it work between us. But it had been four days by now and I was growing anxious.

I had decided to go pay Richard a visit. I needed closure, I needed to see that bastard behind bars. He was hunched down when I walked in, his legs wide open, his arms dangling between them, his head bent down. He was only a fraction of the man he used to be. He looked like he had aged ten years in the span of a few days. He lifted his head when he heard me, surprise and relief bringing some life to his miserable face.

"Rick? Is that really you?"

He stood up and wobbled towards me. I had managed to get a smaller visitation room with him, with just us and one guard in the room.

"I am so glad to see you." He said as he offered me a hand.

For once, I didn't take it. I kept my fists in my suit pockets, otherwise I knew they would go straight to his neck. I don't know if I would be able to stop myself.

"I wish I could say the same" I added as he seemed confused.

"You don't... you don't believe all these things they are saying about me do you?" he looked horrified, as if I had betrayed him.

"What am I to believe Richard? There are videos of you killing that man. They are everywhere."

"I know that, but it's not what it looks like."

A smirk drew on my face as my shoulders tensed further. He was really going to try to lie his way out of this.

"Is it not you in those videos Richard?"

"Yes... yes, it is. But it's not what it seems. I didn't mean to... it... that man, he stole from me. I was trying to get my property back. It was really self-defense."

I chuckled. Anger burned through me and before I knew it, my hand was at his throat, as I violently pushed him until his back hit the wall. The guard I had paid off did not budge.

"He was unarmed, you son of a bitch. He was unarmed and because he saw your face you fucking killed him in cold blood."

"What? Rick, what the fuck?"

"Yeah, what the fuck is right," I said, squeezing his neck tighter as his face turned plum, his eyes wide. He was fighting me, to no avail. The guard finally came next to me, as a silent ask that I let go.

I wasn't going to kill the bastard. I would much prefer to watch him rot in here. I loosened my grip, and he fell to the ground, coughing aggressively, his hands around his neck.

"Why? Who are you?" he managed to ask between coughs.

"Your worst nightmare. I will enjoy seeing you spend the rest of your miserable fucking life in here, with no one, and left with nothing. There is no escaping this Richard. You are done for."

"What's it to you? Who the fuck are you?"

I slowly squatted down on the floor to face his terrified gaze. He couldn't pull himself back up.

"That man you murdered? He was my brother."

I watched as realization drew on his face.

"Rick, I didn't know."

"You didn't have to. It didn't matter."

"Was it you? Did you take my daughter?"

I slowly got up. I was tempted to kick him, remove Amelia from his thought. But I had done what I had come there to do. To confront this murderer, and let him know who was behind his incarceration.

"Take care Richard. I hope you burn in hell."

"This is not over asshole!" he screamed as he tried to get himself up.

"You will either die here Richard, or, if you somehow manage to set yourself free, you will die out there, simply because, I will kill you. I would love for you to give me the opportunity."

"Fuck you! Fuck you!" he yelled as he struggled to get himself up. The guard put himself in between us.

I bore into Richard's eyes one more time. He put on a brave act, but it was terror I saw in his gaze. And his fear brought me peace. I swung around to leave.

"Oh, before I forget" I added as I turned around. "A little souvenir from Mathias."

I removed the small diamond from my pocket and threw it at him. Richard painfully bent to pick up the diamond that fell right at his feet. His hand was shaking, under the intrigued gaze of the guard.

Richard started to breath heavily as he studied the shiny stone in silence. I turned back around and left the room, as I heard the guard and Richard struggle for possession of the stone. I had given that gem to him for payment, with the condition that he pry it from Richard's hands and rough him up in the process, and he gladly took the deal.

As soon as I made it to the parking lot, I checked my phone. Nothing. She hadn't answered my calls or my texts. I took a deep breath to avoid the panic that threatened to consume me at the thought of losing her. I was quickly losing hope. But I wouldn't stop fighting.

CHAPTER 51

Amelia

> I'm told to be patient. I'm told to give you space, to give you time. But I don't know how to do that when you are in every breath I take, in every step I make.

> Amelia, you are the best thing to have ever happened in my life. Answer me, text me, give me something, anything.

IT WAS FIVE DAYS before I could finally meet with Nicholas face to face. He came to meet me at the Airbnb. The woman next door stopped watering her plants for a minute, admiring Nicholas's height and his muscular build, appreciating his custom-made blue suit that flattered his broad shoulders, and his pitch-black hair and brown eyes. Nicholas was a Greek god—quite literally, as his father's family was from Greece. His square jaw and Mediterranean tanned skin used to cause uproar among the girls at school.

I had been the lucky one he had set his eyes on at the time. We had dated for barely two months when Richard made us break up because Nicholas's family was nouveau riche, his grandfather having made a fortune in the real estate business. Richard only wanted to establish himself within the old-school rich of California. We had remained friends since, and while our breakup really had been of our own accord when we realized we were much better as friends, Nicholas hated Richard.

Nicholas had, of course, done well after that, becoming a highly coveted attorney, and he was now progressing to manage the family empire. He was one of the most sought-after bachelors in California, enjoying his single life more than most. He reminded me of Alejandro, I realized—similar features, similar drive.

Although, no one could match the fire that Alejandro lit inside me.

Nicholas gave me the hug I desperately needed. I saw him glance in my neighbor's direction. The woman almost fell in her bushes. I rolled my eyes with a smirk.

"I'm so happy to see you," he said as he hugged me.

"Me too!" I said as we walked in the apartment, and I closed the door behind him. "I don't know how I would deal with all of this without you."

I had rented a one-bedroom, one-bathroom apartment, and it was just the right size to feel airy. I loved the beach theme and the light-blue and green colors. They reminded me of Alejandro's beach house.

"Why are you not staying in the house?" he asked.

We proceeded to the living room, and I invited Nicholas to sit next to me.

"I had intended to move to New York this week," I explained, "and I didn't want to be near Richard. He is the reason I got kidnapped in the first place."

"What do you mean?" He frowned.

"I, uh... I don't want to talk about it, to be honest."

"Well, okay, that's fine. But things are different now. That man will be in prison probably for the rest of his days because he killed someone. The house is yours. Your mom bought it with him before her death."

"Are we sure he didn't kill her?"

That had been the most important question for me—the one that had haunted my dreams this past week. Now that I knew Richard would stop at nothing for money, I wondered.

"I am still investigating, but it really does seem like it was an unfortunate drunk driving incident, in which the drunk driver who hit her car also died. Nothing seems to indicate that Richard lied about that. I think, if it was him, he would have made sure to take your shares beforehand as opposed to holding them for you after the fact. It seems like they had intended to move to the US, but then the accident happened. That would explain why your mom was an owner of the house as well."

"I see. I still can't believe this is happening." I ran my fingers through my hair. "I know I should be happy, but I'm disturbed, confused, and angry at him—and at myself."

"I know," he said, taking my hand in his, "but it will all be different now. You have your independence, and you can focus on running YOUR company."

"I know. You're right. I still can't believe this is happening. But to be honest, it feels so right. Like part of me must have known this was my destiny."

We talked for another couple of hours, as he was helping prepare me for what was to come. Chloe joined us as well for a few hours, providing me with support and to help me gather my thoughts into concise arguments. If I wanted justice, I would need to roll up my sleeves and be involved, go to court, take this to the very end. I had also called a special board meeting at Hotel Estrellas. I was quite scared. I had to look a lot stronger than I felt, earn the trust of some directors and shareholders while being suspicious of every single one of them. I had no way of knowing if any of them were Richard's accomplices, but it was very likely. I felt better with Nicholas by my side. I opted for a simple black dress with a black vest. I wanted to look professional and ready to get straight to business.

When we marched in the meeting room at Hotel Estrellas headquarters, the nine directors were all staring at me, clearly uncomfortable. Steve came to welcome me.

I felt like I was in a haze, my brain doing its best to protect me from any sort of strong emotions. I was at my wits' end, but this was the time to change my life. I recalled always being in awe but also intimidated by those huge conference rooms, everyone sitting around a vast thirty-person, rectangular, gray marble conference table, the high-tech room being used for important meetings.

"I called this special meeting today," I stated, "because this past week has been a revelation. I am sure that at least some of you feel the same way. Richard's arrest has caused a lot of issues in my personal life, and I imagine that it hasn't been easy here either."

I paused for emphasis.

"I am not one to waste my time with pleasantries, so I am going to cut to the chase." I took a strategic break. "Richard has managed to fool me, and he's managed to fool at least some of you, by pretending to be a good and honest man. I want to say that he took my money from me, but that doesn't feel right as I had no idea it was mine in the first place, and I did nothing to deserve such a windfall. I wasn't allowed to. He never wanted me around here too much, and now I know why. He was an awful father, owner, and man, but I don't want to dwell on the past. I just want to focus on the future."

"Well said, Amelia. Well said. And I want to add—"

"I am not done, Charles," I said, giving the man who had interrupted me a cold stare.

He silently sat back down, a look of exasperation and surprise on his face.

"As some of you might know, even if Richard has presented me to you as the capricious little girl he took care of, I do have ambitions, and I have the required preparation to manage my own affairs in this company. I do have an MBA from Stanford, and I did work at companies before, in managerial positions. I know my rights, and I know what our bylaws authorize me to do and not do. While I don't think I have the right experience for what used to be Richard's position, I do believe that I have the experience and frankly the right to belong on this board. Richard fooled me, but he also fooled all of you. You were comfortable enough believing his tales. Never once did it occur to any of you that Richard was taking advantage of me, that I might have any interest in what was rightfully mine. His tax attorney was on this board as of a few days ago—until I sued him, of course."

I took another break, letting it sink in that I was coming for any other accomplices.

"I won't discuss why you were so comfortable believing him, how you enjoyed his yacht parties, his eccentric trips, the ridiculous donations he has made to Claude's private accounts from mine. It is very clear to me that there was enough there to cause concern, and while some of you really didn't know, others turned a blind eye, and I do think the outcome would have been different had you seen me as an equal."

I looked at the distorted faces around the room.

"I take responsibility for having been foolish, but some of you were purposefully ignorant. I ask that we put a special independent committee in place to investigate our books, our minutes, and our records. We are under scrutiny now as a company, but I won't let my mother's legacy be destroyed by greed."

Once I established my strength and frankly my anger and disgust, I could see a few of these men struggling to pay attention and becoming a bit nervous. But Steve was encouraging me, backing me up in every decision. The meeting lasted four long hours. The other shareholders and I added me to the board, and the board voted on a temporary CEO. I pushed for Steve while we handled the investigation and the public image of Hotel Estrellas.

There was a lot of work to be done. I assigned Nicholas as my temporary representative. Nicholas had enough work on his plate in his complex law practice, but he agreed to do me the favor.

My mental health was more important, and I needed some time away before I was ready to take the reins of my future. I needed to heal. Nicholas wouldn't make any decisions without my consent, but all I wanted to do for the next two weeks was disconnect as much as I could, let Nicholas bother me when needed. Chloe would also be involved, as I wanted her to handle the corporate governance aspect of this company going forward. For now, though, I had to focus on myself.

CHAPTER 52

Amelia

MY HEART WAS IN shambles, rebelling against me for not answering any of Alejandro's texts. This morning, I had found two bouquets at the front door. They were Dahlia's, so I knew they were from him. I couldn't throw them away, so I put them in water and allowed my heart a minute to enjoy them.

Today, I had the energy to have what promised to be the hardest encounter to date. I had decided that I needed to go see Richard and confront him.

Nicholas came to get me in the afternoon, and we drove together. The jail was a much worse experience than a hospital. I could feel all the hair on my neck rise. I was very uncomfortable with the idea of being surrounded by certain people who had broken the social contract. When they took me and Nico to see Richard, I almost walked back to the car, but I could no longer be a coward. I had to face my fears.

"You came!" exclaimed Richard, and he got up from the table he was sitting at in the visitation room.

"I did," I said, keeping my distance.

This wasn't a social visit. We both sat down at opposing ends of the square table.

"Amelia, I can't imagine how you must feel, but I… it… it was a mistake. I didn't know that man was there… I thought he was one more of those lowlife fucks…"

"You have no right to take anyone's life like that, Richard, no matter who they are. That's part of what is wrong with you, what's broken inside of you. This false sense of self, this chip on your shoulder, making you want to prove to the world and yourself that you are better than others. I think you actually managed to convince yourself of that, of your superiority. That delusion made you decide that it was okay to take what wasn't yours, that it was okay to kill, that it was okay to steal from me and treat me like your fucking charity case."

Richard's face was distorted. He looked shocked and horrified. This was the first time I ever saw him cry. Part of me wanted to grab his hand, console him. After all, he was the only father I ever knew. But he didn't deserve it. He didn't deserve whatever love was left in me for him.

"I just wanted a better life."

"You were a cartel member, weren't you?"

"Yes. I was born into terrible circumstances. I had no choice. But when I met your mother, I saw an opportunity to get out. She had some money from her parents, and she had invested in an American business. I wanted a different life. I needed to belong here. I needed my past gone. I needed to be an American. We decided to move here, but she died. And I kept you. I kept you. Remember that."

"You did. But you were never a father to me. You kept me for my mother's shares. That's it."

Richard looked like I had slapped him, his eyes wide.

"Yes, I know."

"No, you don't. When your mom invested, the company was nothing like it is now. I built it up, made it the empire it is today."

"By stealing from me. You used my money for everything."

"Didn't I take care of you? Give you everything you ever wanted?"

"No, not everything. I didn't have your love. I didn't have a dad. I had a man who treated me like an inconvenience."

"Don't say that," he begged, his eyes wet.

I didn't want to feel sympathy. I didn't want to take pity on him.

Time had passed, and, the sleep-deprived man who had already lost some weight tugged at my heart. His frown lines were more pronounced, and he had more wrinkles around his eyes. This was no longer the strong man who used to terrify me. My heart wanted to go to him, even if he didn't deserve it. I had to get out of there.

"Don't leave me like this, Amelia" he begged, panicked, looking at the prison guards walking around us. "After all I have done for you. I need you. I need you to testify in my favor in court."

I laughed, the sympathy I had left washed away by his audacity. He was once again trying to manipulate me, and I almost let him.

"You did take care of me, Richard, but for interest. And I know you don't love me. You never did. I got kidnapped because of you! Because of your greed! Those people you stole from… I know, Richard! I know what you did!"

"It was you? It was you!!! YOU! YOU took my diamonds!"

"I don't know what you are talking about," I said slowly, a devious smile on my face.

Richard stood and took a step back, recognizing in me his biggest and most dangerous enemy. I enjoyed the fear and shock in his eyes for a few seconds more.

"You never loved me. You used me. The worst part is, I would have let you do exactly as you did. You were my father, Richard, whether you wanted it or not. And for your love, I would have given you all of it, without blinking an eye." I held my tears.

"I was just a kid who wanted the love of a parent. You chose not to give me that. You chose your greed, your need to belong. You chose your hatred for your own country. You took classes just to get rid of your accent. You hate me because I remind you of that life you left behind. But I was innocent. I was just a girl, who desperately wanted a dad."

"Amelia... I'm so sorry."

My throat closed. I wouldn't sob in front of him. I wouldn't give him that satisfaction, so I walked away before it was too late.

"What was he talking about?" asked Nicholas as we got to the parking lot.

"I am swearing you to secrecy as my attorney."

"Of course."

I sighed.

"The people who took me... they did it because Richard stole their diamonds. That video of him killing that man... that's what it was about, stealing diamonds."

"I can't believe this!"

"You better. That's why it took so long for me to be released. He left me there to die. He wasn't going to give them back."

"How do you know all of this?"

"I, uh... overheard some conversations when I was in captivity..." I turned around, avoiding his gaze, ashamed that after all he had done for me, I was lying to protect Alejandro.

"Did you take those diamonds?"

"No, I would have no idea where they are."

Nicholas stared at me for a minute, clearly suspicious. I kept a cold face this time and held his eye contact. When it came to protecting Alejandro, there was no strength I couldn't conjure. He sighed.

"Well, now that he is in prison, he won't be enjoying them anyway. Are you going to file a complaint for this?"

"No, there is a video of him clearly killing a person. He stole some of my money, committed fraud... he is done for. I just want to move on."

"I know."

Nicholas got closer to me and wrapped me in his arms. I enjoyed feeling another person's warmth and strength, but I slowly pushed him away. I did not want to cause any confusion.

Nico treated me to dinner as a thank-you for bringing him what he called *"a Wild Wild West case."* I gladly accepted. The less I was left alone with my thoughts, the less likely it was that Alejandro would haunt me. It had been a few days since he had called, and even if I was not answering him, just knowing that he had been trying to reach me gave me a sort of masochist comfort.

I snapped awake to my phone's incessant ringing in the middle of the night.

"Hello?"

"Amelia, I'm sorry for calling you so many times. Something happened..." explained Nicholas.

"What's wrong?" I immediately sat up, not knowing what to expect, hoping nothing had happened to Alejandro.

"It's Richard... he... he committed suicide. He's dead, Amelia."

CHAPTER 53

Alejandro

THAT LAWYER WAS STILL standing next to her. I knew they had been high school friends, but it didn't mean I enjoyed knowing how much time they spent together, especially when he was in the apartment she was renting. Amelia was surrounded by the three women who had been with her since she came back to California and the person I knew to be Martha. All those people had been investigated, in case any of them had a concerning connection with that fucker.

They had finally lowered his coffin into the ground, and they were covering it with dirt. I had been in my car the whole time, watching her. I wanted to be with her, console her.

Even though Richard's death was good news, I understood that, for better or worse, she was burying the only father she had ever known. She barely cried during the ceremony, but she looked skinnier in her black dress and cardigan, her eyes hidden behind black sunglasses. She finally broke, turning around into the arms of that fucker. That was the last straw. She was in pain, and I needed to be there for her, not him. I stormed out of the car and told Carl, my driver, to wait for me.

They were all staring at me as I closed the distance between us, the grass crushing under my feet.

Amelia lifted her head and looked in my direction.

God, she was beautiful, her hair arranged in a ponytail, that dress unable to hide those curves that haunted my dreams. By the look I was getting, if I had to bet, those friends had an idea of who I was. I was hoping it was a good sign, but the death stare the brunette gave me said otherwise.

They all stood next to her, as if any of them would be able to stop me from talking to her.

Amelia took a timid step in my direction. My heart lost it, wanting nothing more than to take her with me and never look back. She wrapped both her small hands around my lapels. I wrapped my arms around her shaking shoulders, holding onto her like my life depended on it. The friends backed away, giving us some privacy. I kissed her head, caressed her back.

"It's okay, mi niña. Everything is going to be okay. I promise."

"I'm sorry," she said as she lifted her head.

"You have nothing to be sorry about." Her words gave me a sliver of hope.

"I am crying in your arms over the death of the man who killed your brother," she explained.

"It's normal for you to feel pain. He was family—however shitty."

"He was... both things," she said as she straightened up and took a step back.

"Thank you for coming," she said as she lifted her head in my direction.

That wasn't good. She was putting some distance between us again, treating me like any random person who would have come to give her their sympathies. My heart sinked, the pit in my stomach growing wider.

"There is nowhere I would rather be than by your side, Amelia."

She shook her head. "Alejandro."

"Please, Amelia."

"Just, please... don't," she begged when I got closer to her. I gently took her face between my hands.

"I'm not losing you, baby," I promised as my throat closed up.

"I can't."

"You're scared. I get that. Your life got turned upside down in a matter of months. Pero no me voy a dar por vencido. Me entiendes?"

"You know we were doomed from the beginning, Alejandro. This will never work between us."

"Why? Richard is dead. Mathias is gone. There is nothing stopping us."

"I can't do this," she said as a sob escaped from her mouth.

God, I would give my life to remove the pain that haunted her, darkening her aura. My strong girl, my loving girl, my loyal girl... Seeing her in pain was a knife to the stomach. Her tears burned a thousand times more than the bullet. I took a step closer, wrapped my hand around her wrist and pulled her close to me.

"I love you," I said, and before she could say anything, I kissed her.

She gasped, but I didn't care.

I was desperate.

Desperate to feel her, desperate to love her, desperate to hear that she loved me too.

I needed her, body and soul, and I was running out of options. It felt as if she was slipping through my fingers the longer we were away from each other.

"Please, Alejandro," she begged as she pushed slightly against me.

"I need time. I need some time."

My heart shattered into pieces.

But I took her face between my hands again, not giving a fuck about all the eyes staring at us. I kissed her again, tasting her tears. I would have given anything to erase them, to make her feel better.

"Ok, mi muñeca, if that's what you want, even if I am breaking inside, I will give you space. But understand this, I am not losing you. I am not going away. I belong to you, mi niña, and you belong to me."

She put her hands on mine, still framing her face. She nodded her head up and down ever so slightly before she turned around and went to Martha and her friends. The brunette I knew to be Chloe took her in her arms as she stared at me, her anger gone. There was only sadness there, a deep need to take her friend's pain away. The blonde I knew as Iris walked up to me.

"Thank you for saving her life. Give her some time… just a little more," she whispered, seemingly making sure others didn't hear her.

She had no idea how much her words meant to me. It meant Amelia didn't hate me. It meant she confided in her friends. It meant they knew she loved me, even if she wouldn't admit it to me, or to herself. I looked in her direction one more time. She had her sunglasses off and was looking at me, a small smile on her lips. There was hope. There had to be. Because a life without Amelia… that wasn't a life worth living.

CHAPTER 54

Amelia

A WEEK LATER

IT HAD BEEN A few days since I came to Napa. After attending Richard's funeral, it all was more than I could handle. I had been feeling a bit guilty about his demise. I had helped get him charged with murder, after all, but I couldn't think like that.

The funeral had been a discreet affair that I could not have put together without Martha and my friends. I toyed with the idea of not doing anything. But I did it for me, for closure. Barely anyone showed up, which was what I expected. After all, no one wanted to be seen at the funeral of a murderer.

But Alejandro... he came.

He came and held me in his arms while I cried for his brother's murderer.

"*I love you.*"

His words, not my imagination. I burned to tell him the same, but the fear that I would put my heart in his hands took over, and I couldn't say it. I asked him for time, and he gave it to me.

I had established my place on my company's board, with my eyes on a position in the executive office when I had enough experience under my belt. For now, there was a close-to-clean slate of the board of directors and officers.

I also had decided to sell the house. It was way too big anyway. I had sort of started to search for my dream house. I would get something smaller, more my style, somewhere by the beach, and Martha would come with me.

But for now, I was on vacation, by myself, enjoying all the wine Napa had to offer. I had booked a nice villa in a five-star, all-inclusive resort that was associated exclusively with my favorite California vineyard, Robledo Estates.

I had arranged a few wine tours and visits for the week. I was having brunch with Francesca, a wonderful woman I had run into on my first day in Napa. I had met her in the lobby as I was checking in. We instantly connected and spent the last few days drinking and eating together. Francesca had explained that this was her third escapade in three months to Robledo Estates. She enjoyed the solitude, and the scenery was perfect for when she needed inspiration.

As an artist, she spent hours a day in her own villa, with a backyard and breathtaking view, painting the wonderful images and sensations nature had to offer. She promised to let me see her work soon.

"Come on, what better way to spend the afternoon than sampling some cold wine and eating some cheese?"

"I know, I know, but I told Nico to meet me here at three."

"Then cancel" she insisted.

"I can't just cancel for no reason! He is only in town for three days," I said, laughing.

"A wine tour with me seems like the perfect excuse. Just tell him to come tomorrow! He works for you, not the other way around," declared Francesca with a final tone.

In the past couple days, I had quickly learned that Francesca did not take no for an answer, and I liked that about her. Francesca was a woman in her early sixties with impeccable style.

She loved wearing linen dresses accompanied by gorgeous pearls of all colors and sizes. She always walked around with a large hat to protect her eyes from the sun. She had long black hair that went all the way down her back. She was beautiful, with a straight nose and sensual lips, but at times, when she got lost in her thoughts, her eyes looked sad and distant.

I did not dare ask what was haunting her. So far, we had very fun conversations about politics, philosophy, music, wine, and food, but I avoided anything having to do with my kidnapping. Francesca had told me she avoided the news like the pest, and thankfully, since she didn't live in California, she had no idea who I was.

Her ignorance made her the perfect companion. Someone to talk to and confide in without the baggage of knowing everything I had been through.

"Fine," I said, caving to Francesca's now shining eyes, "since you insist."

Francesca was basking in her victory as I pulled my phone out of my purse to reschedule my appointment with Nicholas.

"There, it's done," I added after finishing texting. "He was bummed, but now he wants to take me to dinner tomorrow instead, so it worked out."

"Oh," teased Francesca, "do you think he wants to date you?"

"Hmm, I'm not sure. I don't think so. We used to date. He was my first crush... but we were younger. It's been so long. I am not the same person I was before, and neither is he. I am most certainly not ready for any type of relationship right now."

"Because of George?" inquired Francesca.

"No, not because of George..."

"Well, then, is there someone else?" she pushed.

I couldn't really explain to Francesca that I had fallen for my irresistible captor.

"Something like that," I responded, fighting the sadness I felt every time I was reminded of Alejandro.

Francesca put her hand on mine, shaking her head in silent understanding.

"Seems like the wine tour with me is just what you need to cheer you up, then," said Francesca smiling, trying to help me fight the tears she could see rising in my eyes.

"Indeed!" I said, wiping my face. "So, shall we meet here in, say, forty minutes and head there together? I can believe it's already 1:50!"

"We can't be served all this wine and be expected to keep track of time!" joked Francesca as we got up. "See you in forty minutes," she said, giving me one of those long, warm hugs that instantly reassured me. "I promise you, everything will be okay. You just need some time to heal."

I hugged her back, taking in every one of her words as if it was my faith. I then walked to my villa.

I had been lucky to find a perfectly secluded villa very close to the water when I was looking. It was a highly coveted spot that I had tried to book a few times before without any luck. I was told this villa was almost always reserved by the vineyard owner's family, so when they told me it had just gotten released for reservations, I jumped on it.

It was a gorgeous three-bedroom, three-bathroom, luxurious, two-story villa with balconies and state-of-the-art amenities. It reminded me a bit of Alejandro's beach house. The colors took me back to the room Alejandro and I had shared, the memories mending my heart and breaking it at the same time.

I quickly changed into a bright-red dress that buttoned in the front. I added a thin gold decorative belt and made sure to grab my glasses and floppy straw hat after I put some sunscreen on. The hat was a gift from Francesca who clearly wanted to share her love of hats with me. I had welcomed the gift and really enjoyed feeling like a 'madame,' as Francesca described it.

I ran my fingers over the bracelet I always wore, now not only a reminder of my mother but also a reminder of the man I loved.

We met in the lobby by the villas and walked together to the parking area. A golf car driver was waiting there to take us to the specific vineyard where the tasting was to take place. I loved it here—the smell, the air, the sun. Everything was perfect.

"I can understand why you come here so often," I told Francesca as I got out of the golf cart. "It's paradise. I wish I could just stay here forever."

"It really is."

"I would love to partner with Robledo Estates for Hotel Estrellas. Maybe serve their wine in the restaurants of our hotels or something. I just love this place so much."

"I think that is an excellent idea! You know, I could help with that. I know the owner," explained Francesca with a smile.

"Welcome to our wine tasting this evening, ladies and gentlemen," greeted a man as he came out of the building and approached the small group of eight people that had gathered. I will be your tour guide this evening, and we are going to have fun."

"He is my favorite!" exclaimed Francesca with the excitement of a first timer.

Her joy and passion were intoxicating, and I decided to relax and enjoy the feeling of the buttery chardonnay one of the guides was distributing to the crowd.

These tours were always very informational, with the guide taking the group through the winery and showing us the vineyards used for the wine we were enjoying.

"Everyone, come closer," said the guide as we followed his instructions. "I have a wonderful surprise for you."

I kept myself slightly turned to the side as I was texting with Nicholas a bit to pin down our next meeting.

"I have such a treat for you today! I was just told that the man who made Robledo Estates what it is today decided to join us for the rest of our evening together, so without further ado, I want to introduce you to Mr. Alejandro Robledo Carvajal."

CHAPTER 55

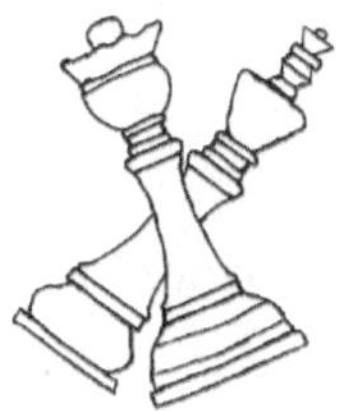

Amelia

THAT NAME RESOUNDED THROUGH me, twisting my lungs as time seemed to slow down. I let out a shaky breath as awareness crawled on my skin. I slowly lifted my gaze as Alejandro walked out.

"Thank you, John," responded Alejandro as the crowd applauded.

My heart stopped, and I froze, unable to move, my iPhone falling to the floor.

Alejandro was talking, but I could not hear anything other than my heartbeat drumming in my ears. Maybe it was the alcohol. Maybe I was hallucinating. This could not possibly be.

Francesca gently squeezed my arm, a concerned look on her face as she picked my phone from the ground and handed it to me. In an attempt to appease her, I swallowed hard and turned around as the group was laughing at a joke Alejandro must have made.

He was there, dressed all in black, his sleeves rolled up, his hair blowing in the wind, and his skin golden and glowing under the sun. I wasn't dreaming. If only I could run, but all I could do was stare at him as he smiled and accepted the handshakes some of the tourists were giving him. He was slowly making his way to Francesca and me, but I couldn't move.

"Amelia? Everything okay?" inquired Francesca.

"Yes, yes, I'm fine," I managed to say. "I, uh… I have to go."

"What's wrong? You look like you've seen a ghost. Have some more wine," she said as she passed her glass to me. I chugged it in an unladylike fashion, without hesitation, wanting to feel anything else but this.

"This is the guy I wanted to introduce you to, since you wanted to meet the owner," announced Francesca, pointing to Alejandro as he joined us.

"Amelia and I have been acquainted," said Alejandro with a smirk, hands in his pockets, having overheard Francesca's comment.

"Oh, you two know each other? Well, then this is just perfect!" said Francesca as she and Alejandro kissed on the cheeks. "And here I was, about to introduce you two! Amelia is just in love with your vineyard, Alejandro. She was even talking about being interested in doing business with you to supply your wine in her hotels!"

"Is that so?" he teased. "Well, in that case, would you give us a second?" he asked Francesca.

She looked a bit confused at the request but did not retort. "Of course! See you both later!"

Alejandro just stood there, studying my every reaction, waiting for me to process. The shock made space for anger as dots were connecting in my head.

The label-less wines we drank, the villa being available when everything at this estate is usually booked about a year in advance, the special vintage wine bottles I got—'courtesy of the hotel,' I was told. It all made sense now. They reminded me of the label-less wine, but I hadn't put two and two together until now.

"Shall we take a walk?" he asked, offering his hand.

Without so much as a sound, I turned around and started walking in the direction of the vines to the side of the building, painfully aware of his presence behind me. When I was satisfied that we were far enough from the group, I brusquely stopped and turned around to face him.

"I'd ask what you are doing here, how you knew where I was when I barely told anyone, but given that all this is yours, I guess I have my answer."

"I'm here to see you," he said casually, like we had an appointment.

"Did I miss a diamond or something? Do you need me to go back?" I mocked.

His jaw clenched a bit. "Are you really going to pretend that's all this was between us? Don't offend me, Amelia. Don't."

He looked more hurt than angry as he got closer to me. I needed to look away. I needed to regain the upper hand.

"You asked for space. And I gave it to you. But at this point, it feels like you are avoiding me. You left L.A. without a word."

"I left because there was nothing to stay for," I said, trying to hold back the tears. The few seconds of silence felt eternal.

"Stop lying, Amelia," he said as he grabbed my arm. "Stop fighting me, please. I am not going to hurt you. I would never hurt you, and if you want me to stay, I will never leave your side."

Eyes opened wide with terror, I stood there like Alejandro had tried to stab me. What was he doing? Still trying to get me to admit how I felt, what I wanted, when we both knew I wasn't the woman he needed. I hoped that with the passing of time, he would stop trying, and I would live with this love, feed off the memories, and pray to all the gods that they would be enough in the long run.

But seeing him here, the need I felt to my core was like dynamite that could explode at any minute. I was confused, and all I could feel was sheer panic as I took a step back.

"Elena and you, are—I can't—I won't be another one... I can't just..."

"Elena means nothing to me, mi niña. Por dios. She was helping me with this. She was involved in this before I met you. You know this. I've told you a thousand times. I needed to keep up appearances with Richard. That's why she was part of the plan—as my fake girlfriend, that is all. I'm not saying that we were just friends then, but we have been just friends since you, and we were never seriously together."

"But—"

I was interrupted by Alejandro as he pulled me closer into his arms.

"Stop talking," he sighed. "I am here now, with you, Amelia, not with Elena. I came here, alone, for you. You are the first thing I think about when I wake up and the last thing I think about before I fall asleep. I need you. I want you. I need you to be mine, now and forever. If what you want is to wait me out, to wear me down, it's not going to work. Don't you get that? I feel you under my skin, baby. I have you in my blood. You are mine. I am yours. Stop fighting this."

I couldn't stop the tears. I felt weak, happy, terrified. He grabbed me by the back of my neck and pulled me closer as he leaned down and took my lips. I was pushing him away but to no avail. He kissed me, long and hard, his need for me invading every one of my senses. And I kissed him back with every bit of frustration and longing I had for him that I had been fighting each day.

When I finally took a step back, we were both out of breath, the heat emanating from his body enough to burn the world down.

Part of me believed him, because that was all I ever wanted—him, offering to be mine and only mine. But to accept that I was entitled to so much happiness was naive. And to trust him, to trust that he meant his words, that I was enough for him... Well, that would be like diving into dangerous waters headfirst.

"I need some space. You need to leave. I can't do this," I said, avoiding the hurt in his eyes as I ran past him back to the tour location.

To my surprise, Francesca was still there, alone, just sitting and sipping some wine. She quickly rose up to take my sobbing self into her arms. Together, we took the long walk to Francesca's villa in silence.

Francesca forced me to take a seat while the maid prepared us a strong cup of coffee. The walk hadn't done much to calm me down.

"What's wrong?" asked Francesca.

All I could do was cry, but I needed to let it out.

"I'm sorry," I sobbed. "I'm sorry. I know you just wanted to have a good time, and here I am, crying all over the place."

"You have nothing to apologize for," assured Francesca, putting an arm around my shoulder. "I'm here, and you need to talk. Talk to me. I'm all ears."

I took a few sips of the hot coffee the maid had just brought in, in an attempt to compose myself.

"I, um... this man, Alejandro... he, um... he is... I love him. I am in love with him. I love him with every fiber of my being. I don't know how it happened. I've been careful all my life, always in control of how I felt, always safe in my cold, rational self, and he threw all of it to shit. I don't know how to go back to before, when I didn't feel so much. Now all I can do is miss him, need him."

"But that's a beautiful thing, Amelia," she said with tenderness.

"It's not!" I shouted between sobs. "It's horrible! It's my worst nightmare."

"But he seems to love you as well, no?" pushed Francesca tenderly, trying to calm me.

"That's what he says. But how can I believe him? How can I believe that we could be together when we have a dark past looming over us?"

"How did you meet him?"

I stopped in my tracks, gaining a bit more composure. I desperately wanted to tell Francesca about the past few months of my life. But that would be telling someone who knew Alejandro that he had committed a crime, keeping me hostage, even if he didn't intend to. I couldn't put him in harm's way.

"It doesn't matter how we met," I answered. "I just can't put myself in that position."

"I see," said Francesca. "It's a secret." She smirked.

I frowned but sat there in silence, taking a few more sips of coffee.

"I have to leave tonight. I have to go back to LA, start my life over and move on."

"My darling," said Francesca in the most tender voice, "it's pretty clear to me that you love each other. You love him, and no matter how far you go, you will be as miserable as you are now if you don't give him a chance. You are keeping his secret at all costs. I have been asking you what was wrong for days, and you've never wavered, not even once, not even drunk."

My eyes squinted as I grew confused.

"Elena has been trying to get his heart since they were children, but the way he looks at you, the way he fights for you, the way he has been staying in the shadows the past couple of weeks, making sure you are safe, even from a distance... you are the love of his life."

I slowly turned to look Francesca in the eyes. "Who are you?" I asked. "How would you know all this?"

Francesca got up and started pacing, clearly a bit nervous.

"Amelia, I... I didn't know who you were when we met. I just saw a beautiful woman with the saddest eyes, a sadness that seemed to match my son's broken heart. And I couldn't help but get close to you, my motherly instincts wanting to take your pain away. I wanted to introduce you to him as you seemed like a wonderful, intelligent woman after we had dinner. I thought you two could help mend each other's hearts.

"I didn't know... I didn't know until I saw you with him today. I didn't know that you were the woman he has been telling me about, the woman who changed my son's life for the better. I didn't know you were the girl he had abducted to protect while he got revenge and ended up falling in love with. And I didn't know the man you were so clearly avoiding talking about all week was him."

"Alejandro is... your son?" I could hear my heart pounding out of my chest.

"Yes," she admitted, a tender smile on her lips. "And now that I have seen how he looks at you, I realize there is nothing I could possibly do, no one he could possibly meet, that would take away what he feels for you."

I closed my eyes and put my head in my hands, trying to process. This familiarity I had with Francesca, those eyes that I now understood were Alejandro's, the firmness in her voice... that was why I felt this innate attachment to her, like we had known each other already.

"He took a bullet to save you, Amelia," continued Francesca as she sat back down next to me and grabbed my hands. "He chose to die... to save you. He had even given up on his quest to avenge his brother, so he didn't hurt you, so he didn't have to put you between him and that murderer. He was going to move on and forget, just to be with you, don't you get it? I know it all started in an... unusual fashion, to say the least, but he is being honest with you. My son loves you more than he loves himself."

I got up. I needed to move, anything to help. Francesca sat there, patiently waiting for my pace to slow down. I finally came to a halt. Francesca got to her feet and went to give me a hug. I was still crying, but my melted heart was letting it all in. I had to believe Alejandro, because even my most rational self could tell that he was being honest. I had been too alarmed to see it, and Francesca... she peeled some of my fears away.

"Thank you," I whispered. "Thank you."

Francesca, with tears in her eyes, took a step back, holding my hands. "Go to him," she said. "Please go to him. He needs to know how you feel. I don't want to see my son haunted by your absence anymore," she teased.

I wiped my eyes immediately, with a smile.

"He's staying in a villa two doors down, if you go left when you leave."

I didn't need to be told twice.

I grabbed my bag from the couch, gave Francesca another hug, and ran to Alejandro. I didn't stop until I got to his door. I still had doubts. I still was unsure. I could still leave. I didn't have to knock. I knew if I did, I could never go back. That was terrifying, but also exhilarating, and the thought of never seeing him again was too hard to bear, so I knocked three times, my heart in my throat. A man opened the door, surprised to see me there.

"Can I help you?"

"I am looking for Alejandro."

"Please wait here. Who is asking?"

I ignored him and barged in. I ran up the stairs at full speed, the poor man scrambling behind me in an attempt to stop me. I entered through the first open door I saw. There he was, putting his clothes into the luggage open on his bed.

"Sir, I told her to wait!" said the man, clearly annoyed.

"It's fine, Jason. You can go home now. Have a good night."

"You too, sir," he said, relieved, as he left and closed the door behind him.

Alejandro let out a deep sigh but finished putting the last of the clothing on the bed into the luggage.

"Are you leaving?" I asked in a low voice, unable to get any closer than the door.

"Isn't that what you want? Me gone so you can start fresh with your lawyer friend?" he asked, now facing me, his hands in his jean's pockets.

He took me by surprise.

"What are you talking about? Nico? He's just a friend who is helping me get back what Richard took from me."

"Do you let all your male friends hug you like that?" he asked dryly.

"Are you spying on me?"

"No, not exactly. But I had to make sure you were safe. That Richard wouldn't retaliate. That Mathias wouldn't harm you for knowing too much. I had to know where you were at all times—at least until the dust settled."

"Alejandro," I said sweetly as I dared to get a little closer, "I promise, he is just a friend. He came to meet with me, but that was it. He didn't stay here. He left. Nothing happened."

Alejandro looked sad, angry, disturbed. My heart was aching. I felt stupid and selfish, for not seeing the pain in his eyes sooner—or rather, not understanding it. I dared to believe now that it was because of me—and that, I couldn't have.

"Alejandro, I... I don't really know how to do this. I don't know if I have it in me..."

"Tell me to stay, mi niña. All you have to do is ask. I have been waiting for you. I will always wait for you. I will never leave your side." It looked like he was holding his breath.

"I don't want you to leave..."

Before I knew it, he was in front of me, and he lifted me off the floor and into his arms.

I grabbed his face with both hands, and I kissed him, letting out a whimper.

His possessive tongue soon made me forget my pain, making butterflies course through my body instead. I needed to feel him inside of me with urgency, need blinding my senses. He carried me to the bed right after he shoved the luggage onto the floor. He laid me on my back and proceeded to undress me. With trembling hands, I unbuttoned his shirt and then reached to remove his pants.

He climbed on top of me. I frantically guided him until he was throbbing inside of me.

"You have no idea how much I missed you," he said between ragged breaths.

"I missed you to, so much!" My voice wobbled.

Alejandro sinked himself in me over and over again, and everytime he did, pieces of my wall crumbled.

"I'm scared. I've never felt like this about anyone," I confessed, trying to hold back my tears.

Alejandro slowed down, grabbed my face with both hands, and kissed me.

"I love you," he said as we stopped for air. "I love you, and I promise I will never stop loving you." He kissed me again, his need for me all too apparent.

"I love you too," I admitted, still searching his eyes for reassurance.

"Tell me again," he whispered as he kissed my neck.

"I love you, Alejandro."

"I love you."

Alejandro took his time, kissing and caressing every inch of me, making me feel everything he did, driving me to complete surrender with every touch, every caress. He had me now and forever, body and soul.

EPILOGUE

Amelia

ALEJANDRO WRAPPED HIS ARM around my waist as we stood on the balcony of our home in Mexico—the hacienda where it all began.

"I never tire of this view," I sighed as I rested my arm on his, my head leaning back on his chest.

"This is our first vacation in a year. We could have gone anywhere in the world," he said.

"I know, baby, but I wanted to come back to where it all started for us."

"Well, now that things are less chaotic at Hotel Estrellas, we can start spending a few months a year here."

"I'd love that!" I squealed as I turned around and wrapped my arms around his neck.

"I am so proud of you, the way you stood up to the task, took over your seat on the board. You worked so hard. They are so lucky to have you."

"Thank you," I said, feeling my cheeks flush a bit.

Even after a year together, he could still make me blush and feel a little timid.

"It certainly helped that I was able to secure an exclusive contract for wine distribution across our hotels with the best vineyard in California." I smiled at him. He grabbed my chin and kissed me, sending small currents down my spine.

"It was a win-win for both of us."

"I just wanted an excuse to live at the villa with my fiancé," I joked.

"Hmm," he grunted, "I like those words from your lips."

"I love you," I whispered before I took his lips with mine.

"Te adoro, niña mia."

Alejandro's hand traveled up and down my naked back, sending shivers through my body, while his other hand cupped my face. I whimpered, frustrated that we had to head to dinner, wishing he could take me here in our room—his old room.

So much had changed since then. I had stepped up to the task of being part of the management of Hotel Estrellas. I had enjoyed every second of it, earning the trust of the board, the officers, and all the employees. I had managed to contribute good and innovative ideas, and between the rebranding Iris had assisted with and the exclusive line of wines from Alejandro's vineyard that I had suggested we add to some of the renewed high-end restaurants, the company had had a great year of profit and ended up not taking a hit from the scandal with Richard. I had thrived, with Alejandro by my side every step of the way.

Alejandro had been on edge for the first few months, insisting that I always had two bodyguards with me, in case Mathias somehow became a problem. He only relaxed when Mathias died in a confrontation with a competitive gang, in a matter unrelated to the diamonds. Even then, it took a few months for me to convince him I no longer needed the bodyguards.

"If you keep touching me like this, we won't make it out of the house," I teased, almost wishing he would cave, the feeling of his thickness against me making me crave the feeling of him inside of me.

I never tired of him. My need for him was unscathed by the passing of time or repetition.

"Hmm, those reservations were quite hard to get," he whispered as he kissed my neck in that specific spot that made my toes curl. "But"—he sucked a little lower—"I think they can wait."

"Hmm, are you sure?" I breathed as he proceeded to lower the strap of my yellow sweetheart neckline dress, leaving a trail of kisses from my shoulder, to my collarbone, to my breast.

"Uh-huh."

He groaned and lifted me, carrying me inside the room. He put me down and turned me around, continuing his exploration of my neck. I ran my fingers through his hair from behind, biting my lip in anticipation.

"Bend for me baby. Keep the heels on."

I obeyed, lowering myself onto the bed. He parted my legs farther and slid my panties down as he hissed out a breath.

"So sexy, so fucking wet for me," he said gruffly as he lifted my dress up, cupping my buttocks.

He positioned himself between my legs, tightening his grasp on my hips.

I moaned as he penetrated me, deep, fast, and efficient. He pulled me against him over and over again.

"Hold on tight," he said in a hoarse tone as I dug my nails into the bedsheet.

My eyes glazed over as a rush of pressure built up in the lower part of my stomach, my senses heightened, my body enjoying the brutality with which he was slamming into me.

"Oh, god. Oh my god, baby. I'm coming!" I couldn't help it. I was always so ready for him.

Alejandro grunted, his movements both accelerated and less controlled, almost sloppy in a passionate, need-filled motion that sent me across the edge with an orgasm so strong my eyes blurred as I saw lights.

We were both panting when Alejandro slowed down his rhythm, holding me so I didn't fall, my wobbly knees unable to hold me.

Alejandro

A FEW MINUTES AFTER I came so deliciously inside of her, we cleaned up and put our clothes back on. I shouldn't have encouraged her, considering that people were waiting on us, but what could I do when she gave me that look that resulted in an instant boner every single time?

I would have preferred to just stay there with her, eat her up. But she would like what was to come. I seized her hand to head downstairs. She grabbed her purse, checked her reflection in the mirror, and followed me out of the room.

"We need to stop in the living room for a second. I forgot something."

We walked in there together. Amelia got startled, her hand reaching to her throat as voices screamed, "Surprise!" toward her in unison.

"Oh my god!" exclaimed Amelia at the sight of her best friends, Iris, Chloe, and Keisha. The girls squealed as they all gathered into a hug around Amelia.

When I gave Amelia all the journal entries she had left at my houses last year, she had no idea what to do with them, but she said she wouldn't just get rid of them. She had decided to pass them onto Chloe, the lawyer friend who somehow had the time to also write what I understood to be spicy romance books that women loved.

After I made her sign a non-disclosure agreement, Chloe worked on a book, implementing some of Amelia's journal entries. Chloe had received the first physical copies of the book's and had brought the girls—with me as their partner in crime—to surprise Amelia with an intimate book party.

Amelia turned around to me and jumped into my arms.

"I love you so much, baby. Thank you."

"I love you, niña amada mía."

Those words from her lips were all I ever wanted to hear. The joy on her face, the shine in her eyes—that was what I lived for. Her happiness. While I hated that she had ever suffered at my hands, her kidnapping had been the best thing to ever happen in my life. Now I had the woman I never knew I needed in my arms, in our house, forever. I wouldn't trade it for the world.

ABOUT THE AUTHOR

STÉPHANIE IS AN AUTHOR of angsty love stories with assertive female leads, who go toe to toe with alpha heroes. Stephanie's love for romance stems from her teenage years, when she was secretly reading her grandmother's Harlequin books under the covers, coupled with spending every weeknight avidly watching telenovelas with her mother.

Stéphanie grew up in the Caribbean and currently lives in Illinois. She enjoys spending time with her cat, a romance book in hand.

Want more of the Game Series? Check out Game of Deception!

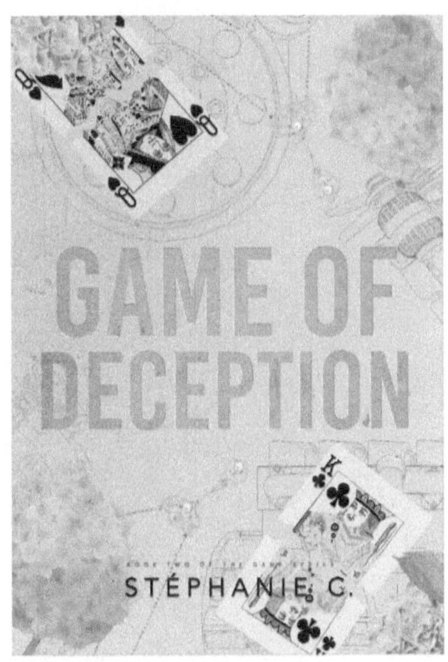

<u>Sign up for my newsletter and receive a link to an extra Game of Revenge Epilogue!</u>

@INBOOKS.ILIVE

Follow me on Instagram for more!

Please also stop by Amazon and Goodreads to leave a review, we LOVE THOSE!